ALSO BY LINDA FAIRSTEIN

The Alexandra Cooper Novels

The Deadhouse
Cold Hit
Likely to Die
Final Jeopardy

Nonfiction

Sexual Violence: Our War Against Rape

THE
BONE VAULT

Linda Fairstein

POCKET STAR BOOKS
NEW YORK LONDON TORONTO SYDNEY SINGAPORE

A Pocket Star Book published by
POCKET BOOKS, a division of Simon & Schuster, Inc.
1230 Avenue of the Americas, New York, NY 10020

Copyright © 2003 by Linda Fairstein

Originally published in hardcover in 2003 by Scribner

All rights reserved, including the right to reproduce
this book or portions thereof in any form whatsoever.
For information address Scribner, 1230 Avenue
of the Americas, New York, NY 10020

ISBN: 0-7434-6273-4

First Pocket Books Export Edition Printing January 2003

10 9 8 7 6 5 4 3 2 1

POCKET STAR BOOKS and colophon are registered
trademarks of Simon & Schuster, Inc.

For information regarding special discounts for bulk purchases,
please contact Simon & Schuster Special Sales at 1-800-456-6798
or business@simonandschuster.com

Printed in the U.S.A.

1

I spent a long afternoon at the morgue. I had left my desk at the Manhattan district attorney's office shortly after lunch to review autopsy results on a new case with the deputy chief medical examiner. A nineteen-year-old, dressed in an outfit she had bought just hours earlier, was killed outside a social club as she waited on a street corner for her friends.

Now I walked a quiet corridor, again surrounded by death. I did not want to be here. I paused at the entrance of an ancient tomb, its painted limestone facade concealing the false doorway to an underground burial chamber. The faded reliefs that decorated its walls showed offerings of food and drink that would nourish the spirit of the dead. I didn't harbor any hope that the young woman whose body I had seen today would ever be in need of the kind of good meal displayed before me.

I made my way past a granite lion and nodded at the uniformed guard, who slouched on a folding chair beside the elegantly carved beast, once the protector of a royal grave. Both were sleeping soundly. The outstretched arms of the neighboring alabaster monkeys held empty vessels that had no doubt been receptacles of the body parts of some mummified dignitary of the Old Kingdom.

Voices echoing from behind me suggested that I was not going to be the last arrival at this evening's festive dinner. I quickened my pace and swept by cases filled with goddesses' stone heads, perched on shelves holding jeweled sandals and golden collars that had been buried with them for centuries. A sharp left turn brought me face-to-face with the enormous black sarcophagus of a thirtieth-dynasty Egyptian queen, held open by two iron posts, so that passersby could see the image of her soul portrayed on the inside of the upper lid. The dark, heavy casket with a faint outline of the slender body it once housed chilled me, despite the unseasonal warmth of the late-spring night.

Then I turned the last corner, where the darkness of the funereal rooms gave way to the glorious open space that housed the Temple of Dendur. The north-ernmost end of the Metropolitan Museum of Art was a sloping, glass-paned wall soaring above the sand-stone monuments, opening the vista into Central Park. It was almost nine o'clock, and the streetlamps beyond the windows lightened the night sky, giving definition to the leafy green trees bordering the great institution.

I stood at the edge of the moat that surrounded the two raised buildings in this stunning wing, searching the crowd for my friends. Waiters in sleek black suits zigzagged back and forth among the guests, stopping to dispense smoked salmon on black bread and caviar blinis. They were trailed by others who carried silver trays filled with glasses of white wine, champagne, and sparkling water, dodging the elbows and arms of the assembled museum members and supporters.

Nina Baum saw me before I spotted her. "You came just late enough to miss most of the speeches. Smart move."

She signaled to one of the servers, and handed me a flute of champagne. "Hungry?"

I shook my head.

"The morgue?"

"Not a very pleasant afternoon."

"Was she—?"

"I'll tell you about it later. Chapman thought he had a lead on a case he's been handling that's reached a dead end, so I wanted to get a clear understanding about the pattern of injuries and how they'd been inflicted. That way, if he picked up a suspect and I got a chance to question the guy tonight, I'd be ready for him. Turned out to be a bad tip, so there's no interrogation, no arrest. It's on the back burner for a while."

Nina looped her arm through mine and started to walk me toward the steps. "Why didn't you bring Mike with you?"

"I tried. Once I told him it was black tie he sent me home to shower and change. No penguin suit for him, not even to see you. He'll catch you later in the week."

Mike Chapman was a homicide detective. Best one on the job, in my view. Nina Baum was my closest friend, and had been for exactly half my life. We were eighteen when we met, assigned to be roommates at Wellesley College when we arrived freshman year. She was married now, living in California with her husband and young son. She had met Mike many times during the decade that he and I had worked together on cases, and she looked forward to spending time with him whenever she was in town.

"First we'll find Jake." She led me up the steps, past the lone palm tree that stood on the platform below the great temple. "Then I'll introduce you to my boss and all the museum heavyweights."

"How's Jake behaving? You still have a job after tonight or is he hounding everybody here, looking for scoops?"

"Let's say we've raised a lot of eyebrows around town. I keep telling people that I've only borrowed him for the evening, but when you read tomorrow's gossip columns, you might begin to wonder. You must have a lot of friends here, 'cause they can't figure out why I'm hanging on to him and why you're nowhere to be seen."

"'Who is that auburn-haired beauty who whisked in from the coast and stole NBC correspondent Jake Tyler right out from under the long arm of the law? Prosecutor Alexandra Cooper has a warrant out for her arrest. And also for the return of the terrifically sexy—and backless—navy blue sequined dress that this interloper slipped out of Alexandra's closet when she wasn't looking.' That's what I'm likely to see in the tabs?"

"I figured you loaned me the guy for the evening, how sore could you be about the sexy, backless gown?"

Nina had arrived in New York a day earlier. She was a partner in a major L.A. law firm, where she had developed an expertise in packaging large entertainment projects for big-screen and television movies. Tonight's event was staged to announce a historic occasion for two great New York institutions. The Metropolitan Museum of Art and the American Museum of Natural History, with some help from Hollywood, would hold the first cooperative exhibition in their histories.

The controversial mix of scholarship and show business had had a difficult birth, struggling to overcome resistance from trustees and curators, administrators and city officials. But blockbuster shows like the Met's "Treasures of Tutankhamen" and the Costume Institute's collection of Jacqueline Kennedy's White House clothing filled the museum coffers and argued for the drama of a spectacular twenty-first-century display of the two museums' collective greatest hits.

Nina's California client, UniQuest Productions, had successfully bid on all the media marketing rights to the new project. "A Modern Bestiary," as the show had been titled, would feature all the fantastic animals of the world, as represented in both collections, from hieroglyphs, tapestries, and paintings to mounted specimens and stuffed mammals. There would be dazzling, high-tech creations and virtual dioramas, IMAX time trips to examine artists and artifacts in their natural habitats, and commercial tie-ins for souvenir sales in museum shops and on the web. There would be Rembrandt refrigerator magnets, triceratops lapel pins, plastic human-genome Slinkys to bounce down staircases across America, and snow globes with endangered species of the Amazon being doused by acid rain.

Nina steered me toward a short, dark-haired man with too much facial hair and a collarless tux shirt. "Quentin Vallejo, I'd like you to meet Alexandra Cooper. She's—"

"I know, I know. The best friend." Quentin did the up-and-down thing. My five-ten frame towered over him, so his eyes just focused at the level of my breasts and worked their way south to my knees before lifting back up to meet my glance. "The sex crimes prosecutor. Nina talked about you for the entire flight yesterday. That's an interesting job you've got. We ought to have a chat sometime, just the two of us. Like to hear more about what you do."

Quentin turned to exchange his empty wineglass for a full one, and I gave him a nod as I walked away. Nina blew him a kiss and followed me.

"That's the guy who's running this show?"

"Worked with Spielberg for twelve years. He's absolutely ingenious at designing interactive materials and futuristic movie images. Makes inanimate objects look like flesh and blood. He sees things in ways that nobody else does."

"That much was obvious to me." I stood on tip-toes, looking over heads and shoulders for any sign of Jake. "Did the big guns at the Met and Natural History ever meet Quentin before today?"

"You think we wouldn't have done a deal if they had?"

"Have you lost your mind? This museum was founded by old men. Very rich, very white, very Presbyterian. Natural History was pretty much the same. The good old boys may be dead and buried, but this place isn't exactly run by the most diverse crowd in town."

"Somebody on the project did his homework. Our advance group managed all the hands-on work to get this event up and running. Probably the preppiest-looking film team I've ever seen west of the Mississippi. Hired a white-shoe law firm here to handle the contract work. Saved the outing of Quentin for tonight's gala, the big announcement."

"How'd that go?"

"Listen to the buzz. The trustees, the press, the upper crust—whoever these people are, they seemed thrilled about the news." Nina steered me to the small recess at the center of the taller building, the gateway to the Temple of Dendur. She was looking for a quieter place to tell me about the presentation that I had missed.

"Do you know Pierre Thibodaux?" She pointed to the podium, where a tall, dark-haired man was being led away from a small group of museum officials. He motioned to his colleagues with a raised finger and stepped into the adjacent corridor.

"Only by reputation. New guy in town." Thibodaux had replaced Philippe de Montebello as director of the Met less than three years ago.

"He's taken all the meetings with our advance crew himself. This show is his baby. Brilliant, mercurial, handsome. You've got to meet him—"

"Ladies, you can't be leaning against the building, y'all hear me?" a security guard said.

We walked out of the narrow opening and searched for another quiet nook.

"Let's get out of this wing so we can have a normal

conversation. There are as many living, breathing jackals in here tonight as there are limestone ones standing sentry over all the Egyptian galleries. I somehow think poor Augustus didn't foresee when he built these monuments that they would become the most prized cocktail space in Manhattan."

I could tell that Nina was annoyed with me, as she tried to follow me back down the steps.

"Who's Augustus? What the hell are you talking about? The temple is Egyptian, right?"

I had been coming to the Met since my earliest childhood, and knew most of the permanent exhibits pretty well. "Half right. It was built near Aswan, but by a Roman emperor who ruled that region at the time. Augustus had it erected in honor of two young sons of a Nubian chieftain who drowned in the Nile. I hate to dampen your enthusiasm, Nina. I've just been around too much death today not to wonder why we find it appropriate to organize our festivities in and around the tombs of all these ancient cultures. Wouldn't people find it offensive to have the next cocktail party at Arlington Cemetery?"

"Sorry they're not serving scotch tonight, Alex. Take it easy, will you? We can leave any time you'd like. Who's the old dame hanging on to Jake?"

He had spotted the two of us and was making his way to the foot of the platform on which we stood. A silver-haired woman with lots of dangling sapphires—from earlobes, wrists, fingers—had grasped Jake by the arm and was bending his ear about something. I stopped on the bottom step and fished in my purse for some coins to toss in the moat.

"Look out for that crocodile, darling. The most dangerous creature in Egypt, the embodiment of the essence of evil." Jake held out his hand to lower me down as I tossed a few quarters in the water, for good luck. The ebony croc mocked the gesture, his gaping mouth poised for eternity, seeking something meatier than the quiche that was being circulated around the room.

I kissed Jake's cheek, which was already covered with the shapes of pursed lips in a variety of colors. "I don't mind that you're *in loco* husband for Nina, but who's the rest of my competition?"

"That last woman? Just one of the trustees. Didn't catch her name. Gushing about how exciting the joint show is going to be and asking whether the networks are covering the fireworks tonight."

"Fireworks?"

"There's supposed to be a preview, a five-minute sound-and-light show to kick off the news about the bestiary exhibition. Here comes Thibodaux. He'll do the honors."

Instead, the director walked straight toward us, smoothing his jacket with one hand and his hair with the other. "Nina, may I have a word with you? Do you know where Quentin is?"

"I'll find him for you. Pierre, I'd like you to meet my—"

"*Enchanté.*" He greeted us tersely but his eyes searched the room over my shoulder. He and Nina broke away, retracing our steps to look for the producer.

I glanced at my watch. "Soon as we tear her loose,

think you'd treat your two dates to burgers at '21'?"

"My chariot awaits you, madam."

Nina, Quentin, and Pierre had their heads together at the top of the stairs. The director did a double take over his shoulder as Quentin pointed down at me. Nina was shaking her head in the negative and trying to block me from Quentin's line of sight. You're right, pal. Whatever it is, keep me out of it.

Pierre Thibodaux didn't wait for the others to descend the two tiers of steps.

"Miss Cooper? Mr. Vallejo just told me that you're a prosecutor. May I have a moment with you, alone, for some advice? Do you mind, Mr. Tyler?" This time, no guard admonished us as Thibodaux led me back up to the platform, removed the rope between the two pillars at the entrance of the Temple of Dendur, and stepped into the quiet archway.

"You're a bureau chief in the Manhattan district attorney's office? I need your help in dealing with the police tonight."

"Here, at the museum?"

"No, actually, in a freight yard. I'm going to make a few remarks to close the evening and send all these people on their way. We'll forgo the drama of the UniQuest Productions pyrotechnics. The last thing we need tomorrow is any bad publicity linked to our splendid new show."

"Perhaps I can make a call to the proper—"

"There's a shipment of exhibits going abroad, stored in containers for transit. It's a very routine occurrence for us. Crates go in and out of the country all the time. Exchanges with other museums, items we've deaccessioned or loaned to foreign institutions. Happens regularly."

"I doubt there's anything that I can help you with. If you've got a problem with Customs—" I said, as Thibodaux continued to speak over my objection.

"What doesn't usually happen is that one of the ancient sarcophagi was opened for inspection a few hours ago. There was supposed to be a mummified princess in the coffin, Miss Cooper. Twelfth dynasty, Middle Kingdom. A couple of thousand years old and quite valuable. Instead, there's a corpse inside. Someone has substituted a body, I'm afraid. A few centuries younger than my princess, no doubt, but just as dead."

2

Rust-colored steel containers, each the size of a boxcar on a freight train, were stacked by the dozens and lined up in rows for acre after acre in the dark shipyard. Pierre Thibodaux's limousine was stopped at the gate by a night watchman, who flashed his beam at the two of us in the backseat. Thibodaux's French accent was lost on the weary sentry, who was probably coming to the end of his shift as the hour approached midnight.

"Say what?"

"We are here to meet some people from the Metropolitan Museum, somewhere in—"

I leaned forward and folded back the leather cover on my wallet, holding my gold and blue badge under the nose of the guard. "I'm Alexandra Cooper, district attorney's office. There are some detectives inside the yard who are waiting for us."

I checked the rear page of the evening's program, on which I had scribbled down the location Mike Chapman had given to me when I called him from my cell phone fifteen minutes earlier. "They're in front of lot G-eight. Which way is that?"

The watchman pressed the buzzer that unlocked the chain-link fence and pointed his finger, illuminated by the lighted end of his cigarette. "Go to your left, couple of hundred yards. Can't miss the big oranges on the side of the stack of Tropicana containers. Hang a right and drive in past them. Your cops are already there."

The fact that the freight yard happened to be across the river from Manhattan in Newark, New Jersey, hadn't put Chapman off in the least. The Port Authority of New York and New Jersey had control of the property, so he figured it was worth his time to explore the situation. Any fears that my New York County identification would not serve to get us inside were short-lived.

The Lincoln Town Car glided like a swan among the huge, awkward metal bins, piled high and patiently awaiting shipment to myriad destinations around the world. It came to a stop against the rear of a tractor trailer truck, which was parked between two containers, and had a ramp rolled up into its gaping end.

Thibodaux was out of the car before the driver shut the engine off. I saw Mike approach and introduce himself to the director, on his way over to help me out of the car.

"Lon Chaney coming, too, or can we get right to work?"

He took my hand and I climbed out onto the graveled roadway, grateful that Nina had borrowed my gown and left me wearing a black satin pantsuit. After I had called Mike at home and asked him to meet me here, I sent her off to dinner with Jake.

"Who's the frog?"

"New director of the Metropolitan Museum of Art. He got the call about this in the middle of a reception he was having tonight. Asked my advice about what to do when he learned the body had been found. It took a while to make him understand that reporting the fact was not optional. He's hoping this is a story that won't have legs." I shook my head.

"Cleopatra taking the big sleep in Port Newark? Probably worth only eight or nine days of tabloid headlines."

"Who's here, besides you and Lenny?"

"The two suits are museum flunkies. They're the ones that got the call from the truck driver, just before six o'clock. Came out to see for themselves before they screamed for the big cheese. The trucker is sitting in the cab, finishing his hoagie and listening to the ball game. Extra innings, Yanks and Red Sox all tied up after ten. Your boy Pettitte pitched great the first seven innings. Joe should never have taken him out. The two square-badges are security for the shipyard. It's their dog that sniffed out the stiff."

Square-badges was police slang for civilian guards hired by private businesses, shopping malls to ship-yards.

"Where is she?"

Mike's back was to the truck, and he pumped his thumb over his shoulder. "Up the ramp. Resting comfortably in the care of Tri-State Transit."

"Never unloaded?"

"Nope. Routine is they start hauling the goods off the truck as soon as they drive into the yard. Most of the items are packed inside wooden crates, labeled and ready for overseas shipping. Truckers set them down on the ground, and then they're winched over into containers that get loaded onto the freighters for transport. Whole place looks like my Lionel train set on steroids."

I looked around at the endless rows of giant boxes, towering over us and stretching in every direction as far as I could see.

"Once they're out of the truck, security has the dogs smell around them, incoming and outgoing. Looking for drugs or dead bodies. Back in the nineties, there were an embarrassing number of incidents out here. Wise guys were using the yard as a wide-open warehouse for cocaine storage and a staging area for shipping nose candy everywhere in Europe you could imagine."

"Jersey police? Port Authority cops?"

"Not involved yet. That's why the square-badges. Shippers worked out a compromise that the owners of these lots would hire their own patrols. Only call in the cops when they got a crime."

"I think I'm getting what they call mixed signals here. Thibodaux believes there's a corpse in the sarcophagus that doesn't belong there. That's why I called you to meet us out here. Isn't there a crime in this?"

"Lucky Pierre might be right. But the mopes who found Cleo have seen too many mummy movies. Curse of the Pharaohs and all that crap. They cracked open the crate, but then the lid was so heavy they could barely move it. Took four of them to lift it just a couple of inches—expecting to find a stash of white powder—but one guy sees a head sticking through some dangling pieces of linen instead. Dropped the stone so fast I'm surprised it didn't splinter into a million pieces."

"So they never bothered to call the Jersey authorities?"

"They're afraid to open the box up again. Think they're doomed to the fate of Lord Carnavon if it turns out to be an actual mummy and they disturb it. They called the museum and got switched over to the curator in charge of Egyptian art. He's the tall, bald guy talking to your buddy Pierre. The rent-a-cops told him that if he wants to know what made the dog howl, he better get his own ass out here and have a look inside."

"And the other one in the business suit?"

"The heavyset one in the middle is in charge of the shipping department. He's responsible for the whole load that came out on the truck. The two of 'em are sweating up a storm. That's more excitement than they've had in any museum since Murf the Surf made off with the crown jewels."

"Why's she still on the truck?"

"'Cause once the crates are down to two rows per stack, they just walk the dog onto the ramp and let him cruise around before they do all the work of unloading. Saves time and aggravation in case they have to seize a truck or ship something back to its place of origin. Rin Tin Tin was frothing at the mouth when he hit the crate with the body."

Pierre Thibodaux took a piece of paper from the hand of the shipping manager and walked back over to talk to us. "I don't understand how this could have happened, Mr. Chapman. We've got a state-of-the-art security system at the Met, as you might imagine. Billions of dollars' worth of paintings and sculptures, priceless masterpieces. It's . . . it's inconceivable—"

"Slow down. Let's work this backwards. Is this your tractor trailer?"

Thibodaux looked at the tracking order in his hand and then back to the truck, to check the lettering on its side. "This is one of our contractors. We own a number of vans, of course, since we're constantly moving pieces about. But on many of the larger jobs like this," he said, gesturing around him at the dozens of cartons that had come off the back end, "we hire out the work to companies like Tri-State."

"Common carrier," I said quietly to Mike.

"What's that got to do with anything?"

"Just hold the thought, Detective. I'll connect the dots for you later on."

He turned back to Thibodaux. "So there's no question but that this mother lode left the Met early today?"

The director handed me the receipt he had just taken from the shipping manager. Mike aimed a flashlight on the wrinkled paper, which was stamped with today's date: Tuesday, May 21, 10:43 A.M.

"Was the whole shipment from the museum, or did the driver stop anywhere else along the way to pick up or drop off other crates?"

"No, we keep a pretty tight financial rein on things like this. Mr. Lissen, he's the fellow over there who runs the department, knows the dimensions of the trucks we rent. And he's got the measurements of all the lots going out. Makes a point of trying to fill them as full as he can, so we get our money's worth."

"How do you inventory the contents?"

"An age-old system, Mr. Chapman." Thibodaux was rubbing his brow as he stepped back to lean against the adjacent container. "We've got more than two million objects at the Met, and the moment one arrives it's assigned a number. An accession number."

"Hey, Lenny," Mike yelled to the detective he'd brought to Newark with him, who had his notepad out, talking to the truck driver. "Wanna gown up, hike up that ramp, and check something for me?"

Thibodaux looked up at us again. "The very first work of art to enter the Met's collection back in 1870 was a coffin. Ironic, isn't it? The Garland Sarcophagus. Roman marble, from the third century B.C. Every employee at the museum knows that. Item number 70.1. The first gift acquired in 1870, the year we were founded.

"Anyway, Mr. Chapman, that's the system. After 1970, all four digits of the year were used, followed by the order in which the piece came into the collection."

"You see any markings on that crate?" Mike had walked to the foot of the ramp. Lenny Dove, who was assigned to the same squad as Mike at Manhattan North Homicide, had put on a crime scene outfit, complete with lab gown and plastic gloves. He was squatting beside the packing box, shining his light across the slats, which had been broken apart by the security officers.

"Got a label for you. Has the Met logo. Says, '1983.752. Limestone sarcophagus.'"

"Handwritten?"

"Typed."

"C'mon, blondie. Alley-oop. Better leave those spikes in the car." He handed me the proper cover for my clothes, hands, and feet.

I kicked off my shoes and followed Mike up, stepping with my gauze booties on the rungs of the metal ladder that hung off the left corner of the truck and swinging my leg over onto the hard wooden floor. Pierre Thibodaux started up after me.

"Not so fast, Mr. T. We'll call if we need you."

"But, I—uh—I'd like to know—"

"Give us a few minutes up here, okay? It's not exactly like viewing hours at your local funeral parlor. Have a little respect for the dead. We're not open for business yet."

Thibodaux backed off and rejoined his two colleagues.

The truck's well was pitch-black and airless. Mike pulled on latex gloves and he and Lenny trained torch-sized beams along the floor so we could see our way over to the exposed sarcophagus.

"Stand back, Coop. It's not gonna be pretty."

"I've seen—"

"You've seen nothing, kid. Take a few steps over there till I say otherwise."

I moved a few paces away, backing into another crated package.

"On the count of three, Lenny," Mike said, positioning himself on the same side of the ancient box as his partner, but at the end closer to me.

"One, two, three." At the same moment, they

attempted to lift the stone lid from its base. Unable to move it more than an inch, they couldn't look inside before dropping the weighty piece in place. But the brief exposure had released a powerful odor. Not the hideous stench of putrefaction I had expected. There was the sickly sweetness of heavy perfume, laced with a bitter, pungent smell that kicked its way out of the coffin and into our dark, crowded space. I gagged on the thick combination that filled the truck's hot confines. Even the dog, resting his chin on his paws as he sat at his master's feet a few lengths away from the eighteen-wheeler, picked up his head and softly howled. He had scented some unmistakable marker of death hours earlier.

"Slide it, Lenny. Just lift and slide."

This time, Mike had walked around to the opposite side, facing his sergeant at the far end. On the third count, they hoisted the lid just high enough to clear the lip of the coffin and eased it back six or seven inches. Mike picked up the flashlight, looked in, and I started toward him.

"Hold it right there, Coop. Close it up, Lenny."

I had my nose and mouth covered with both hands, fighting the urge to be sick. The dog was on his feet now, pacing and whining, straining at his lead.

"I'll draw you a picture, kid. Go on back down." I knew Mike's moods and this wasn't one to mess with. I'd called him here to help me, and I had no choice but to follow his orders.

As I held on to the ladder and stepped off the truck, I saw him drop to his knees and move the flashlight slowly across the lower sides of the casket.

Every now and then he ran his gloved hands back and forth along the surface, as though feeling for imperfections.

I joined Thibodaux and waited for Mike and Lenny to stop whispering to each other. Within minutes, they stripped off their gloves and threw them on the floor beside the crates, climbing down to tell us what they had found.

"You okay? You look like a beached tuna, gasping for breath."

I hadn't realized that I was ferociously gulping in the clean night air to rid my lungs of the foul smell. "What could you see?"

"First of all, you oughtta get your money back for that coffin, Mr. T. Full of holes. It's the fluids from whatever that body's been wrapped in that leaked through the cracks and attracted the dog's attention this evening. I had my snout right up against them, on the floor, and couldn't smell a thing. But that's just what those shepherds are trained for. Drugs and death."

"So the box and body probably could have made it into a container and out of the country without detection?"

Mike nodded at me. "Till you pull back that lid, it takes a professional nose to get what's just beginning to seep through."

"Could you—"

"There's a body, no question about it. And somebody tried to wrap her in linen cloth, to give it the semblance of a mummy, I guess. But we can't play games with something like this out here in a filthy shipyard in the middle of the night. We've got to get this whole setup to the morgue."

"Her? Are you sure it's a woman?"

"It's just a good guess at this point. Hair a little longer than yours," Mike said, as I instinctively reached for mine, hanging limply against the nape of my neck. "A bit darker in color, with a shiny silver barrette. Small physique, and thin. That's all I can give you tonight."

Mike poked the small of my back to move me away from Thibodaux. We left him talking to Lenny Dove, who was taking down his office telephone number and making arrangements to see him the following afternoon.

"Where was she being shipped to?"

"A long cruise. A sweltering summer voyage to the Cairo Museum on the high seas. There wasn't even a date set for transport yet. Cleo would have been like soup by the time she got home to Egypt."

"What do you want to do?"

"There's only one place to go with this, and the oxymoronic nickname 'Garden State' doesn't figure in my plans."

The last case Mike and I had worked together, the previous winter, had involved a prosecutor's office in New Jersey. Charges of corruption and incompetence had complicated the murder investigation of Lola Dakota, a distinguished professor who had been the target of hired killers in an operation that our Jersey counterparts had completely bungled.

"We're on the same wavelength here, aren't we? You want to take the body back to our medical examiner's office, right?" I asked.

"No better place. Why risk this anywhere else? You worried about a little legal technicality like jurisdiction?" Mike beamed his best grin at me. "I'm the beauty of this operation. You're the brains. Figure out how to get us there, blondie."

"Ignore the fact that we're standing in the middle of a shipyard in Newark, New Jersey. Battaglia always says he's got global jurisdiction." The district attorney, Paul Battaglia, was a genius at capturing cases well beyond the borders of New York County. He had gone after international banking cartels when every other prosecutor in America had ignored them, recovering millions of dollars in restitution and fines from financial institutions worldwide. He liked creative lawyering.

"It's a beautifully clear spring night and I can practically touch Manhattan island from here. Strawberry Fields, roses in Spanish Harlem, the great white lights of Broadway . . . we're just a hop, skip, and a jump away. Doesn't that count?"

"Don't expect to see that reasoning in my brief for the court."

"I'm ready to tell the truck driver to rev up his engines. You got the balls to do this?"

I retrieved my cell phone from the car and dialed my secretary's number, reaching her voice mail to leave a message for the morning. "Hey, Laura, it's Alex. As soon as you get in and pick this up, would you Xerox a few copies of the Criminal Procedure Law, section 20.40, on geographical jurisdiction? I'll need to have one set ready for Battaglia and me, and another set for McKinney."

"Cleo was never actually in the state of Jersey, right? Never left the back of the truck. Never made landfall."

"And the truck is a common carrier, Mr. Chapman. If we've got a homicide, it can be prosecuted in any county in which the carrier passed during the trip. We don't know how long our victim has been dead, do we?"

"Well, I could make an educated—"

"I'm begging you not to do that. Right now I'm still operating in good faith that she may have died on Tenth Avenue, on her approach to the Lincoln Tunnel, or before she got on the entrance ramp to the George Washington Bridge. Either way, it establishes jurisdiction for us. By the time a forensic pathologist states an accurate time of death, I'll be more likely to know exactly where she was when she was killed, which may not be something I want to hear this very minute."

"And she'll be more likely to have a professional autopsy and a shot at a successful prosecution if we get her home. Let's get the truck back on the road and explain all this to the medical examiner. I'll be in your office in the morning, after you break the news to Battaglia. Have Thibodaux get you home safe and sound."

"Will you guys ride shotgun behind the truck?" I asked Mike. "I'm about to hijack my first corpse."

3

I slipped my key in the lock, opened my apartment door, and went to the kitchen without turning on the overhead light. I held a glass against the edge of the automatic ice maker and let four or five cubes drop into it. The decanter on the bar had been refilled by my housekeeper, and I listened as the Dewar's I poured crackled over the frozen pieces and floated them to the top. The glass cooled my hand, and I held it pressed against my forehead for several seconds before I took my first sip.

Walking to the bathroom, I removed my watch and set it on the dressing table. It was almost 2 A.M., and I had to be at my desk before eight, ready to meet with a detective who needed help with a complaining witness whose story about a sexual assault did not make sense. I took off my wrinkled suit and draped it over the back of the chair. It was unlikely I'd ever want to see it again after it was returned from the dry cleaner; it might be headed to the thrift shop. I was sure I could never wear it without thinking of the body in the coffin in the back of the truck.

I turned the water on and waited until steam filled

the room, clouding the mirror so I didn't have to look at my own reflection. I was too tired to deal with that. The circles under my eyes had as many rings as the oldest redwoods in the forests. I opened the cabinet to find some kind of bath oil that would have a calming effect. I pushed aside the rosemary and lavender to read the label on the chamomile. Nina Baum and Joan Stafford, my closest friends, would know exactly what to use. My luck, I'd slather myself with something invigorating rather than soothing.

I showered and washed my hair, then toweled it dry as I carried my drink into the bedroom. The alarm was already set for six-thirty, so I folded back the soft cotton sheet and settled onto the bed, relishing the comfort of the cool, dark room.

A hand stroked my thigh beneath the covers. I turned my head and saw Jake's dark hair against the pale yellow bedding. "Smooth marble finish, perfectly sculpted. Must be the Venus de Milo."

I rolled over and caressed his head, kissing him on the ear. "Wrong museum, wrong continent, wrong broad. This one's got arms." I ran my hand along the length of his spine.

He started to sit up and turn on the light.

"Please don't. The light, I mean. I'm just trying to wind down for a few minutes. This is a nice surprise." I continued to rub his thigh.

We had tried living together at his place for a few weeks around the New Year, but I had found it too difficult to give up my independence. I was in love with Jake, but not ready to make a permanent commitment while we both had such strong professional pulls. His job took him out of town for long and erratic periods of time, and mine required an intensity of focus that made it hard to be available when he was between assignments. I did not need the artificial compromise of one apartment to stay faithful to him.

Jake turned onto his side and crossed his leg on top of mine. He put his hand on my chin, turning my face to his and kissing my mouth, over and over again until I responded to him. I rested my head on the pillow and he played with the ringlets that were forming around my face, first with his fingers and then with his lips.

"When you didn't call within the hour, Nina and I figured that the message she heard delivered to Thibodaux at the party was right. There's a dead girl?"

I nodded my head, sat up, and reached for the scotch.

"Somewhere downtown, Nina said."

"Newark, actually. Mike's got her over at the ME's office now. We'll have a better idea of the whole thing tomorrow. I'm just wired from being out there at the shipyard. You're supposed to be calming me down and taking my mind off my work. Isn't that why you're here?" I slid down lower on the bed and wrapped Jake in an embrace.

"I'm mostly here so you didn't worry all night about me being seduced by the old dame dripping in sapphires. She doubled back for me the minute you left. Ruth Gerst's her name."

"Is she really a trustee of the Met?"

"Most definitely. Toying with giving them her late husband's entire collection of Greek and Roman sculpture. Wants me to come up to her country house in Greenwich and see it sometime."

"Where was Nina when I needed her?"

"Quentin was making her crazy. He was furious that Thibodaux didn't do the big fireworks finale. Quentin had apparently sold a highlights special to one of the cable networks and now he's got no grand ending to deliver. Nina and I finally rescued each other, had a lovely dinner, and I managed to cross-examine her mercilessly about all the crazy things you two used to do together. I dropped her off at the Regency."

"At least she gets to sleep late and have room service in the morning. No such luck for us."

"I wasn't sure that you'd be happy that I let myself in. I know your stalker hasn't been heard from in a couple of months, but I didn't think this was the night to experiment with letting you come home alone."

"Much as I hate to wish her on someone else, she's obviously found a new target." One of the witnesses in an old case of mine had been harassing me all winter, showing up at my apartment lobby from time to time, with doormen and cops scrambling unsuccessfully to snare her. "No sign of her in ages. Maybe her parents had her institutionalized after all."

"Shhhhh. Don't think about her now. Don't think about anything." Jake's mouth brushed down the side of my neck, finding my shoulder blade, and then moving on to my left breast. "No, it's not Venus. This is definitely not marble."

He looked up at me and saw that my eyes were open. "I'm not doing a very good job of distracting you, am I? I know, I know. It's hard to go from what you've seen tonight to making love to me. Come here." He lay flat on his back and pulled me against his side, cradling my head in his arm and holding me tight. "Close your eyes, darling. Think about something else. Pick a place, anywhere in the world. Let's plan a vacation for the end of next month. Someplace with turquoise water, no police department, and funny drinks with little paper umbrellas stuck in them that magically start appearing at noon every day."

I picked up one of his hands and pressed it against my lips. "Good night, Jake. I'm glad you're here. It means the world to me."

I stared at him as his eyes closed and he tried to position himself for sleep. I knew how fortunate I was to have a lover who understood the demands of the work I had chosen. It seemed like an odd career to many of my friends and acquaintances, but Jake understood the great emotional satisfaction the job provided for me.

Nights like this one always made me wonder about what it was in my life that had prepared me for such an unusual occupation. I had grown up in a close-knit family of great privilege and personal strength. My two older brothers and I were young children when my father, Benjamin Cooper, revolutionized the field of cardiac surgery with an ingenious invention that he and his partner created. The Cooper-Hoffman valve, a tiny piece of plastic tubing, was a critical component in every heart operation in this country for more than fifteen years after they introduced it to the medical community. Still, he and my mother remained grounded, raising the three of us in suburban Westchester County, with an emphasis on superior education and a commitment to giving back to society in any way possible.

After my education at Wellesley College, with a major in English literature, I had surprised them by going on to law school at the University of Virginia. My commitment to public service was to try a stint in the greatest prosecutor's office in the country, working to do justice with a district attorney whose integrity was legendary. Although I had planned to stay for only a few years before going on to private practice, Paul Battaglia's innovative approach to combating crime had given me a unique foothold in the legal community.

Battaglia's office had pioneered the idea of a specialized unit to investigate and prosecute crimes of violence against women and children. For so many decades, victims of sexual assault were denied access to courts of law, these intimate violations handled differently from other criminal cases. The word of a woman had not been legally sufficient to take her case into a courtroom because of myths and misconceptions that had actually become embodied in the legislation that this country had adapted from British common law. Throughout the 1960s and 1970s across America, the legislative reform that enabled these cases to proceed sparked the birth of police and prosecutorial units, evidence collection techniques, and continued lobbying efforts for improvements in the criminal justice system. Nowhere were these changes more boldly employed than under the guidance of Paul Battaglia.

It had been a dozen years since I had joined his legal staff and been promoted to run that distinctive unit. When I tried my first rape case in front of a jury, my three favorite letters of the alphabet—DNA— although sequenced that way in a laboratory several years earlier, had not yet been accepted in the scientific or legal communities or developed enough to yield the forensic results that are so decisive for victims today. And now, not only do we use it on a daily basis to exonerate men wrongly accused of crimes, but we achieve victories in cases of homicide and sexual assault that would not have been possible a decade ago.

Those triumphs, those days that we could give a just result to a victim of violence, were what made every moment of this job a joy to me and my colleagues. The rewards were much richer than the experience of an evening like this, when the enormity of a particular tragedy and the loss of a single life overwhelmed all our good work.

Jake stirred beside me and rolled onto his side again.

"You're not still writing your summation for the trial about this body you found tonight, are you? You haven't got anyone to prosecute yet. C'mon, Alex. Shut it down."

I closed my eyes and nestled my body against his.

"Did you say Newark?"

"Newark what?"

"A couple of minutes ago, when I asked you if you went downtown with Thibodaux to see the girl's body, did you say you were in Newark?"

I was finally beginning to feel drowsy. "Yeah."

"So what morgue is Mike going to with the body?"

"Ours."

"How'd you get the body back over here from Jersey?"

"I stole it."

"No, seriously."

"I'm being serious."

Jake had propped himself up on one arm now, just as I was getting comfortable. "Did you give this story to anyone yet?"

"Don't be ridiculous. This neck that you were kissing? It may not be marble, but I'd still like to keep it intact. The cardinal rule is that I need to tell the district attorney about the case before anyone writes a press release. Remember?"

Paul Battaglia had more media sense than anyone I had ever encountered. He had the wisdom to call in chits and favors owed from reporters with valuable information and unnamed sources, and he knew how to repay them with a great scoop carefully timed and planted. An exclusive, if the subject matter was right for it. This one was his to deal out.

"You think this story's going to stay quiet, just amongst your little circle of friends?"

"For the moment, yes. Thibodaux has no interest in publishing a rumor that some unfortunate young lady shuffled off her mortal coil on her way out the door of his museum, if that's what happened. Nobody knows who she is, or where and how she died. And Mike Chapman hates the press. All the guys in his squad do. The media does nothing except make their work more difficult, especially in a high-profile investigation. Then there's me, and I have the good sense to drop this right in Paul Battaglia's lap. Not to mention that I'm exhausted now. Can we talk about this tomorrow?"

"That's my point, darling. I'm having breakfast with Brian Williams." Jake subbed for Williams on the nightly cable news desk, and they had become good friends.

"Don't even think about it."

"I'd never discuss your cases with anyone unless you gave me permission. You know that. But this one's going to get out before the day is over. You can't sit on the story of a dead girl in an ancient sarcophagus shipped out of the largest art museum in America, and a controversial prosecutor who spirited the body out of one jurisdiction back to Manhattan. We'll do it tastefully, darling. It might as well be our story to break."

"Save the *darling* for another time, will you? Tell anyone and I swear that I'll never talk to you again." I pulled the sheet up over the top of my head to end the conversation.

It wasn't enough that the coffin had developed cracks. Now I had to worry about leaks from my own bedroom.

4

"I'd like to be in the room when you interview my daughter, ma'am."

"I'll answer all your questions, Mrs. Alfieri, when I'm done speaking with Angel. In the meantime, I'm going to give you a newspaper to read and ask you to take a seat in the waiting area. The detective and I need to be alone with her."

"But she's only fourteen. I got a right to—"

Somehow, everybody had a laundry list of rights that I couldn't find anywhere in the Constitution. "We're preparing your daughter to testify about her case before the grand jury. That's what the law calls a secret proceeding. I'll be the only person in the room with Angel, aside from the jurors and the stenographer. I need to get her used to talking about what happened without you holding her hand."

She frowned at me and waddled behind Detective Vandomir as he led her down the hallway. I waited for him at my door. "I couldn't shake her loose the other night," he said. "Good move."

"My first rule of thumb with a dishonest witness:

get the mother, the boyfriend, the sister out of the picture. Find some way to do it, whatever works. You never get the truth when they have to admit to someone close to them that they've been lying. Where are you with her?"

"Mother works for one of those overnight mail services. Ten P.M. to four in the morning, five nights a week. Ex-husband lives in Florida. Angel and her two kid brothers are home alone. Perp is a livery cabdriver who drove Angel to her house from the hospital about a month ago, after she visited her grandmother, who had some serious surgery.

"Kid says he showed up at the door the other night, forced her up the stairs into her bedroom at knife point, and raped her."

"Brothers hear anything?"

"Sleeping in the room right up against her wall. Not a peep."

"Outcry?"

"Immediate. That's on her side. Called 911 a little after midnight, a few minutes after she says he left."

"Medical exam?"

"Inconclusive. She says he didn't ejaculate, so there's no semen. No way to do DNA. And she's sexually active. Three partners."

"Some little angel."

"Yeah, she's already got chlamydia. Mother doesn't know about that either."

"Tell me about the perp."

"He's a real dirtbag. Forty-eight years old, has a bunch of collars for drug possession, boosting cars, doing break-ins. Nothing like this. Nothing violent.

Floor of his car full of kiddie-porn magazines and condom wrappers. No knife."

"He got a story?"

"Yeah. Starts the same way. Picked her up outside of Metropolitan Hospital. By the time they hit 110th Street, she was sitting in the front seat, writing down her beeper number so he could page her at school the next day. Met her a couple of times after class. Drove her around with her friends. Oral sex once or twice in the backseat. Even did a threesome with Angel and one of the other cherubs in her pack. Says she invited him to come over this past Monday night when her mother left for work."

"You tell her what he said?"

"Yeah. She denies it. Says the only way he knew where she lived was because he had driven her home from the hospital that one time. Gave her his card with his cell phone, in case she needed to use him again. That's how we got him. I called and asked him to pick me up in front of the deli next door to our office, and then invited him to step inside to help my clearance rate for the month. Collars for dollars."

"She understands we're going to get her beeper information and his cell phone records?"

"I don't think it had the same impact on her as it does when you tell an adult. She didn't seem to grasp that all of this is computerized now. I explained to her that every time he beeped her or she called him, it's just like leaving a fingerprint. Not sure she believes me."

"Or wants to. Let's give her a go." I turned the door handle and went into my office, where Angel had been waiting for us.

She smiled at Vandomir as we entered, and closed the small mirrored case in which she had been examining herself, rubbing one last application of a fruity-smelling gloss over her lips. She tugged at the straps of her bright yellow tank top, pulling it into place so the rhinestone letters that formed the word *Gangsta* stretched from nipple to nipple.

"Angel, this is Ms. Cooper, the lawyer I told you about. She's going to be handling your case. She's got some more questions for you."

"You understand why you're here today, Angel?"

"Not really. I told him everything that happened." She jerked her head in Vandomir's direction. "I don't know why I have to explain it over again. You just oughtta keep Felix locked up so he don't do this to nobody else."

"In order for that to happen, we have to find out exactly what he did. I'm going to ask you the same things the detective did, maybe even more questions. And what you say stays in this room, do you understand that? If there's something that went on between you and Felix that you don't want your mother to know about, then *this* is the time and place to let me know about it."

She lifted her eyes to look at me, without moving her head.

"What do you mean?"

"Do you have any idea what goes on at a trial, Angel?"

"I don't want to be at no trial. I just want the judge to sentence him to jail."

"That's not how it works. You watch television?"

"Yeah."

"Ever see any of those cop shows where the guys go to trial? You know who's in the courtroom when the witness testifies?"

"Me. Him. The judge. You. That's when I gotta tell what he did to me."

"And what do you think Felix does, after you testify?"

"I don't know."

"He gets to talk to the jury, too, if he wants to. He gets to tell them the story the way *he* says it happened. Those twelve people don't know you, and they don't know him, so they have to try to figure out which one of you to believe, whose story makes more sense."

"How come he gets to talk?" That part of the process clearly bothered her. "He's gonna lie anyway. He's gonna say I invited him to my house."

Angel's tongue clicked against the roof of her mouth, sounding a strong note of disapproval at the defense she had just offered on Felix's behalf, and she slumped farther down in her chair. Her shoulders sagged forward, the *g* and *a* rhinestones disappearing from my view. All that was left were the letters forming the word *angst*.

"Let me tell you about lying in a court of law. Did the detective tell you that it's a crime, too? That if you take an oath to tell the truth but you lie on the witness stand, you can be arrested?"

"Felix raped me. I'm not lying about that. You can't arrest me for nothing. I'm too young." The pout had passed momentarily, and she was emboldened by the thought that her age would protect her from my lightly veiled threat.

Don't test me today, Angel. "Actually, we *can* arrest you. Your case is heard in family court because you're not sixteen. But the judge there can send you to a foster home upstate, take you away from your mother—"

That snapped her to attention. "I don't want to be doing this now. I want to go home."

"I'm afraid that's not one of your choices. A man has been arrested because of the story you told Detective Vandomir. He's been in jail for a couple of days, charged with the most serious thing one human being can do to another, short of murder. And he belongs there, if he held a knife to you and raped you. He belongs there for a very long time.

"So we're going to go over your statement one more time. There's only one thing you can do wrong, from this point on."

"What's that?"

"Lie. You cannot tell any lies, Angel. Not about anything. No matter how insignificant you think the question is, no matter what it concerns, you can't lie about it. If I ask you whether it was raining or sunny the day you met Felix, you've got to tell me the truth."

"Like what does that have to do with my being raped?"

"Every single thing you say has to do with how we know what to believe when you get to the point of telling us what happened with Felix in your bedroom. If you lie about the little things that led up to that, then it means you're very capable of lying about the big ones. Tell me you never gave him the number of your beeper, and I get records back from the phone company in a few days showing that he beeped you every day last week, then I know you've told enough lies for me not to trust anything you say. And if you do it under oath, before the grand jury, I'll have you arrested before you leave the building."

There were gentler ways to do this, but I was out of patience and short on time. It was almost nine-thirty, and as soon as my assistant, Laura, clocked in and got to her desk, she'd be leaving a message for Battaglia that I needed to see him.

Vandomir was a smart cop with good instincts. If he doubted the veracity of Angel's narrative, he had reason to do so. Four and a half hours with her in the emergency room at the hospital had given him a concrete sense of where the holes in her story were. I tried to soften my tone and get back to the beginning of her meeting with Felix.

Each time she answered a question, Angel looked at Vandomir for a reaction. I had become the bad cop, and she was sticking with the version that she had originally given, even though the details did not hold together. But I couldn't discount the complaint of any rape victim on a hunch, so I drilled away at every hour that had passed between the first cab ride in which they met and the night in question.

I was up against a stone wall. Angel wasn't convincing, but she was tough. Vandomir wrote something on a piece of paper and handed it to me across my desk.

His note suggested a weakness to get us over the

threshold. "Ask her if one of her girlfriends has a tattoo on her butt. The word *Ralphie*, inside the outline of a bull."

"Who are the girls you hang out with at school?"

"Jessica. Connie. Paula. Why you gotta know?"

"Last names."

"I don't know their last names." She was pushing me.

"I'll go to the school myself and find them."

She murmured "Bitch" just loud enough for me to hear it.

"Tell me about Ralphie's girlfriend."

Angel glared at Vandomir. "You been to my school already?"

"Which one is Ralphie's girl?"

"She ain't got nothing to do with this. You stay away from my—"

"Every single person you know who Felix met has something to do with this. The fact that he knows that one of your pals has Ralphie's name engraved on her ass tells me that he knows more about you than I do right now. And that's okay for me but it's very bad for you."

She was as startled as I was when the intercom buzzed and Laura interrupted us. "Now's your chance, Alex. Rose said to get in there as soon as you can. Battaglia wants to know what you've got before he starts his ten o'clock with the deputy mayor, okay?"

"Tell her I'll be there in five."

I turned my attention back to Angel. "Do you know what a lie detector test is?"

"Yeah. I seen them on TV."

"You know how they work?"

"Some cop puts like a . . . um, I don't know. They ask you questions, that's all."

"We've got brand-new ones now. Computerized. Impossible to beat. They're hooked up to your brain waves, your pulse, your blood pressure. First, we put a needle in your arm—"

"A *needle*? I don't want no f—"

"It's not a question of what you want. This is the point you've taken us to, and it's full speed ahead from now on. It's a big needle. It just stings for a few minutes when they inject you."

Her bottom lip was quivering. "I don't like no needles. I'm afraid of needles." She had turned her whole body toward Vandomir and was begging him to intercede. The fourteen-year-old kid hiding inside the attitude of a thirty-year-old was beginning to reveal herself.

I pressed the intercom and Laura came on immediately. "Get me Detective Roman, will you, please? Immediately. Tell him I need a lie detector test in one hour. Juvenile subject. May have to make an arrest, so he better bring his handcuffs."

Tears were poised on the bottom lids of Angel's eyes, ready to pour down her cheeks.

"I'm going to have you wait across the hall until the detective gets up here. Come with me."

"I *hate* needles."

"And I hate people who lie to me. Especially about being raped. You know how busy Detective Vandomir and his partners are? They get called out on three, four, five cases a day. Young girls and grown women who need their help. Badly. They work all night most of the time, just trying to keep families like yours and mine safe. Every extra minute we spend trying to get the truth out of you is time taken away from someone else who was the victim of a crime, some other person who wants to cooperate with us."

"Can I talk to my mother first?" She was whimpering now.

"Here's what we're going to do. You've got one hour until the detective comes to give you the test. I'm going in to talk to my boss. Sit in that room and think about the choice you have. If there's something about your story that you want to change, you just tell Detective Vandomir. He's your best hope. If you tell him a story that makes sense, you won't need the needle."

I kneeled beside her chair and tried to make contact with her moist eyes. "Felix was wrong. It's against the law for a man as old as he is to have sex with you. That's a crime. We can still punish him for that. But if he didn't have a knife, Angel, then you're making up an entirely different kind of crime. If you made a mistake by starting that story and you got in over your head without meaning to, then tell us the truth *now* before you dig yourself in any deeper."

I grabbed a legal pad off my desk and told Laura to hold everything while I went over to see the district attorney.

My identification tag released the security lock on the door to Battaglia's inner sanctum. The chief assistant was refilling his coffee mug as I walked past him.

Rose Malone, the DA's executive assistant, had the phone wedged between her shoulder and her left ear, working at the computer as she waved me into the boss's suite. I tried to stall long enough for her to get off, so that I could get a reading on his mood, but she gave no sign of ending the call quickly.

I had practiced my approach several times on my way down to the office in the cab. A casual "By the way, I thought you'd want to hear what happened to me at the museum last night" wouldn't work. I was confident Battaglia would back my shipyard decision if it was presented as an homage to his style, and smiled in anticipation of his reaction as I pushed open his door.

The first thing I saw was the smirk on Pat McKinney's face. He was standing, arms akimbo, between Battaglia and me, and I knew before a word was spoken that he had gotten wind of last night's maneuvers. The deputy chief of the trial division and my most driven in-house adversary, McKinney would have delighted in pitching this to the boss as a political embarrassment.

"I knew you and Chapman were movie buffs, Alex, but *The Mummy Returns* meets *Invasion of the Body Snatchers* wouldn't even rate buttered popcorn in my house."

No point asking him how he knew. He'd be only too happy to regurgitate the details. His fingers tapped excitedly on the conference table behind him and his mild overbite looked like it had grown into fangs overnight.

"Paul, I'd like to—"

But Battaglia seemed content to let McKinney play out his hand. "Your pal Chapman was a bit out of control last night. Tried to push the Crime Scene Unit to drag themselves down to the ME's office to take photos in the middle of cleaning up a job at a triple homicide in Midtown. Chief of D's had to call me at three-thirty in the morning to referee the decision."

I had no idea that some other sensational crime had occurred after midnight.

"Jeez. And I know how you hate to be bothered at home about anything job-related." More than half the legal staff of six hundred lawyers were on felony call at any given point in time, and all of the supervisors knew that being beeped and contacted twenty-four hours a day came with the territory. Most of us welcomed the opportunity to have input on case actions that would affect the way they would later move forward through the system. McKinney was an exception to the rule. He lived without an answering machine, didn't give out his beeper number, and punished all but his handful of pets who dared to find him once he left his office.

"I hated having to say no to something you were working on, Alex. But we had a real serious investigation going on, not some cute publicity stunt."

Battaglia usually couldn't stand that kind of bickering. There was no point defending my actions in front of McKinney. But I had insisted that Chapman get the sarcophagus photographed before it was removed from the back of the truck at the morgue and was incredulous that my own colleague had prevented such critical documentation of the findings.

"Paul, may I talk to you about this alone?"

"Not until I return the phone calls I've got here."
He flapped a stack of messages at me. "I'm trying to
understand why the press found out this happened
before I did."

My face reddened. "Boss, I've talked to no one
about this, except—"

"Just find out who the girl is, where she was when
she was killed, some reason for anyone to want her
dead, and then we'll figure out what to do with this
mess you've created for me."

"I'd like you to understand that I had Jake's word
that he would not tell anyone about the case."

I tried to convince myself that I believed what I was
saying, but Battaglia wasn't even interested in my
denials. "Maybe McKinney's right about this. You
can't be expected to keep confidences while you're
personally involved with a newshound. We should
leave you off some of these high-profile cases."

I opened my mouth to protest, but McKinney
spoke over me.

"This might be the perfect place to start."

5

"What did you do to that pitiful-looking kid who's sitting in the conference room crying?"

"Get away from my office before Pat McKinney sees you talking to me or I'm dead."

"That case anything I should know about? She the girl who was attacked outside Port Authority last week?"

I grabbed Mickey Diamond's sleeve and dragged him to the top of the stairwell opposite Laura's desk. The *New York Post* courthouse reporter was trolling for stories and he had come to the wrong place at the worst possible moment this morning. "You do remember, don't you, that it's against the law for me to identify a rape victim to you?"

Diamond had been a fixture at 100 Centre Street for more years and more tabloid headlines than anyone could remember. Our public relations director was headquartered a short walk down the corridor from my office, and Diamond hung out in her anteroom when he wasn't watching trials, trading tales with reporters from the other papers in the pressroom on the ground floor behind the information rotunda, or making up stories out of whole cloth to keep his byline lively.

"Is she crying in spite of you or because of you?"

"Somebody ought to put a 'Do Not Disturb' sign on the entire eighth floor, meant only for you. Just stay here a minute. I need your help. Did you call Battaglia this morning?"

"What for? I got that triple from last night with the transgender victim and the two thugs who were three-card-monte dealers on the Deuce. Right in front of one of the Disney theaters."

Forty-second Street—the Deuce, in perp parlance—had undergone a major face-lift during my tenure in the DA's office, but it still attracted sharks who preyed on the tourists who flocked to that neighborhood. "My editor wants to know if the deceased was shtupping Minnie or Mickey, but I didn't think to bother your boss with that."

"That's all you're working on?"

"Unless you've got something sweeter."

"Nothing yet. But somebody leaked a breaking story and Battaglia's blaming me. I need you to check with everyone in the pressroom, keep your ears open, be discreet—"

"I was with you until you got to that part."

"Then forget I said it. Just listen. You're going to hear something interesting later on. That much I can promise you. Find out for me who had it first. Find out where it came from."

"I'm gonna give you a source when you won't even give me a clue about that bawling little adolescent you got in there?"

"You're going to give me a direction. I don't need a name, I need to get out of the sinkhole I'm in right now."

"What's in it for me?"

"You got any space left on the wall of shame?" Diamond had wallpapered the courthouse pressroom with his page-one *Post* headlines. He turned every human tragedy and violent crime into an alliterative eye-catcher or tasteless punch line to help sell the tabloid rag. Unfortunately, the work of my unit had provided a rich source of material.

"I might have to cover up some of your old cases, but they're turning yellow anyway."

"Get me what I need and I can assure you you'll be so busy for the next couple of days that you won't know what hit you. Meanwhile, get lost before Mc-Kinney eyes the two of us together."

"Give me a hint."

I pushed at Diamond's shoulder and pointed down the stairs. "Go see Ryan Blackmer. He's taking a plea this afternoon on the case with the oral surgeon who sexually abused a patient after he gave her nitrous oxide."

"Today? I already have my piece written. 'D.D.S.— Dentist Desired Sex.' Would have been a cover story if the triple hadn't happened."

"Where's Cooper?" McKinney's voice echoed in the stairwell. I heard Laura tell him that I had gone to the ladies' room and would be back in a few minutes. Diamond waved over his shoulder and trotted down to the seventh floor.

"Tell her I want to know whose side she's on. She's

got some witness out here crying and the kid's mother is complaining that Cooper was going to give her a lie detector test and take her away from home. What kind of crap is going on around here? This office hasn't used a lie detector since 1973. I want to see her immediately."

I waited until I could hear McKinney's footsteps walking away from my office and crossed back to find Vandomir standing beside my desk. "When did you come up with this tactic? You oughtta patent it. Worked like a charm on Angel," he said.

"Remember those old Dick Tracy cartoons that were called 'crime stoppers'? My favorite was the one that said the best lie detector was the threat of a lie detector. I haven't yet met the teenage girl who isn't afraid of a needle. I just designed the most unpleasant-sounding imaginary machine I could think of, wait until I catch them in the first concrete fabrication before I describe it, and then give them an hour to decide which is worse—the big needle or 'fessing up. I've never had to wait more than fifteen minutes."

"This one took exactly eight. She pleaded with me to let her tell me what really happened. Anything but sticking a needle in that skinny arm of hers, and having to see *you* again."

"What did she give you?"

"Felix was telling the truth. She fell in love about two minutes after getting in the cab and he began to pick her up at school every day. It was her friend Jessica they did a threesome with. She's the one who's Ralphie's girl."

"So why the 911 call?"

Every false report had a motive, some reason that person decided to pick up the phone and invite the NYPD into his or her otherwise private life. Find that spot, and the need for deception usually became crystal clear to the investigator.

"'Cause Felix didn't bring a condom with him that night, and when she told him to pull out or she'd never let him have sex with her again, he told her she wasn't that good anyway. Said he got it better from Jessica. She was jealous and angry. Figured she'd get back at him by getting him in trouble with the cops. Never thought anybody would take it too seriously."

"The knife?"

"Didn't exist."

"Force?"

"Nope. She invited him in and led him right to the bedroom."

"And there's her poor mother, working all night to try to give her kids a good life, and this one's going to break her heart. Let's bring this to an end."

Angel refused to pick up her head when I walked into the conference room. She had a box of tissues in front of her and had gone through a handful before I arrived. Mrs. Alfieri was standing at the window and staring out, with her handkerchief balled up in her hand.

"Does it feel any better to tell the truth? Isn't it a relief?" I asked Angel. She didn't seem to agree with me.

"You both lied to me. You told me what I said to you was just gonna stay with us."

"I had to tell your mother the truth," Vandomir said.

"She's got to know she can walk out every night and do her job without having you bringing men into the house. Miss Cooper was right. Family court will take you away from your home if your mother can't control you."

Mrs. Alfieri turned to look at her daughter, too pained to raise her voice above a whisper. "You lied to him, Angel. You lied to all of us. Now you know how it feels when someone does that to you."

I tried to get her to understand the gravity of her encounter with Felix. "Do you know how lucky you are to be alive? You meet a total stranger in a taxicab and start having sex with him. Bring him into your house, where your two little brothers are asleep, not knowing what he's capable of doing to you or to them."

"So?" Angel was still sullen and angry.

It ripped me apart to see a kid like this who had a roof over her head and a parent who cared, and was still on a clear path to self-destruction. "You know where I spent my night? Standing beside the body of a young woman—not much older than you, probably. Somebody killed her and then stuffed her inside a box, hoping she'd never be found. She'll never be going home again. The people who loved her will never see her alive."

Angel looked at me now, trying to figure out whether I was serious. "And yesterday afternoon I was at the morgue, looking at the autopsy pictures of another girl who was murdered, probably by a guy she met at a club the night before. Ever hear the word *autopsy*? Know what that means?"

"Tell her what it is, Miss Cooper." Her mother walked closer to us, resting her arms on the back of one of the chairs. "Listen to her, Angel. This is what happens when somebody kills you. It ain't enough that you're already dead. They gotta cut you all up and take you apart, piece by piece. Then they sew you back up like you was a rag doll."

Better than my own big needle, I thought. That image grabbed the kid's attention and had her looking to Vandomir for salvation from the two women who were making her day so difficult.

"What happens to Felix now?"

"He stays in jail. But it's a different charge. It's called statutory rape." I explained to her that even though she had been a willing participant in her sexual relationship with the forty-eight-year-old man, the law deemed her incapable of consent. She was under-age, and he would still be punished, although the sanctions were far less serious than those for forcible rape.

"Laura will type up a new complaint," I said to Vandomir, "and Angel can sign the corroborating affidavit. I want you to take the two of them down to the witness aid unit to get them hooked up for some counseling, okay? They can both use it."

I walked back to Laura's alcove, almost tripping over Ellen Gunsher, who was on her way down the hall to Pat McKinney's suite. The pair spent an inordinate amount of time behind his closed door, leading to endless office gossip about the inappropriate nature of their friendship. If Ellen needed as much supervision as McKinney claimed he was providing, she must have been even more dense than she revealed at trial division meetings on those rare occasions when she opened her mouth.

Gunsher's arrival gave me breathing room. McKinney wouldn't look for me while she was hanging out with him, so there was no point even knocking on his door.

I picked up the phone and dialed Jake's number on my private line, trying to find a tone of voice that was not too accusatory. His assistant, Perry Tabard, answered and told me Jake was in the studio in the middle of a taping. "Would you ask him to call me as soon as he wraps it up? It's pretty important."

"Shall I give him a message?"

There was no point telling him what the problem was. I needed reassurance from Jake that he had not betrayed my confidence last night, and I didn't want a middleman to get it.

Before I could finish my conversation with Perry, Laura buzzed me on the intercom. Mike Chapman was on the phone.

"Hey, Coop, how fast can you get your ass up to the ME's office?"

"Half an hour. I just need to turn over the rest of today's schedule to Sarah." My deputy and close friend, Sarah Brenner, had returned earlier in the spring from a six-month maternity leave. Our professional styles were so similar that I relied on her to run the forty-member unit as my partner. It was shortly after she gave birth that I had my terrifying encounter with the underbelly of the academic community at an elite Manhattan college, without benefit of her guidance and judgment. I was delighted to have her back at my side.

"Great. Meet me at Dr. Kestenbaum's."

"The girl—did you learn anything last night? Will they be able to figure out who she is or when she died?"

"Save your cross-examination for the courtroom and step on it. You're about to have a lesson in theology."

"I've already said my prayers for the deceased. Now I want some answers to my questions." I was thinking of Battaglia's directive and anxious to get results for him.

"Dr. K. will give you all the answers you want. You're going to meet your first Incorruptible."

"My *what*?"

"Unless he was an altar boy in my parish, chances are the killer never set eyes on one either."

"What's an Incorruptible? What does it have to do with our victim?"

"She's perfectly preserved, Coop. No decomposition, no decay. We'll have her identified before the end of the week. It's a natural phenomenon—happened to a few of the saints every now and then over the centuries.

"I'd have to think our perp closed the lid on Cleo and figured all he was leaving behind in his trail was a box of bones."

6

I signed the visitors' log at the entrance desk of the morgue. An interpreter was explaining to a middle-aged man, in Mandarin, what the process would be for the viewing of his father, who had been stabbed to death during a dispute in a gambling parlor in China-town. The attendant pressed the release button on the door that led to the elevators, and I followed a cop carrying an evidence envelope as he got on one and headed to the fourth floor.

Mike was sitting at Kestenbaum's desk, holding a phone to one ear and a cup of coffee in his other hand. "Yeah, loo, we got some good photos. Coop'll take me up to the museum later on. I got a feeling this case is gonna be more culture than is good for a guy like me." He paused to listen to his lieutenant. "No, Dr. K. is still in the basement with Cleo. Call you later."

"How'd you get pictures? McKinney told me he overruled you on having crime scene come in to process the truck. You should have called—"

"Relax. You think you're the only snake charmer who can get some results in the middle of the night? I called Hal Sherman at home," Mike said, referring to the ace Crime Scene Unit detective. "He doesn't need to be stroked by you in order to put in a little overtime on a serious caper. Screw McKinney."

"So who else knew about this before daybreak?"

"Besides Lenny, the two of us, the mopes in the shipyard? Guess it's Hal and the guys and ghouls who work downstairs on the graveyard shift. It was pretty quiet here when we brought the body in."

"Mike, the truth. Did you tell anyone about this?"

"Like who? Whaddaya mean?"

"Anyone you shouldn't have. At one of the papers?"

"Are you crazy? I'm not the one who likes the lime-light. The less frigging coverage I have, the better I work, the sounder I sleep. Today it's news. Tomorrow, it's a stack of garbage tied up in piles and left out on the sidewalk with the trash, dogs lifting their legs to piss all over yesterday's headliners and legends."

"Battaglia's ripped. The story's out, and he's blaming me for telling Jake. He assumes Jake is the leak."

"And?"

"I don't know. I can't believe he'd do something stupid like that, but he was with me when I heard the news, and he was waiting for me when I got home early this morning."

"In bed? As bad as you looked when you left me in Newark?"

I smiled. "I'd better forget my own problems and focus on the more important things. Like Incorrupt-ibles."

"Guess you'd have to be a good Catholic like me to

know all about the saints, kid, and how to preserve a body without any decay."

Kestenbaum entered his office and motioned to Mike to stay at the desk. "It's actually a tradition that started with the Jews. Check out the Old Testament. It's the way Joseph had his father buried by our forefathers, Alex."

"Gospel According to Saint John, doc. Jesus was wound in linen clothes and anointed with spices."

"What are you two talking about?" I had been raised in the Jewish faith, my mother having converted before her marriage to my father.

"Last night I figured it was going to take weeks to make an identification of our victim. That there would be natural decay, speeded up by her being enclosed in the sarcophagus. Maybe there'd be nothing left for DNA, or Dr. K. would have to do mitochondrial DNA on the hair, which takes so much longer. But she's perfectly preserved."

"You mean, someone took steps to do that?"

"Not intentionally. Not by cutting her up, the way they did to the Pharaohs. This one is natural, just like with the saints. You explain it, doc."

"Even as physicians, we learn that for millennia, early Jews and Christians tried to preserve human bodies against decomposition by wrapping them in linens, then saturating them with herbs and plant residues like aloe and myrrh. The Egyptians perfected the method, copied later by Europeans, of eviscerating the corpse and removing the internal organs, to prevent natural gases from causing decay."

"Forget taking out the viscera." Chapman took

over the lead in the conversation. "There's not an external mark on Cleo's body, is there, doc?"

"Not one. This was not a medical preservation. The killer couldn't have dreamed his prey would show up in this condition."

"You gotta think miracles. For centuries the corporal remains of saints were thought to be responsible for miracles in our Church. The Holy Ghost once took up residence inside them, making them sacred. That's how come they healed the sick, made blind men see, and let cripples walk again. In the Middle Ages, Church officials began to dig up the bodies of saints and martyrs and nuns, hundreds of years after their deaths. Like Saint Zita, she's always been one of my favorites."

"I've never heard of her."

"I'll take you to see her myself. Tuscany, in Lucca. All laid out in a little glass case, looking like she's taking a nap. She's the patron saint of domestic servants—that's why my old lady likes her so much. Lived in the thirteenth century. When the medieval wise men decided to exhume Zita because of all the miracles associated with her, they were amazed to find that her body was completely intact, without a trace of decay."

I had never heard of this phenomenon and looked at Kestenbaum to see whether he knew of it, or whether Chapman was bluffing. The pathologist nodded.

"Saint Bernadette, too, in France. She died in 1879, and they dug her up thirty years later."

"Yeah, but the churchmen who did the digging

were all religious people who must have been looking for miracles."

Kestenbaum corrected me. "They had surgeons present to witness the exhumations, along with the mayor of the little village and people unrelated to the Church."

Chapman continued, "They unscrewed the lid of the wooden coffin and there was the sister's body, perfectly preserved."

"It must have smelled like—"

"No odor of putrefaction at all. The only change noticed by the nuns who had prepared her for burial was the pallor of her complexion. She was wizened, but all the skin and hair was right in place, her nails were shining, and her hands still clutched a rosary, which had rusted."

"But surely, beneath the skin—"

"I'm telling you, they did this to her two or three times. They reburied her and brought her up again. There are lots of witnesses. Muscles and ligaments were all in good condition."

"Why did they do it?"

"Incorruptibility used to be one of the requisites for canonization, until some of our boys began to cheat and do it the surgical way. Like Saint Margaret of Cortona. Turns out she wasn't preserved naturally. Had a little medical intervention. Did it by the Egyptian method, then put her back in the coffin and pretended it had happened naturally.

"But Bernadette was a real phenomenon. The third time they brought her up was when they began to take relics. Pieces of her bones that doctors and priests removed from her corpse. Part of the body of the saint to help perform more miracles."

"They cut out the poor woman's bones?"

"Ribs, muscles. If they found gallstones they took them, too. Looking for proof of divine grace, trying to memorialize the person who was responsible for attracting this powerful good."

"So, you're telling me that Bernadette was mummified? Naturally, not like the Egyptians did with the removal of all the body organs?"

"It really was miraculous, at least in the Church if not to science. I mean, the way she was buried, nobody expected it. She'd been very ill at the time she died, and the chapel in which she'd been interred was so humid that everybody expected the flesh had decayed. After all, the rosary was rusty, the crucifix inside the coffin had turned green, and even her habit was damp."

I shuddered at Mike's description. "This must have been very rare. Zita, Bernadette—"

"Saint Ubald of Gubbio, Blessed Margaret of Savoy. You want me to go on? I know my saints and virgins better than I know Yankee statistics. Had my knuckles rapped enough times back in parochial school for catechisms I couldn't follow, but when they got to this kind of stuff, it grabbed me."

"I'm missing something here. You two have figured out who our victim is? You're not trying to tell me she's some kind of saint, are you?"

"She's Saint Cleo to me, working her only little miracle for us. I never thought we'd find anything under those linen wraps. I figured that body would be partially if not fully decomposed. You gotta think the person who put her in that box and stuck a shipping label on it to sit on the blacktop in Newark during the summer heat, or in the hold of a freighter headed for Cairo, wouldn't have expected there'd be anything left to make a visual ID of his victim."

"You've done the autopsy?" I asked Kestenbaum.

"Later today. But we've unwrapped the linen and taken the photos. Mike's right. The body is completely intact, in remarkable condition."

"Maybe she just died recently, within the week."

"Unlikely. I'd say she's been dead for months, maybe the better part of a year. I'll have a better idea after I get to work, but the skin has some discoloration and it's shriveled a bit, the muscles have atrophied, and the lashes on her left eyelid have come out and are stuck to the brow."

"And she's dressed in winter clothing, am I right, doc?"

"Yeah. Nothing you'd wear at the end of May. Heavy woolen slacks and a four-ply cashmere sweater with long sleeves and a crew neck."

Kestenbaum removed a few Polaroid photos from the pocket of his lab coat and passed them to me. I lifted the one on top for a close look and passed the others to Mike.

The young woman stared back at me with a sober expression. It was remarkable to think that she had been dead for any period of time greater than a few days. She appeared to be about thirty years old. Her skin had a strange cast, but I could not tell how much of that was due to the poor quality of the Polaroid shot in the dim light of the morgue basement.

"I'm telling you, Coop, she's an Incorruptible."

Her sandy brown hair seemed to be falling out of her scalp, but otherwise, she appeared to be perfectly preserved.

"She's going to tell us what we need to know. Where she's been all this time—"

"Any ideas, doc?"

"Think about the way the saints were buried. A number of pathologists have studied these cases, just as religious historians have. Most of the Incorruptibles, before canonization, were interred in burial vaults beneath the altars of churches. Not only was it hallowed ground but it was also cool and the area was often lined with heavy stone. The temperature was usually quite low beneath the floor, even when the seasons changed. That's what you're going to be looking for, Mike. Someplace cool and dry that would naturally preserve this body."

"What happened to her?" I studied her small face, with its high cheekbones and thin, straight nose.

"I'll work on that. You and Chapman figure out who she is and who wanted her dead."

"No signs of trauma?"

"None."

"You don't think she could have died naturally, do you?" I suddenly worried that we did not even have a crime victim here.

Chapman shook his head. "Like a premature burial? Cleo just got in the box because she didn't feel well, and someone closed the lid? I don't think so, Coop. How about you, doc?"

Kestenbaum wasn't the guessing type. He'd wait and let the science of the postmortem procedure tell him what had caused the young woman's death. That's why I was surprised when he answered Mike.

"Don't quote me on this before I give you a call later on today. In all likelihood, it's poison. I'd say it's arsenic."

7

Mike was still chewing on his hot dog as we jogged up the several tiers of steps at the entrance of the Metropolitan Museum of Art on Fifth Avenue at Eighty-second Street shortly after 2 P.M.

"Shootings, stabbings, strangulations. Drownings, decapitations, defenestrations. Beatings, bombings, bludgeonings—" He had a manner of death for every riser as we maneuvered our way around sunbathing students and sightseers. "Hey, watch it, Houdini, will ya?" An amateur magician was performing tricks for a crowd of onlookers and from under his cloak released a pigeon that practically landed on Mike's head. "A dove I wouldn't mind, but these guys stink."

He skipped a beat to wave off the bird. "Robberies, rapes, rub-outs. I've had everything else, but I don't think I've ever had a homicide by poison. You?"

"Just the guy who put Drano in his wife's martini."

"Yeah, but she didn't die."

"Almost. Burned a hole in her gut."

"Doesn't count in my squad. She lived to tell about it. Jeez, I forget how huge this place is."

"Quarter of a mile long, more than a million square feet in area."

"How do you know that?"

"I read it in the program last night, before things got crazy."

The four sets of double doors were wide open, freshening the interior with the mild breeze of the May afternoon. The Great Hall was a spectacular space, elegant and airy beneath the high, domed ceiling and filled with light.

"My dad used to bring me here all the time."

"Mine, too." My father began to buy art after the success of his medical invention, and had a small but impressive collection of seventeenth- and eighteenth-century European paintings, Flemish to Florentine.

"Saturday morning?"

"As soon as the doors opened."

"Same for us. It was my reward, after five days of school—my daily torture—and before I had to hang out in church all day on Sunday. You think we would have hit it off if we met here back when we were six or seven? I picture you all decked out in patent leather Mary Janes with starched crinolines and dopey little headbands on."

"Wrong kid. I was a total tomboy, except for my ballet slippers."

"You probably weren't quite so bossy yet, then, were you?"

We were having the identical thought. As different as our backgrounds were, we had probably stood in this very space on the very same day many times during our childhood. Mike Chapman was half a year older than I. His father, Brian, had died of a massive coronary just forty-eight hours after turning in his gun and shield. Twenty-six years as a cop had earned him the respect and admiration of his favorite son, who was a junior at Fordham University when Brian died so suddenly. Although Mike completed college and graduated the following spring, he enrolled in the Police Academy shortly afterward.

Mike had risen through the department like a rocket. He had spent most of the years since his promotion to the detective bureau in the elite Manhattan North Homicide Squad, which was home to some of the best men—and a smattering of women—in the NYPD. His days and nights were devoted to solving the steady stream of killings that occurred on his half of the island, north of Fifty-ninth Street. We had met in my rookie year in the office, when we both had other assignments, and had spent a great deal of time together, on and off the job.

"Wipe the mustard off your chin before we get to Thibodaux's office."

"See what I mean? I take it back. You must have been a pain in the ass already by the time you were six. It's in your blood. Where'd you hang out?"

"Second floor, paintings and sculpture. That's where I saw my first Degas." I had started taking ballet lessons when I was five years old. The elegance of the movement and the beauty of the music had always been a refuge for me, and to this day I continued to take classes whenever I could fit them into my unpredictable schedule. As a child, I had often sat spellbound in front of the painting of two dancers practicing in their white tulle dresses with large yellow ribbons on their backs, stretching their legs along the barre before they began their exercise on pointe, hoping to grow up to be just like them.

"Me, I went straight over here," Mike said, pointing across the hall past the bottom of the Grand Staircase. "Arms and armor." The Met had a stunning collection, and although my brothers spent hours wandering around the cases filled with gilded parade armor, presentation swords, and rapiers, I raced past them to get to my dancers and the other portraiture I loved so much.

I asked the woman at the information desk the way to the museum director's office. She called ahead to Thibodaux's secretary, who told her we were expected.

"This is where I got hooked on battles and warriors. Couldn't get enough of that stuff." Mike had an encyclopedic knowledge of military history. I knew he had studied the field at college, but it had never occurred to me to ask how his interest had originated.

We walked through the galleries of Greek and Roman art to find the bank of elevators to take us upstairs. "They've got more than fourteen thousand objects in there, from knights in chain mail to samurai swords. There's an armor workshop in the basement. Uncle Sam used it in World War Two, copying medieval designs to make flak jackets for the army."

A middle-aged woman was standing by the elevator door when we got out. "Miss Cooper? I'm Eve Drexler, Mr. Thibodaux's assistant." I introduced her to Mike and we accompanied her down the hall-

way. Her ankle-length flowered print dress swished
between her legs as she walked to the door of the
office, ushering us past the secretary and into a lav-
ishly decorated room with large windows. The sunny
view looked across Fifth Avenue to the handsome
town houses that had been converted years ago into
the prestigious private girls' school Marymount. The
perks of the directorate were obvious. An ancient
hero, sculpted in bronze, was battling a centaur on
Thibodaux's desk, a Savonnerie carpet ran the length
of the room, and paintings by recognizable Masters—
Cézanne, Goya, Brueghel—were hung on three of the
walls.

"Miss Cooper, Mr. Chapman, won't you sit
down?"

The director reached out to shake hands with us,
and moved from his chair to join us at a conference
table. An ornate silver tray holding an antique cof-
feepot that had probably served an emperor or queen
had been placed in front of Ms. Drexler, who poured
for each of us into an ordinary mug.

"I've been trying to get as much information for
you about that shipment as I possibly could," Thibodaux began, opening a folder which contained a sheaf
of papers.

Drexler seated herself at the far end of the table,
opposite her boss, while Chapman and I were next to
each other. She opened a leather-bound notebook and
seemed to be dating the top page, noting the time and
writing down each of our names. Mike flipped open the
cardboard cover of his steno pad, a clean one for the
beginning of a new case, and made similar notations.

"I've made copies of the bill of lading so you can take them along. Have you learned anything this morning from the medical examiner?"

"Nope. They'll be doing the autopsy right about now." Mike reached into his jacket pocket and pulled out one of the head shots taken at the morgue this morning. "Brought this along to see whether you happened to know this girl. Maybe she worked here or something."

Thibodaux took the Polaroid shot, glanced at it, almost doing a double take before turning it facedown on the table. "No, she's not at all familiar to me. But we are a very big place, Mr. Chapman, and I can't say for a moment that I know half the people who work here."

"You looked startled."

"Well, I am, eh? Such a young woman, it's a terrible thing. I never expected she would look—so—well, so alive as she does. To be in a coffin like that for some time, well—"

"What do you mean, 'for some time'?"

"I have absolutely no idea how long she was there, it's just that I assume she didn't die yesterday, Mr. Chapman."

"What's that assumption based on?"

"Here, why don't you look these papers over. Eve has made this set for you." He passed a copy of the multipage document and we started to read it together. "While it is clear that the truck went to New Jersey directly from the museum, the shipment was made up of objects from a number of other institutions. As you can see, there are records of which crates came in when, and from which other museums."

I scanned the top few pages, squinting at the tiny typewritten descriptions of the various sources. There were amphorae on loan from the Smithsonian, African masks from the American Museum of Natural History, mummy cases from the extensive collection at the Brooklyn Museum, and Asian paintings from the Getty.

"I think you've just made our job about a thousand times more difficult. These things all appear to be mixed into the same crates as your own stuff. Why'd that happen?"

"Well, Detective, Mr. Lissen, our shipping manager, tells me that's because they were repackaged after they arrived here, depending on where they were being sent. We're in the final planning stages of a huge show that we'll be mounting next year, and in exchange for some of the treasures that belong to us but are on loan in museums around the world, we're sending out some of our other art to help fill in those gaps."

Thibodaux rubbed his eyes before speaking again. He looked paler than he had in formal dress standing on the floodlit platform at the Temple of Dendur yesterday evening. He had probably not slept at all last night, worrying how this dreadful discovery would affect his museum. His French accent seemed more pronounced today, perhaps because of his exhaustion.

"This sarcophagus—number 1983.752—it's listed on page twelve of that inventory."

Chapman flipped to find it. "This coffin came back

to you last fall. It had been on loan to the Chicago Art Museum, right?"

"So it appears."

"And it's been here ever since then. You know where?"

"I don't, but I'm sure someone can tell you where. Exactly." Thibodaux rose and walked to his desk, opening the drawer and shaking two tablets into his hand. He washed them down with some ice water that was in a crystal pitcher next to his blotter. This was a headache that would not go away with pills.

"And the other stuff in that crate was all from local institutions, am I reading this right?"

Thibodaux came back and picked up his folder. "Yes, that particular box was full of things going to Cairo, mostly from Natural History, right across Central Park, and from the Brooklyn Museum as well. Some were to stay in Egypt, others had final destinations in other parts of Africa.

"You see the enormity of this problem, Detective? There are almost three thousand people who work inside the Met. We've got eight acres of buildings, hundreds of galleries and service areas. There's a fire department, several restaurants, an infirmary, and a power plant. I can't even begin to think about having you disturb everyone here, on account of—of . . ." He gestured to the small Polaroid, on which he had rested his mug.

"Of the young woman who might well have met her death within these walls?" Mike had already dubbed his victim Saint Cleo, and he would fight to bring her murderer to some kind of justice whether or not he ever found out who she was.

"It probably makes sense for us to start talking with Mr. Lissen, and with whomever is in charge of the Egyptian department as well. Weren't they the gentlemen who were out there in Newark last night?" I tried to take the conversation over from Chapman, who was clearly put off by Thibodaux's dismissal of the deceased.

"Trustees, curators, artists, students. If you've never been in a museum, Detective, you'll have no understanding of what this all entails."

"Maybe your French flics haven't looped the Louvre too often, Mr. T., but I've probably spent as much time in this place as you spend looking down your nose at people like me. What would make you think I've never been in a museum? 'Cause I'm a police officer?"

Thibodaux had just turned a dangerous corner. Mike hated that familiar upper-class assumption that he was just another dumb cop, and every time we came up against it in a case investigation, it infuriated him more and more.

"It's just a manner of speaking. I never meant to offend you." He looked across the table to Eve Drexler. "Why don't you call and get Lissen up here, for the detective to speak with."

"Came here the first time when I was four years old." Mike was talking to me now. "My dad had his picture taken right in this office, when the police department gave the museum the guns he recovered."

I didn't understand what he was referring to, and Thibodaux listened as intently as I did.

"During a raid on a whorehouse, back before I was

born, my father and his partner recovered a stash of guns, mixed in with a load of other stolen property. Laid in a warehouse for years, the old property clerk's office. Meanwhile, he's telling everyone how beautiful they are, decorated in gold, chiseled steel, and carved ivory with initials on the handle. Story got up to headquarters and someone finally took a look at the stuff."

Thibodaux stared at Chapman with a bit more interest. "Catherine the Great—the empress's pistols and hunting guns?"

"Made by Johann Grecke, the royal gunmaker, 1786. Right before they would have been destroyed to make room for the new evidence storage unit, the department had Pop bring them to the curator here. They traced the original owner, he donated them back to the Met, and we were all right in this fancy room for the ceremony. First time I ever saw a bottle of champagne and ate cake off an antique plate. Used to come as often as I could to look at my dad's treasures."

"Let me apologize, Detective. I didn't mean to imply that I thought you were ignorant of the museum. Five million visitors walk in and out of these doors every year, seeing only the objects encased in glass or the canvases hanging on the walls. They never think about what goes on behind the scenes, out of view, to make a place like this work so brilliantly, to give life to all these inanimate things."

He was turning the charm on now, trying to play up to Chapman and work the hardship angle to his advantage.

Eve Drexler hung up the phone and came back to

the table. "Mr. Lissen will be here in ten minutes. I've ordered a fresh pot of coffee. And I've asked some of the curators who might be useful to your inquiry to be on standby." She was a model of efficiency.

"Thank you." The director picked up his folder again and continued to scrutinize the entries. Eve walked behind us to gather the empty mugs from which Mike and I had been drinking. She left them on an enameled tray on a satinwood commode next to the door, turning back to remove Thibodaux's and replace it with a fresh one. She picked up the photograph of the dead girl that he had been using as a coaster and took it over to his desk, peeking at it with curiosity as she placed it on the blotter.

I watched her reaction as she reached for the picture again. "Pierre, didn't you recognize this young woman? She was here for meetings with us a number of times last year. Look again. I think it's Katrina Grooten."

8

Thibodaux walked to his desk, opened the drawer, and removed a pair of reading glasses from a metal case. He studied the photograph and shrugged his shoulders.

"I meet so many young people here, Detective. You must forgive me." He looked at his assistant. It wasn't a glare, but it seemed to me that it was a signal for her to back off. "I'm sure I don't recall any specifics, Eve. Is there any reason Miss Grooten should have stood out to me?"

Eve had resumed her place at the table and picked up her notebook. "I might be mistaken, Pierre. It's possible you had nothing to do with her at all."

"Did she work for us?" he asked, looking perplexed.

"Not here. At the Cloisters."

Most of the Met's collection of medieval art is housed in the Cloisters, the dismantled elements of several European monasteries that were shipped to America by a prominent sculptor in the early 1900s, and then given to the museum by John D. Rockefeller. The magnificent setting is in northern Manhattan, overlooking the Hudson River.

"Are you familiar with—?"

Before Thibodaux could finish the question, Mike had to prove that his knowledge of the Met wasn't limited to just one branch. "Fort Tryon Park. Thirty-fourth Precinct." I didn't need a reminder of our last trip to that neighborhood, when we had investigated the murder of a prominent art dealer.

"I'm not sure what the girl did there," Eve continued, "but she was working on some aspect of the big bestiary exhibition we're doing with the Museum of Natural History next spring, the one that was just announced last evening. We had several planning sessions in this office. Of course, Mr. Thibodaux is abroad so frequently that I may have been mistaken that he was present for any of them."

"It's a terrible pity that this—this victim—is someone from our own family." The director was exhibiting the appropriate degree of remorse for us now. It was impossible for me to read his expression and know whether he was the least bit sincere.

"Wouldn't someone from the museum have missed her?"

"I'll have to get them to pull her personnel file, Mr. Chapman," Eve Drexler said, turning a page to make a list of things to do. "What else will you need?"

"Everything you've got. Who she worked with, what she did, where she lived, when she started here, and when she left. Of course, we'll need someone to identify the body. How well did you know her, Ms. Drexler?"

The woman was clearly not used to being the center of attention. She was the backup to the boss, but wasn't supposed to be involved herself. "I—uh—I can't say that I knew her at all. I mean, we were both at this table together two or three times, but—"

"You came up with her name pretty quick."

"I'm good at remembering names and faces, Detective. I have to be."

"That's—as you say in English—not my forte, Mr. Chapman. Eve stands at my shoulder at all our receptions, whispering in my ear as people approach." Thibodaux's smile seemed forced. "It seems the larger their collections, the more likely I am to block out their names when I need them most. It's a dangerous thing when you're courting potential donors, trying to get them to include the Met in their estate planning. They each want to believe that they have become my best friend."

"Did you talk to her at all, one-on-one? Find out anything about her?"

"Well, I remember making small talk with her," Drexler said, forefinger pressed against her forehead, as though digging for her recollections. "She had an accent, and since so many of our curatorial staff are from all over the world, naturally I inquired where she was from. You know, waiting for the meeting to get under way. I guessed Australia, but I was wrong. She is—she was, I'm sorry—she was South African."

"Dutch name, right?" Chapman asked.

"Yes, we also talked about that. Her family had been there for almost two hundred years. Boers." Dutch settlers who had moved to the African continent as early as the seventeenth century.

"Keep going. What else did she tell you?"

"That she worked at the Cloisters, of course. Here

on some kind of visa. I don't remember any other conversation. She seemed rather shy. Didn't speak up at the meetings, didn't really participate very much."

Mike pointed at her leather notebook. "You take minutes?"

"Yes, I usually did." She looked down the length of the table, at Thibodaux, as though she was seeking his advice.

"I'd like to see those."

The director took his cue. "I'll have Eve find them. We'll have to figure out the relevant dates in order to do that."

Ten minutes with Eve Drexler and you knew she could put her fingers on them in an instant. She was the assistant we all wanted. Roughly fifty years old, memory like a steel trap, polite to a fault, willing to take the heat for the boss, and compulsively organized. There was probably a diary for every day she had worked with the director.

"How long have you been assisting Mr. Thibodaux?"

"Actually, I've been here a few more years than he has." She was blushing, now that the focus of the discussion had moved to *her* life and actions.

I tried to warm her up by engaging her on a personal level. "Would you mind telling us what your duties are?"

"Certainly, if that will help you with what you need. I came here as a graduate student almost twenty-five years ago. I was planning to spend my career as a museum archivist. That was my training, you see. But Mr. Thibodaux's predecessor thought the things that made me such a good librarian, if you will, would be helpful to him."

Chapman called up his childhood image of the beloved school librarian. "Tight lips? That index finger held over your mouth, going 'ssssssssh' while I was trying to set up a football game after school with the other guys in the stacks, huh? What else?"

Drexler smiled at his reference. "Well, he certainly appreciated discretion, yes. And my knowledge of the collection. I spent a great deal of time cataloging entries and answering questions from staff and researchers—those who were too lazy to do the work themselves. And then, when Mr. Thibodaux took charge, he was gracious enough to keep me on."

"When was that?"

The director answered for himself. "Not quite three years ago, Detective. I'm sure you want to know everything about my background as well. Miss Drexler can give you a copy of my curriculum vitae. I'm fifty-two years old, born and raised in Paris. My experience is all curatorial. I ran the European art and sculpture department at the Louvre for more than a decade. Welcomed the opportunity to move to this gem of a museum. My wife was a New Yorker. She very much wanted to come home."

Eve Drexler heard the knock on the door and went to open it. I recognized the man who had been outside the truck at Newark last night, whom Thibodaux had said was in charge of shipping.

"Come in, Maury." He rose and greeted the shipping manager, a short, chunky man with a round face and thick red hair.

"Miss Cooper, Mr. Chapman, this is Maury Lissen. He is going to assist you with everything you'll need from his department."

Lissen took one of the seats at the table and placed the clipboard he carried in front of him.

"I've been up all night going over my paperwork. I just can't see any way this could have happened here."

"Yes, but obviously it did, Maury, and we're going to have to help the police as best we can."

Chapman stood and reached for the photograph of Katrina Grooten and passed it to Lissen. He winced as he looked at it. "I got a weak stomach for this kind of thing, Detective. Don't make me look at it, okay?"

Not exactly a response that resonates with a homicide detective. Mike and his partners rarely had the luxury of encountering a body that was not decomposed, or gaping with stab wounds or gunshot holes. "Take a good look, Maury," he said, sticking the shot back under the guy's nose. "She can't bite. She's dead."

He wouldn't pick up the photo but stared down at it and shook his head.

"Know her?"

"Should I? There's probably no one in this whole museum who has less to do with human beings than I do. Frames, pots, swords, masks, instruments, artworks. I open boxes and close them up. I unpack them and send others off. Pretty young girls I don't know."

Chapman repeated her name and still Lissen was flat.

"You have anything to do with the Cloisters?"

"Is that where she worked?"

"Do you?"

"I'm responsible for everything that goes in and out of the place. I've got a crew on site to run it, day to day. I don't spend any time up there myself. Small change compared to what we do here. Go to check on things two or three times a year."

"This sarcophagus the body was placed in, where's that been sitting since it got here last fall?"

"We're trying to track all that for Mr. Thibodaux. You know how much floor space I got downstairs? It covers as much ground as thirty football fields."

"I thought everything had a number and a tag and a tidy little home."

"Two out of three, Detective. You gotta give me a few days. Stuff gets moved around all the time down there. We'll get a handle on this as soon as we can."

Thibodaux leaned in on his elbows. "Mr. Chapman, I don't want to make the same mistake as I did earlier and risk insulting you. But there's a simple fact very few people consider when they come to visit us here—in fact, when they go to any museum in the world.

"The Metropolitan collection includes more than *three million* objects and works of art. Three million. At any given time, the most that is ever on display in these vast halls is less than ten percent of that number. That means we've got literally millions of objects stored in our basement."

He was right about one thing: I had never given any thought to that.

"Some are crated away because there will simply never be any room for them in our galleries and on our walls. Many are inferior and came to us as gifts, which will eventually be traded or sold off. There are hundreds of thousands that are far too fragile to ever be on display, and scores that scholars study, here or on loan at other institutions."

Chapman and I exchanged glances. Where would we possibly begin?

"I guess we might as well take a look at your territory, Mr. Lissen. Get a sense of how things are organized and stored, what the situation is with your security force—"

"The system is superb, Mr. Chapman," Thibodaux said. "It has all been upgraded since I arrived here. Every single section of the building has guards, and there are watchmen who patrol the museum all throughout the night, above- and belowground."

"Surveillance cameras?"

"In the galleries, hallways, storage space, exits, and entrances."

"Ever turn them on?" Several years before Thibodaux was appointed as director, I had handled the prosecution of a celebrated murder case in which a vibrant teenage girl had been killed by a drug-addicted prep-school dropout on the Great Lawn directly behind the museum. Because of construction that was being done on the rear wing that projected into Central Park, the cameras that would have captured the crime on videotape had been poised to shoot but never loaded with film. It haunted me that no one had been able to prevent the murder, nor had we had been able to reconstruct the crime for the trial jury.

"I—I just assume they're working."

Lissen knew the answer, I thought, from the glum look on his face, but was silent. "Is there a problem with the cameras?" I asked him.

"I don't think anybody's changed the film in the ones in the basement for more than a year."

"Like those frigging ATMs," Chapman said to me. A young uniformed cop had been shot and killed during an ATM stickup that Chapman had once investigated. The gunman looked directly into the camera lens, but the film had been used over again so many times that it had completely deteriorated and displayed only the grainy outline of a bearded face. As a result, the state legislature mandated that banking institutions change their film on a regular basis. No such requirement existed for museums.

"The detective and I would like to begin with you this afternoon, Mr. Lissen. If there's a telephone I can use first, I'll notify my boss that we've identified the deceased."

"Of course, Miss Cooper. Please use the one on my desk. I'll step out to Ms. Drexler's phone and call the gentleman who's in charge of the Cloisters. He can pull up Miss Grooten's file."

I dialed Paul Battaglia's direct line and hoped Rose Malone would answer. She sounded busy—or distant—and tried to patch me through to the district attorney before getting back on the line to tell me that he wouldn't pick up my call. That hadn't happened to me very often.

"Just tell him we think we got an ID. The deceased is Katrina Grooten, and she was working up at the Cloisters, on a special joint project that involved a few of the museums. ME thinks the cause of death is poisoning. Soon as I know any more you'll have it."

I handed the receiver to Chapman and moved out of his way. "Hey, loo. Got a tentative make on Saint Cleo. Some kind of art maven working in one of the museums. From South Africa, here on a visa. Coop and I'll pop up to the Cloisters tomorrow, when we're done in this joint, see if anyone knows why or when she quit her job."

He put the phone down and picked up a photograph from Thibodaux's desk. The handsome woman in the eight-by-ten frame was smiling back at him, dressed to the nines and standing in front of the glass pyramid in the courtyard at the Louvre.

"Mrs. T.?"

Eve Drexler nodded.

"She have anything to do with the museum, officially?"

"No, Mr. Chapman. She's dead. Killed in a ski accident at Chamonix, winter before last. They had only been here at the Met for little more than a year. I was right here in the office with Pierre when he got—"

Drexler stopped talking when Thibodaux opened the door and reentered the room. "Hiram Bellinger, the director of the Cloisters, will see you anytime tomorrow that suits you. He didn't know Miss Grooten well, but he'll pull her file and be prepared to give you whatever you need."

Chapman turned his back to the director and whispered to me, "Let's get a gander at the setup here this afternoon, meet at the morgue in the morning to see what Kestenbaum has for us, then spend as much time as we need uptown, talking to the people she worked with."

"Fine with me."

He walked back to the conference table to pick up his steno pad. "Tell Bellinger we'll be there about twelve tomorrow. Hasn't he got anything he can fax over to you now?"

"The basic personnel records should be in the database, even if the entire file is archived. I expect he'll have her address and date of birth over to me shortly. What else would you like?"

"Next of kin would be nice. I'd hate for them to find out about this on CNN. Maybe she has family here who can help us out."

"How thoughtless of me. Why don't you start downstairs with Maury, and Miss Drexler will find you as soon as the information comes in."

"Did he say there was anything strange about Ms. Grooten's disappearance?"

"Nothing at all, Detective. He said he remembered that there was a letter of resignation from late last December that he put in the file. You two should be able to track this down better than we can: Bellinger said that Katrina had been planning to leave the city for some time, ever since she'd been assaulted—how do you say, violated?—in that park up at the Cloisters after leaving the museum late one night. She'd never been quite the same after that."

9

Thibodaux closed the door of his office and left us at his secretary's desk with Ms. Drexler, who was waiting to escort us to the basement.

"Could you give us some privacy while we make this call?" Chapman asked. Both women stepped into the hallway.

I watched him dial the number of the Special Victims Squad as he looked at his watch.

"Hey, Joey, Mercer Wallace working today?" He paused while the detective who had answered looked at the duty chart. "When he gets in, tell him to give me a call on my cell. I need him to check an old case. No thanks, no need to bother you with it."

He hung up the phone. "Must be losing your touch, blondie. How is it you wouldn't know about a legit complainant attacked in a public park?"

"'Cause somebody tanked the case. Didn't want to let us take a crack at it."

"That means there's a boss up there who doesn't like you, or even the guy who took the squeal. You sure it doesn't ring any bells?"

"I'll have Laura check the screening sheets, but it's

got too many hot-button items not to stand out in my memory." We had a detailed system of tracking sexual assault cases in the unit, in which every incident was cross-referenced by the name of the victim and the offender, the date and place of occurrence. Reports were made in each circumstance, whether or not an arrest was effected or the case went to trial. Sarah and I liked to think our record-keeping was foolproof, although the police department managed to keep things under wraps from time to time.

"You got a victim who's a foreigner—which would make the mayor ballistic." It was bad enough to assault or murder a New Yorker when City Hall was tracking crime stats so closely, but attacks on out-of-towners led to national headlines that threatened the income tourists fed to the hotel and restaurant industries. "She worked for a major art institution, attacked in a public park. Likely to cause a stir. Mercer's coming in any minute on a four to twelve. He can dig around for the case folder."

Mercer Wallace was the third man in what we liked to think of as our team. At forty-one, he was five years older than Mike and me, and about to become a father for the first time. He had remarried his ex-wife, Vickee, on New Year's Day, after she reappeared in his life to help him through the aftermath of an investigation in which he had suffered a near-fatal gunshot wound to his chest.

Mercer's great height and dark black skin made him a physical standout in any room. But it was his meticulous investigative style and compassionate manner with witnesses that won him the coveted spot as my favorite detective at the Special Victims Squad, which was responsible for handling every sexual assault and child abuse case in the borough. The son of a widowed airline mechanic who had worked several jobs to save for Mercer's college education, he had at the last minute turned down a football scholarship to the University of Michigan to enroll in the Police Academy.

Mike and Mercer had worked together at Manhattan North Homicide for several years, until Mercer decided that he preferred to deal with witnesses who were still alive and needed the strength of a sensitive, smart detective to help restore their dignity and find some kind of justice for their assailant. More often than we liked, the work of the two units overlapped, and the victim of some kind of sexual violence became the subject of a murder investigation.

Eve Drexler was waiting for us in the hallway. She led us back to the elevator and pressed the button for the basement level. When the doors opened, she pointed to the sign across the corridor that had Lissen's name printed on it. They closed before I remembered to ask her to finish her sentence about what had happened when Thibodaux received the call about his wife's accidental death. I told Mike to add it to his list of questions.

The cubicle that was home to the shipping department head lacked the lavish accoutrements of the museum director's office. Unframed reproduction posters were thumbtacked to the scratched walls, much as in a college dorm room. File cabinets ringed the perimeter, the dust on the computer looked so thick that it appeared to have been untouched since it was installed, and the desk was crowned by sloppy piles of yellow and white papers.

Lissen motioned us in and we sat on stools facing his desk. "Mr. Thibodaux asked a couple of the curators to come down. I'm really not supposed to poke around their storage areas unless they give me permission."

"Can we sit somewhere else, so I can take notes while we talk?"

"We don't got a lot of fancy rooms down here, Detective."

I heard footsteps and turned to see several people in the doorway. I recognized the tall, balding man as one who had been with Mr. Lissen in the shipyard last night.

"I'm Timothy Gaylord. I'm afraid the Egyptian art collection is under my direction," he said, extending a hand.

Mike and I stood up in the crowded space and made introductions all around. The second man told us he was Erik Poste, the curator in charge of European paintings, and the third staffer was Anna Friedrichs, who ran the department of the arts of Africa, Oceania, and the Americas.

Gaylord took command of the situation. "Maury, why don't we all move into our storeroom?" He turned to Mike and me. "There's a small office we can work in there, a lot more comfortably than in this."

"Can we access your computer files from that one?" I asked Lissen.

"Only if we had any." He waved a hand behind him at the dusty monitor. "We're not the high-tech section of the museum. They got it all cataloged upstairs. We're just the brawn. Someone tells us to move something, that's what we do. Never had time to go to school to learn how to catch up on these machines. Sooner or later someone picks up the paperwork and puts it in order. I ain't lost much more than a couple of African masks that'd scare you half to death anyway, and some fake statuettes. A few minor paintings that weren't going to get hung."

Lissen locked his door behind him and we all followed Timothy Gaylord into the hallway. We were at the southeast corner of the basement, and we walked for several minutes down a windowless stretch of corridor without a doorway or stairwell to break the long cement barriers.

"What's back here?" Chapman was walking on Gaylord's heels, anxious to find out what was behind the great gray walls.

Gaylord turned his head and smiled at us. "Surely, Detective, you can guess what the most lucrative part of this great art museum is?"

Neither of us had any idea.

"That's the underground parking garage that was built thirty years ago. It's entirely museum revenue. Unlike everything else, the city doesn't get a nickel of that money."

"It's public parking?"

"Yes, the daily museum visitors and permanent tenants from the luxury buildings in the neighborhood. As an art lover, it pains me to say that the garage is probably the most significant source of income for the great Metropolitan Museum of Art."

And I knew Mike was thinking that it was an entirely unexpected headache for him. The fact that one could bring in a private vehicle, park it off the street for days or weeks at a time, and have such immediate access to the institution made it something else to add to his list of facilities to search.

We turned a corner and were walking north now. There were a series of doorways, each with a numbered plaque above the lintel. Gaylord stopped in front of the third one and turned the handle. Inside the large square room two young women sat on opposite sides of a table, wearing magnifying glasses strapped to bands that circled their heads, bent over the model of an ancient boat.

"I'm going to need this area for an hour or so," Gaylord said in his soft-spoken voice. "Would you mind terribly if we interrupted your work?"

Both of them removed their headpieces and assured us the break was welcome.

We seated ourselves around the table.

"Pierre called to tell me this latest piece of news, and I just want to say how distressing this is to me. To all of us, I'm sure. I have met Katrina Grooten." He paused and ran a finger over his lower lip. "She was a very serious young scholar. And I'm holding myself responsible for the fact that Ms. Grooten was found in a sarcophagus that belonged to my department.

"I called Erik and Anna in on this because they might have some information that would be helpful. When Pierre told me it was Katrina, I was aware both of them knew her as well, so I've asked them to come down here with me. Where would you like us to begin?"

I wanted to know about my victim. The kind of person she was, the things she did for a living, and the things she liked to do when she left her job. What kind of people she socialized with, and whether she was a risk-taker. Who her family was and what they thought had become of her. I needed a sketch of Katrina Grooten that would keep her alive for me in my mind's eye, so that I could try to re-create the events that had led up to her death.

Mike, on the other hand, did not want to know the deceased any better than the facts forced him to. He kept his sanity by staying at arm's length from the person whose killer he would try to find. Although he would be dogged in learning every morsel about Katrina's existence, he wanted to internalize nothing that would make him judgmental about her life or lifestyle. He didn't care whether she was liked or despised by her peers, sexually active or a recluse. What mattered most to him was that she hadn't deserved to die, and no one would try harder than he to get the bastard who had brought her to such an ugly end.

"Perhaps each of you could tell us what you knew about Katrina, personally and professionally. We need every detail you can remember."

Gaylord spoke first. "I would say I have the least to contribute, so I might as well go first. Do you know about the project we're collaborating on with the Museum of Natural History?"

"I know there's to be a joint show next year, and that the celebratory announcement was last night. But neither Detective Chapman nor I know any of the details."

"There's been a rather intense rivalry between these two institutions for more than a century now. They were both founded in the 1870s, and in fact, the trustees had actually planned that each museum would occupy buildings on the very same site, known as Manhattan Square, on the west side of the park. Only later was the Met resituated to our present site, on what was then called Deer Park, the area between Seventy-ninth and Eighty-fourth streets on the Upper East Side.

"President Grant laid the cornerstone for the Natural History Museum, while President Hayes dedicated the Metropolitan."

"Why the conflict?" Chapman asked. "Can't they get over it and talk current events here?"

"Our trustees at the Metropolitan, the fabulously wealthy merchants and businessmen of that period, had extraordinarily lofty goals. They had models in all the great museums of Europe, most of which enjoyed the benefit of centuries of plundering their neighbors or being patronized by royalty. Both methods were tried-and-true for establishing collections. Our founders wanted to use art to educate and refine the American masses, and to provide for them a knowledge of the history of art that existed in civilized countries abroad."

"Wasn't Natural History doing the same thing?"

All three of the curators smirked in unison.

"That's hardly *art*, Mr. Chapman. Natural history museums developed from an entirely different type of collecting mania. They are the descendants of what are known as 'cabinets of curiosities.' Fossils, minerals, mollusks, shells, bugs, and the ever-popular dinosaurs. They have a fascinating repository of all the bizarre and wonderful creatures that have ever crawled and walked on Earth."

"They make a good effort at calling themselves scientific in this day and age, but for those of us in the museum business, they're just pickled remains. Lots of dead things in jars and behind glass walls," said Erik Poste.

"But put the best of their exhibits beside a painting by Delacroix or Vermeer, or even next to the faience carving of the Sphinx of Amenhotep III, and it's simply laughable," said Gaylord. "We're not a warehouse of the bizarre and extinct. We are quite simply the greatest repository of art in the Western Hemisphere, a living institution that is not only informative but uplifting, in a way that our sister across the park was never meant to be."

"So, the joint exhibit?"

"Holding hands for the greater good, Detective. It's all about profit-making, as you might guess. When the national economy took such a marked downward shift this year, the trustees had to ask Thibodaux to tighten his belt."

"Why him?"

"Because he's such a big spender. That's what he was brought in here to do three years ago. All the fat-cat trustees had money to throw at him and adored his boldness. I'm not talking behind his back. One of the things we all like about having him at the helm is that great works of art are being offered to us all the time because collectors know that we have a rich board willing to pay for these masterpieces. No haggling, no bargaining."

Erik Poste took over from Gaylord again. "The Met puts on special exhibitions all the time, as you probably know. Some more successful than others. This one has been in the planning stage for more than a year. It was Thibodaux's idea to ask Natural History to partner it with us. It's never been done that way before, and quite frankly, he thinks it has the potential to be a financial blockbuster."

"So does UniQuest," Gaylord said, reminding me of the purpose of last night's party.

"So what's this theme?"

"It's our working title. 'A Modern Bestiary.'"

"Doesn't sound too thrilling to me," Chapman said.

"Don't worry. Our friends in Hollywood will probably dream up a snappier title before we're done. We've already rejected things like 'Satyrs, Sirens, and Sapiens.' It's actually been a riveting undertaking. There's something in it to appeal to everyone, which is what makes Thibodaux such a genius at marketing. He and the woman who runs Natural History—Helen Raspen—she's absolutely brilliant."

"What's a bestiary?"

Erik Poste spoke again. "They were originally medieval books, Mr. Chapman. They purported to depict and describe all the animals in the world, and then—because this was the thought in the Middle Ages—what human traits they each represented."

"Animals with human traits?"

"Bestiaries are the source of all kinds of fabulous beasts, and artists throughout the centuries have used them as guides to literary symbolism. Think of the unicorn. A magnificent pure white beast with a single horn in its forehead. It's long been the symbol of virginity."

"And I used to think that was a blonde prosecutor," Chapman mumbled under his breath.

Gaylord went on. "Lewis Carroll, James Thurber, Jorge Luis Borges—they've all done bestiaries. Much more recent, of course. This gives us a chance to pull together centuries of work from both collections with a common theme. We've got the artistic representations in our paintings and sculpture, while Natural History has the fossils and skeletons. Art lovers or animal fans, kids and grown-ups, there's something for everyone to relate to in a show like this."

Roll out those giant silk banners that announce new shows as they hang from the museums' rooftops, open the cash registers, stock the gift shops, and the masses will come.

Where had we lost Katrina in this? "How was Ms. Grooten involved?"

Timothy Gaylord rolled his lacquered fountain pen back and forth between his palms. "When Thibodaux first proposed this idea in-house early last year, we decided to get together with someone from each collection within the Met."

"How many are there?"

"Eighteen curatorial departments—everything from the three we represent to musical instruments and photography. We started with the heads of each group. Some of the smaller divisions sent representatives. I remember that Hiram Bellinger, from the Cloisters, came to the first meeting in Pierre's office, isn't that right?" Gaylord said, looking to Poste and Friedrichs for confirmation.

"Yes," Friedrichs answered. "It was after that point he designated Katrina to work on the project and pick the exhibits that might be included from the Cloisters, which he runs."

"Mr. Bellinger specializes in delegating assignments, Miss Cooper," Erik Poste said, crossing his legs as he laughed aloud. "Pierre made it clear that even those of us who ran major departments in the museum—well, Timothy here, and me—had to sit on this show ourselves. It was a serious investment of our time and energy, but I knew Pierre would make it worthwhile for us with the money the exhibition could raise."

"Bellinger himself is like a throwback to medieval times," Gaylord said. "Sits up there as though he's a monk in his own monastery, studying illuminated manuscripts. He doesn't seem to realize that if we don't make the money to support the museum, he'll be taking the vow of poverty himself. Unfortunately, a lot of our scholars, like Hiram, have nothing but contempt for Thibodaux and his entrepreneurial vision."

"And you?"

"I quite admire Pierre. I think all three of us do. There's no other way to compete against the other great museums of the world if we don't have the financial means to buy the pieces that come on the market. It can't be any simpler than that."

"Is it in these meetings where you first met Ms. Grooten?" I asked Gaylord.

"It's the only place. Pierre put me in charge of the Met's role in the joint exhibit. I chaired several of the planning sessions."

"Was Mr. Thibodaux himself present for those?"

Gaylord took a moment to think. "Maybe one or two. Once he turned it over to me, I don't remember that he came to many of them."

"And Ms. Grooten?"

"As I said, she wasn't at the first one."

"But were they ever in meetings together?"

The three curators exchanged glances. "Hard to say," Poste answered. "Thibodaux would occasionally stick his head in the room, when he wasn't traveling abroad. Just to make the point that the program was his baby, a directive straight from the top."

"Does he travel often?"

"All the time. Some middleman calls and says there's a krater in the hands of a private owner in Athens who needs some cash, or a Caillebotte coming up for auction for the first time in Geneva, or a rich old dame who's thinking about leaving her Stradivarius to whichever museum will give it the most prominent placement. That's the way the game is played."

"Did any of you ever socialize with Ms. Grooten, apart from these sessions?"

"We both did," Anna Friedrichs said, pointing from herself to Erik Poste.

"What did you know about her? How well did you know her?"

"I was very fond of Katrina," Friedrichs said. "We

had dinner together on occasion, after work; sometimes lunch. She was about ten years younger than I. Twenty-eight or twenty-nine. Studied in England. Oxford, I believe. Got a master's in medieval art before she came to the States three years ago to work with us."

"Single?"

"Yes. Lived alone. Rented a studio apartment in Washington Heights so she'd be close to the Cloisters. She liked to bike to work."

"Did she have any relatives here?"

"None that she spoke of. Her mother had died while she was at university. And I believe her father was quite ill, at home in South Africa."

Erik Poste knew more about that. "It was one of the reasons she was torn about her work here. Her father was failing, and despite how much she loved her job, she talked about going home to care for him."

"Any men in her life? People she dated?"

"Not that she spoke about. Like Anna, I had lunch with Katrina from time to time, if I happened to be working at the bestiary office when she was there. I believe we had dinner one time, with another one of the museum fellows, because they had business they wanted to discuss with me."

"Did you and she ever—?"

"Not what you're thinking, Detective. I'm forty-three years old, with a wife and three children. My relationship with Katrina was entirely professional. There was a good deal of overlap between our two departments, naturally, so we were thrust together on many occasions."

"What do you mean by overlap?"

"I'm in charge of European paintings and sculpture. Katrina's interest was medieval art, which is the reason she was assigned to work at the Cloisters. Her field was a subspecialty of my department's, so I had a lot of contact with Hiram Bellinger and his staff. Quite frankly, I was hoping to lure her away from Bellinger and bring her down to supervise some projects here at the Met."

"So you enjoyed working with Katrina?"

"Yes, I respected her intelligence and her desire to learn. She was mature beyond her years. And very quiet, very demure."

Anna Friedrichs laughed. "Not in the meetings I attended. There was a feistiness about her that I loved in a young woman her age. Despite her lack of experience, she wasn't afraid to take on the old boys who wanted to control the show."

"I never saw that side of her. How interesting."

Why were their recollections so different? "Were you two at the same meetings?"

"Rarely. My department is enormous," said Poste. "It was easy for me to break away and attend things in this building. But once the idea for the big show got started, the action moved across the park."

"I usually saw Katrina over at Natural History, after the joint planning got under way. It's a bit looser over there than it is in this mausoleum, as you might guess. That whole place is a lot funkier than the Met," Friedrichs added.

"Had Katrina worked in any other museums before coming here?"

Poste shrugged his shoulders. "I assume so. But I don't know any details."

Friedrichs gave it some thought. "I'm sure she must have had an internship somewhere. The Cloisters would be a pretty plum place to start out. I just don't know where."

"Did she confide in either of you?"

"About what?" Friedrichs asked.

"Anything personal. Any bad experience she had while she was here?"

"No. She did seem more somber the last few times we were together. In fact, she broke our dinner date after the last meeting we had. Complained about not feeling well."

"That was in the fall, Anna, wasn't it? That's when she began to talk about going home to help with her father. She was very subdued, as I said. What kind of bad experience do you mean, Detective?" Erik Poste asked.

The telephone rang on a side table in the corner of the room. Gaylord got up to answer it, turning away from us to listen to the caller, then he walked back to the table and spoke to us without resuming his seat. "You'll excuse me, Detective. Ms. Cooper. Erik and Anna will continue to show you around and answer your questions. I've got to go upstairs immediately."

Gaylord ignored Chapman and me, speaking to his colleagues. "Pierre Thibodaux has just resigned."

10

"I'll be happy to talk to you tomorrow, Detective. I've just been ordered up to the director's office. We've clearly got a crisis at the museum that none of us had anticipated an hour ago."

"And I got a dead broad in my locker who croaked on your watch, Mr. Gaylord." Mike walked to the phone. "What's Thibodaux's extension?"

"He—he's not there. In his office, I mean. He was already out the door before Eve got on the phone to me. I wanted to talk to him myself. Honestly."

Timothy Gaylord was as rattled as Mike and I. Thibodaux was either a brilliant actor, able to mask whatever professional trouble was brewing when we talked to him half an hour earlier, or this abrupt resignation might have had something to do with the photograph of Katrina Grooten that we had just stuck under his nose.

"It's Chapman here. I want your boss. I want to talk to him before he leaves the museum, do you understand?" Mike was running his fingers through his straight black hair. I knew he was angry, thinking Thibodaux had pulled a fast one on him. "Yeah? Then why'd you ask Gaylord to come upstairs if he's already gone?"

Mike didn't like Drexler's answer. He slammed the receiver back into the cradle.

"Want me to try to catch up with him on his way out?"

Mike looked at me as though I were crazy. "You know how many ways there are out of this place? The man has at least a ten-minute jump on us, we're buried down here in the bowels of the museum, and you don't know which way he's headed. Give it up, blondie."

Gaylord tried to move to the door again. "I'm afraid I've got to get upstairs. Eve has asked me to call several of the board members to convene a special meeting."

Mike pointed at Gaylord like a trainer ordering a show dog to sit. "Stay put." He used the same finger to dial his squad commander, explaining the situation. "Get a couple of guys over here to get Thibodaux's address. They want to be talking to Eve Drexler. He's probably got a car and driver, too. Get the plate number. Have a detail sit on his apartment to make sure he doesn't go anywhere, will you? Lemme know when you find him, loo. I'd like to pay him another visit. Talk to you later."

Erik Poste and Anna Friedrichs both looked as though they were afraid to move. They were whispering to each other, as surprised by the news as Gaylord was.

"Any of you know what this is about?"

"I think it's clear we're as startled as you are," Poste said. He tapped his fingers nervously on the tabletop.

Anna Friedrichs tried to muster a smile. "I don't think you need to treat him like a criminal, Mr. Chapman. I can't imagine for a moment this is related to Katrina's death."

Chapman ignored the comment and spoke to Gaylord again. "Before you run out of here, you want to explain to me where this sarcophagus we found last night has been for the last six months?"

"I'm sorry. It's just hard to balance all this right now. I've got my staff trying to reconstruct the movement of the piece and get you that information as soon as possible."

"How about the innards?"

"Excuse me?"

"Ms. Grooten didn't have a bunk mate in the coffin. Wasn't there a little old princess inside that thing for a few thousand years? Does that mean you got an extra mummy lying around here somewhere?"

Erik Poste stood up and walked to Gaylord's side, putting a hand on his shoulder. "That's a good point, Timothy. Perhaps we should be looking for—"

Gaylord stepped away from his colleague. It seemed this added another problem to his plate that he had not considered. "No, certainly not. If any of my people had come across—well, nothing's been found." He turned to Erik Poste and Anna Friedrichs. "There's no point having word of all this spread through the junior staffers. I know it's an imposition, but Pierre promised Mr. Chapman that he would be shown through the storage area today. Would you two mind very much taking them around?"

Poste appeared to accept the assignment more graciously than Anna Friedrichs. She glanced at her watch and exhaled her annoyance audibly.

"You'll see what a monumental task we have, Detective. The sad truth is that no one can tell you where the piece was at any given moment during the past few months. The best we can do is try. You want to scout through a few million other pieces of art, be my guest. I'll turn you over to Anna and Erik, for the moment."

Gaylord passed a large metal ring with dozens of long keys dangling from it to Erik Poste and walked out.

Chapman took his cell phone from his pocket to see whether there were any messages.

"You can forget about getting calls down here, Detective," Anna Friedrichs said. "Might as well use the phone on that table. We're so deep inside the museum that cell phones don't penetrate. Too many thick steel beams in the foundation. It's the bane of my existence when I'm stuck working in the basement."

He dialed the number from the museum phone and asked for Mercer Wallace, who got on the line. "Don't tell your boss what I'm about to ask you to do, 'cause someone up there dropped the ball on this. See if you can find a sixty-one from spring or summer of last year. Three-four precinct. Your complaining witness is a Katrina Grooten. Female, white, about twenty-eight years old. Sneak a copy of the file out, and Coop is buying us dinner at—?" He looked at me for the answer.

"Primola."

"Hear that? Meet us there any time after seven."

The complaint report, the NYPD's uniform force form number 61, along with the follow-ups from the detective division known as 5s, would tell the story of Katrina Grooten's assault. Precinct cops would likely have responded to the original complaint and filled out the initial paperwork, referring the investigation to the detectives of the well-trained Special Victims Squad. If the case had been closed without an arrest, these papers would have to explain why.

"Shall we get started?" Erik Poste led us out of the room. Mike walked beside him while I followed with Anna Friedrichs, and Lissen brought up the rear.

"Each department has its own storeroom, acres and acres of it here under the museum."

"Turf battles?"

"Of course, Detective. Mr. Gaylord's Egyptian galleries are crowd pleasers, always have been. His exhibits take up an inordinate amount of space. Giant stone sculptures and actual pieces of temples and tombs. Dendur was shipped over here from the Aswan as six hundred and eighty-two enormous pieces of rock, and stored wherever they could find a niche, until it could be reassembled as you see it today."

We reached another doorway and Erik Poste searched for an engraved number on the shank of one of the keys. He found one that matched the lock and opened the door. Ahead of us on either side were endless lines of funerary objects, some exposed and others sticking partway out of packing crates, with painted figurines and jasper animals sitting upon their backs. Many had plastic drop cloths draped over them, while hundreds more collected dust.

"I believe Mr. Gaylord has about thirty-six thousand objects from his collection on display upstairs. If you care to hazard a guess about how many remain down here, I'll be happy to take the bet."

Mike was walking up and down the narrow rows, looking at labels and reading tags affixed to the objects. He called back to Poste and Friedrichs, "But all the Egyptian stuff is in here, right?"

"Not exactly. There's overflow, especially because so many of the pieces are oversize, and that goes into some of our underpopulated areas."

"What would they be?"

"Islamic art, for example. It's one of our smaller departments. Artifacts, miniatures, ceramic tiles. The pieces aren't as bulky, don't take up as much room. Same for musical instruments. It's not uncommon for some larger pieces—whether Egyptian relics or American period furniture—to be moved for the purpose of storage."

"Do the other curators get annoyed at Gaylord for using their space?"

"Of course not. And he's not the only one who trespasses. I've got thousands of paintings in my division. And I need room to do restoration. Many of the pieces are quite sizable and the canvases must be spread out for weeks while workers tend to them. You call on a friendly neighbor, examine his quarters, and find some way to beg for the area you need."

Mike walked back to us. "These things aren't even in numerical order. They're all out of whack."

"That's why we have students and scholars, Detective. Eager young interns. They like nothing better than poring over these treasures and having that 'eureka!' moment when they've put their hands on a missing masterpiece. I can assure you that all of these things are carefully cataloged in each department and in the overall collection. They can all be tracked and traced. At least, we've always assumed that."

"The sarcophagus in which Ms. Grooten was found, do you know about that?"

Friedrichs answered: "Mr. Gaylord told us about it shortly before you arrived here."

"Why is it that no one can tell us where it had been stored?"

"There are several possibilities, Miss Cooper. We expect to narrow it down within the week." Erik Poste played with his key chain. "Mr. Lissen and Miss Drexler are going over all the records. This storeroom is one of them."

"Makes it look like trying to find a dollar bill you've dropped on the floor at Grand Central Station," Chapman said, trying to sketch the layout in his notepad.

"I'll show you some of the other areas as well, where the Egyptian overflow usually goes. I guess you'll have us all looking for the missing mummy now, won't you, Detective?" Poste said as he walked back to the doorway.

"Have you had a good look at the sarcophagus?" Friedrichs asked. "If it was ever considered for the bestiary exhibit, it might even have been carted over to Natural History at some point in the last few months, to be vetted and photographed for the show."

"Why vetted?"

"To be certain it was authentic. We've suffered that embarrassment before. Put on the big show only to learn that the featured artwork was a forgery or a fake."

"Why would the coffin be in the show?"

"Some of those ancient Egyptian pieces are richly decorated with animal paintings. Not just the ones that belonged to royal families, but also just the well-to-do. You'll see baboons with their arms raised in worship of some god, the hippopotamus that was the patroness of women during pregnancy, or a cobra whose tail encircled the sun for some reason I can't remember. There were falcons and scarabs and sacred cats, many of them portrayed on funeral objects of the wealthy."

"I doubt anyone would have gone to the trouble of moving a sarcophagus over to Natural History," Erik Poste said.

"Objects—even large, heavy ones like that—were being carted back and forth every week," Anna said, correcting him. "Somebody must have put it on the list to be shipped overseas. I've asked Maury to check out those intermuseum transfers, too."

We continued back along the long, gray corridor and around another corner, more than a city block away. Again, Erik Poste inserted a key in a lock and stepped away to let us enter. Here, hundreds of paintings were displayed, one on top of another until they reached the high ceiling, all encased in glass for the entire length of the room. The lighting was dim and none of it shone directly on the canvases. It was obvious we had come to the European painting area, Poste's professional home.

"It's a bit easier to store paintings. Although the size varies, and our walls can make the accommodation to hold them, they're all quite flat. I have a much easier time keeping records of what's in here."

Again, Mike walked up and down the long rows, examining tags and sketching the setup. "What's this door?" He was out of sight, at the far corner of the room.

"It's open, Detective. Go right in." We made our way back to find Chapman, who was standing inside a room the size of my office. It was like a carpentry workshop, with pieces of wood and parts of gilded frames against the walls and on the tabletops. "In each department's storage area, there are shops like these. Some are for the conservators who restore works of art, others make frames or do repairs."

"This isn't the only shop?" Mike's question conjured up the image of endless small cubbyholes within the massive storage areas. Pierre Thibodaux's point about several million objects of art below the museum's surface was becoming very real to both of us.

"Oh, no. Must be at least a dozen more like this scattered about within the building, as well as space we rent outside."

"Anybody else getting hot flashes?" Mike pulled out his handkerchief and wiped his brow.

Anna laughed. "All of these fragile works of art have different needs. Those sculptures that survived in the deserts for centuries like it hot and dry inside. My department—things from the South Pacific islands and the ocean people—thrive in a damp environment. There are climate controls all over the museum—

thousands of sensors. You can go to all extremes of temperature, hot or cold, damp or dry, just by moving from gallery to gallery."

"And you can tell me what the weather is in every section, more reliable than those schmucks I listen to every night on TV?"

"We certainly can," Anna said, "because we manufacture our own weather conditions."

I knew Mike was trying to figure out where within a museum Katrina Grooten's body could have been best kept without decomposing. Would her killer have known how these temperatures and conditions would affect a human body? Or would it have proved to be a circumstance that accidentally worked against his interest, preserving the remains so that they were recognized and identified before leaving the country?

"You're welcome to come back here any time to go through all of these storerooms, Detective," Poste said, locking up behind us. "I think you'll need an army to help you do it."

"You got a list of all your employees, Maury?" Chapman asked Lissen as we reentered the hallway. "Names, dates of birth, social security numbers?"

"Yeah, Eve was going to print it out for you. They're all bonded. Won't find any criminals in my department. The thieves all work upstairs in archaeology and anthropology, if you ask me, robbing the graves and stealing these pots and pans from other countries." Lissen wasn't the first one to complain about the ethics involved in museum acquisitions.

"Other workmen?"

"You got a sea of 'em down here. They got offices

in the subbasement for locksmiths, plumbers, electricians. They roam around this place like it was the wide open spaces."

We turned another corner and reached a divide between sections of the corridor. The lights dimmed even more and the ceiling dipped to a mere eight feet. Poste and Friedrichs led us across a low barrel vault, which ran north to south through the center of the building, deep below the museum, and brought us out on its other side.

Mike had stopped in the middle and called out to us, "What's in here?"

"One of the original structural features of the museum," Poste said. "It's long been obsolete."

"Let's have a look."

We all turned back to join Mike.

"This was constructed in the middle of the nineteenth century," Anna said. "An enormous storm drain-off for the Central Park reservoir."

We walked ten or fifteen feet into its mouth, and the temperature dropped noticeably. There were ghostly figures of bronze bacchanals and carved Asian dragons, heavy pieces of furniture and fluted columns. Most of these neglected or unwanted artworks had been dressed in plastic shrouds and left to guard this useless tunnel.

Mike used the point of his pen to lift the covers and poke around the objects.

"Even art goes in and out of vogue, Mr. Chapman. Something that was all the rage for collectors a century ago gets cycled out. Some of the greats have staying power, but—"

"Anything Egyptian in here, Mr. Poste?"

"I'd be surprised if there isn't. We can light this for you more properly when you come back. There are a couple of areas like this which just aren't the first priority to be fixed up with our limited funding."

Our walking tour continued until we had circumnavigated the entire museum basement, peering into storerooms and skirting empty corners. Erik Poste wasn't wrong; it would pay to come back here with reinforcements in serious numbers. Perhaps we could convince the chief of detectives to let us have some cadets from the Academy to scour the vast space for us.

We left our three escorts near the front door, where a uniformed guard was waiting to let us out. The museum had closed at five-fifteen, and it was just after seven in the evening.

Even though it was dusk, the Fifth Avenue steps remained a place for groups of all sorts to congregate. Three rappers were doing moonwalks at the bottom of the staircase, a juggler was trying to keep six balls in the air while playing the harmonica, and a bespectacled kid was reading aloud from *Ulysses* to the accompaniment of her friend's guitar.

We stayed to the far south and descended the three tiers. "You think you could actually kill someone in that museum?" I asked.

"I'll let Dr. K. figure that one out. You could sure as hell stick her there to rest for a few months without any interruption, except by chance. Or probably even have the coffin moved in and out, without anybody being the wiser. I never gave any thought to how big that place is. Kind of like an iceberg below the main display floors."

"Millions of objects that never see the light of day." I pulled my cell phone from my handbag and dialed Nina's hotel, leaving her a voice mail about where to meet us for dinner.

Mike and I were the first to arrive at the restaurant on Second Avenue near Sixty-fourth Street.

"*Buona sera*, Signorina Cooper. You going to be four tonight?"

"Yes, Giuliano. Do you mind if we borrow your office for a few minutes?"

He laughed and told Adolfo to unlock the door at the foot of the staircase. Mike and I went down and turned on the small television set, switching the channel to find Alex Trebek. One of our common bonds was a devotion to the Final Jeopardy! question at the end of the daily quiz show. For the decade throughout which we had worked together, Mike had found a way at almost every crime scene or station house to get to the tube in time for the last question, to bet on it against me and against Mercer.

"Tonight's category, ladies and gentlemen, is 'The Cinema,'" Trebek said, stepping back to reveal a giant screen with those two words printed on it.

There were some topics I didn't challenge Chapman on, and others that were completely my domain. This was one we both knew and loved.

"Twenty dollars."

"Dinner, Coop. For four."

"You're on."

"Tonight's Final Jeopardy! answer is: William Shatner starred in this movie, filmed completely in the universal language Esperanto."

The nauseatingly cheerful music bounced along in the background as two of the three puzzled contestants stared blankly at the board. The only one of them who ventured a guess at a title was wrong, and I told Chapman that I didn't have the faintest idea. Before Trebek read the studio audience the question, Chapman tweaked the back of my neck. "And a good bottle of wine with that dinner, too. Right, blondie?"

I laughed and swatted his hand away. "Anything you say. Just let go of me."

"What is *Incubus*? Nineteen sixty-five. A man possessed by demon spirits. Only Shatner outing worse than that one is *Big Bad Mama*," he said, shutting off the TV and walking out of the office, "where you actually get to see his pubic hair in one of the scenes. Chow time."

"And you make it so appetizing, too."

Fenton had our drinks ready at the bar, where Mercer had greeted Nina as they were waiting for us to come back upstairs.

"Let's have some fried zucchini for the table while we're talking," Chapman told Adolfo. Nina embraced Mike, whom she had not seen in several months, and Mercer finished telling her that Vickee was less than two weeks away from delivering the child Mike referred to as "our baby." He was the first on our team to start a family, and the significance of that was not lost on either Mike or me.

"Cheers!" We clicked glasses and caught up briefly

before Mike asked Mercer to tell us what he had learned about Katrina Grooten.

"I couldn't sneak the folder out so I just made some notes. The sergeant was sitting right next to the Xerox machine."

"Whose case?"

"Cathy Daughtrey's."

"No wonder I don't know about it." I've tried several times to have her transferred out of the squad. She had burned out somewhere along the way, and never went the extra mile needed to solve the difficult cases. She would do anything possible to avoid taking direction from me or from Sarah Brenner, because it always meant more legwork than she wanted to do.

"Happened almost a year ago, just about this time of night. Monday, June eleventh. Katrina Grooten, twenty-nine years old. Employed at the Cloisters.

"Sixty-one says she left the museum a little before eight and was walking her bicycle down the steep path, through the park, on her way home. That was a small apartment near Dyckman. Says a gunman pulled her off the path behind a rock, made her undress, and raped her at gunpoint."

"She give a 'scrip?"

"Male black. Tall, slim."

"That's it?"

"Face was covered with a ski mask. Couldn't see anything but the skin color on his hands and the back of his neck. That's why she refused to pursue the matter. Went to the hospital to be examined. Cathy interviewed her there. But Grooten herself didn't see any point in coming to look at photos 'cause she couldn't make an—"

"But DNA? Forget the corporeal ID." I was impatient to know why I hadn't gotten the opportunity to talk Katrina Grooten into letting us investigate and build the case.

"He didn't ejaculate. No seminal fluid. No DNA."

"Did we have any other cases like that in the park? Any other crimes to which we could have linked this one?"

"A couple of robberies with a guy who used a ski mask. No arrests, no suspects."

"Witnesses? Nobody coming from or going to the museum?"

"The Cloisters is closed on Monday. Just a few of the staff working there. She thinks she was one of the last ones to leave."

"Any record in the file that Cathy called me before closing out the case?" I believe in getting every victim into our office to be talked to by a member of the legal staff of our unit, whether or not it is a long shot, to see if there is any way to develop the facts into a stronger case or determine if the crime is the work of a serial offender or a convicted rapist on parole.

"Nope. Just EC'd it and the boss signed off on it."

"Exceptional clearance? And she didn't bother to call me for approval?"

"Your best friend here likes to think she runs the NYPD, and not just my life," Chapman said to Nina, trying to make sense of this conversation for her. "In case you don't realize it, Coop, a lieutenant can actually close out a case without your permission."

"Whole song and dance in there about Ms. Grooten being from South Africa. She felt that too many black men had suffered in prisons in her country for crimes they didn't commit, so she didn't want to take the chance of starting a manhunt when she couldn't even identify the rapist."

"Great. So we got a bleeding heart. She's got a Dutch name—descended from Boers, who killed more Africans than you or I could count," Chapman said, holding his empty glass up in the air for Fenton to see, ordering another round of drinks. "Meantime, one of the brothers be having a field day in my neck of the woods and she decides she's gonna give him a pass. America the Beautiful. And nobody notices a mope running around the park with a ski mask on in the middle of June, his dick hanging out of his pants."

"Who was the outcry witness?" The first person Katrina called from the hospital might suggest the name of the friend or relative to whom she was closest, in whom she confided.

"She didn't make any calls. She told Cathy she had no family in this country. And she didn't want anyone at the museum to know what had happened. Katrina said she planned to be going back to Cape Town before the end of the year anyway."

"What'd she do at the museum?" Chapman asked.

"Worked on medieval art. How's this for weird, considering her final resting place? Had an expertise in tomb sculpture."

11

"Nobody's touched the story yet. You lead a charmed life, Alex."

Battaglia had the morning newspapers stacked on his desk, and someone from the public relations office had gone through them to check for crime-related clippings before I showed up on his office doorstep shortly after 8 A.M. on Thursday.

I had scanned them myself before leaving my apartment. Below the fold on page A1 of the *Times* was the feature on Pierre Thibodaux's sudden resignation. Trustees gave opinions in unsourced quotes, and art critics gnawed at some of the questionable purchases made during his tenure. Everyone was surprised at the timing of the announcement, and some even speculated at a behind-the-scenes scandal involving fiscal impropriety or a masterpiece of questionable provenance.

No mention was made of a dead woman found in an ancient sarcophagus. Thibodaux himself had made only a vague reference to the unfortunate coincidence of an ongoing police investigation. His assistant explained that he would hold a press conference in a week's time, after he'd had an opportunity to brief the board members in private on his decision.

"Mickey Diamond called me at home late last night," I told the boss. "He said they didn't want to go with it because no one over at the museum would confirm the girl's ID and the paper was spooked about the next-of-kin thing. Afraid to print something and find out she had family here who would only learn about her death that way."

"Since when are they so sensitive? Truth of the matter is, as one of the other reporters put it to me, Katrina Grooten wasn't really 'anybody.' Pretty pathetic commentary on their values."

"Paul, I spoke to Jake about the leak." He had returned my call shortly after I left the office. He'd also tried to get through to my cell phone, but it wasn't working—just as Anna Friedrichs had described— while we were in the museum basement. So Jake had come over after dinner, when he finished working. "He didn't do it. He wouldn't lie to me."

"It's dead in the water. I trust it won't happen again."

"Have you heard from your counterpart in New Jersey?"

"A casual inquiry. I didn't get the sense he'd want to fight for jurisdiction of the case unless he knew it could be solved with very little effort. Or until you solve it for him."

"So I can keep working on it because the press isn't interested?"

"You can stay with it because Katrina Grooten was a rape victim." That would be his answer to Pat Mc-

Kinney. "Any chance that attack last June is related to her death?"

"Very unlikely, but we're going to run it down. She was treated at Presbyterian Hospital. An evidence collection kit was prepared, but it never went to the lab because she refused to cooperate with the investigation."

"Didn't the ME want the genetic profile developed from the DNA to put in the data bank?"

With the astounding technological advances in the science of DNA, it was the practice of the serology lab to develop the "fingerprint" from every piece of crime scene evidence—blood, semen, saliva—and add it to the local data bank. Unsolved cases that had never seemed to be part of a pattern before were connected by the cold hits that the computer made between one violent occurrence and another, all over the city. Some resulted in links to convicted offenders whose samples had been obtained prior to their release from state prison, leading to arrests in matters that had been investigative dead ends.

"If there had been any evidence to examine, of course it would have been analyzed and entered in the bank. Mercer Wallace is going to see whether the kit is still around. Most hospitals destroy them after ninety days, if the victim doesn't want to go forward."

"But you don't doubt the rape allegation was legit?"

"Why would we? Seemed to be an attack by a stranger, with no reason to be fabricating it, and Grooten saying from the outset she couldn't make an ID."

"Suppose she was having a problem with someone at the museum, Alex. A lover, a coworker, a supervisor. Someone who was giving her a hard time, harassing her, frightening her." Battaglia reached forward to light the end of his cigar. I hadn't finished my coffee yet and he was probably on his third Monte Cristo of the morning.

"You scare me. You're beginning to think like Mike Chapman."

"Maybe she reports a rape—no physical evidence, no finger-pointing or framing a suspect—maybe she calls the cops just to send a shot over the bow. 'I'm serious about this, Mr. Whoever You Are. Leave me alone or else. I'm not afraid to bring the police into this.'"

"Anything's a possibility at this point, Paul. But most stranger-rape victims have no reason to make up the story."

"And most of them aren't found dead within a year."

"Katrina Grooten might have had reasons to act the way she did. A foreigner, alone in this country with what seems to be a very small network of emotional support. An incident that she feared would be racially charged if an arrest followed. The great unlikelihood of finding the assailant. In most other cultures, there's still a societal stigma that attaches to victims of sexual assaults. Somewhere in her life, at work or at home, there would be someone to blame her for walking into the park alone."

"Anybody dust her bicycle for prints?"

All I needed at this point was the district attorney

to micromanage my cases. I had thirty-seven open files in various stages of their investigations, and the forty other lawyers whom Sarah and I supervised had scores more. Maybe I could drop them off with Rose, and Battaglia could try to sort his way through some of those while I helped find Grooten's killer.

"Mercer is double-checking all the paperwork to see what was done, and whether anything can be reexamined at this point."

When he lowered his head to look at the weekly figures in the report from the Office of Court Administration, noting the arrest-to-arraignment time lag, I knew Battaglia was finished with me. I was almost out the door before he spoke: "That big-needle thing, that phony lie detector scam you pull, how often is it successful?"

I bit my lip and paused in the doorway, knowing that McKinney had given me up again. "About ninety-eight percent of the time."

"I like it. Might borrow it someday. Just promise me you won't ever do it in an election year, okay?"

"Sure, boss."

No one was in yet on either side of the hallway. The display on my phone reminded me to pick up my voice mails. I punched in my password and the mechanical recording told me I had two messages.

"*Message one. One thirty-four A.M.*" A real human voice kicked in: "Good morning, Alex Cooper. Or should I say I hope there's nothing good about it."

The stalker. Shirley Denzig's biting tone was unmistakable. The young woman with a complicated psychiatric history had harassed me for weeks during the winter months, after a confrontation in my office when I had seized a forged document that she was carrying with her. She had ferreted out my home address and tried to get past the doormen, at the same time that I was embroiled in a dangerous homicide investigation. The detectives from the District Attorney's Office Squad had searched for her in vain, certain also that she had stolen a pistol from her father's garage in Baltimore.

"I haven't forgotten what you took from me, Alexandra. And I haven't forgotten that you told people I was crazy." Denzig rambled on, filling the three minutes of recording time with vitriol, short of threatening but nasty and unwelcome.

The second message picked up seconds later and Denzig finished her tirade. "I'm closer than you think, Alexandra. You'd better stay out of my way."

She was smart enough to know exactly what she was doing. At no time in either message did she express any intent to harm me. The sound of her voice and the fact that she had not forgotten her anger was enough to alarm me. I dialed the extension upstairs in the squad and reached the duty sergeant who had come on at 8 A.M.

"Steve Maron will know what to do when he gets here. He and Roman handled this one last winter. I'd like someone from the tech unit to come down and tape the messages, so I have a record of them. And I'll get Sarah to sign off on a subpoena to dump my phone."

Computerized telecommunications systems were so sophisticated now that even the shortest telephone call or message would leave its source on our machines. We could request a "dump" of my phone line, specifying the date and time of our interest, and within a day would know from what number Shirley Denzig was calling me. It was an expensive process—five hundred dollars for each twenty-four-hour period in question—but it was foolproof.

Ryan Blackmer had walked in and taken a seat opposite my desk. "Got a minute?"

This was one of the assistants who could always make me smile. Smart, hardworking, and with a talent for attracting the bizarre and unusual, Ryan loved to produce results for the detectives and they loved bringing cases in to him.

"Remember that guy who was on-line in the chat room with Brittany in April?"

"Vaguely." Brittany was the screen named used by a male detective from the pedophile squad, Harry Hinton, when he went on the Internet to look for child molesters.

"I'll refresh your recollection. He wants a meet tomorrow afternoon."

"Friday? Right before the holiday?" It was the beginning of the Memorial Day weekend, and for many New Yorkers it signaled the start of three- or four-day summer getaways to beach and country houses, hotels and inns.

"That's the ruse. Brittany said her parents were going out of town and she'd be home alone in the city, having a sleepover at a girlfriend's house."

"Did you review the transcripts?"

Blackmer was always prepared. "Nice and clean,

just the way you like 'em." He passed the folder over to me.

On the World Wide Web, Brittany was a petite thirteen-year-old cheerleader with a ponytail who attended a parochial school on the Upper West Side. In real life, Harry was a muscular thirty-six-year-old cop with lots of facial hair and fifteen years on the job.

When he went on-line to surf for pervs, Brittany-Harry never initiated the conversation. This was not entrapment. It was simply going to the cyber-caves where these creatures lurked, just as Felix steered his cab through city streets looking for underage girls.

"Which chat room?"

"It's called 'I like *very* older men.' The usual profile. Say the magic words—*cheerleading, music videos, parochial school uniforms.*"

You could watch Harry's act in real time. Within minutes of his logging on in that kind of room with his benign teenage-girl profile, sharks would come out of the water and line up for the kill:

"How big are you?" they'd ask.

"I'm only five-three. I'm short," Brittany would reply.

"No, I don't mean your height. What's your bra size?" and then "Describe your uniform," and then "Are you a virgin?" usually followed by "Send me your picture." Harry would press the enter key, and off would go a digital head shot of Joni Braioso, the undercover who actually took the meet, if the case progressed that far. Although she was twenty-four, Joni didn't look a day older than sixteen. When she dressed in a plaid skirt with navy blue knee socks, fake braces on her teeth, hair pulled back in a bouncing ponytail, and weighing less than a hundred pounds, she easily passed for twelve or thirteen.

Harry had downloaded the response to the photo he sent: "This is me at my computer." Attached was a picture of a middle-aged man in a polo shirt, looking like an ad for a sportswear catalog.

"And this is my *monster*." The printed page that followed was a close-up of a penis.

I did a double take.

"Huge, huh?" said Ryan. "Harry and I are betting he borrowed that from a porn site. These guys never have the equipment they claim is theirs. I especially love it when they name their private parts. Just something that never occurred to me to do."

"Shall I read on?"

"Follows the basic outline. Wants to show her the ropes. Meet the monster and learn how to make love."

"Is he explicit?" I didn't want to waste police manpower if he was simply talking dirty.

"Lays out what he wants to do and how he wants to do it. I'm telling you, he's the perfect target for us. Wants her to suggest a meeting place where there are hotels in the area. He'll bring the condoms, the marijuana, and some booze to relax her."

"And you've found out who he is?"

"Faxed a court order to the ISP." The Internet service provider had responded with information about the subscriber whose screen name was MonsterMan. "The response was sitting in my fax machine this morning. Just ran him through Faces of the Nation."

Ryan read to me from the background report he had pulled off the web. "Frederick Welch III. He's a high school principal in Litchfield, Connecticut."

"The meet is a go. Let's decide on a place that makes Joni comfortable and scout out some SROs that the squad has a relationship with." The single-room-occupancy hotels were often hot-sheet operations, renting rooms by the hour. Plagued by prostitutes and junkies, they frequently looked to the NYPD when trysts and drug deals turned sour and became emergencies. Harry would call in a chit with some desk manager who owed him a favor.

"You want to take it that far?"

"I want him to sign in and ask for a room key. We lost one a month ago by grabbing the guy as soon as he showed up and gave Joni a kiss on the cheek. The judge said we couldn't prove that the perp had any intention of following through with his screen banter."

Cyberspace had become a new kind of playground for pedophiles. Not only were there thousands of sites on which to buy, sell, and exchange child pornography, it was an easy and inexpensive way to correspond with children and adolescents all over the world. Parents who enforced rigid rules about playmates and curfews in their own neighborhoods sent their kids to their bedrooms for hours on end, without ever warning them that the dangers of talking to strangers were every bit as real on-line as on the street.

Sarah Brenner came in with two mugs of coffee, one for her and a refill for me. "Got your message and came right upstairs. Hey, Ryan. Something good, no doubt."

"Maybe I'll just skip the coffee and put toothpicks in my eyelids to keep them open. Good morning," I said, reaching for the hot cup.

"Don't complain about sleep deprivation to the mother of three kids. Battaglia's letting you run with this? You know you love it."

"If you can cover my back down here, Ryan's Internet sting might heat up tomorrow. We've got three people on trial and a holiday weekend. The young and the restless are bound to start celebrating the rites of spring." Our numbers always went up in warm weather.

"Do I get to make command decisions?" she said, smiling.

"You even get to suck up to McKinney, if you're in the mood."

I reached for the ringing phone but Laura came in and grabbed it. She greeted all of us and told me Chapman was on the line.

"I'm just setting things up with Sarah. I'll be on my way."

"That's not why I'm calling. Dr. K. isn't even back from a domestic up in Chelsea. What do I need to seize someone's passport?"

"What you don't have yet, in this case: probable cause. Why, has Pierre Thibodaux packed up his bags already?" I had worried that the soon-to-be ex-director would have no reason to stay in town, but figured that there would be a period of transition until his successor was named.

"I just called Ms. Drexler to see when I could pick up a list of all the employees, and get a guided tour of the other Egyptian coffins from Timothy Gaylord, who left us so abruptly yesterday afternoon. Unfortunately, he's leaving the country tonight."

"Business or displeasure?"

"A rather special assignment, down in Chile. He's going to the mummy congress."

12

The morgue attendant at the loading dock on East Thirtieth Street was pushing an empty gurney through the entrance that Mike Chapman was holding open for him. I slammed the cab door behind me and squinted because of the bright sunlight. It was unusual to hear singing at the mouth of this gray tunnel where the night's dead were brought in to tell their stories to the medical examiners.

"See the pyramids along the Nile . . . ," Mike crooned softly, a more doo-wop version than Jo Stafford had recorded in 1956. Mike rested his arm against the opening, for me to pass under, pointing me out to the waiting ambulance driver as he got to the coda of the song, "she belongs to *me*."

"I'll bite. What's the mummy congress?"

"The Fourth World Congress on Mummy Studies. Now, that has got to be a totally happening group of scientists, don't you think? You might be able to find some guest speakers for McKinney's killer camp."

The DA's office held an annual retreat that served as a training session on investigating and prosecuting homicide cases for the senior members of the trial division. It was Pat McKinney's pet project, and he spent the better part of each year lining up the quirkiest experts and the worst lodging that a convention could promise.

"This is the real deal?"

"Ms. Drexler ranks it just below a papal consistory. Every three years, a lively group of paleopathologists and Egyptologists gather together for a serious study of issues related to mummies, old and new. They deliver papers, study techniques, compare hieroglyphics, walk like Egyptians. That kind of stuff."

"Serious subjects?"

"DNA in mummies, human sacrifices at high altitudes in the Andes, parasites that inhabit mummified corpses."

"Can't Gaylord skip a session? Pick it up on satellite? Alan Dershowitz does CNN interviews from the nude beach on Martha's Vineyard; I'm sure we can hook something up for this guy."

"He's delivering the keynote this weekend—'Ethical Considerations in Studying the Ancient Dead.' Apparently, he's got the most serious credentials in the field. Drexler says it's a big issue in museum work. Things that were tolerated fifty and a hundred years ago, digging up sacred graves and messing with the spirits, are taboo now."

"Why Chile?"

"A stretch of road called the Atacama, about the most lifeless desert in the world."

"You knew that?" It must have been a battleground once.

"Never heard of it. Miss Efficiency is my lifeline to

the mummy man. There's a little city in northern Chile called Arica, close to the desert. That one I know. Peru ceded it to Chile after the War of the Pacific. Treaty of Ancón, 1883."

"You know about wars I wasn't even aware were fought."

"What I didn't know is that it has the distinction of being so dry in the Atacama that the long-term preservation of the human body is practically guaranteed. Mummy heaven. Probably more of them there than in the entire Nile valley."

"Is Gaylord going there because of what he knows, or what he wants to learn?"

"Seems obvious to me that he wouldn't need to keep that appointment if he's our killer. Whoever wrapped up Ms. Grooten must have already completed the course. Can we stop him, just to be sure?" Mike asked.

"On what basis? We haven't got a thing. Any sign that he's not coming back?"

"Eve Drexler says it's business as usual come Tuesday."

"I'm more concerned about Pierre Thibodaux."

"She's boxing up his entire office now to send off with him. Want *her* DNA? Betcha there'll be tearstains all over his belongings. I think Eve would like to follow Pierre home to Paris."

By the time we reached Dr. Kestenbaum's office, he had arrived from the scene of the Chelsea stabbing and was changing out of his clothes into the scrubs he would wear in the autopsy room for the rest of the day.

"So what do you two know about poison?"

"Start at the top of the page, doc. We're beginners."

"Katrina Grooten died of arsenic poisoning. I've submitted all the tissue and hair samples for toxicology and mitochondrial DNA analysis, but those results take quite a while, as you know."

"You were just guessing yesterday. But now you're sure?"

"Some very gross indications, Alex. Mee's lines on her fingernails were rather telltale, the minute I saw her hands."

"What are they?"

"White lines running straight across her nails, suggesting toxic levels of arsenic in the body. That strong, pungent odor you smelled when the coffin lid was opened. Remember when I asked you if it reminded you of anything and you told me it was pungent? Garlic, I thought. The alopecia I observed, hair coming out of her scalp and her eyelids—all those things are consistent with high levels of arsenic intake. I'll have the complete report typed up by the beginning of the week, but those were my initial observations before we even started to cut."

"D'you ever see a body preserved like that, doc?"

"Never. Not naturally. Nothing was done surgically to keep it intact, I've confirmed that."

"So we've gotta figure out whether the killer knew what he was doing when he hid the body, or whether it was an accident of the climate conditions where he hid it, right?"

"I'll tell you this, Mike. When I get the tox results

back, I think we'll see that Ms. Grooten's murderer did nothing to disguise the fact that she was over-dosed with arsenic."

"What do you mean?"

"That he didn't expect her to be found for six months, if ever—"

"Or a year later, a continent away—"

"Even better for him. It's not like he was giving it to Grooten in small, subtle doses. I think he was figuring she'd be long out of the way, undiscovered and decayed before anyone realized what had happened."

"Isn't arsenic in our drinking water?"

"It would take one thirsty broad to put out her lights this way, Coop. You gotta call my mother. She'll be so proud of the way my education is paying off in this investigation. Day one, I come across an Incorruptible. Now I can add all the things I know Albertus Magnus—Saint Albert the Great—was good for. He was the first guy to produce arsenic in a free form. Right, doc?"

"Exactly. It's been a popular way of poisoning peo-ple since the Middle Ages, in fact and in fiction. At one time it was such an available means of killing that the Brits referred to it as 'inheritance powder.' Best way to do in the family member who controlled the purse strings.

"And yes, Alex, arsenic is introduced into drinking water through the dissolution of minerals and ores on the earth's surface. Sometimes aggravated by indus-trial waste. It's in a lot of the fish and meat you eat. But if Grooten was exposed to a supply of contami-nated water, where she worked or where she lived, she wouldn't be the only one getting sick. The whole neighborhood would have been in bad shape after a while."

"What are you figuring, blondie? She drank too much tap water, fell into a limestone box and the lid dropped on it?"

"You know Battaglia's going to ask me if there's any chance her death could have been accidental. I'm just trying to rule out the obvious."

"Of course there have been accidental poisonings. We had a case last year where a guy who did professional woodworking breathed in the fumes from some chemically treated lumber. Absorbed the stuff through his mucous membranes because he was just too stubborn to use a mask on wood that had been coated with an arsenic compound. You can inhale it, absorb it, and ingest it. None of those methods are recommended."

"Does it manifest any symptoms over time?"

"Sure. If it were just a mild poisoning, I'd expect the patient to complain of nausea, chills, loss of appetite, intestinal upset, apathy. Small doses would make you sick, but they wouldn't necessarily kill you. The more acute cases begin to show skin lesions, chronic headaches, the metallic taste which results in that garliclike odor, the liver damage apparent here at autopsy."

"Can you give me any idea how long this was going on, doc?"

"The hair sample should be a big help with that. It will give us a poisoning time line."

"How so?"

"Figure that the average growth rate for human hair is one and a half centimeters a month. Every millimeter sample represents about two days' growth. I'd expect to be able to tell when Grooten was exposed to her first significant dose of arsenic once we get that result. And from the looks of things today, we'll probably find a much greater concentration—five or six times as much—in the hair closest to her scalp."

"Did you find any trace evidence on the body or inside the coffin, anything that might link us to the guy who did this?"

"I've saved the linen binding. Has some age to it. Probably was taken off some other antiquity and wrapped around Grooten. So you're likely to have some transfer material or residue from the first subject. More likely that than from the killer."

"Prints?"

"I never thought of you as an optimist, Mike. The lab can look it over. I'd think whoever had this much time to deal with a corpse had latex gloves on. You don't have to be a doctor. Every drug and hardware store sells them."

"And where do you shop for arsenic?" I asked.

"It's in insecticides like Paris green. It's in poison gases. Have you confirmed that she had a connection at the Metropolitan Museum, like you thought yesterday?"

"Yeah."

"Arsenic is a very common ingredient in pigments, Alex. Any art museum would have a surprisingly good supply of deadly poisons. Lye and white lead and arsenic make for brilliant colors but a lousy diet, and they're likely to be in any serious artist's stash of pigments." Kestenbaum turned to Chapman. "I've bagged her clothes for you, Mike."

He tossed us each a pair of latex gloves and pointed at a bunch of brown paper bags standing on the far end of the table at which we were seated.

I stood up and opened the first of them, removing a bra. It was old and worn thin, and the writing on the label had been bleached off after many washings. It was a small size. The second bag held the deceased's panties. Like the bra, they were a dingy shade of off-white, from age and repeated cycles of laundering. The third bag contained a pair of women's slacks, size 6, poorly made of a coarse plaid wool. They were worn around the bottom of the pant legs and had pilling all over the seat. The brand name was that of one of the cheap mail-order companies.

The fourth bag held a woman's crewneck sweater.

"What's so fascinating, Coop?"

"It doesn't belong to the same shopper who bought the other pieces."

"How come?"

"First of all, it's cashmere. It's also not her size." I held the sweater up to examine it. It was much larger than the small-boned Grooten would have worn.

"Third, the label is one of the most expensive shops on Madison Avenue. Where's your Polaroid?"

Kestenbaum pointed to the door. "Turn right, there's one in the supply closet at the end of the hall-way."

"Submit all this to the lab, but I want to do some checking on the sweater. Maybe we can find out whether she bought it herself, or if someone gave it to her as a gift." I handed it to Mike to photograph, to record the detail of the cable stitching and the style of the collar and cuffs. The item had not been mass-produced. It was doubtful that many of these pale peach-colored knits had been sold. "This probably retailed for more than five hundred dollars."

"On a museum intern's salary? I don't think my entire wardrobe between the time I was born and the age of thirty cost that much," Mike said.

Kestenbaum picked up a white letter-sized envelope from his desk. "You'll want to voucher this, too. I found it in the pocket of her slacks. Maybe it will tell you where Ms. Grooten left her belongings when she went for her last meal."

I lifted the flap and took out a square red ticket, one inch in size, bearing the number 248. It looked like the stub of a receipt from a coat-check concession, somewhere between the morgue and Cairo.

13

"See any Hessians?" Mike Chapman called out to Mercer Wallace, who was leaning against the massive granite stones that formed a wall bordering the grouping of monasteries that had been moved from Europe to this rocky cliff three-quarters of a century ago. It was shortly after twelve on a sunny May afternoon, and we climbed the circular walk to join Mercer on the ledge overlooking the Hudson River.

"You are standing, my friends, on the highest piece of land on the island of Manhattan, accessible by the deepest subway station in the city—not that you would give a thought to any form of public transportation, Coop," Mike continued. "Almost lost to the Brits in the affair of the outposts."

Mercer turned to listen to the military history of this extraordinary piece of open public land on the northern end of Manhattan, his huge frame posed against the wide stretch of water below.

"General Washington left the garrison here and headed north, while Cornwallis surrounded this place with warships, Highlanders, British troops, and Hessians. They took the fort, killed most of the Americans, and were encamped here until these heights were refortified. That's why the Long Hill outwork was renamed for William Tryon, the last English governor of New York."

The Cloisters Museum stood on a spectacular hill-top in Fort Tryon Park, the last of the New York City parklands designed by Frederick Law Olmsted. John D. Rockefeller had given the city the buildings and more than sixty acres of unique urban land, with paved walks, terraces, and rocky terrain covering the area from the old ramparts of the original fort to the peak on which the imported ruins had been reset and enclosed in a contemporary setting.

My eyes swept the vista, leaving the river to follow the pathway that led directly down from our perch through the densely wooded area. Katrina Grooten had set off from the museum along one of those sloping walks on an evening last June, into the hands of a modern-day highwayman who had pulled her into the thickets that shielded them from view while he assaulted her.

"Hiram Bellinger is waiting for us inside." Mercer led us around the impressive structure and down to the entrance that faced the parking lot. The Romanesque-style doorway, adorned with animals and birds, both real and imaginary, led to a series of arched steps. We were among only a handful of visitors, and I felt as though I had stepped back a few centuries into a medieval church as I made my way upward, passing the occasional window framed with tiny panes of leaded glass.

"Cool in here," Mike said.

The thick walls, constructed of enormous pieces of stone, lowered the temperature at least ten degrees as we stepped inside. I'm sure Mike was wondering, as I was, whether this nouveau monastery's chill would have been conducive to preserving a dead body. The machine-made wrought-iron hand railings were the only reminder that we had not entered a time warp.

At the top of the staircase a lone guard pointed the way to the curator's office. Beyond the splendid marble capitals of the Cuxa Cloister, one of the five French monasteries re-created here, we crossed through a serene garden and over to the tower that housed the museum's administrative wing.

I knocked on the door that bore the sign HIRAM BELLINGER, CURATOR—MEDIEVAL ART, expecting it to be opened by a churlish old recluse who had spent decades with his nose in his antique manuscripts. Hiram Bellinger didn't fit the description. He couldn't have been any older than Mercer, perhaps forty-two at most. His khaki slacks, tasseled loafers, and cotton turtleneck under an open-collared button-down shirt gave him the look of a country squire.

Books were stacked everywhere around the large room, and from its setting high above the museum, I could see for miles up the Hudson.

"Hard to work on a day like this, so I'm happy to have the interruption. The medieval monks liked isolation, Ms. Cooper. Almost as much as I do. The Benedictines preferred mountaintops while the Cisterians chose remote river valleys. I've been fortunate enough to find the closest imitation of a monastic setting that any big city offers."

Bellinger invited us to sit around a circular table in the middle of the room. He moved several open volumes of books to the windowsill and pushed other mounds of them to one side of the tabletop.

"How can I help you?"

"We'd like to talk to you about Katrina. Katrina Grooten."

"I still can't believe what I've heard," he said, rearranging his papers and sitting next to me.

"Exactly what is it that you've heard?"

"That she's dead. That she never actually left New York to go back home, which is what she told us she was doing." He shook his head. "That someone killed her."

"We intend to find out who. And why. We need to start with some information about Katrina. What she did, whom she knew, how she lived—"

"And who she pissed off." Mike's manner jarred with the refined calm of Bellinger's aerie.

"That last would be a very short list. But I'll give it some thought. Katrina could get under your skin if she found an issue, a passion that engaged her. But most of the time she was quiet, almost to the point of being withdrawn."

"How long had you known her?"

"I hired her, in fact. Almost three years ago."

"Where did you meet?"

"She showed up at the Met, résumé in hand, like most other graduate students with a degree in art history. They teach, they get more degrees, they work in museums."

"There is a medieval art collection in the main building, too, isn't there?"

"Of course. A very good one. That's the reason Katrina applied there. But when her application was circulated, it wound up on my desk. Her interests suited my needs perfectly."

"Why is that?"

"She had just completed an apprenticeship at the Musée des Augustins. Do you know it?"

None of us did.

"Toulouse, in France. It's very much like the Cloisters, except it survived in its original site. The museum is an old convent building, quite sumptuous. In addition to the church buildings, it houses a remarkable art collection. Rubens, Van Dyck, Ingres, Corot. Most people are attracted to the art. Katrina immersed herself in the Gothic and Romanesque sculpture. She had a wonderful eye for medieval treasures. I invited her to join our operation."

"How many of you are there working up here?"

"With support staff, just over a hundred. Librarians, bookshop personnel, security, janitorial. I've got an assistant curator, a good number of restorers, and then half a dozen interns, like Katrina."

"And those others, was she close to them?"

"Professionally. I'd tell you to talk to them, but the interns come and go. The salary is low, this facility is a throwback to another age—so kids just out of school find it a bit inconvenient for socializing—and it's hard to get to. I'll have to check to see who overlapped with Katrina."

"Are you single?" Mike was looking for a wedding

ring as Bellinger gestured with his left hand, but there was none.

"No, I'm married."

"Your wife?"

Bellinger smiled. "Works for a music production company."

"Classical?"

"No. Pop, rock and roll, rap, whatever's hot."

"Kind of a Jack Sprat thing, huh?" Chapman said. "You eat no fat, she eats no lean."

"Just gives me even more appreciation for the quiet within these walls."

"Ever hang out with Katrina?"

"Museum functions. Command performances when Thibodaux wanted to trot us out for the trustees. Nothing personal."

"Guess you won't have to answer to Pierre any longer."

"You've probably heard that I wasn't part of his fan club. Too much P. T. Barnum and not enough emphasis on scholarship and education. I'm grateful to him for some terrific acquisitions he made for the Cloisters, but we didn't have very much in common."

"Is that why you assigned Ms. Grooten as the Cloisters' liaison for the show that was being planned for next year with the Museum of Natural History? Wasn't that a lot of responsibility for an intern?"

"Katrina was extremely knowledgeable, Detective. Far more scholarly than many of her peers, and I worked with her quite closely on the project. I realize the exhibition is going to be a meaningful source of revenue for both museums. To me, anything that takes me away from my research is a waste of time. I thought it would be a good opportunity for Katrina to mix with other people at both institutions, get to make some acquaintances that would give her more of a life in the city. Get her noticed by some of the higher-ups."

"Did she enjoy it?"

"Seemed to. I think she had quite a good time exploring all our treasures to look for the animals that could be featured. Bestiaries were creations of medieval art originally, so they're everywhere in our work. And I also got a sense that she looked forward to the meetings. Making friends, spending time downtown, coming out of her shell a bit."

"Has another intern taken over where she left off?"

"That was my plan," Bellinger said. "But time was getting short so I've taken on much of it myself, as you can see. Seemed like more trouble than it was worth to start training someone all over again."

In the far corner of the room, assembled on a table, were a variety of objects that depicted an array of fantastic animals. "That fresco of the lion is from Spain. According to the old bestiaries, lions slept with their eyes open, as paragons of watchfulness. And this," he said, walking over and picking up a whimsical brass figure, "this was one of Katrina's favorites."

"What is it?"

"An aquamanile. The priests used them to wash their hands during the celebration of Mass. This one's a wyvern."

"A what?"

"A two-legged dragon, swallowing a man. His tail curves over his wings, forming the handle with which to pour." He surveyed the menagerie. "Double-headed eagles, devil's helpers with cloven hooves, lions restrained by apes, Harpies—with their angelic faces and false music—luring sailors to their death. Katrina adored these creatures."

"So when did you take over the exhibition project coordination?"

"After Katrina resigned at the end of the year."

"If she was so happy with this kind of work, weren't you surprised that she was quitting?"

"I've learned not to invest a great deal of emotional energy in bonding with the graduate students. It's usually a short stay. They're parking here briefly before they go back to school for their doctorates, or this place is just too damn unexciting for them. At least Katrina had a valid excuse. I mean, what can you say when someone tells you she's been raped?"

Mercer and I exchanged glances. "When, exactly?"

"Not when it happened. Not for more than a month. But the whole thing had a much more profound impact on her than she had anticipated. It began to affect her work, even her relationships with other people here."

"And that's why she discussed the rape with you?"

"In confidence, yes. Because she was conflicted about what to do. I'll walk you through the areas she spent time in, Ms. Cooper. These buildings are a series of chapels and gardens and arcades. As beautiful as they are, they're rather foreboding, with statues of grotesques and effigies of the dead all around. We don't get the heavy foot traffic that the main Metropolitan museum gets. It can be fairly—shall I say— haunting up here on our hilltop, especially late at night when there's no one to keep you company. I believe Katrina was attacked about a year ago, am I right?"

"In June."

"Well, one night in August, while she was working alone on a sketch of a stone monster in the vault of the Langon Chapel, she was startled by one of the guards who had come in to do a routine security check. She hadn't heard his footsteps, I guess, and she looked up to see him standing over her. She let out a scream. She scared him as much as she scared herself."

"Didn't she know him?"

"That's just it. He had changed out of his uniform to go off duty, and came back to check out everything one more time. Katrina had never seen him in jeans and a T-shirt, with a baseball cap on. She didn't recognize him. The next morning, she was in at the crack of dawn, waiting for me, to explain what had happened."

"Why?"

"She wanted to quit. She felt horribly guilty. The guard was an African-American, and she knew she had insulted him terribly by responding to his appearance with fright. That's the day she told me that she had been sexually assaulted.

"And she told me how ashamed she was, because she kept reacting with fear every time she saw an unfamiliar black face, anxious that it was the man who attacked her."

That kind of response was all too common. Victims whose assailants were unapprehended had a generalized terror, irrational even to them, that the next stranger they encountered, if he was the same race as their rapist, might be the person who was responsible for the crime. They knew he was out there somewhere, and they started at the sight of any person they didn't know.

"Did she tell you whether she could identify her rapist?"

"According to what she told *me*, he'd been wearing a ski mask. That's what had her so strung out. Katrina had no idea if the rapist was someone she'd ever seen before or not. His black hands and neck were all she saw clearly. So here was poor Lloyd, who'd just gone back into the chapel one more time to make sure she was okay that night, and she jumped out of her skin when she saw him."

"Did she quit?"

Bellinger answered softly, "I wouldn't let her. I asked her to tell me the story of the attack, and she did. I spoke to Lloyd about it that very same day, and he sought her out to try to calm her. Told her he understood completely.

"Quite frankly, I thought a lot of it had to do with the fact that she was raised in South Africa. Katrina tried very hard to convince herself that she had no prejudices or racial bias. Her family had been in Cape Town for generations, and she talked from time to time about the horrors of apartheid on a society. I'm not sure she could ever have been responsible for testifying in a case that would have sent a black man to jail, no matter what he had done to her."

"But she did resign eventually?"

"Several months later, just around the Christmas holidays. I found her note in the file," he said, walking back to his desk. "She was anxious to get out of town before the New Year. If I remember correctly, there was a big ice storm predicted right about the time she was supposed to leave. It didn't surprise us that she wanted to get out before it stranded her here."

Mike Chapman rolled his eyes at me. "Yeah, Ms. Cooper decided to hibernate during that one, right? It was a killer."

I had tried to put the images of last December's frigid encounter with a greedy murderer out of my thoughts. Mercer got us back on track. "Between August, when she told you about the rape, and the end of the year, did you notice any change in her behavior?"

"Everyone I knew had a change in behavior, Mr. Wallace. After September eleventh."

I breathed in and bit my lip, remembering the devastating aftermath of the terrorist attacks.

"Maybe that's why I minimized Katrina's distress. We were all so incredulous. So frightened and self-absorbed. She just never pulled out of it. Things like that episode with Lloyd. And her lack of spirit, her general malaise."

"What malaise?"

"I suppose I don't have to tell you three investigators about what occurs. The rape changed Katrina's whole life. She didn't trust anyone after that. Wasn't able to stay here late and work. Had trouble getting to the Cloisters, because she didn't want to walk or bike through the park, yet she didn't have the money for cab fare every day. What is it called? PTSD?"

Post–traumatic stress disorder. Many victims of violent crime suffer from it for months or even years after an attack. Symptoms vary widely, from sleeplessness and eating disorders to weight loss and dysfunctions of every kind. There are scores of survivors whose recovery is fast and full; they never forget the attack but have the emotional and physical resources to move forward. There are far too many others without the support system to regain the stability of their former lives for months or even years after the occurrence of the crime.

"Who told you about that?"

"Her counselor, actually. As soon as Katrina told me, I asked her whether I could speak with the woman who was helping her deal with the rape."

"Do you know who she is? Her name, I mean?" The medical record in the file Mercer had seen had a check mark next to the box that said Katrina Grooten had refused an appointment for follow-up psychological care.

Bellinger was still standing at his desk, flipping through his Rolodex cards. "Loselli. Harriet Loselli. Would you like her number?"

"I got that," Mike said. "What I'd like is to hear her talk for once without that miserable, whiny, you-cops-are-all-insensitive-bastards recording that goes off from her weaselly little mouth whenever one of us hits the emergency room with a victim."

There were superb rape crisis counseling units at hospitals all over the city, run by experienced psychologists and social workers, staffed with volunteers who went out on cases at all hours of the day and night. How did Katrina wind up with Harriet? The most obnoxious, ignorant, and self-centered of the crew, she was unlikely to have dealt with the depth of Katrina Grooten's problems and concerns.

"Did you actually speak with Loselli?"

"Yes, Katrina gave her permission to talk with me."

"About these psychological reactions?"

"Not really. My main concern was her physical condition."

Mercer put down his pen and we all focused on Bellinger. "What do you mean?"

"From the time she disclosed the rape to me in August, I began to keep an eye out for her. When I knew she was going to be working late, I sent her home in a car. If I noticed she wasn't eating, I'd bring an extra sandwich for lunch. By midfall, I'd certainly say by October, I didn't think she looked very well at all."

"Did you speak with her about it?"

"I don't know about your office, Ms. Cooper, but we've got pretty strict institutional guidelines about sexual harassment. Puts a supervisor in kind of a catch-22 position. 'You're not looking very well today, Katrina. Seems to me like you've dropped a few pounds. That old spark I used to see fly when we discussed the one-point-three-million-dollar purchase we expected the museum to make on a tapestry from Bordeaux, it just isn't there in your eyes anymore.' Uh-uh. Only gets a guy in trouble. I talked it over with my wife and she told me it was none of my business. Leave it alone."

"Did you tell anyone else?"

"Sure. Pierre Thibodaux. He's the boss. I put it right in his lap. I told him I thought one of our rising stars had a problem and needed our help if we were going to hang on to her."

"What did he do?"

"Nothing. Nothing at all. You know what his response was? When I told him that she had been raped leaving work a few months earlier, he told me to forget about our telephone conversation. He told me that he wanted me to destroy any records I was keeping about the fact that she had been assaulted."

"What?" Chapman asked.

I whispered to Mercer the same word that Bellinger spoke aloud: "Lawsuit. All he was concerned about was the museum's potential liability. 'Pierre,' I said, 'this girl is suffering. There's something seriously wrong with her, and someone here needs to intervene.' He refused to deal with that aspect of it. It's all about money to him, all the time. He kept insisting that Katrina was probably setting up a case to sue the museum."

"I don't get it," Mike said, looking at me.

"Sure you do. Cloisters employee working late, probably to make a deadline for a research project or exhibition." Bellinger nodded in agreement as I talked. "Leaves the museum alone and is attacked, still on the grounds. No one is ever caught or charged with the crime. Victim suffers from generic psychological ailment. Maybe she's going to feel better some day, after lots of expensive therapy. Maybe she's not. Museum dangles half a million dollars in front of her nose to keep her quiet. Don't scare the tourists, don't upset the coworkers."

"Did Thibodaux know the girl you were talking about was Katrina Grooten? I mean, did you mention her name?" Mike was clearly drawn back to the reaction when he had shown her photograph to the director, who claimed not to recognize her.

Bellinger thought for a few moments. "I'm not sure whether I did. Pierre had met her a couple of times. But that would have been at group meetings or large social occasions. I'm not sure I thought he would have known her. It shouldn't have mattered who she was, frankly, once I brought the gravity of this to his attention."

"Anyone else you told?"

"Yes. I tried two of the women next. Thought that might strike a responsive chord with the sisterhood." Bellinger shook his head as he spoke. "They both knew her from the planning sessions for the big exhibit. Eve Drexler, who's Thibodaux's assistant, and Anna Friedrichs, who's the curator in one of the other departments at the Met."

"Yes, we saw both of them yesterday. How did they react?"

"I was foolish to think that Eve would do anything to cross Thibodaux. She listened to everything I told her and asked me to keep her informed. But she basically advised me not to worry about it. It was just a 'woman's problem' and Katrina would get over it."

"And Anna?"

"She was good. She's the one who urged me to call the counselor. Anna had noticed the changes, too. She felt the phone call would have more weight coming from me, since Katrina worked directly for me. So I called."

"What did Harriet say?"

"I told her my concern. I described the changes in Katrina since the summer. How she had lost weight and become listless. That lately, she had become apathetic about her work, which was very uncharacteristic of her."

It not only sounded like post–traumatic stress, but also like the beginning of an overlay of arsenic poisoning.

"I asked Harriet whether she thought Katrina should see a physician, whether there was something medically wrong that might be causing this deterioration. You haven't told me how Katrina died, of course," Bellinger said, looking at Mike, "so perhaps my second-guessing is all irrelevant."

Mike didn't offer any assistance. "What did she say?"

"Harriet? That she could handle this herself. That counseling like this was her specialty. She had only been seeing Katrina since late summer, so the differences were not as startling to her as they were to some of us who had known her before she was assaulted. But she led me to believe that she was the expert, so I left it alone. Harriet told me all the symptoms I mentioned were consistent with rape trauma syndrome."

"Did you and Katrina continue to talk about it, too?"

"Not really. By the beginning of November, she was already hinting to me that she was thinking about going home, to Cape Town. Her father was there—"

"Do you have a telephone number for him?"

"It's in the personnel folder here. I don't think it will do you much good. She told me her father was in a nursing home. Early-onset Alzheimer's, if I'm not mistaken. I told her I thought it was crazy for her to go back there, for two reasons."

"What were they?"

"I thought she needed to get well before she went home. Brought out that stubborn streak she had. She got all fired up about the medical care in South Africa and how advanced it was. That if there was something psychological impeding her recovery, it would do her good to get out of this environment, where the rape occurred. And that if it was medical as I suspected—and she doubted that, by the way, because she placed such faith in Harriet—then the best doctors in the world were in Cape Town."

"And your second reason for thinking she shouldn't leave?"

"The work she was doing."

"They don't have tombs in Africa?" Mike asked. "They don't have museums?"

"Of course they do. But nothing like her specialty. She had already applied for a job. I'd written a letter of recommendation, which you'll also see in the file."

"For what kind of position?"

"The McGregor Museum. It's in Kimberley, South Africa."

"They've got a medieval art department?" I asked.

"Botany. Archaeology. Cultural history. Zoology. Natural history. Science, not medieval art. They're what you do at the McGregor. That was my point, Ms. Cooper. Katrina was such a promising student in this highly competitive field. But all of the medieval studies programs are limited to the European and American institutions. She was throwing away ten years of her education."

"But it was her home, Mr. Bellinger."

"Her mother was dead. Her father didn't know her any longer. She'd gone to university in England, so her friends were scattered all over the world. *That* wasn't home, in South Africa. She was beginning to make herself a decent life here." Bellinger was pacing now and was getting more agitated as he spoke about his efforts to stop Katrina from leaving New York. "Anna Friedrichs and I were hoping to restore her health and well-being. I'd talked to Eve about letting her transfer her work to the main branch of the Met so she didn't have to deal with coming through Fort Tryon Park every day."

"Sounds like you wanted to keep her around," Mike said.

"Very much so. I even suggested a leave of absence. Go home for the holidays. Visit her father. See that there was nothing left for her in Cape Town. Now I can only imagine the pressure she was experiencing if someone here was trying to kill her all that time."

Bellinger hesitated, then looked across his desk to Mike and Mercer. "Are you going to tell me? Am I entitled to know how she died?"

"Poison, most probably."

He pulled out his chair and sat down, throwing his head back and studying a gargoyle in the arch of the ceiling. The last thing I expected to hear him do was laugh.

"I hope to hell it wasn't arsenic. I've got enough of it here to do in all of us."

14

"Do you mean that Katrina Grooten worked with arsenic here at the Cloisters?"

Bellinger fidgeted now, swiveling in his chair as though he were looking for something north of the heavy traffic crawling across the George Washington Bridge.

"No, no, I can't say that she did."

"But a lot of the other staff members do?" Chapman asked.

He thought before answering. "I wouldn't say very many. Four at the most. Those who work under my direct supervision. They'll all tell you *I'm* the one who uses it most."

"Why? In what form?"

"My particular scholarship is in the field of illustrated manuscripts." He stood up and walked to some of the open volumes that had been moved to accommodate our gathering. "From the earliest monastic houses on, the production of books was an essential task the monks performed for the greater ecclesiastical community. Each of them had what was called a scriptorium, where scribes and illuminators copied classical texts. Here, in the building we call the Treasury, we've got a unique collection of these exquisite books."

Bellinger picked one up and carried it back to us. "Certainly our most prized possession. Perhaps you know it. The *Belles Heures*."

"Only from the museum catalog."

"This one was described in the inventory of the Duke of Berry in 1413. These were made by the monks for the rich patrons and royal families, who were supposed to say their prayers at the same canonical hours that were observed in the monasteries—book of hours."

The two pages he displayed were ornately decorated in gold leaf around the text of the prayers. There were stunning paintings in vibrant colors, and I studied the heavy pages before moving out of the way for Mike and Mercer.

"How has this survived in such good condition?" I asked.

"The books always suffered less damage than things like tapestries. They couldn't be melted down into bullion, like jewelry or pieces of gold, so thieves and rogues didn't perceive them to have very much value. It's just that their colors fade over time, and we restore them here. That's the work I like to do."

"And the materials?"

"We try to imitate what was done in medieval times." Bellinger pointed at parts of the elegant page. "Powdered gold for these elaborate drawings was made by grinding the actual metal with honey and mixing it with egg whites. Black came from a carbon-based ink. They made blue in a number of ways. The most expensive was actually ground from lapis lazuli, or indigo mixed with white lead—which is actually quite poisonous itself. And yellow, that's where the orpiment comes in. The monks used saffron to produce a yellow pigment in the early days. But it wasn't permanent."

"What's orpiment?"

"It's an arsenic compound, Detective. Very widely used to give us a fine yellow color. You can see how effective it is right on that page you're examining now. In our workshop downstairs, we've got more than enough to make someone quite ill."

"Is it secured?"

"Do we keep it under lock and key? Of course not. Our little restoration area doesn't get a lot of outside interest. It's very intense labor and doesn't excite much of the general public."

"Did Ms. Grooten have access to the room?"

Bellinger paused for a moment. "Certainly. But she wasn't in the habit of licking paintbrushes, Mr. Chapman." He was beginning to snap at Mike.

"And Napoleon didn't chew on his wallpaper, either."

"What?" the puzzled curator asked.

"There was arsenic found in locks of Napoléon's hair. Lots of it. There were theories that his captors did him in, and some wild conjecture that he was poisoned by the vapors from the wallpaper color in his room at St. Helena's, during his exile. Copper arsenite."

"Scheele's green, probably. A brilliant pigment.

We've got some of that, too. Don't use as much of it because it wasn't created until after the Renaissance, so it wouldn't be authentic to our pieces."

"That's exactly why we need to know what Grooten was working on and who she dealt with," I said. Mike knew more about the great Corsican general than Pat McKinney knew about the law. If he got off on a Napoléonic tangent, we'd be here until midnight. "I assume you have a way to tell us whether any tubes or vials are missing?"

"I'm sure I don't. The workmen get all the supplies they need by ordering from the Met. Ask Pierre Thibodaux. Ask Erik Poste. Ask the other medievalists."

His counterparts at the main branch were obvious interview subjects. "Why Thibodaux? Why Poste?"

"I'm sure the director's office has all the billing records for the goods that are purchased for our needs. The ever-rigid Ms. Drexler must be able to put her fingers on that. There are a host of toxic substances in paints and pigments, varnishes and cleaning agents. And we're not the only ones who restore old artworks, Ms. Cooper. Mr. Poste's European collection has far more extensive restoration projects than do I."

I didn't think he was pointing the finger at other colleagues as much as he was highlighting how frustrating our search would be in an institution that apparently needed poisons to enliven the glorious holdings the public came to view.

"May we have this copy of Ms. Grooten's personnel file to take with us?" I asked.

"I've reproduced the entire thing for you."

I opened it from the back and saw the letter of resignation first. It had been written on a word processor and dated December 24 of the previous year. In place of a signature was the capital letter *K*, drawn with a marker in almost a stick-figure print.

"Is that how she usually signed things, not spelling out her whole name?"

Bellinger took the document from my hand. "Straight and simple, just like that. She usually used both initials, but her *G* was more Gothic, if you will." He closed his eyes as if to call up an image of her signature. "The *G* would have been harder to imitate, come to think of it, if someone else did the writing."

I hadn't suggested that the letter wasn't written by Grooten. "Why would you think she didn't write this herself?"

"I—uh, I don't know. When did she die? I just mean she never came back to work after the twentieth, if I'm not wrong. Maybe she'd already been murdered, and the killer wrote this so I wouldn't be worried about her disappearance."

"And were you?"

"I was out of town that entire period, visiting my in-laws for the holidays. I never knew Katrina had quit until I returned in January. She was gone, and I thought she had left the country. There wasn't much I could do about it until she sent me a forwarding address, as that letter said she would do once she got set up at home."

"Did she have a computer when she was working here?"

"Yes, of course."

"With an e-mail address?" I could see where Mike was going.

"So far as I know, the only e-mail address Katrina had was through the museum system. You'll see in her file some correspondence that arrived for her after she left for South—" He caught himself. "After she resigned. We bought an entire new computer system, hardware and software, which was installed after the first of the year.

"When they dismantled Katrina's equipment, I authorized the head of our management information systems to go into her account with her password, to make sure that nothing had come in for her that was related to museum business."

"Did they find anything?"

"Minor correspondence, really. There were a few responses to requests for materials from museums overseas. We've got a good number of objects out on loan that she wanted to see photographs of, for their possible inclusion in the bestiary show. I forwarded those to the committee she had been working with. Gaylord, Friedrichs, Poste, and the others."

"Anything personal?"

"Those should be in that packet you're holding. A bunch of Christmas and New Year's greetings from people she knew, here and abroad."

I opened the file from the front this time, to skim through it to find those letters. I was arrested by the photograph of the young woman that appeared on the museum identification tag dated almost three years ago. The contrast to the Polaroid that had been taken the night we found the body was stunning. Grooten had smiled at the camera when she first came to work here, her face fuller and her light brown hair alive with chestnut streaks, as bouncy as a commercial for a home permanent.

I twisted the folder and showed the shot to Mercer, who shook his head.

"Something wrong?" Bellinger asked.

"I hadn't seen her before, except the photographs made the night before last. I realize this was taken a few years ago, but is it a pretty good likeness?"

Bellinger reached across and looked at Grooten. "A very good one. Until last fall. That's when she began losing weight and developed that awful pallor."

Mike pulled the more recent picture from his jacket pocket. Bellinger looked at it and again closed his eyes. "It's not the way I like to think of her, but it's certainly how she began to look by October."

Perhaps Thibodaux hadn't been lying to us. It was hard to imagine the physical transformation this young woman had undergone in the short months before her death.

"How about her apartment?" Mercer asked. "Did you ever check there to see what happened to her belongings?"

"My wife and I went to see the super in—let me think—it must have been the middle of January. When she was ten days late with that month's rent, he called the museum. No one in his small building had seen her in weeks, and my secretary said she had resigned to leave the country. He cleaned out the apartment and rented it again before—"

Mike interrupted. "How about her things? Her belongings?"

"Katrina hadn't accumulated much stuff. He figured she just bolted on her last month's rent. She left no forwarding information, so the super held a tag sale in the building to get rid of what he could, and threw everything else out on the sidewalk."

Mike was thinking about potential evidence. I imagined the possessions of the young woman's life, meager as they were. Family photographs, treasured art books, perhaps an heirloom—a ring or bracelet that had belonged to an ancestor or friend. All discarded or sold for a few weeks of back rent in a cheap tenement building by a landlord who didn't think to question her disappearance.

"This work that Katrina did, with medieval tombs and their sculpture, what was it exactly?" Mike asked. "Did she *want* to do that, or did you assign it to her?"

"It was the specialty she chose, Detective."

"Grim, wouldn't you say?"

"Not as grim as your job, Mr. Chapman. That's what most people in my line of work would think. Would you like to see what she was doing here? I can show you on our way out."

Mercer took the Grooten file and we followed Bellinger back to the elevators and downstairs. Clouds were forming above us, casting shadows over the crosswalks in the cloistered garden. As we reentered the building on the far side from the tower, nearly every archway in the arcade seemed covered with fantastic animals.

"She loved those, Ms. Cooper. I'd often see Katrina out here, no matter how cold or wet the day, sketching these odd beasts." He saw me slow my step to look up at the stone menagerie. "That's a manticore—a man's face, lion's body, and a scorpion's tail. Quite a combination, eh? And she'd had a cast made of that pelican, to use in the big exhibit. It pierces its own breast so that its blood, falling on its dead brood, can bring them back to life."

We walked behind him into a two-story building at the southwest corner of the museum property. Mike whispered to me, "It looks like a stone deadhouse."

I shivered at the sound of the words, an old name for a morguelike place where bodies are stored, and shuddered again at the cold interior of the Gothic chapel. Everywhere I looked, against each wall and in the middle of the room, were funereal monuments.

Bellinger clearly felt at home. "By the eleventh century, it had become quite fashionable in Europe for noblemen to commemorate themselves and their families with carved effigies. These tomb sculptures are what Katrina studied, back in France. Famous masons of the time would plan and execute these, including details of the patron's coat of arms and the particular costumes and possessions of their ladies."

"And Katrina, what did she do exactly?"

"Everything at the Cloisters, including the stones of the chapels themselves, was purchased from ruins in Europe and reconstructed here. Some were of provenances that were easily traced and proved, while others were just scraps of rock, vandalized as the monasteries broke up over the centuries. This poor fellow," Bellinger said, crouching as he spoke, "was found facedown, being used as part of a bridge to cross a stream in the Alps."

I kneeled beside him and rubbed my hand over the enormous black slab bearing the praying figure of a man.

"So Katrina studied the art form, learning who the sculptors were and how to recognize a particular style of carving or identifiable family traits. It's a continuing effort to verify what we have, and to know when to purchase valuable pieces should they come up for sale on the European market."

I circled the room, looking at all the dead figures in whose company Katrina Grooten had spent her days.

"These sarchophagi," I said, gesturing at the many tombs that lined the walls, some piled on top of each other. "Are there more like these in storage?"

"Plenty of them."

"Here?"

"Some here and some at the Met. They've got a vast basement, you know."

"Any reason for Katrina to have some of the others shipped up to the Cloisters? I mean, from periods other than the Middle Ages."

"She's done it, I know. To compare styles. To help scholars who come here to research the way funereal art has changed over the ages."

"Ever had any Egyptian pieces here?" Mike asked.

"I wouldn't doubt it. Shipments come in and out from the Met all the time."

Mercer was moving in another direction. "Was Ms.

Grooten involved in anything controversial while she was here?"

Bellinger turned to walk us back toward the exit. "Not that I can think of. She didn't normally operate at a high enough level to cross the big shots at the Met. The bestiary project was an exception, and there she was just on the committee acting in my stead. I wouldn't have thought she'd ruffle any feathers while sitting in for me."

Mercer was thumbing through the file as we moved along. "What's the reference in here to the 'flea market fiasco,' two years back? It's in a memo from you to Thibodaux."

Bellinger stopped in his tracks. "The young scholars are so idealistic. It wasn't a big deal. Katrina just had to be made to understand the commercial side of museum work."

I repeated Mercer's question. "What exactly was the fiasco about?"

"We got word—"

"Who's *we*?"

"I was with Pierre Thibodaux and Erik Poste at a convention in Geneva. Word got around the place that one of those unusual finds had been made at a local flea market. A small medieval ivory, a carving of a hound chasing a rabbit, very similar to the large version that appears in the stonework outside." Bellinger took a few steps. "I wanted it, for obvious reasons. And Thibodaux was willing to pay the price."

"Was Katrina there?"

"Oh, no. But it's a small world, this museum business. She had heard the rumor about the piece even before I flew back here. Anyway, we tried to buy the ivory but it was too late. It had been promised to the Copenhagen museum."

"What was Erik Poste's role in this?"

"Just that it made him furious while the squabbling about who would get the piece was going on, before the Danes firmed it up. Poste wanted Pierre to spend the money on something major for his European painting department rather than on some little rabbit that I coveted. A great portrait, or an artist like Bazille who's underrepresented in the Met collection, rather than a six-inch piece of walrus tusk. We argued, but that happens among us all the time. You can't hold a grudge around here, Ms. Cooper."

"And the carving?"

The reclusive scholar smiled. "One of Thibodaux's favorite smugglers—"

"Smugglers?"

"Yes, Ms. Cooper, you heard me. Pierre has a few favorites he relies on when he doesn't get his own way with his checkbook. It's an old tradition in this field. Anyway, Pierre's man managed to get the piece out of Switzerland in about a week's time, before the arrangements were made to ship it to Copenhagen. For his usual four percent commission. A month later, it was in one of our storerooms deep below Fifth Avenue."

"You stole the carving."

"Surely you don't prosecute crimes that occur in Europe?" Bellinger laughed. "That's been the nature of this work since museums first opened their doors. Some treasures came home in grand style, like Lord Elgin stealing the Greek marbles and setting them up for all the world to see in the British Museum. Others arrived more quietly and were bartered around town in secret. If there weren't grave robbers and petty thieves, I'm afraid there would be far fewer works of art in public institutions everywhere in the world."

"And your precious little object?"

"Will go on display after the summer. There wasn't much of a scandal. We sent the Danes something of ours that they'd been longing for, and I got my ivory. All that was needed was a cooling-down period. People forget after a year or so. They quiet down."

"And Grooten?"

"She learned as we all did. If you're looking for a selfless way to help humanity, Detective, join the Red Cross. If you're going to work in a museum, get used to the fact that most of what you see has been stolen from beneath someone's nose. The great archaeologists who dug in Egypt and Turkey and Pompeii, they all believed what they recovered belonged to them personally. Took the urns and coins and jewels home to display on their own mantels and bandy about at their gaming clubs. Gave them away as gifts. Sold them to the highest bidder."

I looked around the room at the assortment of tombstones from France, Belgium, Spain, and England. Lords and ladies at rest together, far from their intended graves.

"The spoils of war and the looted booty of imperial rule, Ms. Cooper. The Trojans did it, the British did it, the Germans did it, and may I add, even the American troops serving in the European and Pacific theaters did it during the Second World War. The only pretty part of this museum acquisition work is what you finally see behind the glass display cabinets."

I was standing beside one such case, mounted on a pedestal, as Bellinger spoke to us. It held the upraised statue of a man's arm, completely silvered and bejeweled, with its long golden fingers raised in a position of blessing. The legend at its base described it as the reliquary of a bishop, and I could see the crystal windows in the arm that once displayed his sainted bones. I wondered what had become of the rest of the poor man's remains.

When we reached the top of the staircase through which we had entered, opposite the gift shop and the cloakroom, Bellinger started to say good-bye.

Mike withdrew a small glassine envelope from his pocket. "What kind of tickets do you use for checking coats here?"

Bellinger looked over his shoulder but there was no one inside. The day had been too mild.

"The usual. A small square with a number on it."

"Like this?" Mike asked, showing him the stub that Dr. Kestenbaum had given to us.

"Identical. Ours are blue. All the city-partnered museums use the same system, just different-colored tags."

"Who uses red ones? The Met?"

"No, they've got white ones, if I'm not mistaken. The one you've got there is from the Museum of Natural History."

15

Mercer led us down the steep incline from the Cloisters exit ramp and across the cobblestoned parking lot. Using a map that the case detective had sketched after her interview with Katrina Grooten, he tried to reconstruct the route the young woman had taken the night of her attack almost one year earlier.

"What did you think of Hiram Bellinger?" Mike asked.

"Not what I expected. I thought we'd get old and stodgy." As soon as we reached the bottom of the shallow steps down which Grooten had steered her bicycle, we were engulfed by the thick foliage of shrubs and bushes.

"Somebody could have been waiting for her back here," Mercer said, pointing into an area where the greenery stood as high as his shoulders.

"Like Grooten was a particular target?"

"Yeah, if it was someone from the museum who did it, or who set her up."

"I thought you'd had some ski mask robberies in Fort Tryon Park."

"So this was either one more random victim in the

pattern, or a copycat trying to make it look like the others."

"How about Lloyd, the guard who freaked her out?"

Mercer tapped Mike on the back of the head, steering us up the hill again. "Don't be putting the blame on the old black guy, Chapman."

"There's no question the rapist was a black man. Everybody's in the mix till we say they're not. And besides, I didn't like this Bellinger guy a fraction as much as Coop did."

"He's white, Mike." Mercer laughed.

"Too white for my taste. How do you know he didn't set her up? Claims he didn't know her all that well, but seems to me he went out of his way to try to urge her to stay here. What was that about? C'mon. We got stuff to do. I'm going right down to Central Park West, check out this coatroom business. You with me?"

I nodded my head. "What was your beep?"

Mercer had been paged toward the end of the meeting and returned the call when we stepped outside the museum. "Beth Israel North. A nurse walked into the room of a ninety-one-year-old patient and found a man in bed with her. His pants were down and he had removed her hospital gown. The nurse screamed but the perp pulled his trousers up and ran out. They think it's a guy who delivered flowers to the room next door. Crime scene dusted the vase and we got a call in to the florist. I'm going to stop by the hospital and see if I can get statements from the staff."

"The patient, too?"

"She's *non compos*."

"Call the florist?"

"Hospital security already did. The guy hires homeless men from local shelters to make his deliveries."

"That's comforting." I looked at my watch. "It's almost four-thirty. Want to meet at my place when you're done? We'll go through Katrina's personnel file and figure out how to tackle this thing. I'll have Sarah assign someone to work with you on the new case."

I got into Mike's department car and we wound our way down the circular drive to get on the West Side Highway going south. I took out my cell phone and dialed Ryan Blackmer.

"Any more e-mails from your cyber monster?"

"All quiet. Harry works a four to twelve. So that means Brittany doesn't get home from her after-school activities till almost dinnertime."

"I got an idea. Why don't you suggest tomorrow's meet be at the Museum of Natural History? What kid doesn't love that place? Dinosaur bones, butterfly exhibits, the planetarium. They could meet in front by the statue of Teddy Roosevelt. That gives the backup team lots of cover with the crowds around. I'm sure the guys can find a crummy hotel within a block or two, between Columbus and Amsterdam."

"Not bad. I'll suggest it."

There were a few places in town that were naturals for pedophiles. In winter, the Christmas tree and ice-skating rink at Rockefeller Center were a magnet for men who wanted to rub up against the rear ends of little girls who stood mesmerized by the lights of the huge evergreen and the practiced spins of the twirling skaters. Summer guaranteed a slew of girls and boys in public swimming pools, jumping on top of each other and enjoying the horseplay.

Among the year-round havens were the city's museums and zoos, which delivered busloads of kids every day to wander through the exhibits, usually oblivious to the hungry adults who lurked in rest rooms and around the concession stands.

"Can you switch me over to Sarah?"

Ryan put me on hold and forwarded the call. "How bad has it been?"

"I'm fine," she answered. "You making any progress?"

"Just getting some background filled in. Anything new?"

"Awful case up at the hospital."

"Mercer was just with us. He's on his way over there now. I told him I'd ask you to put someone on it, but you're already ahead of me."

"I checked out the name and social security number the perp gave to the florist, who pays him per diem. Doesn't match. So we have no idea who the guy really is. Staked out the shelter but he hasn't been there very long, so they don't expect him to show up tonight.

"And I've had one walk-in you should know about. Thirty-nine-year-old woman who claims she's been in an S and M relationship with a guy for two years. I'm doing a search warrant now for his apartment."

"For the equipment?"

"Whips, chains, a pulley system in the ceiling that

drops out with restraints for her hands and feet. And the videotapes."

"Of what?"

"Of every time he whips her. I don't think we have any sex crimes, 'cause she consented to everything sexual. But the assault charge will stick." New York's highest court had made it clear that you can't consent to being assaulted. "She's got scars and bruising all over her back and buttocks. Permanent. It's painful just to look at her body."

"Need any help with it?"

"Will you have time to look over the tapes in the morning, if Lieutenant West comes back with anything from the warrant?"

"I'll be there first thing."

"I don't want to authorize an arrest until you give us the go-ahead. You took so much heat the last time we had one of these. What'll really make you sick is that the perp is a lawyer. Brooklyn Law School, master's in taxation from NYU."

We had prosecuted another high-profile sadomasochist recently, and despite the fact that he had beaten his victim with wooden batons and dripped hot candle wax on her body, one of the tabloid columnists—fueled by his excessive daily intake of alcohol—saw fit to criticize our unit, and the college student who had been restrained overnight in his apartment.

"See you in the morning."

There was no place to leave the car on Central Park West. The great old museum, made up now of twenty-three interconnected buildings, was ringed by the buses that had come to pick up students at the end of the day. Mike turned onto Seventy-seventh Street and parked in front of the original building facade, throwing his parking permit in the windshield.

We were conscious that it was getting late in the day, and we walked briskly down the path and under the immense arch, below the chiseled granite markings: AMERICAN MUSEUM OF NATURAL HISTORY.

This was probably the first institution visited by every child who grew up within range of New York City. Indian artifacts, dioramas with mammals of all sorts, fossils, skeletons, bugs, mollusks, meteorites, minerals, gems, and now a hall of biodiversity. It was more fun than every other colossal collection of things, and any kid you talked to would be likely to name it as his or her favorite city destination.

As I brushed past the guard at the door, he put out an arm to try to slow me down. "We close at five forty-five, young lady. That gives you less than half an hour."

Mike went up to the information desk and asked for the nearest coat check facility.

"Are you a member?"

"I'm a cop." He flashed his shield and the elderly volunteer blanched.

"Oh, well. It's, um, just follow that blue arrow across the lobby."

The spaces within the museum were vast. We zig-zagged through the crowds of classes and Scout troops on field trips, making our way around the sixty-foot-long war canoe, peopled by half-naked natives from British Columbia who had been paddling against the same current since I'd first come here as a toddler.

The line was long as kids stood restlessly to retrieve backpacks and lunch boxes that had been checked on their arrival. Mike didn't have the patience to wait. Again, he flashed his badge at the man who was returning their belongings.

"Let me see your claim checks, please?"

"I don't understand."

"The ticket stubs. I'd like to see them."

The attendant offered up a giant roll of numbered claims in his left hand. "Like this?"

Mike reached for the end of the check that was dangling and ripped it off. He held it against the one Kestenbaum had found in Katrina's pants pocket, which Mike had taken with us to voucher as evidence, and it matched exactly. "Where's the lost and found?"

"Something you misplaced today, sir?"

"Nope. My girlfriend here is kind of absentminded. Left her snowshoes and gloves at the museum last year and wants to get them ready for the season."

"You want to be going to security then. Follow the signs past the IMAX theater and around to the front of the building. It's right before you get to the Hall of Planet Earth."

Mike was practically trotting now, as I raced behind him. The Northwest Coast Indians hall seemed endless, with its displays of men in loincloths and women in animal skins cooking over open fires and curing meat on racks above their heads.

"You know what's completely different from the Met in the way this place is laid out?"

"The light, for one thing."

I had never realized how dark it was in these huge corridors. Once inside the exhibits, there was no natural light, and none of the openness of the art museum. The cases were backlit, but there was a cool darkness that enveloped the entire place.

I followed as Mike turned the corner and entered the enormous central gallery reserved for North American mammals. Again the darkness of the hall was striking, with dim, glass-fronted cabinets displaying the familiar great-antlered caribou and herds of bison in clusters.

Past the bank of elevators to another information desk, and this time the volunteer, closing up her papers for the evening, pointed at the door to the security office. Mike held it open for me. Like most institutions in the city, whether financial or philanthropic, the security forces were run by retired NYPD bosses. They frequently went off the job young and healthy enough to collect a full pension and start a new career with a good salary and benefits.

Mike identified himself to the square-badger sitting at his desk. "Who's in charge here?"

"You're looking at him."

"On the job." Once more, the blue and gold detective shield did its magic. "You got a lost and found here?"

"You're looking at it."

"This is a claim check for something left here months ago."

"How many?"

"Maybe five, maybe six."

"Five, I got it. Six makes it last year."

Mike passed him the glassine envelope with the ticket stub in it. The guard studied it, then picked up the telephone and made a call to someone, telling whoever had answered to look for an item tagged under number 248 and left behind during the previous winter.

"They'll let me know shortly if they can find it, Detective."

"Can they also tell us the exact date the item was checked?"

The guard screwed up his face and thought for a few seconds. "Probably not. Not exactly, that is. Each cycle of tickets goes up to ten thousand, then starts again at one. They may be able to place it within a week or so."

"Is there a separate checkroom for employees?"

"Of this museum? Yes."

"How about if they work at another city museum, like the Met or the Cloisters?"

The guard looked Mike in the eye, trying to convince us of his effectiveness. "After September eleventh, nobody went through these doors without checking coats and packages right at the entrance. We were on high alert last fall and winter, like every other public institution that draws large crowds. Doesn't matter where anybody worked or what kind of passes they had. It all got checked. Us private security guards were as busy as you guys."

For the ten minutes during which we waited, Mike used the museum phone to call his office and tell the sergeant what we'd been up to before he went off duty for the evening, and I checked with Laura for all the day's messages.

As I hung up the phone, a teenager with a museum-logo pin on her lapel came into the security office. "Is this what you're looking for?"

She held up a faded blue pea jacket, army-navy-store issue, with a wool scarf draped around underneath the collar. It looked like a perfect fit for Katrina Grooten.

16

"What's the extension for the office of the museum president?"

The guard tugged at the top drawer and shuffled the papers to find the directory. This was not a man who spent a lot of time dealing with the executive wing.

He handed the receiver to Mike, who dialed the number, then said, "I'd like to speak with"—he turned to the front page and looked at the list of names—"President Raspen?"

"Sorry to be holding you up," I said to the guard, who kept looking at the time. He was ready to close up shop and go home.

"Oh, yeah? For how long?" Mike didn't like the response he got. "Well, who's in charge? Can you put him on?" Another bad answer. "Eleven tomorrow morning? Fine, just tell him to expect me when he gets in. Michael Chapman, NYPD." And he *really* didn't appreciate whatever was said next. "No, but if you mention the word *homicide*, he might find he has a spare moment or two to squeeze me in."

He turned to me. "President Raspen's off ogling

turtles in the Galàpagos. Gone for a week with a tribe of donors. Those poor critters will probably be hanging from a giant sky hook next to that friggin' fiberglass whale that's been down the hall here since I first walked in the door."

"Who'll be hanging, the donors or the turtles?"

"The donors have a shot at immortality. They just plaster their names all over a wing or an auditorium or a species of lizard. It's the lousy turtles who get screwed every time."

"Who are we going to be talking to in the morning?"

Mike looked at the name he had scribbled on a piece of paper. "Elijah Mamdouba. Vice president in charge of curatorial affairs. He's got a full schedule, but he'll try to see us. The routine bureaucratic hand job."

We made our way back through the quiet hallways and were escorted out by another guard. Mike squared the block in his car, then headed east through Central Park at Eighty-first Street.

"Drop me at Grace's Marketplace. I'll get some hors d'oeuvres and meet you in the lobby of my building." I got out of the car at the corner of Seventy-first Street and bought an assortment of cheeses and pâtés to hold us until dinner. Mike and Mercer were chatting with the two doormen when I got home. Mercer took the shopping bag from my hand, and I pressed the elevator button for the twentieth floor. "How's Vickee feeling?"

"Tired, cranky, excited. Went to the doctor this afternoon and she said we're about two weeks away from the delivery. First baby, may be a few days late."

"How can you concentrate on anything? This new little life coming along . . ."

"Yeah," Mike said, leaning back against the wall of the elevator. "Our first kid."

Mercer beamed.

"At least for the time being it is. Can't seem to get blondie here interested in the how-to's of making one of those things. I remember being at the Natural History Museum once, must have been fourteen or fifteen years old. They had these beetles, they were called feather wings. The whole friggin' species was female. Reproduced without any fertilization by a male. I'm gonna check tomorrow and see if they still have any of those bugs around. Must be the way Coop plans on doing it."

Mercer tried to get me off the hook. "I think Jake's got the program under control."

I reached into my bag to get the keys and unlock the door. Mike kept talking. "One minute the man's in Washington, next day he's in Jerusalem or Hong Kong or Moscow. How can he score any action from long distance? Now it's getting worse, 'cause Ms. Cooper here is trying to deprive *me* of a little tender loving care."

"Female bonding in the country." I smiled at Mercer. "Nina Baum arranged to come on this business trip with her boss so she could stay east for Memorial Day weekend and go up to Martha's Vineyard with me. I've invited Val to come with us, too," I said, referring to Mike's girlfriend. "Food, wine, massages, beach walks, girl talk all night. No testosterone." I flipped on the light switch and dropped my things on the ottoman in my living room. "I'll get the ice."

"You think people don't wonder why you like being in charge of sex crimes prosecutions? You should hear the crap people ask me about you. 'Is it because she hates men?' 'You figure she thinks about it when she's in the sack with a guy?' or 'You think it turns her on to listen to those stories all day?'"

I walked from the kitchen to the den, carrying a bucket of cubes. "I can't even begin to imagine the clever answers you dream up to amuse them."

"I used to shut a bunch of 'em up by telling them we lived together, but then they began to look at me like *I* had some kind of problem, too, so I quit with that line."

Mercer poured the drinks while I went to my bedroom to change into casual clothes. When I reentered the room, he was telling Mike what he learned at his hospital interviews after leaving us at the Cloisters, the television muted in the background. This would be an easy case to prove, despite the victim's inability to testify, because the nurse had witnessed the assault. It would just be a matter of tracking down the assailant, and then helping a jury to understand why an incontinent ninety-year-old bed patient had been the object of someone's sexual appetite—or rage.

I picked up the phone and dialed Hal Sherman's cell number, letting it ring until the crime scene specialist answered the call. "Catch you at a bad time?"

"Bad for who? Me or the dead guy?"

"Where are you?"

"Not Chapman's beat, Alex, if that's who you're

looking for. Manhattan South. Some poor schmuck from the 'burbs picked up a hooker in his wife's new Beemer for one last fling before the long weekend. Must have been quite an argument. Five stab wounds to the chest."

"Who's wailing like that?"

"The widow. Not because she's in mourning. She's screaming like a banshee because the chief of D's won't release the car to her. 'But it's *mine*,' she keeps saying. 'It's registered in *my* name.' Kind of lost sight of the fact that it's the murder scene. I'm wrapping up. What do you need?"

"Mike's with me. Just want to know if you've had a chance to do blow-ups of the photos you took for us in the truck Wednesday morning."

"I'll have them on your desk tomorrow. Came out great."

"Could you make out any designs on the sarcophagus?"

"Like hieroglyphics?"

"Exactly."

"Yeah, it's covered with them. It's carved all over the place."

"Any symbols you remember? I didn't get close enough to see when I was up on the truck."

"You must be kidding. I just take the pictures. I don't airbrush out the bloodstains or bullet holes, and I don't do translations."

"I mean, was it all writing, or are there any figures on it, too?"

"Loads of little Egyptians."

"Any animals?"

"More than they got in *The Lion King*. All kinds of monkeys, enough cats to make my allergies act up, rams and lambs, ducks and falcons and—"

"Great. Thanks for coming out on this one. I owe you."

"I'll add that to Chapman's list. I could be a very rich man some day if you clowns pay up."

Mike clicked on the TV volume as I hung up. "Hal says there are a lot of animal symbols on Katrina's sarcophagus."

"I could have told you that. I was right on top of it with the flashlight. Sssssh."

Alex Trebek had just told us that tonight's Final Jeopardy! category was "Greatest Hits."

"Everybody in for twenty?"

"I wish you *had* told me that. It means the coffin could easily have been designated as part of the exhibition. Katrina could have been studying it up at the Cloisters, or it could have been on site at the Museum of Natural History."

"Obviously. 'According to ASCAP, this song has been played on American radio stations more times than any other hit.' Mike was doing his Trebek imitation. "What's your question, Coop? How about you, Mr. Motown?"

Mercer held his arm out straight, palm forward. "I'm guessing The Supremes, early. 'Stop, in the Name of Love.'"

"We're going to be all over the map with this two-ton sarcophagus. How is that possible?" I couldn't fathom that something as large and heavy as the ancient coffin could be so difficult to keep track of.

"It's gotta be something Sinatra. 'Strangers in the Night'?"

"Exactly what I mean, Coop. There's a lot of people would read a personal clue into the answer you just gave. Strangers in the night, one-night stands. Too much sex on the brain. Me? I'm going with Elvis. 'Love Me Tender.' 'What is . . . ?' of course."

"I'm sorry, ladies," Trebek feigned dismay at their three wrong questions. "And that brings our Campus Winners Week to an end. The correct answer would be, What is the Righteous Brothers' 'You've Lost That Lovin' Feeling'?"

Mike zapped off the television set, as Mercer sang, "'Now it's gone, gone, gone . . .' Can't believe that blue-eyed soul gets all that airtime."

"Game plan. I can see we're not going to get treated to any dinner here tonight. You've got two mouths to feed at home, Val's waiting for me to take her to a movie, and the blonde's still got murder on her mind. What assignments you giving out? Anything I have to do before I get to your office in the morning?"

"While you're pining away for Val and me this weekend, you might check out Bellinger's story. Speak to his wife, confirm the dates they were out of town in December, get a feel for what she thought the relationship was between her husband and his protégée."

"I'm also going to try to get my hands on anything else Katrina might have signed. It's curious that Bellinger's gut reaction was that might not have been her handwriting on the resignation she submitted."

I didn't have to tell Mike what to do in the course of any difficult investigation, but it helped for us to split the duties between us. He went on, "I'll try to check out these museum documents and see if they help us pin down exactly where she spent her time between June and December, and why she would have been in close proximity to the sarcophagus."

"I'll copy the personal e-mails tomorrow and take them with me to the Vineyard. I'd like to see what she was telling her friends about her health and her job, and her decision to go back to South Africa." I reached for the telephone and got it on the second ring.

"Hey, Joe, got anything?" It was the detective from the DA's squad who was going to order the dump of my office phone to see where my old stalker, Shirley Denzig, had been calling from. I turned my back on Mike and Mercer, hoping they wouldn't pick up on my recurring problem as they talked with each other about the weekend.

I listened as Joe told me that because of the holiday, and the fact that the harassing calls were coming in to a trunk line—the central telephone operations center of the district attorney's office, with hundreds of individual extensions—the phone company might not be able to have results for me until early next week.

"That's fine. I'm skipping town tomorrow. Taking some friends and going to the country."

"You won't be alone?" he asked. "And you promise you won't be in the city?"

"You've got my number on the Vineyard. Call if you get any news."

I hung up and walked the guys to the door, just as Jake opened it with his key. I relieved him of the shopping bag that held whatever he was going to cook for dinner, and let him greet Mike and Mercer, whom he had not seen in several weeks.

"Plenty of food. I'm cooking some fettuccine for the overworked prosecutor tonight. Any takers?"

"Gotta run. You booted out for the weekend, too?"

"For the long haul. I leave on Saturday for the defense secretary's mission to Australia and Southeast Asia. Nine days."

"Mercer and I'll watch out for the little princess. Be good to her tonight. Maybe she'll tell you about the other body we found today, stuffed in a suit of armor at the Met. That's got to be the most dangerous place in town."

Jake's head snapped around to make eye contact with me as Mike pulled the door shut behind him. "Is he—?"

I stretched my arms around his neck and clucked at his gullibility, kissing him on the tip of his nose. "He's just baiting you. No more bodies. No progress on Katrina."

"I guess he really believes that I was your leak. Maybe I can buy back a bit of goodwill."

"Have you solved the case for us? That would be a good start." I was sorting through the wine cabinet to find a serious bottle of red to go with our dinner.

"There was a voice mail in my office late today. Must have come in while I was taping the piece I did for the evening news. Remember the woman who

THE BONE VAULT 193

attached herself to me on Tuesday, while you and Nina were talking?"

"That good-looking old girl with the silver-rinse hair job?"

"Ruth Gerst. Museum trustee. She asked if I had any well-connected sources in the NYPD. She wants to give them some information about Pierre Thibodaux."

17

"You've already missed the cartoons and first feature, Alex. Pull up a chair and tighten your seat belt. This one's really a bumpy ride." Colin West was a lieutenant in the detective squad of the First Precinct, an area that covered a primarily commercial part of the city—Wall Street—and a fast-growing residential community as older buildings were converted into lofts and apartments. He was a big man, with a broad, handsome face, shaved head, and terrific mind.

"The squad commander himself? To what do I owe this honor?" West, one of his detectives, and a tech guy from our video unit had set up in the small conference room opposite my office and had a stack of tapes piled up on the table. One of them was playing on the monitor as I walked in. It was only a few minutes after 8 A.M. "Sorry I'm late."

"You're not. We seized forty-six tapes with the warrant Sarah drafted. We got down here an hour ago so I could start running through them and pick out the highlights for you."

"How about the weapons?"

"A regular torture chamber. More than twenty whips, an assortment of things that look like hairbrushes with metal spikes on them, restraints at the foot and headboard of the bed, sex toys you can't begin to imagine, and a metal pulley that's recessed into a panel in the ceiling, with handcuffs attached to it. All the comforts of home. Black?"

West reached into a cardboard carton and pulled out some coffee containers and doughnuts.

"I hear the perp's a lawyer."

"Yeah. Kalder. Peter Kalder. Lives in Battery Park."

"You lock him up?"

"Nope. Just knocked on the door, showed him the warrant, waited while he went into the bathroom to throw up, then cleaned out the joint. Sarah told us to let him be until you viewed the evidence."

"What's the story on the victim?"

"That's her, handcuffed to the pulley." West pointed at the monitor, which was frozen on a frame that showed a woman I guessed to be about my age, anorexically thin, stretched out across a disheveled set of striped sheets on a king-size bed, her lower face covered with a gag.

"Cooperative?"

"She is now. But it took her a while to get to this point. Met him through a personal ad in the *Village Voice*. No pain, no gain kind of thing. The relationship started off fine, moved into verbal abuse, then to some mild S and M. The last few months have been this heavy-duty stuff."

"More than once?"

"Our girl kept going back. A perfect target. She'd

been an incest victim for most of her adolescence. Low self-esteem, every kind of eating disorder you can imagine, inability to maintain any stable relationships. Kalder has her convinced this is what she deserves. You'll find a shrink who can explain it to you better than I can."

"Is she coming down here today?"

"She's in a better place. Last night she checked herself into a private clinic in Connecticut. For her addiction."

"What to?"

West picked up the clicker and forwarded the tape a few inches, then froze it again when the woman turned onto her side. "He's about to come into view, Alex. Watch her flinch. She's turning away because he's got a six-foot whip raised over his head, poised to slap down on her left thigh."

As the woman rolled her body, her entire leg and buttocks came into view. They were bloody and swollen, flesh stripped away and welts seeming to form on top of other open wounds.

"Painkillers. She dopes herself up when she gets to the apartment. Gotta be the only way she could let herself be subjected to this."

A squat man wearing only gray briefs and white athletic socks appeared at the side of the bed. He had a hideous hairpiece, which he must have knocked askew in his excitement. He turned his head to smile into the video camera he had set up on his bureau to capture himself and his playmate for posterity.

"Promise me one thing, Alex. When you give me the go-ahead for the collar, I get to pluck that cheap toupee off the top of his fat head and voucher it as evidence, okay?"

I nodded as I watched the tape roll, and Kalder hauled back with his arm and cracked the whip down against the woman's broken body. I rested my elbow on the conference table as I sat beside Colin West, lowering my head and closing my eyes, rubbing them with my thumb and forefinger.

"I don't think I could take much of this under the best of circumstances."

The lieutenant fast-forwarded the tape as he talked. "I know you have to sell this one to your supervisors. I mean, after that other case you lost. You've got to watch some of this to see just how vicious he gets."

"The chief assistant will back me on this one, Colin. No human being should be allowed to do this to someone else—it's pretty extreme. The one that got dismissed? That was just McKinney overruling me, and a young prosecutor with no balls who flacked for him. They made a decision to redact some of the evidence in that case without telling me—took it over my head to McKinney—and then when the appellate court threw out the verdict, the woman who had tried the case the first time just walked away from it. Claimed to be sick. Seems to have gone to Lourdes in the interim so now she's back doing McKinney's bidding again. Don't worry—we can handle Kalder. How much of this do you think you have here?"

"I don't know yet. This is only the eighth tape we've gotten through."

"Any sound to go with the video?"

"Yeah. Lots of time spent putting her down, calling her his slave. And games, he plays lots of games with her."

I couldn't conceive of anything frivolous happening in the middle of these beatings. As West rewound the tape Mike Chapman walked into the room and closed the door behind him. He leaned over the table to shake Colin's hand, then put a finger on his lips and pointed outside, mouthing to me that I had company.

"Anyone I know?"

"Some broad who claims she represents a lawyer you're investigating. I thought maybe you were expecting her, so I told security I'd bring her up with me."

West and I exchanged glances. "She can wait," I said as West played a portion of the tape I hadn't seen.

Kalder stood at the foot of the mattress, shouting words at his companion. She was handcuffed and had her ankles in leg irons, but there was no gag on her mouth. On the bedside table, next to a studded dog collar, was a Barbie doll, her head and wrists locked into a colonial-style stock.

The pathetic-looking lawyer yelled at his subject. "Exegesis!"

The woman squirmed on the bed, and in a tentative, whispered voice began to spell the word she had just heard. "E . . . x . . . i . . ."

Kalder snapped the length of leather whip back over his shoulder and brought it down on the trembling woman's bloody thigh. "No! That's not right." She continued to guess at the spelling.

"They're both screaming pretty damn loud."

West ran his finger across the top of the screen. "It's all been soundproofed in here, Alex. The whole apartment was rebuilt to suit his needs. We canvassed the neighbors last night and they've never been disturbed by any noise, although you can hear how loud the volume is on the tape."

"Syzygy!" Kalder shouted out, over our chatter.

Now she was writhing and whining at the same time. "I don't know that word," she cried. Then, choking as she tried to talk, she made an effort to spell out loud. "S . . . y . . . z . . . z . . . ?"

This time the whip licked the ceiling on its way down to her thigh, streaking it with blood from its last contact with her body.

Chapman helped himself to one of the coffee cups. "Shit, Colin, who is this perv? I'd hate to play a game of Scrabble with him."

I stood up and West put the tape on pause. "Just think of it as one of those reality TV shows. We're calling it *Survivor Jeopardy*.

"Let me see what Kalder's pal has to say for him."

Mike held the door open and I motioned for the woman who was waiting outside my office door to come in. "Good morning, I'm Alexandra Cooper."

"Marcy Arent." She extended a hand and introduced herself to each of us. "I represent Peter Kalder. I'm here to find out what your intentions are in this case."

"My intentions? Right now the detectives and I are reviewing evidence that was taken from your client's home last night. I didn't ask for this meeting. You did. That's about all I'm prepared to tell you this morning, so feel free to explain what brings you here if you want this conversation to go on any longer."

"Are you planning to arrest Mr. Kalder?"

"If there is information *you* want to give to us, I'm happy to take it from you. I'm not going to answer any of your questions now."

Arent's facial expression was as severe as her dark brown lady-lawyer suit and thick-heeled shoes. "There's no sex crimes case here, Ms. Cooper. All of the sexual activity between Mr. Kalder and his friend was consensual."

"I'm aware of that."

"Then why is this any of your business? What does your unit have to do with this?"

Mike spoke. "Something unpleasant happens to a woman, between her knees and her neck, on the island of Manhattan, it's Coop's territory. Anything else we can help you with today?"

"She consented to the physical assault, too."

I bristled. "Our court of appeals says you can't consent to be beaten and whipped, Ms. Arent. Want the cite? I happen to agree with them."

She reached into her jacket pocket and pulled out her business card. "You obviously don't have a clear understanding of sadomasochism. We'd like to help you with that."

I didn't reach for the card so Arent set it down on the conference table.

"You decide what kind of injury is acceptable for a human being to sustain?" I asked.

"As long as the sex is safe, sane, and consensual, you've got nothing to prosecute."

"I think where you and Coop here don't see eye to eye is on the sane thing. It's okay with you to draw blood, to rip skin off another person, to leave permanent scars—"

"And who might you be?" Arent glared at Mike, thrusting one of her cards at him. "I'm with AASF— the American Alliance for Sexual Freedom. We've got more than sixty-five hundred members across the country. The simple truth is that whether or not you know it, fifteen percent of your friends—each one of you—engage in some kind of bondage or sadomasochistic behavior."

"Speak for yourself, sweetheart. Me, Coop, and the lieutenant just like to cuddle. No leather, no flogging, no dripping candle wax."

Arent's unsmiling gaze flipped back and forth between Chapman and West. "Which one of you was at my client's home last evening?"

"That's me. Colin West."

"You're with . . . ?"

"First Precinct."

She pointed at Mike. "And you?"

"Mike Chapman. ADU."

"What does that stand for?"

"Acronym Designation Unit. You see, Ms. Arent," he said, studying her business card, "everybody's got some catchy phrase that describes their organization. Me, I would have come up with a better name for yours. The one you've got captures none of the flavor you're trying to express here. Like, uh, National Union for Thrashing Someone during Sex. Then you could all just call yourselves NUTSS. Okay?"

I bit my lip to keep from laughing out loud and turned to roll my eyes at West. Battaglia would get a letter of protest about my insensitivity to the S and M community. So be it.

Mike ushered Arent to the door simply by taking two steps in her direction and watching her recoil. "Ms. Cooper's got a lot on her plate today. Go tell your client to relax. The lieutenant's not in any rush to lock him up. We know Peter'll get a hard-on when we put him in cuffs, and we'd hate to make him that happy."

Arent ignored Chapman and directed her ire toward me. "We're going to go over your head on this one, Ms. Cooper. I'll get an appointment with the district attorney."

I walked across the hallway and unlocked my office as Mike followed me in. "I wish everybody would go over my head for a change. I might actually get some ordinary work done if I didn't have to deal with every psycho who knocked on my door. I think there's a support group for all the misfits in this country except cops and prosecutors. Let's let Colin work on the videos in the conference room. Did you have a chance to look over Katrina's file last night?"

Mike spread some of the papers from her personnel folder out across the top of my desk. "She didn't punch a time clock, but a lot of these computer printouts reconstruct when she left the Cloisters to work at one of the other museums. It's clear she spent a fair amount of time last fall going to both the Met and Natural History. She had passes that got her into each of them, and nothing to limit her access to any parts of the collection in both places."

We spent the better part of the next hour trying to chart a time line of Katrina Grooten's fall schedule. I told Mike about Jake's message from the rich Mrs. Gerst, and we waited until after nine-thirty to call to set up a meeting with her. I couldn't get past her social secretary, who invited us to come to Gerst's Park Avenue pied-à-terre at the end of the afternoon, so we had no sense of whether the visit would be a complete waste of our time.

I was on the phone setting up the rest of the day and weekend with Sarah and Mike when Mickey Diamond came into the room, a rolled-up copy of the day's *Post* under his arm.

"You got an answer for me?" I still wanted to know who had been the first leak on Katrina's story.

"Good news or bad? What do you want first?"

"No bad. Not for another month or so."

"You'd better look now. Otherwise you'll just call and yell at me later." He passed the newspaper across the desk and I unfolded it to see a half-page picture of Pierre Thibodaux. The photograph of his head was attached to the body of a Hollywood-style mummy, and in typical tabloid fashion, the headline read: TUT! TUT! MUSEUM BIGWIG DEPARTS UNDER WRAPS.

I skimmed the story, which linked his sudden separation from the institution to the discovery of the corpse in the coffin. "Very classy, Mickey. A lot of dignity over at your operation."

"I didn't write it, really. I would have made up a quote from you if I'd done the story myself."

That was a technique that the dean of the crime reporters had perfected over the years, often enough so that even Battaglia knew I wasn't breaking his rules to talk about my cases.

"What have you got for me if I tell you what I know about the leak?"

Mike was reading the Thibodaux story. "What has she got? For once will you just do the right thing and tell her what she wants to know? We promise to call you before we call Liz Smith the next time some rich and famous bastard confesses to killing his wife."

"It's nothing you don't already know, Alex. Pat McKinney is just trying to make your life miserable."

"Don't tell me he's found a new way to do it."

"His friend, Ellen Gunsher?"

"Yeah. An expendable member of our brilliant legal staff."

"Do you know who her mother is? Well, who her mother *was* says it better."

"No, should I?"

"Before your time. Her mother, Daniella, used to be a network commentator. Like Jake, only never quite as established. Career washed up ages ago. She did something unprofessional, like sob on-air during some speech at a political convention. She's supposed to be a bit unbalanced. Still works in production for a news-magazine show. My source tells me the call about your case came in from Daniella Gunsher's assistant. Like they were calling from the network to check on whether we had heard the same story before they went with it."

"My apologies to Jake," Mike said.

"If you ask me," Mickey Diamond continued, turning to leave the room, "I'd be willing to bet Daniella doesn't even rate an assistant at this point in her career. Your pal McKinney probably made the call himself, using Daniella Gunsher's name to establish press bona fides, so the call would be noticed. That guy hates your guts, Alex."

"Always a pleasure, Mickey." His news confirmed my own beliefs, but made it impossible for me to report it to Battaglia. He didn't want to hear any more of the grousing that had become commonplace between McKinney and me. I'd just have to put the information away for future use.

Mike packed up the Grooten file and we waited for Laura to Xerox a set for each of us before we drove uptown to keep our eleven o'clock appointment at Natural History.

I reminded Mike that we needed to stop at the East Side shop to try to identify who had purchased the sweater that was found on Katrina's body. We got off the FDR Drive at Sixty-first Street and went north on Madison Avenue until I spotted the store marquee that matched the logo on the cashmere label. We parked and went inside.

Mike identified himself to the saleswoman, who was alone in the small store, using the quiet morning hour to refold and shelve her stock in neat columns. Like most everyone we encounter in the course of a murder case, she seemed to hope that the two of us were mistaken that any connection—no matter how casual—could be made between her life and our investigation into the death of someone else.

I showed her the Polaroid photograph of the sweater that Mike had taken at the morgue, and then a copy of the label that had been sewn into the collar. She studied the picture, bringing it up close to her nose to examine the stitching and inset design. There was a trace of an accent—Italian, I thought—when she looked up to speak to us. "But it's not from this year, is it?"

"We're not the fashion police, ma'am. It's what the girl had on when she died. We don't know when it was purchased, or by whom. That's why we're here."

The earnest young woman picked up the slip of paper with the information about the label. "This manufacturer, we don't carry his things anymore. Ah, perhaps if I check our computer, it will tell me something."

It seemed to take forever as she sat at the monitor and entered the name and code numbers into her machine. Refusing to give in to the need for reading glasses, she leaned in close again and squinted at the display.

"Ah, yes. Two years ago, in the fall. We had a shipment of nine of these in a crewneck style, from the fabricator in Milano who hand-knits them."

"Just nine?" Mike asked.

He seemed pleased, realizing that it was not like trying to track down some mass-produced piece of department-store clothing.

"One in each size—small, medium, and large. And three colors only. Lime, raspberry, peach." She looked at Mike as though he must surely know the reason. "Our customers, sir, they don't like to see themselves—how you say?—going and coming. This was a very expensive sweater."

She paused. "And you are interested in which one? The medium size, in peach, am I right?" She pressed ENTER, and an answer that seemed to please her popped onto the screen.

"*Allora*," she said softly, in her native Italian. "Of course, I should have remembered. Her favorite color, and she was such a beautiful lady. I'll write down the address we had for her, but I don't think it will do you much good. She's dead now, also. We sold this one to Penelope Thibodaux."

18

"Not exactly a lucky charm, that pricey piece of goat hair. Both broads who wore it got more bang for the buck than they bargained for. Can we see him?"

I turned off my cell phone as we walked up the Central Park West entrance to the American Museum of Natural History. "No. That was Ms. Drexler. Thibodaux took the shuttle to Washington this morning for a speech he's giving this evening. We can meet with him after the weekend. He'll be at his desk on Monday. She assures me he has several weeks to clean up his affairs at the museum."

"Let's hope he can mop this one up for us. What the hell is Katrina Grooten doing in his dead wife's sweater?"

The guard at the front door had been told to expect us. He asked me to sign the log before directing us to Elijah Mamdouba's office on the fourth floor of the south wing.

This time, entering from the opposite side of the structure, we retraced our steps through the massive hallways of ground-floor exhibits. It looked to me, as we traipsed past the dioramas of North American mammals, that today they were being prepared for medical procedures. Some kind of restoration, no doubt, which must be a constant need in an institution with this vast array of collections. In front of the tableau of the Grand Canyon, two solemn mountain lions were being examined by a pair of young scientists, who were dressed in lab coats with small white surgical masks covering their mouths and noses.

Arrows pointed us to the public elevators. "Skip it," Mike said, tugging at my sleeve as I stood behind a rowdy group of eight-year-olds. "Check out the stairs."

Whenever possible, Mike opted for the unmechanical route through a building. It was a logical way to get to see more of a scene, often including parts of a location that weren't meant to be observed by outsiders.

Like everything else in the old buildings, the staircases were enormous—easier to fly down than to climb up. Because the height of the rooms was so grand—high enough to house a dinosaur skeleton or whale model—there were four flights of steps between each floor.

When we reached the second landing, Mike stopped to crack open the door that led into the corridor. He closed it behind him and started back for the staircase. "Birds."

We loped up to three, and I paused to catch my breath while he opened the door to look. "African mammals. Monkeys and apes everywhere." He tried another door that stood directly opposite the entrance to the exhibits, but it wouldn't give. "Remind me to ask. I want to know what's behind every locked door."

"Good luck. There must be several thousand of them in this place."

I was relieved to get to the fourth level and leaned on the banister to catch my breath.

"Wait here." I was happy to rest while Mike went on up to the fifth level, past the signs that announced NO PUBLIC ACCESS. He pushed open the pair of double doors and was gone for several minutes.

"What did you find?"

"The longest hallway I've ever seen in my life. Offices and cubbyholes everywhere. And lockers. Floor to ceiling, as far as you can see. Gray metal lockers, like a storage facility, that stretch from one end of the building to the other. C'mon. Let's go see how many ways there are to stuff a monkey."

More arrows on four led us around corners, past the Dinostore, the cafe, and the extinct mammals to a receptionist who worked for Mr. Mamdouba. She pointed us to his open door just as he must have heard our voices and walked out to welcome us.

"Mamdouba here. Elijah Mamdouba." The slight black man who stood before us was barely five feet five inches tall, but had a powerful voice and hand-shake to match. "Miss Cooper? Mr. Chapman? Won't you come in?"

I followed him into the room, a perfectly circular space that occupied a corner turret, looking out on the intersection of Seventy-seventh Street and Columbus Avenue. I couldn't recall ever being in a round office before, and the delightful whimsy of the shape was enhanced by the assortment of treasures that sat on his desk and bookshelves. Not sterling tea services and Old Masters, as we'd seen at the Met, but priceless pieces of cultural history from all over the world. Four identical doors were set back into the walls, two behind his desk and two across the room, all covered with decorative exhibition posters.

Mamdouba grinned as he watched me take in his surroundings. "I'm sure you are both quite familiar with our museum, am I right?"

We talked for several minutes while I wandered around the room, examining specimens, skeletons, and photographs of Mamdouba that had been taken in deserts and jungles all over the world. The gentle lilt of his African accent belied the credentials that were hung on his wall among the pictures. There were undergraduate and graduate degrees from Cambridge University and a Ph.D. from Harvard in cultural anthropology.

"But I'm sure you're not here to listen to me go on about the latest species of fish we've just discovered." All trace of the smile disappeared. "You want to talk about Ms. Grooten."

"Yes, we've got quite a lot of questions. About her, and about the exhibition she was working on while she spent time here."

"Anything we can help you with. I liked Katrina a great deal."

"You knew her personally?"

"Not terribly well, Miss Cooper. She was quite junior, of course, so the other members of the bestiary exhibition team often used her as a gofer, I think you call it. She ferried information back and forth between their quarters downstairs and my office. We shared some professional interests, too, not least of which was our love of Africa."

"Are you from South Africa, too?"

"No, Mr. Chapman. Ghana. Born there in fifty-two, when it was still the Gold Coast. But my travels have taken me all over the world."

"Did you meet Katrina here, at the museum?"

"Yes. I'm supervising our involvement in the big joint show. I saw her here often."

"Why did you take notice of her? I mean, she wasn't one of the most important scholars or contributors to the project."

"Actually, it was she who asked for *my* attention at the time. She was working at the Cloisters, as you know. But by the end of the summer, she was interested in going back home. She wanted a job at an institution there, and she was thinking of changing her entire field of concentration. Katrina's background was in medieval art history. She'd become interested in anthropology along the way, and came to me for guidance."

"Why the change in focus?"

"Perhaps her friends can tell you that, Miss Cooper. I don't know which came first—her desire to go home, and a realization about the shortage of European art collections in Africa, or the subject matter itself. Once she was exposed to the extraordinary collections we have here, I assume she became more interested in them."

"Did you socialize with her? Outside the museum?"

"No, no. I can't think that we were ever anywhere together except right in this building."

"Did you know anything about her personal life, her problems?"

He reflected for a minute before answering. "Not really. She told me, in the fall, that she'd been ill. Nothing she wanted to discuss with me. She apologized from time to time, at meetings, for being distracted when I called on her to answer questions. She didn't look terribly healthy, but then, have a glance around at some of these young scientists. Not the heartiest-looking lot. We don't pay them enough to eat very well, and then they spend all their time in these windowless laboratories, with fluids and preservatives that would give a funeral home a bit of competition. Can't say as I thought she looked worse than many others."

Mamdouba smiled and then said, as an afterthought, "Besides, most of them look awfully pale to me."

Mike leaned forward, his notepad resting on his left knee, his pen in his right hand, with which he was gesturing. "So exactly what is it you do around here?"

"I'm the administrative director of the museum, sir. The keeper, as they call us in England. Everything in this wondrous place is under my care. We have to know how to maintain all these specimens, how to display them appropriately, when to acquire something new."

"You got a body count?"

"Ah, Mr. Chapman. A little more respect for our dead. The closest I can give you is about thirty-two million species and artifacts. Mammals alone—I presume that's your area of interest—we've got over 270,000 specimens, and that includes their skeletal material, their skins, and their innards, which are in jars all over the building."

"On display?"

"Just like an art museum. Maybe one, maybe two percent of what we've got is out on view. But you know about that. I understand you've already begun your questioning across the park, at the Met."

"You've spoken to someone over there?"

"Well, I could simply say I've read today's newspaper, couldn't I? In fact, Anna Friedrichs told me first. She was here yesterday, in the afternoon. She was very fond of Katrina."

"Are you close to your colleagues at the Met?"

"To begin with, Mr. Chapman, many of them don't even consider us to be in the same business. Our institutions may both be called museums, and we've each got vast holdings, but most of the similarities end there. Anna's interests have a bit more humanistic content than those of her other colleagues. I think that brings her closer to us. More simpatico. What do you know about the history of natural history museums?"

"Not a thing," I answered. Mamdouba's smile was magnetic. He stood up and came out from behind his desk, walking over to sit on a sofa that was on the far side of the room. We both turned to look at him.

"The British did it first, you know. Seventeen fifty-three. There were earlier collections, in Paris and even at Oxford, but it was the British Museum that was open to the general public, to all 'studious and curious' persons, as its grant allowed. It was never meant to be just art, but cabinets full of all kinds of odd things that people had collected. Birds, animals, and human 'monstrosities'—all kept in spirits. Wine, frequently. Alcohol proves to be a wonderful preservative. Even the royals had the bug. You don't know about Peter the Great?"

"Know what?" Mike was always ready to take on historical data.

"When he discovered his wife had a lover, he had the man beheaded. He actually placed the head in a large jar and had it pickled. Deposited it in the empress's bedchamber, as a painful reminder of the price of her infidelity. Peter kept an entire collection of biological oddities. Centuries later, his descendants found them— even the fermented head, in rather good shape—still on their shelves in the palace."

Surely, Mamdouba would get us beyond the sensational. His entire career was invested in this work. "And *this* museum?"

"The greatest in the world. With a very similar start, actually. I can show you the first annual report, from 1877. Bones of an extinct dodo; three thousand bird skins form the 'cabinet' of Prince Maximilian of Neuwied; hundreds of beetles; private vaults of the French consul general in New York; mollusks and shells that—for lack of a formal home—had been stored in the Wall Street offices of Brown Brothers, the old investment firm."

"Where in the world did the money come from to build such an enormous showcase?"

"Aha, Miss Cooper. This was the golden age of

exploration. Theodore Roosevelt, Junior—every schoolchild knows that statue out in front. But there were so many other extraordinary men of great vision. J. P. Morgan, Morris Jesup, Albert Bickmore, and Teddy Roosevelt's father, too." Mamdouba reeled off the names, standing now and pointing at photographs on the wall.

"These men had the vision that led to the discovery of the North Pole, the charting of the Gobi Desert, with the richest dinosaur fields on earth, the penetration of the deepest jungles on the African and South American continents." The fingers of his left hand spread across the length of his chest as he pressed against it. "*We* are the living history of the evolution of life on this planet, constantly changing, always interpreting and incorporating new data. A tremendously vital research organization, also. Not just a bit of oil and canvas left to hang for a century or two in a gilded picture frame on a museum wall." He grinned again as he returned the salvo of his friends across the park at the Met.

"Would you mind showing us where Ms. Grooten worked when she was here?"

"I'll be glad to have someone take you around. We've dedicated an entire acre of basement space to arranging and archiving the exhibit."

"An acre?"

"Yes, Mr. Chapman. After all, we've got twenty-five acres of floor space within our buildings. Come this way." He guided us out past his receptionist into the main hallway.

"What's upstairs?"

"The fifth floor? The longest corridor in North America, outside of the Pentagon. There may be something that rivals it at Versailles or Windsor, but it's the length of three city blocks. Goes a lot farther than the entire village in which I spent my youth."

"Can we see what's up there?"

His hesitation was almost imperceptible, but the rest of his delivery had been so smooth that I'm sure Mike caught it, too.

"When President Raspen returns from her voyage, I'm certain she will approve." He went right on with his polished performance. "Surely you know Margaret Mead? Well, she had the turret office above mine all to herself. A remarkable woman. More than fifty years she was associated with this museum. Half a century of work in the field, all in the most primitive areas of the world, if you can imagine that."

Mamdouba pressed the elevator button and we waited for the slow machine to grind its way up to four. We took it down to the first floor and again entered the North American mammal hall. He stopped at a guard desk and used a telephone to call someone to take us the rest of the way.

"What's going on with the animals? Somebody sick?" Mike asked, referring to the crew of gowned and masked scientists still at work inside several of the dioramas.

"Aren't these wonderful? It was one of our original explorers, Carl Akeley, who designed the first diorama here. Before his time, people stuffed animal skins with straw. It was not only bad aesthetically, because of all the lumps, but there was frequently insect infestation. Akeley was a great sportsman and hunter. He knew the animals intimately."

Mike was more interested in the taxidermy technique than I was. He listened closely as Mamdouba described the famous Akeley innovation. "The first thing Carl did was pose the actual animal's skeleton. The real one, after the body was cleaned. Then he used clay to sculpt the creature's muscles and tendons, on top of its very own bones. Completely true to life. Finally, he'd take the original skin and place it over the reconstructed animal. That's why they look so lifelike."

More than I needed to know about the lost art of taxidermy.

"So the little men and women in white, what are they up to today? Plastic surgery for the old animals? BOTOX?" Mike and I watched as they dabbed with Q-tips at ears and hooves and antlers.

"Precisely, Mr. Chapman. Just the occasional touch-up. Keep their teeth white and their coats shiny. The surgical masks do look a bit serious, don't they? We make our workers take that precaution when they're in the cabinets. You see, one of the surefire ways to kill the bugs when you're preserving the natural skins is to make certain there's enough arsenic in the treatment."

Mamdouba looked serious. "It's a staple in our conservation department, Detective, and we wouldn't want any of the workers to breathe it in. Could be deadly."

19

"Forgot your pass, Mr. Mamdouba?" A bespectacled young man, about thirty, dressed in a denim work shirt and jeans, came up behind the curatorial director and tapped him on the back.

"Ah, Zimm. Perfect man for the job. Meet Alexandra Cooper here. And Mr. Chapman."

"Mark Zimmerly. Entomology."

"Bugs?" Mike asked as they exchanged handshakes.

"Yeah, well, spiders in particular. Gnaphosoidae. Australian ground spiders. Six hundred and fifty species and still counting."

"No offense, but I was hoping for something with fewer legs and no stingers."

Zimm turned and led us back to a tall doorway behind the bank of elevators. There was a laminated photo ID around his neck, and he bent over to scan it in against the security pad.

Mamdouba followed Zimm, taking us down a poorly lighted staircase that wound around for three flights. The dull gray paint was chipped and faded, and there were smudged handprints on the wall where people before us had tried to balance their footing on the narrow treads.

Chapman whispered in my ear as I turned a corner, "Remind me to tell Mercer and Vickee never to let the kid go to a museum. Friggin' arsenic everywhere. Did you have any idea?"

"Takes us back to square one. Whoever poisoned Katrina Grooten knew the field of suspects would be wide open. He didn't have to go into a pharmacy and ask for a prescription. Just point the finger at someone else who worked in any of the institutions."

At the bottom of the steps was a large sign: BES-TIARY. A red arrow pointed to the right, below the words THE MET. And a green arrow headed left: AMNH. We all followed Zimm around to the office in which he worked.

"Miss Cooper and Mr. Chapman are investigating Katrina Grooten's death."

"What a shocker," the young man said. "Saw the story in the *Post*. Couldn't believe it was someone I knew. Someone who worked here with me."

"Why don't you tell them about what you're doing here, and what her role in it was. Zimm's been with us since he was a high school student."

"I'm a graduate student at NYU. Started to come here when my family moved to Manhattan, fifteen years ago. Thought this was the coolest place in the world. Spent all my free time here, so my teacher encouraged me to do an internship while I was at Stuyvesant." Zimm had gone to one of New York

City's premier public high schools, specializing in science and math, for which kids had to pass a special test for admission eligibility.

Mike smiled at him. "So you started working at the museum when Pluto was still a planet, huh?"

"Ah, Mr. Chapman. At least we're always controversial here," Mamdouba said. "You disagree with my friends at the planetarium?"

"All I know is that for the first thirty-five years of my life, there were nine planets in the solar system. Now your museum decides Pluto's just an icy comet. I don't deal with change that well."

"Don't hold it against me, man." Zimm laughed. "I've got nothing to do with the astrophysicists. What we're doing down here is assembling and cataloging all the specimens that are under consideration for selection in the exhibit."

"Who's in charge?"

"Well, Elijah has the final word. I'm just the functionary. People bring me their artifacts, or photographs of the items. I inventory them, scan them into the computer, and pass the lists along to the joint committee, and to Elijah." He moved over to his desk and clicked the mouse of his computer; the program for the big show appeared on the screen. He scrolled down to give us a sampling of the thousands of proposed artifacts.

Mike stopped him halfway down the list of *B*'s. "Whoa. You got a namesake here, Coop. They've got their own Blondie."

"Right behind you, Detective." Zimm pointed, and I looked at the large mason jar on the counter at my elbow. "Blondie—my personal favorite."

"Mine, too," Mike muttered to me. "Golden hair, lots of leg, and very painful when she lands on top of you."

There in the jar was an albino tarantula, about the size of a soup dish. Dead, I hoped.

"This one was raised in the museum and lived here all her life. Kinda the department mascot. She's my candidate for the bestiary show."

I stepped away from the large spider and drew the conversation back to our mission. "Katrina, did you work with her on this?"

"Sure. I guess I saw her whenever she came to the museum."

"How often was that?"

"Last year? I'd say at first it was a couple of times a month. But by last fall, probably two or three times a week."

"I didn't realize she had to be here that often."

Zimm blushed. He looked over at Mamdouba but didn't offer any more information.

"What's your hesitation? She's not exactly going to get in trouble for anything at this point."

"Oh, well, I'm not sure how much of it was business she had to do for the Cloisters. I mean, I think she just discovered how interesting this place is. She'd do her work, all right. Faster than the rest of us. Then she'd just take off and wander around."

Mamdouba frowned. This seemed to be news to him. "In the museum, son?"

"Yeah."

The director took over the questioning. "Are you

talking about areas open to the public, or did she have a security pass, like yours?"

"No, sir. Katrina had the basic ID to get into the building and access this office, but she couldn't get into any of the other departments—without help."

"What kind of help would that be, Zimm?"

The entomologist was fidgeting with a jar full of stiff bugs, rolling it around with one hand, gripping it by the lid. The label read, *Lobster Roaches*.

"Katrina made some friends here, Elijah. Borrowed their swipe cards. Nothing wrong with being curious about this place."

"Who loaned her their cards?" Mike asked.

Mamdouba tried to cut that avenue off. "Why don't you see me later on this, young man? Detective, this is an internal security matter. It has nothing to do with your investigation."

"I hate to disagree with you, but it might be exactly what we're looking for. And what would have stopped her from walking off through the basement from right here, finding her way up into any part of the building?"

"Because, Mr. Chapman," the director snapped back, "this museum consists of twenty-three separate building structures. Most of them have no interconnection from this level, belowground, to any other."

"How did that happen?"

"It's called cash flow. The founders ran out of money early on, so the master plan was never completed. Wings were added piecemeal, and most of them are free standing structures that only connect on

the main floor or some corridor above. Who were
Katrina's friends, Zimm?"

He was still twisting his bugs, their legs and
antennae seeming to catch and entangle in each
other like a delicate jigsaw puzzle. "I'm really bad
on names. There was a woman, a postdoc in
anthropology—they used to have lunch together all
the time. But she doesn't work here anymore. I think
she was British. And a few researchers in the African
peoples department. Honestly, Elijah, I never hung
out with any of them. Oh, the Rare Book Room—she
loved to go there."

"Why?"

"Mr. Chapman, we have perhaps the most superb
collection of books, journals, documents, and photographs ever assembled about the diversity of human
cultures and the exploration of the natural world.
Very fragile, some of it. And not accessible in our
library. They must be kept in a restricted area, of
course, or these papers would just walk out the door.
Terribly valuable."

"Where is it?"

"Adjacent to the library. But again, in a separate
building that you can only get into with a special security pass." Mamdouba was not pleased. "Very well,
Zimm. After you show these people what they need to
see, I'd still like to have a chat with you in my office."

He told us he would be available for any further
questions that we had, but excused himself to go back
upstairs.

"Didn't mean to jam you up."

"Not a problem, Detective. Everybody's so jumpy

here about security, but you get a feel for people who respect the same things you do. It's not like Katrina was going to make off with first editions of hand-colored Audubon drawings from the collection. This place intrigued her, in a positive way. I don't think she'd ever been exposed to phenomena like this before."

Mike parked himself on a stool across the counter from Zimm. "You have anything going on with her?"

The kid blushed again. "Nah. Went out for margaritas a couple of times after meetings, but she really wasn't interested in anything else. Not with me."

"How about Mamdouba? He and Katrina have any special relationship?"

Zimm looked at Mike as though he were crazy. "Him? That guy is all business all the time. You know what he's most interested in now? Burning whoever let Katrina break the rules. He's probably more concerned about that than the fact that she's dead. This may be the only kind of bureaucracy worse than academia, and I'm bouncing back and forth between the two of them."

"Don't try city government next. The two of us could outdo you in a flash with bureaucratic rules. And one other piece of advice: You meet a nice kid like Katrina and you wanna get laid? Get rid of the spiders. Especially the ones you got at home next to the bed." Mike kicked the stool away and stood up. "We want the same back-door view she had. The museum you don't see on the school tour. Is that going to be a problem for you?"

Zimm seemed energized by the idea. He rested his

jar of roaches next to the tarantula. "I get my degree next month. I'm outta here." He jerked his thumb back over his shoulder like a hitchhiker. "Off to Chicago, to the Field Museum. Assistant curator of the department. Want to see anything else about the exhibition before we start walking?"

"If I give you a museum acquisition number, can you tell us where the piece is right now?"

The entomologist was ready to show off his computer program. He clicked off the screen with the alphabetical list of items and waited while Mike opened his notepad to the page he wanted.

"It's from the Met: 1983.752."

"Limestone sarcophagus, right? Mamdouba had me looking this one up yesterday."

Mike nodded and Zimm double-clicked, bringing up a color photo of the ancient coffin. The pale beige slab that had looked so macabre in the darkened hollow of the big truck seemed almost elegant as photographed against the faux-marble backdrop of the museum display.

As he read aloud a description of the markings, Mike and I studied the image on the screen. Just as Hal Sherman had told me, there were ornate carvings with rows of wild animals inscribed in exquisite detail, everything from boars and hyenas to wading birds and elephants. But for its grisly diversion to Port Newark, it would have been a perfect object for the bestiary show.

"Is this, um—the newspaper said Katrina was found in—"

"Yeah, this is it. What else does the entry mention?"

While Zimm printed out two pages of information, he straightened up and recited the rest from memory. "The piece came in on December first of last year. Timothy Gaylord—he's the Egyptian curator—sent it over from the Met for consideration in the exhibition."

"Where was it kept while it was here?"

"The oversize things like that? They were all in the basement of ichthyology."

"Fish?"

"Yup."

"Why there?"

"I guess it was just a question of where there was the most room for storage on the lower level. They've got a back door there that opens onto the loading dock. It would be the logical place to bring the heaviest pieces in and out."

Mike scanned the printout. "This doesn't say when the sarcophagus left here."

"According to our records, it never did."

"Can you reverse the process? Can you plug in the dates—say, last Monday or Tuesday—and see what items shipped out of here?"

Zimm went back to his computer program. He entered May 20 and May 21 into the search for outgoing loads. "Looks like one of our own trucks picked up some things to be transferred to the Smithsonian. Light stuff, though. Birds, shells, mollusks."

"The week before?"

"Yeah, here's a bigger truck. See? Here's a shipment going back to the Met on the fifteenth of May. Some heavy limestone in it. Probably stuff that's been rejected from the show. This sarcophagus wasn't the only one they were looking at. They had lots of Egyptian objects that were submitted. Hmmm. An Indian funeral stele with scenes from the life of Buddha." He brought up a picture, which showed Prince Siddhartha, who later became Buddha, riding off on his horse to renounce his nobility.

Mike leaned in over the young man's shoulder to read through the list. "Sandstone. A four-foot-tall Cambodian statue of Ganesha, the Hindu god with an elephant's head. And a bronze statue of Theseus fighting the Minotaur. What do these initials mean?"

"Somebody from the Met team has to sign out the pieces here, sending them back. That last one, that's signed by the head of European sculpture."

"Whoa, here's some Egyptian stuff going back."

"Like what?"

"The coffin of some guy named Khumnakht. A false door from the tomb of Metjetji. Who signed for this?"

Zimm brought up the signature. "Timothy Gaylord. I'll print it out."

Mike grabbed the pages as they came out of the machine.

"Want this one, too? Looks like another big sarcophagus that we shipped up to the Cloisters the week before. May eighth. Some guy named Ermengol, also carved in limestone. The whole block of stone is supported by three lions, and I think one of them has a pig in his mouth." He was more riveted by the animal images than by our mission.

"Signed out by?"

"Bellinger. Hiram Bellinger."

"Can you search through your programs to see whether Katrina signed in or out on anything?"

"Did that already, for Mamdouba. Nope. Somebody over her head would have to do that. She wouldn't have had that authority."

"How about a cross-check, to see whether any other exhibits are missing. Things that have not been signed out—like the sarcophagus—but have disappeared."

"Ditto on Mamdouba. That's going to take a lot longer to do, but we've got a team of students who are trying to do a hand count right now. So far, three other items can't be located. But they're all small things. Pilfering, probably. Like a seven-inch silver drinking vessel from medieval Germany, shaped like a stag. Kinds of things that people could easily sneak out of here. Not quite as startling as shipping out that coffin."

Mike straightened up. "Can you take us to where the fishes sleep?"

"Ichthyology? Why not?" Zimm locked the door behind him and led us back up the drab stairway we had descended earlier. "Sorry for all the steps. It's the only way in and out of this basement. We're kind of landlocked down here. So you guys do any DNA on her body?"

I could tell from the expression on Mike's face that he was as surprised by the question as I was. "You know anything about Katrina's murder besides what you've read in the papers?"

"Nope. But I wasn't sure whether Mamdouba told you that all of us who work here, they've got our genetic profiles on record. They've got our DNA."

No one had mentioned it to us, and the idea had never crossed my mind.

"Much of the work we do in the labs here is identifying different species and subspecies of animal life within our fields of specialty. See what their similarities and differences are, and which characters are threatened with extinction. The bird guys can tell you whether a spotted owl on a mountain range is a relative of the ones that live a mile away, or in Northern California, or if it's more closely linked to a particular family of owls in Mexico."

"What does that have to do with you scientists?"

"We sit at the microscopes all day, looking at and breathing onto our specimens and slides. A sneeze, some sweat—well, anything that one of us contributes to the mix would obviously throw off the research results. So they take an oral swab from each of us when we start working here. Thought you might just want to know that."

The same procedure was followed at most morgues and serologists' offices. It should have occurred to me that anyone working with genetic samples would be required to have his or her own DNA on file. If Dr. Kestenbaum found something of serological value on any of Katrina's crime scene evidence, it would be a good place to start.

We crossed through several corridors until Zimm came to another unmarked door behind a row of service elevators. Again he swiped his identification card and took us into a dingy staircase that led four tiers below the main lobby.

The hallways were dark and he flipped on light switches as he walked along. "A lot of people took the day off, before the long weekend. But I've got friends who work in this department, and it's where I spent my first two summers, back when I was in high school. I can show you most of what you need."

There were compact laboratories on either side of us, filled from floor to ceiling with fish tanks and glass jars of all sizes. Then came storerooms of fish samples—some two million of them—each drifting in some kind of watery solution, carefully labeled and housed in stacks of rolling metal cabinets, like so many books on library shelves.

"What's that smell?" Mike asked.

"Which one? Dead matter? Preservatives? The odor of death is all over this museum. We've just learned to mask it pretty well."

I studied the markings on scores of fish skeletons, their whiteness standing out in striking contrast to the dull painted gray of the basement floors and ceilings. "How do you do that?"

"When I was first an intern here, they brought in a huge whale skeleton that had washed up on a beach in Long Island. I'd never smelled anything like it. Couldn't shake the odor. My boss sent me to Columbus Avenue, to a drugstore. Oil of bergamot, he told me to ask for. I bought the place out."

"What is it?"

"It's an essence made from the rind of a citrus fruit. Bergamot—it's like an orange smell with mint in it. We'd just douse some cloths in that and leave them draped over the specimen when we weren't working on it. Everyone here has tricks like that. It's the only way to deal with the smell of the dead specimens."

Mike was writing in his notebook. He'd make Kestenbaum test the linen cloth that was wrapped around Katrina's body. Perhaps the mummified linen had been soaked in a substance that had masked the odor of death while she was in storage somewhere. That sweet smell that hit us when the coffin lid was opened on the truck, before the stronger blast of garlic, might have been something like bergamot.

"Suppose you wanted to kill someone, Zimm. How would you do it down here?" Mike was checking to see whether the availability of arsenic was common knowledge. The cause of Katrina's death had not yet appeared in the press.

He steered us past the ichthyology X-ray department and into a room crowded with three-foot-long fish tanks, alive with samples. "Know anybody with a weak heart? This sucker's an electric catfish. African. He can pump out about three hundred volts when he's riled up."

The whiskered brown creatures darted about, one pressing his nose against the glass as though he wanted to prove Zimm's point to us.

"Over here's where we keep the tissues, for molecular work." He turned on another light in a small lab across the hall. There were two enormous vats, with DANGER signs printed on their sides. "Liquid nitrogen. Eighteen degrees. If I stuck your head in this for just a minute you'd burn to death from the intense cold. Painful, fast, quiet."

"But you'd still have the problem of getting rid of me."

"I could at least keep you in cold storage till I figured out how to do that. Us bug guys? We don't get many things that won't fit in a jar. A couple of giant insects from the Amazon or the African jungles. You wanna talk to some people in mammalogy? They just got a new degreaser."

"What's that?"

"Hey, you're the detective. How do you figure they get their skeletal samples clean? They got this brand-new degreasing machine. You can fit an entire elephant skull into it, submerge it for a few days. This thing takes all the fat off the bones. Then we give them some of our beetles to nibble off whatever's left, before they stick it in the freezer to kill off all the germs. Dip somebody in there and they'd be clean as a whistle."

I ignored the midday rumblings of my empty stomach. Museum work was killing my appetite.

He was leading us down a long, dim corridor and around one more corner. "Ever hear of a coelacanth?"

"No."

"It's the missing link of the fish world. All anybody had seen for centuries were fossils of this thing. Scientists thought it had died out several million years ago. Five feet long, very unusual fin structure, gives birth to live young. In 1938 a trawler off South Africa came up with one. A young scientist working down there sketched it and then sent the fish over to this museum. We've had it here ever since."

"That same fish?"

"Yeah. She's pickled."

"How come everyone in your business uses that expression?"

"Because alcohol is such a great preservative. This beauty has lasted more than sixty years, just as she was pulled out of the water, in a solution that's seventy percent ethyl alcohol." He was around the last nook and into an open space.

"Have a look. There's her coffin."

We were standing in front of a six-foot-long metal container with a hinged lid. It was three feet high and a couple of feet deep, large enough to hold a prehistoric fish or a large shark, and most human beings I knew.

20

Zimm lifted the lid on the heavy metal casket. "Stand back. The smell of the alcohol can knock you off your feet."

He was right. My head jerked away and I was reminded of the overwhelming stench of formaldehyde that had been so pervasive when I viewed my first autopsies at the medical examiner's office as part of my training for homicide investigations.

I covered my mouth with one hand and rested the other on the end of the case. Mike and I stared in at the behemoth, whose single glassy eye gazed back at us. Zimm reached into the murky fluid and lifted up the head of the coelacanth for us to admire. The fish was larger than the body of Katrina Grooten.

Mike was more interested in the container than the fish. "What's this?" he asked, tapping on the inside.

"It's completely lined with stainless steel. You couldn't have odors like this escaping into the room for very long, and still have people working around here, could you?"

"You'd lose me at the end of a day. How many of

these have they got?" Mike helped lower the lid into place.

"Maybe four. Maybe six. I'll ask my friend next week."

"Where are the rest of them?"

Zimm shrugged his shoulders. "This is the only one that's got a permanent resident. They move the others around as needed."

We had walked through most of the department and had not seen any similar coffinlike vats. "They're certainly not small enough to conceal."

"People don't hide them intentionally. There are endless numbers of small offices in which the research is done. Some are probably tucked away in corners of those rooms, and others are in storage areas. Believe me, Ms. Cooper, you'd need an army to go through this place from top to bottom to figure out everything that we've got in here. And Mr. Mamdouba isn't about to let that happen."

"Those other friends of Katrina's you mentioned, can you take us to meet them?"

"I'm not really sure who's in today." He hesitated, and I thought he was afraid to make trouble for any other graduate students.

"We're just trying to talk to people who might have known she was in distress. People whom she may have confided in about her return home to South Africa."

"I wasn't kidding about her friend, the one who left. I didn't know her by name. Only by sight. I just know she was an anthropologist who was asked to resign and—"

"Fired?"

"Yeah. That's why she's in London now."

"What do you have to do to get fired from a natural history museum?"

"Steal things would be the easiest. But that wasn't her problem," Zimm said. "Rumor was she crossed someone in administration."

"Mamdouba?"

"No, but he'd certainly know the story."

Mike looked at his notes. "And the African peoples connection?"

"They're up on the second floor. I can take you up there. Maybe I'll recognize her pals."

We trekked again, up the stairs and out into the public space, past North American forests and through the Hall of Biodiversity, among the birds of the world, and into the African Peoples hall.

Zimm asked the guard if he knew where any of the interns were, but the man just shook his head.

My beeper began to vibrate as I stood before a photo exhibit of an early African expedition. "Cell phones work up here?"

"Not in the basement, and not in most interior areas like this. Better walk back to the birds."

I checked Ryan Blackmer's number and returned his call. "I've been trying to page you for half an hour. Black hole?"

"Yeah, sorry. These museum foundations are too thick in places. What'd I miss?"

"The meet with the Internet pedophile that we had set for three o'clock today? The perp canceled."

"You think he smells something?"

"Nah. Wants to do it Monday. Sounds like he just couldn't get into town early enough. I didn't want you hanging around the museum for no reason. And Sarah said to tell you one other thing. We're on the lookout for a limo driver from a company the talk shows use."

"What for?"

"The producer of one of the shows brought in a bunch of wild-child types for a show called 'Easy Teens.' Would it surprise you to know that after the taping, a spunky fifteen-year-old took off with the limo driver? Last seen giving him a blow job in the backseat of the stretch limo, parked right in front of the hotel where they were waiting to pick up her mother. Wire services have it."

"How'd they get it?"

"Mother gave it out. She's looking to sue the show."

"Where the hell was she while the kid was on the loose?"

"Back in the hotel room."

"We're almost done here. If I don't have to wait for your sting to go down, we've got another witness to interview," I said, thinking of Ruth Gerst, the Met trustee.

Our eager guide took us through many of the back corridors and unpeopled areas of the museum before we left: hallway after darkened hallway filled with cases of forgotten bird displays, rows of unmarked lockers, and blocks of empty containers covered over with thick layers of plastic tarp. By the time he walked us out the door, it was close to three o'clock.

Zimm had known nothing about arsenic sources within the museum, since his department did not use any in their work, but he was now alert to endless ideas about how to dispose of a body within the vast network of buildings.

On our way east to the Gerst apartment on Park Avenue, Mike and I stopped for a sandwich and cold drink. He called the ME's office and left a message on Dr. Kestenbaum's voice mail. If there was anything on Katrina's body or clothing that indicated a need for DNA analysis, the profiles of the Natural History staff were on record. He also suggested testing the linen cloths in which the body had been wrapped for some natural oil substance that might have been used in an attempt to suppress odors.

The doorman admitted us to one of the toniest buildings on Park Avenue, just north of Seventieth Street. Mrs. Gerst answered the door herself. "Come in, darlings. Ruth Gerst. You're Miss Cooper and Mr. Chapman. Come right in."

She looked as though she had just returned from an elegant luncheon. She was a large woman whom I guessed to be in her eighties, dressed in a light tweed walking suit, perfectly coiffed, and wearing enough jewelry to sink a rowboat.

She ushered us into a sitting room off the main living area. The furniture was covered in a luxe silk fabric, and the walls were hung with an assortment of small paintings, each undoubtedly as valuable as the emerald-cut diamond ring that tried to balance itself atop Gerst's gnarled finger.

"You're Jake Tyler's girl, is that right?"

I answered her politely, while Mike stifled a laugh. "Yes, ma'am. Alexandra Cooper."

"I hope I didn't smother him the other night, at the Met, with all my attention and questions. You shouldn't let a good-looking fellow out around town by himself."

"What am I, chopped liver? You available, Mrs. Gerst?"

"That's the spirit, son. I've been available for way too long. Eighty-six, I am now. Think you can handle me? Been a widow almost thirty years. But let me get right to the point. I've been involved with the Metropolitan Museum for an awfully long time. Seen directors come and go. Scandals, too. I read about this young lady's death and I've been terribly concerned."

Ruth Gerst pushed herself up off her armchair and walked to a small wet bar in an alcove against the far corner of the room. "Can I fix you a drink?"

We both said no, and watched as she poured herself a neat shot of bourbon.

"You have something you want to tell us about Pierre Thibodaux?"

"Goodness, no. I see the newspapers could hardly wait a minute before they started damning him about the girl's murder. You need to know something about the politics of the place, and who's out to get him. I thought I could help."

"Have you been affiliated with the Met for a very long time?"

"My dear, my father was a trustee. In 1925, he gave his first million. Old banking family. His father came to this country in the 1880s. You can't begin to imagine how this whole business has changed over time. Gaylord and Bellinger, pointing fingers at Pierre? Curators used to know their place in the old days."

I knew Bellinger was not a fan of the director's but I wasn't aware of any public finger-pointing, yet. "Really?"

Mrs. Gerst picked up on her own story. "In my father's day? The curators at the Met weren't even allowed to sit when they made a presentation before the trustees of the purchasing committee. They came into the meeting, described their research on a piece, and they left. As it should be. Each of the trustees' wives was expected to donate evening gowns from her own wardrobe, after the season, to the wives of the curators so they could make a respectable appearance at museum events.

"I remember the year I went off to college, I howled when I learned Mother had given a strand of her South Sea pearls to the Greek and Roman curator's wife, along with a couple of Chanel gowns. It's a different world now. Very high and mighty they are."

"Why do you think Hiram Bellinger didn't get along with Pierre? Style? The quiet scholar versus the showman at the helm?"

"Hiram's just a crybaby. No matter how much money we poured into acquisitions for him and the Cloisters, he's never been satisfied. He embarrassed Pierre terribly with that purchase of the tapestries that he claimed were from the Gobelins' workshops. We gave him a fortune to complete the deal. He gets them here, to be restored at the textile laboratory at the Cathedral of St. John the Divine, and it turns out they had an entirely different provenance. Weren't worth the price of the plane ride to America."

I glanced down at my watch. Gerst's gossip was interesting but hardly going anywhere.

She rested her glass on a side table and looked at Mike. "What I wanted to know is whether anybody told you about the vaults."

"Vaults?" I looked at Mike and he shook his head from side to side.

"I should have figured. There aren't many people around from the early days. It's quite possible Pierre doesn't even know about their existence."

Mrs. Gerst lifted her glass to her lips and took several sips of the bourbon.

"This goes back almost fifty years, when there were some very lean times at the museum. There was a trustee named Arthur Paglin, who had a mediocre personal collection, but an awful lot of money. The director at the time was after him to make a donation that would enable a massive renovation of what was then called the Great Hall. The man knew how to drive a deal like the devil."

"What did he do?"

"He agreed to donate the money. But he had two conditions. The first was that the Met sell to him most of their collection of Egyptian art—which they'd bought many years earlier—at the original prices."

"Why do that?"

"So he could bequeath the objects back to the Met, and this time they would all bear the designation 'Gifts of Arthur Paglin' in perpetuity. He'd get the credit for having put together the collection, and a brilliant tax deduction as well. Worth far more than the cost of the art at the 1930s prices."

"And the second condition?"

"He demanded a storeroom in the basement of the museum. A private vault. He wanted a storage space that only he and his personal curator could access. Rent-free."

"And they gave it to him?"

"With great reluctance. Imagine, to other collectors, the value of having this perfectly secure vault right inside the Met, without having to pay for any of it."

"Why did they go along with it?"

"Because the museum director wanted its contents eventually. Subsequent directors courted Paglin for the rest of his life, without even knowing what treasures were inside the room."

"How'd they do?"

"*Chacun à son goût,* Detective. My husband used to say that the tax scheme had more value than anything Paglin had the taste to collect. There were some great pieces, but he'd been taken to the cleaners as often as the rest of us."

"And this vault, this was common knowledge at the time?" I could neither remember reading about it nor hearing of it before today.

"*Common* would be the right word for it. Mr. Paglin and my father had similar taste in one regard: they shared a mistress. Just for a year or two, but long enough for her to see the splendors of the vault and tell my father about it. I don't think many other people were aware of it. Starts that whole 'mine is bigger than yours is' thing. Men are such babies about that, don't you find?"

"Do you know how many private vaults there are in the museum?"

"I have no idea. But Timothy Gaylord would be a good place to start. Anyone who's involved in our Egyptian collection, even today, would know the Paglin story. I'd bet Timothy was working in the Egyptian department as a curatorial apprentice at the time of Paglin's death. The old boy lived well into his nineties, like I'm hoping to do. Cheers!"

Mike turned to me. "Wonder if they have anything similar at Natural History. Private vaults, I mean." We were both thinking, like Ruth Gerst, that a vault would be a great place to hide a sarcophagus.

"Not that I've ever heard."

"How familiar are you with *that* museum?"

"Herbert was on their board."

"Herbert?"

"My late husband. Refused to have anything to do with the Met because my father was such a strong presence there. Loved the romance and excitement of exploration. Have you met Erik Poste yet? European paintings?"

"Only briefly."

"His father, Willem, was one of the great adventurers of the last century. Right out of Hemingway, my dear girl. Fearless, handsome, sexy. Took Herbert to Africa with him on many of his trips. I think my Herbie was the only one, in those days, who had no stomach for the hunt, no desire to kill the magnificent beasts. Never got caught up in that."

"What were your husband's interests?"

"In Africa? Anything that wasn't nailed down. After those early trips with Willem, my husband brought back every fossil he could find. Reptiles, tortoises, mammals. As long as someone else had done the shooting. The man just loved his bones. Believe me, if they'd had any private vaults in that museum, Herb would have finagled one for himself. Ask Erik Poste. He'd know. He lived with all those tales."

"Well, where did they store the bones?"

"My boy, they've got an elephant room in the attic, a boar closet somewhere else, lizard vertebrae in herpetology. Do you know how many bones they've got in that place, scattered everywhere? Fifty million of them. Now what the hell for?"

"Well, what exactly did your husband want with them?"

"Same thing those others wanted: immortality. J. P. Morgan gets a hall of gems named after him, for giving the museum the Star of India. Gertrude Whitney gave birds—enough of them to give Hitchcock the creeps—and she's got a hall of her own, too. Herbie? They never quite figured out what to do with all his bones. Couldn't possibly display them in one place, because they cross over into too many departments. So they just sit there collecting dust."

Gerst hoisted her glass again, drained it, and walked briskly to the bar for a refill. She turned to look at Mike as she spoke. "I met that girl once, you know. The dead one."

"Katrina Grooten?"

"Yes. I've got a good mind for faces. They showed

a photo of her, from the Cloisters, on the morning news. Sweet-looking young thing."

"At the Met?"

"No, no. At the Louvre. There was a search committee made up of some trustees, when we invited Pierre to take the position with us. After he accepted, a few of us flew over to Paris, and they held a reception for him at the Louvre."

She walked to her chair and steadied herself on one of its arms as she sat down. "I'll have to ask him if it's the same girl. I remember chatting with her about the small museum she apprenticed in, in Toulouse, I think."

"Musée des Augustins?"

"That's it. My husband and I had been there a few years earlier, so I was intrigued to hear about her scholarship. When did the Grooten girl come to work at the Cloisters?"

Around the same time—almost three years ago—that Pierre Thibodaux accepted the directorship of the Met. "I'm not sure."

"Maybe he was mentoring her," Gerst said.

"We'll have to ask Ms. Drexler about that."

"Eve? I call her 'Evil.' I wouldn't ask her anything about another woman." Mrs. Gerst had a rowdy twinkle in her eye and a quick smile. "She'd have put a knife in the girl's back if Katrina had been getting too close to Pierre."

21

"So do you think she buried the lead or what?" Mike asked.

"I can't figure it out. Ruth Gerst is way too smart to have brought us over there, just to drop in that fact about meeting Katrina Grooten as an afterthought."

"When she started out, I thought maybe Thibodaux had set her up to put in a good word for him. Shift some suspicion to Timothy Gaylord. But if that's the case, she wouldn't have dropped the bombshell about Thibodaux and the girl."

"I had never put Pierre and Katrina together until the salesgirl placed the sweater on Mrs. Thibodaux's back. Now suppose it goes even further, with them arriving in town within a month or two of each other, and both coming from France."

"We're going to have to get a road map to find out where these private storage rooms are hidden in the museum."

"Someone else made a reference to a 'vault' the other day."

"This case? You mean the vaulted ceilings that we saw in the Met basement?"

"No, something I saw in a report or—I know. In one of those e-mails from Katrina's friends."

"What did you do with those?"

"I've got them packed to take with me to the Vineyard tonight. I was planning to write to each of her friends and tell them about her death. See who that brings out of the woodwork."

"Val's waiting at my apartment. I told her we'd pick her up after we get Nina."

"Nina's at my place. I have to run up and throw some things in a suitcase. The traffic leaving the city on a holiday weekend is going to be a nightmare. You sure you don't want us to grab a taxi to the airport?"

"And miss the chance to be with the three of you?"

It was after five o'clock as we pulled up to the front of my building. Unlike most Manhattan apartments, mine had a driveway off the side street, where cars could actually park and wait. Mike stayed there while I went upstairs, changed into jeans and a sweater, and filled a canvas-sail bag with some casual clothes and my folder of case reports. Nina was on the phone with her office in Los Angeles and motioned with her hand that she was winding up the conversation.

"Great," she finally said, turning to me. "Just getting confirmation on the plane. Quentin's spending the weekend in Sag Harbor. He wants to fly back to the coast early Monday morning. It's all ours till then."

The UniQuest jet was sitting on the tarmac at

Teterboro, a small field for private aviation in northern New Jersey. "Wheels up?"

"The pilot's ready for us." Her suitcase was next to the front door. "It's so bizarre to be running off for a weekend without a husband and kid. Like old times, huh?"

We were inseparable during our years at Wellesley. And like the great friend that she had been, Nina continued to include me in her travels even after her marriage to Jerry and the birth of their son, Gabe, four years ago.

Mike opened the trunk for our bags, and we drove a few blocks downtown to pick up Valerie Jacobsen, the thirty-two-year-old architect whom he had been dating since the previous summer.

He double-parked and went upstairs to his studio apartment on the fifth floor so Val wouldn't have to carry the suitcase down. When Mike met her, Val had been recovering from a mastectomy and an aggressive course of chemotherapy to combat breast cancer. She had rebuilt her strength over the winter months and was much stronger than when she and I had originally met, during the Christmas holidays.

I climbed into the backseat with Nina and did the introductions when Val reached the car. "You can't imagine what a godsend this weekend is, Alex. I've been working around the clock on a proposal the firm is doing for a new baseball stadium. Mike's idea of a long weekend is having me spend even more time at the office, while he covers homicide for all the guys who've got family graduations or weddings."

"Have you ever been to Martha's Vineyard before?" Nina asked.

"No. But I understand we're in good hands. Best food, best view—"

"And thanks to Nina, best way to get there. What a luxury."

One of the key virtues of the island was its remoteness from the rest of the world. Ferry reservations were essential at this time of year, and it was more than a four-hour drive from Manhattan to reach the terminus. Direct air service varied in its regularity from year to year, but rarely started before early June. It would have been almost impossible to plan a short stay like this one without the well-timed availability of the UniQuest plane.

We got to the airport shortly after seven o'clock. The four of us went inside to find the crew and have some coffee before we took off. By the time we were ready to board, Mike had found the television and had it primed to *Jeopardy!* for the final question. "C'mon. I got one world-class architect and two shopping mavens. The category is 'Furniture.' I'll be a good sport. Everyone in for twenty bucks?"

"Double or nothing. How often do I get to do this?" Nina asked.

"I must be crazy. I don't have a shot." Mike put his money on the counter while the receptionist tried to figure out what was going on.

Trebek read the answer as it dropped into place on the game board. "'Pedestal-style circular table named for Moorish slave whose heroism gave Venetians the victory at the Battle of Lepanto in 1571.'"

I looked at Nina and laughed. "I'm clueless. You, too? How'd we get the one decorating question you couldn't answer?"

Mike swept the jackpot off the table. "I'm heading right to Patroon for a great steak dinner. Anybody have second thoughts about the weekend? 'What's a gueridon?'—that's your question, Mr. Trebek."

"Of course. Like those little round bistro tables. How'd you know?" Nina asked.

"Never heard of the tables, but Gueridon was the name of the slave who helped the Christians defeat the Turks during Lepanto. One of the most famous warrior legends of the Middle Ages. Okay, ladies, now scat. I've got places to go, people to see."

He helped us get our bags to the plane, gave us each a hug, and watched as the copilot pulled the staircase up into the plane and locked the door.

The sky was clear and, looking down, you could trace the path of the flight by the lighted towns and villages that stretched out east of New York City. The three of us gabbed the entire way, cruising into the landing strip and coming to a stop directly in front of the new terminal before the hour was out.

My caretaker had opened the house for the weekend and had left my twenty-year-old Jeep Cherokee in the parking lot. It was too dark to show Val any of the lush spring scenery on the twenty-minute ride up-island to my farmhouse in Chilmark. There was a wonderful crisp chill in the air as we stepped out of the car on my hilltop and looked up at the blanket of stars covering the sky. I was immediately calmed—as always—by coming home to this peaceful haven.

"Anybody else hungry?" Nina asked. "C'mon, Val. Let's pick our rooms. We're upstairs."

I dropped my bag in the master bedroom, with its wide vista out over the water, which was shimmering in the moonlight. The answering machine light was blinking, and I played back the message, which was Jake calling from somewhere high above the Pacific Ocean. I'd have to wait until tomorrow to speak with him.

In the kitchen, I unpacked the sandwiches and put out dinner plates. I breathed in the rich smell of the lilacs that my caretaker's wife had clipped and placed in the living room. The pale lavender and white trees surrounded the front door of the house, filling the air with that unique scent for just these last weeks of May.

Nina was the first to come back downstairs. "Not a trace of Gabe. What did you do with all his toys?"

Nina and her son, my godchild, had spent ten days with me the previous July. I adored the opportunity to spoil him, loading up on toy trucks and trains, building blocks and books of all sorts, and dozens of beach toys. "Stashed away till this summer. Coming back, aren't you?"

"I'm begging Quentin to give me some time off. Gabe says he'll be here with you, whether or not I come."

"Only thing you risk is that I keep him forever."

Nina had her elbows on the counter, watching me pour the drinks. "Jerry's ready for another one. Kid, I mean."

"You told me that a year ago. I think it's great."

"Yeah, well, it just hasn't happened. And if you like the idea so much, why don't you start giving some thought to—"

I could hear Val's footsteps on the staircase. "I'll make you a deal. This weekend? No advice. I won't spend any time telling you that you're insane to put the kind of effort and intelligence into a job that pays you a bloody fortune but has absolutely no emotional rewards, no personal satisfaction. And you keep your mind out of my uterus, okay?"

I lifted my glass and clinked it against hers as Val joined us. "What a little piece of paradise this is. I may lose myself in that down comforter, with a stack of old books next to the bed. What time is reveille?"

"Any time you want. Tired now?"

"Yes. I'd prefer to make tonight an early one."

Val soon headed upstairs to her room to read, Nina got on the phone to call home before Jerry put Gabe to sleep, and I sat down at my computer.

I opened the file that had the e-mails Bellinger had collected when Katrina Grooten's computer had been dismantled at the beginning of January. There were nine from acquaintances in Europe, all wishing her a merry Christmas and a healthy New Year. None seemed to know her well enough to have been aware that her physical condition had been deteriorating for months. Several asked what she was doing at work, and wondered whether she would be traveling abroad in the months to come. Someone named Charles, writing from the cyber address of the museum in Toulouse, gave her the local staff gossip and ended by asking about her love life.

A few of the messages were administrative e-mails from the Metropolitan, in response to circulation of the memo that Katrina had resigned: "May I remind you to turn in your keys to the ladies' room at the Cloisters?" "If you have any books outstanding from the Metropolitan Museum library system, will you please return them to the employees' desk in the main building?" "Unless you complete all the necessary steps for clearance before separating from the organization, we will be unable to process any references for future employment."

There was nothing to suggest that anyone suspected foul play at the time the young woman disappeared from the institution.

In the middle of the pile I came to the note I had been seeking. It was dated December 27 and signed with the single word I assumed to be the writer's name: Clem.

> *I was beginning to worry about you until this morning, when I got back to London after a trip home and found your message. I'm glad you have decided to go back to South Africa. You can focus on regaining your strength. I'm still curious. Have you gotten into the vault since we last spoke? I visited the grave when I was at home. It made me happy to see that he could be at rest after all this time. We are doing a very fine thing.*
>
> *Let me know as soon as you have a new e-mail address and contact information.*
>
> *Clem.*

Who was *he*? I wondered. What grave? Where? I went back up to the header and typed the screen name, hoping it would still be valid these five months later. Omydarling@Britmail.uk.co.

I took the cursor down to the subject line and wrote Katrina's name. Then I moved it to the body of the letter. Without any knowledge of the nature of their relationship, I could not imagine breaking the news to Clem that Katrina had been murdered in this first cold contact.

Instead, I introduced myself as an acquaintance of Katrina's, said that I did not know when their last contact had been, and asked whether I might get a telephone number so we could speak about her. I signed my name, without identifying my professional position, and pressed the mouse to send the message across the ocean. I composed similar e-mails to the other correspondents before shutting off the computer and going to bed.

When I awakened at seven o'clock, Val was already outside on the lawn. She was sitting on the grass at the edge of the wildflower field, sketching the poppies and loosestrife that stood defiantly upright in the strong morning breeze, against the backdrop of Menemsha Pond.

"I'm going down the road to Primo's, for coffee, blueberry muffins, and *The New York Times*. Special requests?"

"Want company or shall I wait for Nina?"

"No mother of a four-year-old is going to miss the opportunity to sleep in on an unencumbered Saturday morning. We won't see her for hours. Stay put. I'll be back in fifteen minutes."

I made the short run to Beetlebung Corner, where

the Chilmark Store was my lifeline for the season's provisions. When I pulled up and saw Justin Feldman sitting on a rocker on the porch of the general store, relishing his daily coffee and bagel while he tried to pick out the regulars from the renters, I knew I was home.

"Who's keeping the big city safe if you're up here, Alex?"

"Haven't you heard? Crime is down." He was the smartest lawyer in town, frequently sought by corporate executives for complicated securities litigation. "I've got some friends up for the weekend. Want to stop by for cocktails before dinner tonight?"

He tapped his hand against the newspaper, which was folded in half to reveal the Metro page headline. "I'm going back this morning. Got a call in the middle of the night." He pointed to the bold print, which I leaned over his shoulder to read. "Freak accident, but the Metropolitan's a client, so I've got to go deal with it."

I straightened up, bringing the paper with me: WORKER DIES IN PLUNGE FROM MUSEUM ROOF.

22

I sat in the Jeep and read the story again.

A twenty-eight-year-old maintenance worker, Pablo Bermudez, fell to his death from the museum roof while performing a routine inspection of the water tanks used in the large complex's cooling system. Mr. Bermudez had done the same checks every Friday for the past two years, without incident. The reporter described the man's death as "mysterious," citing coworkers who had seen him half an hour before the accident but had lost sight of him when he climbed outside to complete his testing. What was it, a museum spokesman wondered, that could have caused him to lose his balance on this occasion?

At the bottom of the story was an architect's rendering of the area involved. That part of the roof was flat, and enclosed by a parapet that was knee high and a foot wide. A museum guard who joined the search for Bermudez noticed his body lying on the ground a hundred feet below, at the bottom of an air shaft, in the narrow courtyard between the Chinese galleries and the wing housing the Temple of Dendur.

I raced home with containers of coffee for Val and

me. "I've got to call Mike. Want me to bring the phone out when I'm done so you can say hello?"

She was shading the two-hundred-year-old stone wall that ringed the perimeter of my property in classic Vineyard fashion, and didn't look up from her sketchpad when she spoke: "I called him earlier. He was already out working on something. I won't bother him again till he's finished for the day."

I walked up to the house and dialed his cell phone number.

"Yeah?"

"You sound like you're in the middle of something. Just saw the paper and wanted—"

"The jumper? The happily married maintenance worker with three kids, who the museum wants me to believe threw himself to his death 'cause the water wasn't quite as tepid as it should have been? Or that he suddenly developed a brain disorder that made him keel over and drop off the roof, only now his brain went *splat* all over the cement so we'll never know quite what the disorder was? Yeah, I'm at the Met, why?"

"They're reporting it as an accident, so I just wasn't sure you'd have any reason to know."

"I had just sliced into a sixteen-ounce New York strip with garlic mashed potatoes when the shit hit the fan. The Hells Angels and the Pagans were having a motorcycle prom at Roseland, which was interrupted by gunfire and resulted in one heavenly Angel making an early visit to Saint Peter. Then some yupster in Yorkville got pissed at his live-in for doing belly shots with another guy at their local watering hole, so he clubbed her over the head with a ten-pound weight from her Richard Simmons workout program when she came through the door, which only goes to prove my point that exercise can be a very dangerous thing. And then this."

"Someone from the museum call you about Bermudez?"

"You've used up your quota of stupid questions for the day. Of course not. I'm sitting in the emergency room at Mount Sinai Hospital, waiting to talk to the distraught lover of the girl who died from the fractured skull he gave her when another bus pulls in with Bermudez. DOA."

"The ambulance didn't get him to the hospital till the middle of the night?"

"He was missing all afternoon, so they were scouring the museum for him. Mostly the basement, where he usually works. Finally, after dark—about nine o'clock—they're back out on the roof when a guard has the good sense to shine his light over the edge, into the courtyard down below. Gets to this spot. Poor Bermudez had those orange neon strips on the trim of his work boots. The guy lit up like a pair of fireflies, only one leg was practically planted in the Chinese collection while the other one was in Egypt."

"Any police involvement?"

"Yeah, it was Emergency Services that had to get into the tight space and pick up the pieces. It was their bus that brought him to the hospital, which is the only reason I had a clue something deadly had happened at the museum. Then your girlfriend showed up."

"Who might that be?"

"Eve Drexler."

"Of course. She'd be taking Thibodaux's calls while he's away."

"Yeah, still in Washington. Eve came over to do damage control with Bermudez's family, and with the media."

"So what other kind of maintenance work did he do at the Met?"

"Jack-of-all-trades, like most of the guys in that department. And yes, if you're curious about whether he moves pieces that are being shipped in and out of the museum, he certainly helps. I'm on the job, blondie. I told Eve we want all his employment records for the last year. Activity logs, time sheets, work orders. I'm waiting in her office to see what they can put in my hands today. We'll talk to his coworkers and his buddies, see why he was doing a high-wire act without a safety net. Now get back to your company. There's nothing for you to do here."

I checked my e-mail to see whether Clem had responded to my message. There was no reply from him yet. I wondered what vault he was talking about, and whose grave site he had visited on his trip home. Three of the others had sent innocuous answers, wondering what my connection to Katrina was and why they hadn't heard from her in so many months. I decided not to give out any details for another twenty-four hours. I didn't want to take the chance that one of them might also be corresponding with Clem, and would alert him to my news of her death before I had a chance to explore what he meant about Katrina and the museum vault.

Now I was restless, almost sorry I had left the city. I walked off the deck and down the hillside to Val. "Can I tear you away from this vista? I can give you the Vineyard tour while Nina catches up on her sleep."

We drove down-island, away from the sheep pastures and rolling, open farmland of Chilmark. For almost three hours, we traversed the twenty-two-mile length of the island, in and out of the separate towns, stopping along the side of the road for Val to take photographs of scenes she wanted to paint later on. Sailboats tacked in the distant waters and lobstermen pulled up their traps in the local salt-water ponds.

Everything was beginning to blossom, not only the ancient lilac trees, which were everywhere, but azaleas and forsythia and beach plum. It was a spectacular time of year to be in residence, as all forms of life shed their bleak winter garb to reawaken in the deep green palette that spread from Vineyard Sound to the Atlantic Ocean.

By the time we pulled into the driveway, Nina had made a pot of coffee and was sunning herself on the deck. "No carpooling, no play dates, no sugar-coated breakfast cereal sticking to every countertop. I've forgotten what life can be like. Feeding time?"

"I left the motor running. I figured you'd have a craving for your favorite lunch."

This time, we took the ride past Beetlebung and hooked around to the little fishing village of Menemsha. There was already a line of discerning eaters who knew that the tiny gray shack on the side of the road, with two picnic tables and a couple of benches on the porch, was the unlikely place to find the best fried clams in the world. The Quinn sisters, Karen and Jackie, sweated over their deep fryers with their staff at The Bite for a very short season, from Memorial Day weekend to Columbus Day, but managed in that time to draw islanders and tourists, hardworking locals and mega movie stars, to eat the most delicious seafood on the coast.

I stood on the back of the line while Nina and Val tried to stake out the end of a table. By the time I got to the screen door to place my order, Karen was already fuming about a customer.

"Clam rage. Can you imagine? We're not even open twenty-four hours, and some guy just docked in a stinkpot is mouthing off about how long he's had to wait for his oysters and calamari. What'll it be, Alexandra?"

"We've got a first-timer with us. Definitely clams. But you better give us a sampling of everything else with it."

The three of us sat at a small table, shaded by a striped beach umbrella, and devoured the finger food in ten minutes' time.

"Ready to work off that fried stuff?" I asked, heading back to my hilltop. I parked the car and unlocked the door of the barn. I kept four ten-speeds there, since the island had miles of bike paths through forestland and along beach roads. "Val hasn't seen Aquinnah. I thought we'd do it this way."

We changed into biking clothes and mounted up, heading right out of my driveway and down the last steep, curving hill in Chilmark to cross over the town line. We rode past Herring Creek and out onto

Moshup's Trail, a stunning strip of roadway that ran along the ocean, named for a legendary Wampanoag Indian chief. We biked up to the lighthouse, then back past the Outermost Inn and down Lobsterville Road, before doubling back up the winding slope we had cruised down so easily at the start of our ride.

Nina rolled her bike into the garage. "Pooped. Done. Easy for you with your weekly ballet lesson, my friend. This is why we have cars in Beverly Hills, so we don't have to do this stuff."

"Your reward is waiting. Remember Pamela? Bodysense?"

"The massage therapist? Divine."

"A house call for three. By the time we shower, she'll be here. Then all I have to do is pick up dinner— already cooked for us—before seven."

"Explain that part," Val said.

"Larsen's Fish Market, in Menemsha, will boil and split three lobsters for us, to be picked up steaming hot from the pot. Around the corner to the Homeport, for clam chowder and a wonderfully refreshing key lime pie, and all we have to do is light the logs in the fireplace if you'd like a little ambience to go with your meal."

While Val took the first massage, I went back on-line. There were several messages for me from friends in between blind solicitations for Viagra and products to enhance the size of my penis. Then I saw the one I wanted, from Omydarling.

I clicked on the symbol that said *Read Mail* and the letter opened. Not exactly warm and friendly: "Who are you and why do you want to know?"

I typed a response. There was no point lying to Clem. I was not going to win him over any more quickly unless I revealed myself. "I'm a prosecutor in the office of the district attorney of New York County. If you give me your telephone number, I'd like to call you to explain my concern about Katrina." I included my own number on the Vineyard, in hopes that Clem would trust me enough to call tonight. I hit *Send*, noting that it was four-thirty daylight saving time, and probably five hours later where the letter was being delivered.

When it was my turn to lie down on the massage table, I was too wired to relax. Often, it was my calves that were tight, from hours of doing trial work, standing in the courtroom in high heels. Today, Pamela worked the tense muscles that had knotted themselves in my neck and upper body.

Nina had started a fire in the living room and opened the first bottle of Sancerre by the time I got back with our dinner. I emptied the chowder into a pot on top of the stove, stirred it, and left it on low to heat up.

"Be honest. I'm just telling Val that I've saved you from at least four bad romances in the last decade. Is that fair?"

"Probably five."

"Oh, yeah. I forgot about that horse's ass you fell head over heels for when we spent the week in Aspen. What a con artist he was. Alex was ready to throw out her penal law and take up life as a ski bum. I practically had to use a winch to get her down the mountain and out of town."

"I hate to think what I missed when I went for dinner if we've already raced through most of my men. Have we dissected Jake yet, or did you wait for me to do that?"

Val was quick to protest. "She was just giving me a summary of how close you two are, how long you've been friends. I envy you. I've never had the one great girlfriend who goes that far back with me."

I couldn't imagine my life without the loyalty and love of my dearest friend. We had been through every triumph and tragedy at each other's side, and I had been able to confide in her about each decision—personal and professional—that had shaped my life.

I served the soup, opened the second bottle of wine, and then brought the platter of two-pound lobsters to the table. Nobody worked the meat out of every crevice of a crustacean better than Nina. She stopped talking to savor the sweet little legs, while Val went right on asking questions about each of us between bites.

"Jerry?" Nina answered as she ripped off a large claw and pulled the meat out of the cracked shell. "Summer after our freshman year at Wellesley, I was working at the State Department. Met him at a Fourth of July party."

"And you're still together, seventeen years later? I can't think of any of my friends who are still with the guys they met in college."

"Get back to Alex. This guy is so juicy and delicious."

Like everyone else, Val tried to get gently around to

why I wound up specializing in sex crimes prosecution.

"No, I've never been raped, if that's what you're asking. I came to the office to do public service when I graduated from law school. Battaglia runs the finest prosecutor's office in the country, and I wanted to do trial work, to learn from the best.

"Sex crimes have had a terrible history in the criminal justice system of this country. Before the 1970s, the word of a woman was legally insufficient for a rape conviction, unlike any other crime. The laws of most states required independent proof—evidence from some other source to identify the attacker—before she was allowed to testify."

"It must have been impossible to win cases back then."

"Worse than that, they couldn't even go to trial unless this corroboration existed. And all that was before there were evidence collection kits. DNA hadn't been dreamed of as a scientific technique back then."

"How did it change?"

"Very slowly. But because there were district attorneys like Battaglia, who believed in devoting resources to this issue when few others did, the woman who ran the unit for fifteen years before I took it over was given the backing to do creative things and begin to change the way these crimes were viewed by the legal system and by jurors. They were really aggressive about investigating these cases as partners with the NYPD, about changing the laws as well as informing public attitudes."

"And you've stayed for so long. Doesn't it get depressing?"

I smiled as I dipped my last piece of lobster tail in the drawn butter. "The good days far outweigh the bad, Val. You can't imagine what it's like when a woman puts herself in our hands, having lived through the terror of the assault. You start with detectives like Mercer, who are not only compassionate and emotionally supportive, but who are dogged investigators with the brains and talent to get the bastards who commit these crimes.

"Now there are trained sexual assault examiners at all the better hospitals, who know what medical evidence to look for. And then you come to my team. Best in the business. The victim usually fears that the system won't work for her, or that even if the police catch the guy, he'll never be convicted. But one of the lawyers in our unit takes her through it brilliantly. We're all trained to handle every aspect of the case and make the survivor as comfortable as we can in the courtroom. And when we give her a victory? There's nothing more rewarding anywhere in the practice of law."

"Trust me," Nina said, licking her fingers as she spoke, "she's had offers. Alex has had the chance to work at some of the best legal firms in the city. And to go on the bench. She stays there because every day is a different challenge, because she really feels great about making the process work for people who've been victimized. The rest of us should look forward to going to work as much as her teammates do."

I cleared the table and filled the dishwasher while

my companions talked and Nina poured us each another glass of wine. When I got to the living room, Nina was stretched out on the floor in front of the fireplace, a pillow under her head, wineglass in her hand, and a box of chocolates by her side. "Here's my contribution to the postprandial hour. I carried these truffles all the way from California."

Val was resting on one of the sofas, and I lay down on a second one that faced the fire.

"So let's turn the tables. What's with you and Mr. Chapman?"

Val smiled and reached for a piece of candy. "He certainly came along at the right moment in my life. I'd just about reached an emotional bottom when he showed up next to me in the hospital. He was giving blood and I was getting it. I'm sure Alex has told you—"

Nina nodded.

"And now he's given me something to live for. Besides that, it's never dull. The man loves his work so much that I'm never quite sure when I'm going to have an uninterrupted evening with him. He's always on, always engaged."

"You've got a real mensch there, Val. Hang on to him."

I listened to their conversation, thinking back on how close Mike and I had become in the ten years we had known each other. I knew him as a superb investigator and a faithful friend. I had never imagined him as a lover or husband. Val deserved this happiness, so why was I feeling so envious of her tonight?

"I'm trying, Nina. I don't know if Alex told you,

but I was married for six years. An architect, too—
guy I met in grad school. He walked out on me. No
fight, no other woman, no problem he could identify
for me. It was the cancer. He couldn't handle the fact
that I lost a breast. He packed up and left two days
after I was released from the hospital."

Nina rolled over onto her stomach and stared at
the fire. "Then there's Mike. The most stereotypically
macho exterior, but his gut is just loaded with senti-
ment."

"You two have known him for so long. And he's so
close to you, Alex. How do you get him to open up
about himself?"

I didn't know how to answer her.

"I'll bet Alex could give you hours on that. She and
Mike have been through—"

I interrupted Nina before she could finish the sentence. "He'll give it up when he's ready. These last
nine months, since September eleventh, have been
devastating for him. You've been a godsend, Val. You
were so fragile when he met you, and I think it gave
him enormous strength, emotionally, to be able to
wrap himself around you, to protect you, but at the
same time to get such fortitude from *your* courage."

"Everybody I know was crushed by the attacks."

"But Mike was—well, *impotent* is the way he
described it. It was one of the few times in his life that
he couldn't make things right in the world, catch the
bad guys. And then there's all that survivor guilt. The
fact that he got out alive, and so many others didn't."
I said quietly, "Val, you were someone to save, and he
feels he helped to accomplish that."

She stood up and came over to squeeze my hand. "He did do that. He doesn't want to hear it from me, but he rescued me from wallowing in my own self-pity. I can't tell you how much I love him."

Nina propped herself up on her elbows. "Dammit. We're just getting to the good part. You fading on us, Val?"

"Yes. All that country air and biking. And a bit too much vino. See you in the morning."

Nina reached up to the glass-topped coffee table and emptied the wine bottle. "Sheesh. Just when I thought we'd be moving into the sex. Haven't you always been curious about that? I bet Mike Chapman is one hell of a good lover."

23

"Maybe you have been married too long." I pulled a throw over my legs and sipped more of the Sancerre, having opened another bottle. "You do that at work? Look at the partner in the next office and undress him when he's standing in front of you talking deals? I work with the man every day. I don't fantasize about wrapping my legs around him and—"

"Bullshit. Maybe you should. How about that first guy you worked for when you got to the DA's office? What did it take, about a minute for him to wriggle your pants off, for the simple price of an evening at Yankee Stadium, a ballpark hot dog, and a brew?" She was laughing as she tried to remember the story.

"Truce! I never did him. I just, well—"

"Fantasized all the time. See? I'm right."

I heard Val come out of the upstairs bath and close the door to her room.

Nina whispered to me, "You promised you'd tell me what happened last September when we had some time alone together. I didn't want to ask in front of Val."

I had avoided the subject every time Nina had tried

to bring it up. It was impossible to have witnessed the events of the World Trade Center attack and describe it without reliving the pain of that morning. Nina and I had lost a mutual friend who had been on one of the planes that hit the towers, and in our grieving for Eloise I had sidestepped the memories that had haunted me from the first moment of the crash.

Like most weekdays, I had gone to the office before eight o'clock, enjoying that hour or more of work before the phones started ringing and the corridors filled with lawyers, cops, and crime victims. My desk on the eighth floor of the district attorney's office faced south, causing the room to flood with light from early morning on. The twin towers stood sentinel, just ten blocks farther south, visible beyond the gargoyles of our annex building's rooftop twenty feet away, every time I glanced out the window.

I was composing a memo on my computer when the first plane hit. It sounded like a massive explosion and the glass panes behind me rattled and shook. At the time, there was only one other person—Judy Onorato—on my hallway, the executive wing of the trial division. My window shades were drawn to keep the sun's glare off the screen of my monitor.

I stood up and raised the blinds, thinking that a car bomb had exploded and knowing that the courthouses—the one in which our offices were located, and the federal building across the street—had been targeted before. There from my desk I could see the gaping black hole near the top of the north tower, less than ten blocks southwest of me. It was framed against the most exquisitely clear blue sky I had ever seen.

Judy ran into my office moments later. She had turned on the conference room television after hearing the blast. "Did you see it? A plane flew into the World Trade Center."

We both figured it was an accident, a small aircraft that had veered off course and hit the tower. By the time the newscaster was confirming that in fact it had been a large jet, it was still impossible to believe. I couldn't fathom that an entire 767 had been swallowed into the core of the tall building.

Phones started ringing everywhere on the hallway. I went to the desk of McKinney's secretary—neither he nor she was in—since her console had all the executive extensions on it.

Lobby security was the first to call, telling me that they were locking the building and no one else would be allowed to enter. The Fifth Precinct, just east of the office, was ordering the evacuation of every office south of Canal Street.

Rose Malone was the next call. "Battaglia's here. He wants McKinney immediately."

McKinney was rarely in before ten on a good day, and it wasn't even nine yet. "He'll have to settle for me." My heart was racing. The news stations were already broadcasting that witnesses were describing the crash as deliberate.

"Alex? Ignore the order to evacuate. How many people have you got over there?"

"Just two of us."

"We're law enforcement, not civilians. Whoever is here, stays here. Whatever the cops need, get it done."

I turned to look out the window at the towers. As I

watched, a colossal explosion ripped through the south tower, blasting a fireball in my direction. I dropped back into the desk chair and buried my face in my hands. The radio on the desk reported what I had not seen coming: a second plane that soared in from the south to cause the eruption I had witnessed.

Now the only street noise was sirens, a shrieking cacophony blitzing the area from every direction. Directly below the window on Centre Street, the scene unfolded like a 1950s movie about nuclear warfare. Hordes of men and women, dressed in business clothes, carrying briefcases, began to head north, some walking, others beginning to trot.

The only people moving south were those in uniform. I knew that every fire truck in the city and beyond must have headed to the towers when the first plane hit. Now every one of the hundreds of police officers assigned to the DA's office for trial appearances or preparation, each of the thousands who had business at headquarters, and all of the uniformed court officers who supervised activity in our buildings, were running to the World Trade Center. At that point in time, I couldn't begin to imagine what they would encounter. I only knew that something inside these people's heads and hearts gave them the courage to go help when everyone out of uniform was moving in the opposite direction.

I picked up the phone and started to make calls. I found my parents first, and my brothers, assuring them that I was out of harm's way. By the time I reached Jake at the NBC studio in Washington, where he was assigned for the week, he was scrambling to put a crew together to go out to the Pentagon. Another plane had just hit. "It's Bin Laden again. They should have taken the bastard out after the ninety-three attack. How are you going to get out of there, Alex?"

"Don't worry. There's a group of us here," I lied. "Do what you've got to do and I'll find you later."

The phones didn't stop ringing. Parents and spouses of young lawyers were calling to see whether they had reached work, especially those whose subway routes took them through the World Trade Center hub. Assistant district attorneys who were stuck belowground on trains or in cars that were stopped at bridges and tunnels called to offer help, not knowing when or how they would ever reach the office.

"Hey, Alex, it's Mercer. What the hell are you doing there?"

He had just been released from the hospital a week earlier, recovering from a bullet wound that had almost killed him. "There are no words to describe what's going on down here. Thank God you're grounded. Have you tried to find Mike?"

Before he could answer me I heard a new wave of wails from the street below and looked out the window. "Oh my God! It's collapsing. Mercer, the south tower is going down!" The implosion seemed to be playing itself out in slow motion, and nausea gripped my stomach as I thought of the thousands of people being buried alive under tons of concrete and steel.

"Mike's way down there somewhere. He didn't get home until six this morning. His mother called to check on him when she heard the news about the first plane. He would have slept through the whole damn thing if she hadn't been worried. He wants you out, *now*." Mercer raised his voice to bring home his point. "My orders are to hound you till you leave."

I closed my eyes and hoped against hope that Mike hadn't gotten there in time to be near the buildings when the second tower crumbled to the ground. Half the kids he had grown up with were cops or firemen, and he would follow them into the mouth of hell if he thought there was a single man he could save.

There was no need for me to argue with Mercer. The phone line went dead. I looked at the other desks and could tell by the unlighted consoles that all service had been cut off. Our provider's antennae must have been part of the communications center located on top of the World Trade Center complex.

Smoke began to drift down the corridor. The mild wind was blowing our way now, carrying with it an acrid odor and soot-filled debris. I went from office to office, shutting the windows, coughing as the downtown air spread its coating of pulverized concrete and burning jet fuel—a toxic mixture that stung my eyes and irritated the lining of my throat.

I walked to Battaglia's wing, crossing the main hallway, which was as deserted as a ghost town. Three of his executive assistants were in with him, while the other two had not been able to get near the office. They were making a triage plan for the rest of the week, already knowing that we would be at war, with no way to carry on the ordinary business of the criminal justice system. The four of us plotted with him for almost two hours, cut off from the city around us except for some of the cell phones, which worked some of the time.

When I got back to my wing, shortly before 1 P.M., the streets below, which had been teeming with fleeing workers after the two towers had collapsed, were eerily still and empty. Coffee carts had been abandoned on every corner, and empty cars were lined up in the municipal lot, many of them belonging to the officers who had sped downtown on foot. Papers swirled everywhere in the breeze, and now ashes were settling on the sidewalks and roadways.

I looked out the window and cringed at the sight of the sky without its landmark towers. What was it that was said of people who had limbs amputated? That the missing arm or leg ached forever, in some kind of phantom phenomenon. We, too, would ache forever as we looked for those towers in the sky, thinking of the thousands who would never be seen again by loved ones, and never be found.

By four o'clock, Rose came around to tell me that Battaglia had gone to meet with the mayor and governor. The police commissioner's office had sent a cop over to see her, insisting that we close our doors and send everyone home. The air quality had become so bad that if we did not leave immediately, no one could guarantee that we'd be safely evacuated that evening.

I pulled a pair of old loafers out of the back of a filing cabinet, closed up the office, and took the elevator to the lobby. Four uniformed cops from the precinct were guarding the entrance, handing out face masks to each of us as we left the building. I spoke to one I recognized, who had arrested a man who had been doing stickups and rapes in Chinatown a month ear-lier. Now he was gray from head to toe, covered in residue and reeking from the stench of burned flesh.

"I need to get down near the towers. You got any patrol cars going over? There must be something I can do to be—"

"Forget it, Miss Cooper. Nobody's getting in but cops, firefighters, Emergency Services. No amateurs. It's a war zone." He thumbed his hand northward. "Be grateful you can't go, ma'am. You'd never sleep again."

I stood at the intersection of Centre Street and Hogan Place, adjusting the mask to ease my breath-ing. How many men and women did I know who at this very moment were risking their lives—or had already given them—to try to rescue people from this cataclysmic event?

Tears had formed, and I tried to convince myself they were caused by the debris in the air. I wanted to find Mike Chapman. I needed to know he was safe. I took my cell phone out to try to dial his number but got no signal. A cop with a bullhorn shouted at me and two other pedestrians on the nearly deserted street. "Move along, miss. D'you hear me? Move it north, guys. This is a frozen zone."

I headed uptown, past empty Chinese restaurants and across Canal Street. The trendy shops of SoHo were all closed and shuttered as I continued walking across Houston Street and up Fourth Avenue. The only vehicles moving south were emergency trucks, now bearing the gold lettering on their sides from counties in upstate New York, and neighboring areas like New Jersey and Connecticut.

Two hours had passed when I reached the approach to Grand Central Terminal. As with all the landmark buildings in the city—potential targets—the small amount of traffic that was moving on the streets was being diverted away from the station. I walked east, breathing better here but exhausted from the day's emotion. As I waited for the light on Forty-fourth Street, a cop called out to me from the driver's seat of his RMP—radio motor patrol car.

"Hey, Al. You comin' from downtown? We'll give you a lift the rest of the way."

Lester Gruby had been a detective in special victims years before. He'd been flopped back to uniform when he lost his gun in a drunken brawl outside a racetrack in Nassau County.

"Still on Seventieth Street?"

I nodded and got in the back of the patrol car. "What do you hear?"

"Real bad. The numbers are staggering. Engine Forty, Amsterdam Avenue at Sixty-sixth Street? Twelve guys missing or dead. A whole company." His voice broke. "It's like that every time I check in with the desk."

"Maybe you could drop me at New York Hospital. At least I can give blood."

Gruby looked at me as though I were crazy. "Guess you haven't heard. They're turning people away from the blood banks. They're not gonna need much. People who escaped, most of them have minor injuries. Anybody in range of the buildings that collapsed, they're dead."

The police radio crackled the rest of the way to my

building, with urgent calls about falling beams and hazardous shifts in the settling structures. It was after seven when I unlocked my door. There were eighteen messages on my machine, family and friends becoming more frantic as the day wore on. I returned the most urgent calls, then asked two friends to get in touch with a list of the others for me.

Jake had left two voice mails, telling me he was fine but that the airports were closed both in D.C. and New York. He had no idea when he'd be coming home.

What was the point of sharing your life with someone if he was never available when it really counted?

I undressed and balled up my clothes to take to the incinerator later. I stepped into the steamy shower and stood beneath the head for almost five minutes, tears streaking down my cheeks as they mixed with the hot water. I got out and toweled off, putting one of Jake's business shirts on with my jeans. It was not a night to be alone.

For the rest of the evening I sat in front of the television, forgetting to eat or drink as I watched the towers fall over and over again, listening to survivors tell miraculous stories of their escapes, and watching the distraught families of women and men who had not been heard from since 8:46 A.M.

I caught Jake on MSNBC, doing remotes from the Pentagon, and later that night, from the steps of the Capitol. What does it take to be a newscaster? I wondered. I could never have reported this story—or many less tragic than it—without being overcome by emotion.

At midnight, I called Mercer for the last time that evening.

"Any word?"

"Your prayers have worked before, Alex. Just get some sleep." I didn't know then that Vickee's cousin, who worked as a secretary for the Port Authority, had been missing from the time of the second crash. Vickee and Mercer had more to worry about than my concern for Mike. I hung up the phone.

Sometime after two I must have dozed off. The doorbell awakened me at four-thirty. I had told Nina that much of the story before, and now I picked it up from Mike's arrival.

"I knew it was Mike when I was startled out of my sleep. The doormen would never have let anyone up who wasn't a close friend. When I pulled the door back, I threw my arms around his neck and held my head against his chest until he pushed me down."

I breathed in and bit my lip. "You can't imagine what he looked like. You'd never have known his hair was black. He was absolutely caked in cinders. His clothes, too—sweatshirt and pants. There were dark stains on his chinos that looked like dried blood. I told him to go in and take a shower, but he wouldn't do it. He didn't want to wash off anything from the scene, like it was sacred to him. He took me by the hand and led me into the living room. All he wanted to do was talk."

"But that's what I mean. Wasn't he going out with Valerie then? Why wasn't he at *her* place?"

"Well, I didn't even know about Val then. He hadn't told me."

"But when you found out about her, that he had started to see her last summer, don't you think it's weird that he didn't want to be with *her*?"

"I, uh, I don't think I've ever thought about it."

"Maybe nobody else knows when you're full of crap, but I certainly do."

I paused. "I guess it was two things. I don't think anybody understands what a cop puts himself on the line to do for other people—for total strangers—unless you are one. Or in my case, unless you've been with him to see him do it. You think even one lawyer, one person in a business suit, ran *toward* the towers that day?

"And the second thing, about Val, is that she had been facing the possibility of her own mortality for most of that year. Mike saw so much death in the space of those twenty hours that I don't think he could bring himself to her doorstep to talk with her about it."

"Are you just blind to the third thing, Alex? Didn't everybody in America want to be with the person, the people, they cared most about? Do you know anyone who didn't want to find whoever meant the most to them and just cling to them like the world was going to end? I brought Gabe into bed with Jerry and me and just rocked him in my arms all through the night."

"I'm telling you, Nina, you're seeing something in this that just isn't there."

She knew she was irritating me and moved on. "Did he tell you what it was like, being there, I mean?"

"Yeah. He couldn't stop talking for hours. I had seen the explosion. I had smelled death. I hadn't heard anything except sirens. The first thing he heard when he got out of his car were the screams. He's still got nightmares. You don't want to hear what he told me about, I promise you."

"Where was he when the buildings fell?"

"When the south tower went down, he was in a stairwell of the other one. There was a pregnant woman who'd been walking down from the seventy-eighth floor. A bad diabetic. She'd collapsed after she reached the tenth floor landing and was getting trampled by the others, so she crawled off into the landing and just refused to move. She didn't want to slow anyone down. She just gave up.

"Her coworkers got firemen to try to help her. Mike ran into them a few flights up and offered to carry her down. He was just coming out of the stairwell and setting her down in the lobby when the first building went. Picked her up again and didn't stop moving till he got her up to Vesey Street. His last image was the single-file line of firemen heading up the stairs, as he scanned their faces to look for guys he knew."

"Did he—did he lose many friends?"

"A cop who's lived in this city all his life? He went to funerals and memorial services for months. That's why he stayed most of that first night at the scene, helping to pull bodies out and keeping up the hopeless vigil for signs that anyone was still alive in the rubble."

"The girl you said you'd tell me about, is that the

first time since you've known Mike that he had ever talked about her?"

I nodded my head. "Her name is Courtney. Yeah. That's another reason why he probably didn't want to go to Val's, to talk about his unrequited love."

"Who was she?"

"Neighborhood kid who grew up with him. Prom queen, good student with big dreams. They dated on and off through high school. When he was a junior at Fordham, studying history, she was chasing him like crazy. She was pushing him to go to law school, make something of himself, buy her all the things she wanted.

"Remember what I've told you about Mike's dad? Spent twenty-six years with the NYPD. Then two days after he retired, turned in his gun and shield, he dropped dead of a massive coronary. Mike finished college, but he idolized his father. Took the test and went to the Academy right after his graduation."

"And this Courtney?"

"Dumped him. Broke his heart, the way he told the story that morning. She pursued one of his roommates, who went on to Fordham Law School and got a job on Wall Street. Married him five months after she walked out on Mike. Big house in Manhasset, three kids, two cars—all the material things she wanted. She told him she'd never marry a cop, she didn't want to live her mother's life. Not because of the danger of it, not because of the hard work and unpredictable hours, but because she wanted to escape from her background, her milieu."

"Did you know anything about this?"

"Never. I've known women he's dated. All very casual till now. I just assumed that he was so busy with sports and school and friends that he'd never had a serious romance."

"What happened?"

"Courtney had come into the city that morning for an early breakfast meeting at Windows on the World. She was planning a celebration for her husband, who had made partner at his firm. The banquet manager was helping her do a menu, select the wines, make the seating arrangements."

"And Mike knew she was there?"

"That's one of the reasons his mother called him. Courtney's mom called Mrs. Chapman, begging her to send Mike to try to find Courtney, to get her out of the building and safely away from the disaster scene."

"You think that's why he went?"

"Wild horses couldn't have kept him away. He didn't go because of her, but he was damn determined to try to save her once his mother gave him that mission."

"That's another difference between guys like him and people like you and me. Some creep had dumped me years ago? I wouldn't have had a charitable bone in my body."

"It didn't matter. She never had a chance, like everybody else up there."

"Mike told you all this?"

"He must have talked for three hours."

"About Courtney?"

"Sure. About how he had always felt so inadequate after she broke up with him. That there was only one thing in his life that was a passion, other than his love for her, and that was police work. That he was afraid to become involved with other women for fear they would reject him, ultimately, for the same reasons. You know the great irony of it?"

"I can guess. Here's the one event that makes everybody in the world stand up and pay their respects to the cops, the firemen, the everyday heroes who did such extraordinary things in the face of certain death."

"Yeah. And Courtney doesn't live to see him right in the middle of it all."

"What'd you tell him?"

"I didn't have to tell him anything. He wasn't there to listen to me. He just wanted to vent some of this, to let me in a little bit. Explain some of his behavior to me, in a way."

"Didn't he—um—"

I shook my head. "He needed an anchor, Nina. That's all he wanted. He was lying down on the sofa, his head in my lap as the sun came up. I was stroking that beautiful black hair. And he cried. He just cried softly until I thought he was going to dissolve in his own tears.

"'No one who wasn't there can ever understand the magnitude of this, the agony of these victims,' he kept repeating. 'I close my eyes and it's all I see and hear. I've been to hell, Alex.'"

Nina sat up and blew out the candles on the table. "No wonder Val can't get him to open up. It's something that none of the rest of us can even begin to imagine."

"She'll do fine with him. She's got the patience to let him move at his own speed. As painful as it was for him to feel so helpless that day, and as unspeakably tragic as it was, I think Courtney's death freed him from a lot of the insecurities that had plagued him."

"And you, Alex? What did it all do to you?"

"I don't even begin to know yet." I looked out at the moon, clouds dancing across its face.

"You sleeping in tomorrow?" I asked.

"Absolutely."

"When do we get to talk about you?"

"If you hadn't just yawned in my face, I would have suggested doing it now."

I embraced her and kissed her good night. "Midnight. That's a good time to knock off."

Nina walked upstairs and I went to get ready for bed. I turned off the alarm clock and shut off the lights. I was too tired to even flip through my pile of monthly magazines.

I must have fallen asleep immediately, because the neon dial on the clock showed twelve-fifteen when I reached to answer the telephone. Jake was somewhere in Australia or New Zealand, and was doing no better a job keeping track of the time differences than was I.

"There's a big empty hole in this bed, right next to me, where you should be sleeping right now. Well, maybe not sleeping, exactly. How's that for a long-distance greeting?" I was tired and intoxicated and hoping the sound of my voice would pass for sexy instead.

"What'd you have in mind, blondie?"

I rolled onto my back and felt my face redden in the darkness of my room. "Not that you wouldn't be entirely welcome, Mr. Chapman. I just wasn't expecting it to be you."

"Glad it wasn't Battaglia. You could put some men into an early grave with that offer."

"Thanks a lot. Something break on the case?"

"No." He paused, thinking I would make the connection before I did. "I just called to say good night to Val. Lost track of the time. If she's gone up I'll just let it be."

I put the receiver back in the cradle. I suppose I was glad that Mike had fallen in love with Val. I turned on my side, away from the empty half of the bed.

24

I was a bit more cautious when I answered the phone on Sunday morning. It was eleven o'clock, and we were spread out on the living room floor with sections of the *Times* while we finished our coffee.

"Alexandra Cooper?"

"Yes."

"This is Clem."

I had assumed Clem was a man, but this was the soft voice of a woman on the line. I sat up and reached for a pen and pad from the drawer of the table beside me.

"Are you going to tell me what's happened to Katrina?"

I fumbled for the right words, not certain of the nature of their relationship. "Last Tuesday, the police found Katrina's body. She was murdered, sometime last winter."

Clem didn't speak for more than a minute. "In South Africa?"

"No, here in the States. She never got back there, it seems." I did not want to give more details than necessary.

"Do you know who killed her?"

"No, we don't. The detectives are working on the case now."

Her questions flooded out in typical fashion as she began to absorb the shocking news. How did she die? Where did they find her? Has anyone tried to communicate with her father? Did I know she'd been raped? Did I know she'd been ill? It was clear to me that Clem knew as much about Katrina as anyone with whom we'd spoken.

"The reason I wrote to you, Clem, is that yours was one of the last e-mails that came through to Katrina's account before the end of last year. You had sent a message after the holidays, after you had returned from visiting your family. Do you remember what you said to her?"

Silence again. "Nothing specific. I imagine I was just anxious to know why I hadn't heard from her."

"I've got a copy of that correspondence. You do ask about her well-being, but you also make a point of inquiring about whether she had gotten into a vault. Do you recall that?"

Longer silence. It was impossible to question someone by telephone. There was no way to assess her demeanor or physical response. "Not really."

"Let me read you the actual e-mail." I went inside to my office and opened the folder.

"Look, Ms. Cooper, I'd like to be helpful. I don't know who you are or why this is useful for your investigation, but I'm not anxious to have this conversation by telephone."

Neither was I.

"Would you be willing to come to New York, at our expense, to talk to us?"

No answer.

"We can't seem to find many people who were close to Katrina. This could make an enormous difference in our work."

"I've got a job. I've got responsibilities here in London."

"Then can you suggest someone here whom Katrina trusted as much as she seemed to trust you?"

"With whom have you talked so far?"

"Museum people. Thibodaux, Poste, Friedrichs, Bellinger, Mamdouba. A kid named Zimm. Oh, and Gaylord."

"That won't do. None of them knew her the way I did." She hesitated. "How certain are you that it was murder and not an accident?"

"Someone poisoned Katrina Grooten. It was a slow death and a very painful one." I said that as firmly as I could. "I can reserve a seat for you on a morning flight from Heathrow. A detective will meet you at the airport. Have you back in a couple of days if you can give us the help we need."

"I'll need to take emergency leave from work."

"Would it help if I called your office and explained the situation?"

"That would make matters much worse, Ms. Cooper. No one at either museum must know yet that I'm coming to talk to you. Is that possible?"

"Of course. We'll put you up in a hotel. You'll be working with me and with the homicide detective assigned to the case. Now, I'm going to need your name. The complete name and address, so we can book the e-ticket. You'll just have to show your passport when you arrive at the desk to pick it up."

"Clementine Qisukqut. Let me spell it for you. It's an Inuit name."

I copied it onto the pad as she spoke the letters. "So when you told Katrina in your e-mail that you had gone home for the Christmas holidays, that was to—?"

"Greenland. My father and grandfather were both miners. Worked the zinc mines in Canada, right up near the Arctic Circle. My mother loved that old American folk song about the miner—the forty-niner—and his daughter, Clementine. I might be the only Inuit with that given name."

She was beginning to loosen up. Her chosen screen name—for the "oh my darling" of the song's refrain— became more obvious now.

"May I ask what kind of work you're doing in London?"

"I've got a job in the British Museum."

"Anthropology?"

"Not yet. You may have learned from Mr. Mamdouba or your other sources that I was let go. It's an awfully incestuous world, this museum business. I would never have landed a job here if I needed my references from Natural History. I tried something different."

"Doing what?"

"They've just reopened the great Round Reading Room in the British Museum. I've used my undergraduate degree in library science to get a position here for the time being. But they mustn't know I'm going to the States to work on a museum matter. They'd sort the whole thing out if someone were to tell on me."

"You have my word on that. Let me make your travel arrangements and get back to you within the hour. I can't thank you enough for doing this."

"I've lost a good friend, Ms. Cooper." Clem's voice dropped off. "I hadn't really worried too much at first, knowing she'd have her hands full once she reached home in South Africa. New job, readjusting to life there, dealing with her father and his dreadful illness. Has anyone told Mr. Grooten about Katrina?"

"Our detectives notified the police there, who went to the nursing home to pay him a visit and explain it to him in person. His dementia is so advanced he didn't even seem to know who Katrina was."

"It's such a tragedy, on every level. And then once I heard that she'd been here on business in January, I assumed things were fine. That she'd settle in back home and once she did, she'd get in touch with me."

The morgue would give me final word on this, but it seemed unlikely from what we knew at this point that Katrina had been abroad this winter. "January? Are you certain that she was in London then?"

"That's what one of my mates told me. Used to work in medieval art, and he'd met her in the States. Said that Katrina Grooten had spent the afternoon in a meeting at the museum with two other people from the Met. He'd seen her name signed in for a visitor's pass. I thought she'd been here briefly, on her way home. Many of the U.S. flights to South Africa stop in London. It's not unusual to break up the trip that way.

Just figured she didn't have enough time to see me on her way out."

"That visitors' log, do you think you can find me a copy for that date in January?"

"Perhaps the friend who told me about it can scout it up. I'll leave him a message now. Why don't you give me a fax number, and if he finds it he can get it to your office tomorrow, while I'm traveling?"

"That's a good idea." I knew our office would be closed, so I gave her the number at the homicide squad. "It's awfully good of you to do this."

"Of course I should be helping you." She almost whispered her response. "I'm afraid it may be my fault that she's dead."

I tried to get her to explain what she meant but she refused to talk about it.

I dialed Ed Flannery's home number. He was in charge of all our witness travel arrangements. "You're flying her in without McKinney's approval? No Saturday-night stay-over? No reduced fare?"

"Battaglia'll sign off on it, Ed. Promise. Get the best price you can. And she can't stay at one of our usual flophouses. Security's an issue. Book a room and put it in my name. I don't want her to appear anywhere on the register."

We usually put witnesses up at midprice hotels in the city, bound by our per diem budget. On more than one occasion, violent crimes had been committed in the same facilities. Push-in robberies, room burglaries, and on one recent occasion a businesswoman was assaulted in the suite adjacent to our victim's as she was followed by a serial rapist after she checked in and wheeled her suitcase to her room without a hotel bellman.

"You tell me. Our credit isn't all that good in the five-star hotels."

"I'll call the Regency. They've done it for us before." The owners were among the most philanthropic family in town, and the nicest, and I was certain they would do a favor for us in the midst of a murder investigation. Nina had stayed there last week and I was familiar with all the amenities. "And nobody would think to look there for one of our witnesses, that's for sure. Call me back when you've got the flight information."

Then I called Mike. "Our Clem? He's a she. Clementine. We're bringing her over tomorrow. Can you meet her at the Jetway when she lands at JFK and speed her through customs and immigration?"

"Don't we have some interviews to do tomorrow at the museum? And then Pierre Thibodaux. I'll get Mercer to pick her up."

"Fine." I repeated all her information for him, and told him I'd get back to him about the flight and hotel.

"What kind of name is that?"

"Inuit." I laughed. "She's from Uummannaq, Greenland."

"Oh, Eskimo."

"Used to be. Inuit now."

"Like the friggin' Washington Redskins, huh? Now it's gotta be the Uummannaq Inuits. Well, Clem'll be my first Eskimo. Don't introduce her to that sadomasochist you're prosecuting. He ever makes someone try to spell this one's name, they'd get beaten to a pulp. What are you guys doing today?"

"Val's set up on the dining room table. She's got to finish drafting some plans before we go back in the morning. Nina and I are going riding. And you?"

"Might actually catch a break. Last night was quiet so I'll stay home today, unless I get called in on something new. Took my sainted mother to Mass and now I'm good for six months."

I waited until Ed called back with firm plans before passing the travel details on to Mike.

Nina and I drove to the stables off South Road and rented horses for an afternoon beach ride.

We made our way slowly through the thickly wooded area until we crossed through the tall beach grass of the wetlands, around Tisbury Great Pond, and onto the wide expanse of pristine white sand that bordered the Atlantic for miles. Nina and I came to Black Point Beach whenever she visited me on the island, and I came often when I was here alone.

More than a decade ago, during the summer after law school when I had taken the bar exam, I was engaged to be married in a ceremony at my home on the island. I had bought the house with my fiancé, Adam Nyman, who had been a surgical resident at the University Hospital in Charlottesville while I was a student there. Nina had been with me for the week before the wedding. She was going to be the matron of honor, as I had been the maid of honor for her several years earlier. And it was Nina who had to break the news to me that Adam—the last person scheduled to arrive because of his inflexible rotation in the residency—had been killed by another driver, who side-swiped his car on the highway in Connecticut, sending it crashing over the side of an old bridge and into the riverbed below.

We came here always, Nina and I, to remember Adam and talk about the things that had made him such a unique influence in my life.

For too long, I had been unable to trust myself to become seriously involved with another man. Afraid to have my heart stabbed at its core, and by immersing myself in the intensity of my new job, I had stayed emotionally remote for several years. Now it seemed to me that Mike Chapman, for quite another reason, had functioned the same way. Perhaps that explained why we had such an unspoken understanding of each other for all this time, even though I had not known why until the morning after September 11.

Nina and I walked our horses along the water's edge as she reminded me of some of the weekends she, Jerry, Adam, and I had spent together while I was in law school. We laughed together at the memories, and I tried to suppress thoughts of what my life would have been like if Adam hadn't been killed.

"Let's stop at the market before it closes. Val and I are going to cook dinner for you tonight." Nina turned her horse around and headed for the dunes.

When I pulled on the reins to get my horse to follow her, I could see that Nina had stopped to watch me. "You know something, Alex? I realize you put a weekend moratorium on advice, but I love you too much not to tell you."

I smiled, expecting the usual lecture on working too hard and becoming too caught up in the lives of my victims.

"Jake Tyler's not the one."

My back stiffened and I sat up straight in the saddle. No wonder Nina hadn't wanted to talk about him last night.

"You know I'm right, Alex. He's too self-centered, too distant. You need a guy with more heart."

I dug my heels into the side of the horse and she carried me up and over the dunes, back toward the woods. The wind had kicked up and I could let Nina think I hadn't heard what she said as I rode away from her.

I was quiet on the short ride home, letting the car radio fill the heavy silence between us.

"Call Mercer," Val said, greeting us at the back door. "Kind of urgent. He's at SVU."

I speed-dialed the number and Mercer Wallace answered. "Thought you ought to know. Bad scene. I'm here with Vandomir. That kid you interviewed with him last week, Angel Alfieri?"

"Yeah, the fourteen-year-old. What about her?"

"Disappeared during the night. Told her old lady she was sleeping over at her girlfriend's house. Be home today. Mother calls over there a few hours ago to find out whether she'd be back in time for dinner. Finds out Angel never got there last night."

"Shit. Any ideas?"

"Mrs. Alfieri came in here all hysterical. The precinct won't take a missing person's case yet." That was typical. The NYPD usually required that someone be gone for forty-eight hours before they took police action.

"Anyone tried Covenant House? The Eighth Avenue strip? Video arcades?" Teenage runaways had a regular network in the city. The usual suspects often went straight to the usual hangouts.

"Vandomir's doing that now."

"Can't be Felix. He's still on Rikers."

Mercer was slow to comment. "I think maybe you were so busy working on the murder case that you forgot to get his bail raised. He got out before the weekend."

I cursed again. There were too many things on my plate, and dropping the ball on any one of them could be a matter of life or death.

"I, uh, I could come back tonight. I can get right on this."

"Stay put. You're the last person she wants to see. Her mother says she hasn't stopped talking about how mean you were to her since she left your office. Thinks it's your fault the kid ran off. I'm just calling to give you a heads-up. Nobody wants you back around here."

I pleaded with Mercer, even though the matter was not in his control. "Please find her for me. Find her before she gets hurt."

25

We flew out of the Vineyard at 7 A.M., as soon as the veil of fog lifted from the short runway, on Monday morning, the twenty-seventh of May, which was the Memorial Day holiday.

Quentin Vallejo was to reclaim his plane at Teterboro to fly back to California. I greeted him, hugged Nina good-bye, and walked outside the chain-link fence with Val to find Mike Chapman, waiting in his car.

He whistled a familiar Dylan tune as he opened the trunk of the car for the two suitcases. I knew it was "The Mighty Quinn," just as I knew he would change that name when he sang the chorus. ". . . when Clem the Eskimo gets here, Alex Cooper's gonna jump for joy."

"Glad to see you're in such a good mood. See if you can find a song by this afternoon that won't offend her before she even opens her mouth. You hear anything from Mercer on my missing kid?"

"Still missing. So is the perp. Felix seems to have skipped out of town as soon as his brother posted bail. He's in the wind. Vandomir's thinking maybe he took Angel with him."

My stomach started to churn. "Ouch. Won't they make an exception to the forty-eight-hour rule and put out an interstate on it?"

"Done. Detective Wallace was very persuasive, on your behalf." We were on the highway on our way into the city.

"Val, we'll drop you at your office and head over to Natural History."

"Fine," Val said. "Any news?"

"We had the entire squad, and Special Victims, running raps all weekend on museum employees from both sides of the park."

"Surprises?" I asked.

"Not too many. Anna Friedrichs is the only one of our people with an arrest. Disorderly conduct, about eight years ago. Looks like some kind of civil disobedience thing. A demonstration about some African political situation at the UN."

The sober anthropologist was an unlikely looking radical.

"And Erik Poste's been fingerprinted. No record."

"Why?"

"Routine application for a gun permit, five years back. Must have changed his mind 'cause he never got the gun or completed the application."

"Son of the great white hunter thing, I guess."

"The rest of the professional crew is just what you'd expect. Very few with criminal histories. A couple of young staffers with drug priors. But belowdecks, watch out. You got a locksmith at the Met with a long sheet for burglary, a handful of guys with petty thefts, and about five in both houses with physical assaults. We'll talk to all of them, but nothing seems to be an obvious connection."

We had almost reached Val's building when my beeper went off. I looked at the dial and saw that it was McKinney's extension. I took out my phone to return the call.

"Isn't your office closed today?" Val asked.

"Yeah, but if McKinney sits home with his wife and kids," Mike explained, "then his idiot girlfriend doesn't get to sit under his desk and give him a blow job all day. Heard they created a new position for Gunsher."

I dialed the number and pressed SEND. "Yeah, this new position's even more useless than her warrant apprehension unit, which caught nobody. Here's an acronym for you: GRIP. Gun Recovery Information Program. Firearm trafficking stuff."

"Don't the feds do that? Isn't that what the United States Attorney's expertise was?" Val asked.

"They do it better than anybody. Just meant to be a feel-good thing for Gunsher. Gives her a title with no work to do. Cops recover a gun from a perp and she calls the feds and asks them to track the piece. A chimp could do her work."

"Maybe not the blow—"

"She sits in McKinney's office all day and tells him he's a genius. Every time she comes up for air. Hey, Pat, what is it?"

"Where are you?"

"On my way to interview a witness." I could tell from the tone of surprise in his voice that he figured he had caught me out of town and unable to respond to whatever he was about to ask me to do.

"I hate to seem like I'm picking on you when you've got so much to do. How's the murder investigation coming along?"

"I didn't realize there was a gun involved in the Grooten case. Why else would you be the least bit interested?"

"I'd like you to get right over to the Waldorf-Astoria this morning before you do anything else. Ask for the head of security—Rocco Bronzini. One of your buddies is staying at the hotel, causing him big headaches. Get over there and clear it up before you drag the office into your personal life."

"I don't know what you're talking about. I don't know anyone who's—"

"Do me a favor, take ten minutes out of your day and get to the hotel."

I flipped the lid to end the conversation. "Slight detour, Mike. Val we'll drop you and then swing by the Waldorf. Was there a full moon? I didn't notice."

By nine-fifteen we were at the concierge's desk in the lobby of the old hotel, waiting for Rocco. He led us to an empty table in the Peacock Alley bar and spread out his paperwork.

"We've been stiffed for twenty-five grand. Third time it's happened. Looks like the broad is a friend of yours."

I had no idea what he was talking about.

"Hard to believe. Don't you return her calls? She leaves you plenty of messages."

"If you'd stop being cryptic and give me her name I'd be happy to help."

"That's just it. We need you to tell us who *she* is?"

"Back it up a step, Rocco. Whaddaya got?" Mike asked.

"Let's use the latest one as an example. I know part of the story now 'cause I had the guy on the phone yesterday. Call him John Doe. Businessman from Omaha, here for a sales convention. Checks in almost two weeks ago, on a Tuesday. Junior suite, reserved through Friday. Five hundred fifty bucks a night, plus some room service. Figure the whole thing should run his company about three thousand for the week, even with the best wines and biggest steaks."

"Nice boondoggle."

"Last night in town, he's drinking alone in our other pub, the Bull and Bear. Picks up a girl, buys her a cocktail. Invites her upstairs for a nightcap.

"In the morning, he's got to dash for the airport and report back to the Nebraska widget company. She's bathing in the afterglow, spread out on top of the bedsheets like she really had a good time. She's sipping on a mimosa from the breakfast tray. 'Mind if I stay an hour or so, take a bath before I leave?'"

"John's not a bad guy, right?"

"Not a mean bone in his body, Chapman. Tells her she just has to be out of the room by noon, and gives those breasts one more squeeze on his way out the door."

"What's your problem?"

"That was Friday morning. 'Mrs. Doe' waits for him to scat. She calls the front desk and tells my receptionist that they're having such a ball they've decided to stay on for another week."

"That works?"

"Hey, he's got the room on his AmEx card. The front desk calls up the credit card company, which says the corporation is good for it. And lovely Mrs. Doe is in business. You start with the five-fifty-a-night suite rate. You add a week's worth of room service—champagne morning, noon, and night, shrimp cocktail and filet mignon for dinner. Make that dinner for two, whoever the lucky guy may be. Make some charges at the shops on the concourse level, everything from clothing to a gold watch, all billed to the room. And then you walk out the door a week later."

"And Mr. Doe?"

"Opens his American Express bill at his office yesterday and almost had a stroke. Instead of three thousand dollars in charges that the company expected, he's got a bill close to thirty thousand. He calls our accounting office, and they tell him Mrs. Doe authorized the payments."

"Only Mrs. Doe never left Omaha."

"How could she? Three little Does, a whole bunch of PTA meetings and soccer games."

"So he can't cry to her, and he can't cry to his boss. So he calls the Waldorf to complain."

"Yeah, and it wasn't until his fourth attempt at a story that he got close to the truth. Someone stole his room key, must have lost his credit card, maybe it was the maid. He tried all that crap first. But this one was recent enough that when I went back to the bartender to see if there was anything he remembered from that final night's bar bill, he actually recalled watching the pickup. Mr. Doe had been there for the last call, chatting up the barkeep about the Cornhuskers' prospects for next season, till the girl came in. She worked fast, and the guy's hands were all over her within ten minutes."

"How'd you put it together?"

"Thanks to Miss Cooper, here. She and her little friend did that for me."

I looked at Mike and shrugged my shoulders.

"I pulled the last two cases we had like this. One guy from Kansas City and another from Austin. Both got beat for thirty large. There's only one common denominator. On each of the bills, the girl calls your number, Miss Cooper. Sometimes three, four calls a night. Checked with the phone company and they said it was an extension at the DA's office. Spoke with the head of the division—this guy McKinney—and he told me it must be one of your crazy pals. You want to straighten this out for me?"

He passed the telephone records to me and I broke into a wide grin. "Crazy, yes. My pal, no. Mike," I said, "this is Shirley Denzig, the woman who's been stalking me since last winter."

"You serious? How can you tell?"

"Because she called again last week. Leaving messages in the middle of the night. The squad's doing a dump on my phone. They should have results tomorrow but this beats them to it." I pointed at the times of her outgoing calls, which corresponded with the messages that had been left on my office voice mail. "All they thought they had on her was a harassment case. Looks like there'll be a grand larceny charge, too. Three of them."

"You know where we can find her?" Rocco asked.

"That's been our problem. She must have come up with this scam because she needed a place to live. She was evicted from her apartment and that's why we couldn't find her to lock her up during the winter. What's she had, three weeks under your roof in the past few months? You checked with any of the other hotels to see if they've been hit? It's pretty clever. She probably goes from joint to joint doing the same thing. One night as a hooker and then she lives like a queen for a week."

"Is she that unstable?"

"Rocco, she's not only psycho, but she's been known to carry a gun, too."

"Don't go public with that," I said jokingly to Mike. "McKinney'll put Ellen Gunsher and her new firearms unit on my case."

Shirley Denzig had been stalking me for more than half a year. She had stolen a gun from her father's home in Baltimore, and become unhinged enough that we feared that she might use it.

"You got a file on her?"

"Sure." I gave Rocco the number for the DA's squad detectives who were working on the case. They would be happy for the wealth of information the Waldorf files would add to what they knew about Denzig's recent whereabouts. "May I ask, why didn't you just call me yourself, instead of going over my head?"

"It never occurred to me. She was phoning you so often I figured you must have been a good friend of hers. The only one she's got. Why would I think she might be annoying you?"

This morning's call from Rocco would give McKinney one more reason to think that I was drowning in my own overload. I could either go down to the office and take the time to explain the story to him or get on with the day as planned. "Shall we get over to the museum, Mike?"

We walked out onto Park Avenue and back to Mike's car. "There's probably a reason you didn't tell me Mad Shirl was back in your life again. I'd like to know what that is."

"Look, I called the squad. They'll get it done. It's not like she's back after me, out on the street. You always overreact to situations like that."

"Like a woman who's walking around with a gun, thinks you're the devil, knows where you work and where you live, and you don't have a clue about how to find her? Damn right I want to know about it. Anything in that set of facts you don't understand?"

"Sorry. I'll keep you up to speed." I glanced at my watch. "So we're supposed to have most of the people who were working on the big exhibition gathered at Natural History. We're a bit late, so they should all be assembled by now."

"They opening up just for us?"

"Nope. The only two days the museum closes are Thanksgiving and Christmas. Who do you want to start with? Any ideas?"

"We're gonna go with the group approach first. See some of the dynamic between the—"

"Among them."

"That little grammatical dictator can't ever shut off, huh? You're just pissed off 'cause the group meeting left you with such a bad headache last time we tried it." He grinned at me, and I remembered our interrogation up at King's College last December.

We parked and made our way past the entrance guards, who recognized us now, and called down to the basement, where the meeting was to be held. A student led us through the maze of corridors and staircases, down past the signs that read THE BESTIARY and into a makeshift conference room in which the mostly familiar faces were talking over their coffee.

Anna Friedrichs poured a cup for each of us and pointed to seats at the table. I sat next to Erik Poste, who was examining a large woodcut, discussing it with a man I did not recognize.

"Hello, I'm Alexandra Cooper."

"Richard Socarides, African mammals."

Poste moved the black-and-white image so that I could see it. It was a stunningly detailed drawing of a rhinoceros with its singular horn, whiskered neck, scaly legs, and armored-plated body. "Can you imagine this, Miss Cooper?"

I studied the wonderful print, which seemed a perfect example for the show.

"Albrecht Dürer drew this beast. There he is, in Germany, 1515. No magazines or books or television to let him see the animal. The only rhinoceros ever shipped to Europe from Africa drowned on its way there. All he had to work from were the verbal descriptions of other people. And still to this day, no one has ever produced a better drawing of a rhino. From my collection, of course." Poste, I remembered, was in charge of European paintings at the Met.

Socarides appeared to be about forty years old, with a serious mien and a more elegant style of dress than most of the Natural History staff. He was wearing a pinstriped suit, tasseled loafers, and a shirt with his monogram on the barrel cuff. "Better than the real thing, Erik. How goes your investigation, Ms. Cooper?"

"Fine, thank you. We're making progress, slowly."

"I would think the odds are against you. I watch all those forensic shows on television. The statistics are rather appalling. If the matter isn't solved within the first seventy hours, the odds of identifying the killer drop off the charts."

"And every now and then we get lucky, Mr. Socarides."

"Yeah, the perp drools on a body and the first place we come is the Natural History data bank, making sure it wasn't one of your taxidermists getting some practice. Mike Chapman. Homicide."

"What data bank?" Poste asked.

"Not quite like your shop, Erik," Socarides said. "We've all given samples of our DNA. Have to do it so we don't confuse a new species of woolly mammoth with some hair that's rubbed off my alpaca overcoat."

Elijah Mamdouba called the meeting to order. "What you have here, Mr. Chapman, Miss Cooper, is the organizing committee of the joint exhibition. From our museum, that is myself and Mr. Socarides. From the Met," he said, pointing around the table, "you have Mr. Poste—European paintings, Miss Friedrichs—the arts of Africa, Oceania, and the Americas, and Mr. Bellinger—from the Cloisters. So we are missing . . ."

He scanned the room, trying to recall the other curator.

"Gaylord. Timothy Gaylord. Egyptian art," Mike said. "Still at the mummy congress."

"Certainly. Well, let's see if we can answer some more of your questions."

Mike let me start the conversation. We both had a preference for the bad cop role—me out of a penchant for cross-examination, and Mike because he was naturally distrustful and impatient.

"We've found out a great deal more about Katrina Grooten than we knew when we met each of you the first time. Some of her friends have been very helpful to us."

Every head in the room seemed to respond to that bluff. Mamdouba was the first to jump at the bait. "So, the people here at the museum that we spoke of on Friday, you've located them?"

"It wouldn't be wise to identify our witnesses to you, sir. We've had some contact with a few of her acquaintances in other lines of work, too. One of the things that has us a bit stymied are the differing snapshots of her personality."

"You mean before she became ill versus afterward?" Bellinger asked.

"No. There are those who have described her as very quiet and, well, meek and shy. Others have said she could be feisty if she was passionate about something. You, Mr. Poste, and you, Miss Friedrichs, each described her differently. We're trying to account for that. See if you can tell us what her passions were, exactly."

Poste spoke first. "As I told you, I only knew Katrina as a serious young scholar, a bit aloof, if I had to use one word to describe her."

"I'm the one who told you she had another side," Anna Friedrichs said, clasping her hands and leaning forward on the long Formica table. "I certainly saw it. Hiram, I think you did, too."

"Well, there was a good deal more of it in evidence before the attack. Before she was raped, I mean."

"*Raped?*" Poste asked. "You mean the killer raped Katrina?"

"No, no. Not that I'm aware of. Is that right, Detective?" Bellinger looked at Chapman. "When she was raped in Fort Tryon Park last year, leaving work."

"I never knew about that," Mamdouba said.

"Neither did I," Poste was quick to add.

Anna Friedrichs was annoyed. "I told both of you, I know I did." The two men looked at each other and were either truly puzzled by her statement or had a similar talent for playing dumb. "Erik, really. Elijah. I made a point of telling you and asking you to keep the confidence. I was afraid she'd be jumpy if she was alone in this place late at night."

This was exactly what Mike wanted to happen. He wanted to divide the united front, which was most often an artificial response to the unwelcome entry of a law enforcement agency, and find out what fractionalized these colleagues. What drew the fire in the belly of both museums, where ninety percent of their collections lay under wraps?

"It's clear Katrina had a long-standing interest in medieval art. That was her training and education. That's what she came to the Met to do. And yet here she was, leaving New York and returning to Africa in December to pursue an entirely new direction."

"If I may say, Miss Cooper"—it was Mamdouba speaking,—"I believe it was her father's health that was the main reason for her decision to go home."

A bit late for that, I thought to myself. Something else had to be at the bottom of her change of focus. I counted on Clem to help us figure that out later tonight, but we also needed to see what these curators thought.

"We haven't heard from you, Mr. Socarides. Tell us your impressions of Katrina."

He had seemed content to be resting his head against the back of his chair, letting the others take the lead. He sat upright, slowly. "Never met her until we started to put the show together. Loved her animals, the girl did. Endeared herself to me."

"What was it about them that you think attracted her?"

"Who doesn't like animals, Ms. Cooper?" He became animated, wagging a finger at me. "Now on your television crime shows, *that* would be your serial killer. Someone who hated furry creatures, tortured them as a child. Isn't that always the way to find the killer?"

"I'm talking about the victim for the moment. What was it she liked about your animals?"

"This exhibition is all about animals, young lady. Katrina found examples of dozens of symbolic beasts from her medieval art, and then I introduced her to the real ones. Okapi, elands, Grevy's zebras, reticulated giraffes."

"Dead ones."

"Well, obviously, Mr. Chapman. This is a museum, not a zoological society."

"The ones you stuff for display?"

"Precisely."

"She ever watch you—or your staff—prepare one of those mountings?"

"No. Not that I'm aware of. The beasts and the bones, she liked both of those. I don't think she liked the whole process of using the skins to re-create the animals. A bit too Hannibal Lecter for her, I'm sure."

"What do you mean by 'the beasts and the bones'?"

"Well, Ms. Cooper, Katrina loved the animals. They were all African, keep in mind. Maybe that's what she liked. And she had a real fascination with the bones. Never tired of looking at the bones. Wanted to know everything I knew about the bones."

Millions of them, as I recalled. Not so unusual, I thought to myself, for a woman whose specialty was funerary art.

"And I must interject, Anna," Socarides said, before he slumped back into his seat. "Nobody ever told me the girl had been raped. I don't know what you're making such a fuss of it for."

"I never claimed to have told *you* about it, Richard. I had no idea she was so taken with your, your . . . beasts," she said dismissively. Anna was determined to show off her close relationship to Katrina. "In fact, I had no idea you'd paid her a bit of mind outside this room."

It was ordinarily my habit to interview each witness alone, which we would attempt to do later on, but Mike's idea to bring the group together brought out talons on each that might not have been visible one-on-one.

"You seem to think you had the market cornered on her friendship, Anna. She was actually quite surprised to learn how weak the Met's history was in your very own specialty, African art."

"Katrina was hardly what I would call African, would you, Elijah? She was Dutch. Boer. About as primitive as Erik." Anna laughed at her inside joke.

"Are you Dutch, too?" I asked Poste, remembering that Ruth Gerst had told us his father was a great explorer and hunter who had taken museum trustees on African safaris and shoots.

"Yes, by birth. But we moved here when I was a child, and I grew up in the States." He seemed embarrassed by the petty squabbling among the museum staff members.

"What did Mr. Socarides mean when he said your department at the Met was weak?"

Anna went on, "Until very recently in museum terms—the late 1960s—the Metropolitan had no interest in what we call the primitive arts. We were terribly underrepresented in my field. The trustees at the time looked on all of it as sort of airport art— Mayan sculptures, African masks, New Guinea ancestor poles. It wasn't until Nelson Rockefeller gave his entire collection to the museum that we began to be competitive in this field."

Mamdouba's irrepressible grin reemerged. "Ah, tell the truth, Anna. Most of your distinguished trustees think all these aboriginal faces belong in *our* museum, don't they?"

Bellinger and Poste had to smile along with him. But Anna snapped, "These are works of art, Elijah, every bit as beautifully crafted as the sculptures of the ancient Greeks. In your museum they just become cultural specimens, totem poles stuck next to igloos and canoes."

"I'm glad Timothy Gaylord isn't here," Socarides said. "He'd be apoplectic hearing you compare some of those drooping-breasted *National Geographic* figures of yours to his precious Egyptian carvings."

Mamdouba bowed his head in my direction. "This is a centuries-old dispute, Ms. Cooper, not likely to be resolved today. Miss Friedrichs and I often battle for acquisitions. My colleagues and I believe that primitive objects are much better respected under our aegis."

Friedrichs walked to the coffeemaker and refilled her cup. People shuffled papers and pretended not to notice the silence.

Mike Chapman tried another topic. "I'm gonna ask you to do some word association now. What do you think of when I say the word *vault*? What does it mean in your work, or in the museum?"

Friedrichs didn't want to play anymore. She looked straight ahead and ignored the question. I thought of her disorderly conduct arrest and imagined her planted in the middle of the street with her picket sign in defiance of police instructions to move on.

Erik Poste leaned forward, his hand on his chest. "I suppose I can give you the definition, Detective. It's an architectural term, illustrated quite often in paintings. In fact, you both saw vaulted areas the day we took you around the basement of the Met. Vaults are a series of arches that radiate from a central point, used to make a roof in a building's interior."

"In my business, that's what the medievalists called burial chambers. They were mostly underground, in churches and cathedrals, so they were called vaults," Bellinger said.

"Funny how it conjures such a different image to me," Socarides said. "Those are our storage cabinets. I've got my assorted mammal bones in tusk vaults and boar vaults and shrew vaults. But then, Erik's my expert on museum history, if that's what you're looking for. Grew up in these places—it's in his blood."

I thought again of our conversation with Ruth Gerst about Poste's father. Erik might be the one to know something about private vaults.

"I understand that there are some personal storage rooms that wealthy contributors were able to keep in the museums." I looked to Mamdouba. "Might you have a list of those names?"

"Not here, madam. We've had no such thing that I'm aware of." The smile had vanished and he was quite firm in his denial.

"Are you saying you're not aware of any, or that there aren't any? I'm going to ask you to check with President Raspen and consult your archives. Surely, Mr.

Poste, you know something about that tradition."

Everyone turned to stare at Erik Poste. "I, uh, I know they've been rumored to exist at the Met. Three or four of them at most."

Mike wanted to prove to the group that he had this on better information than rumor. "The Arthur Paglin vault. Others like that?"

Poste shrugged his shoulders. "Paglin had the great Egyptian collection. Gaylord would know more about that than I do."

"What became of your father's collections?" I asked Poste, who had pursued such a different line of scholarship from Willem, as Ruth Gerst had described it to us.

"You know about him, do you?" He looked pleased that I was familiar with his father's work.

"Not very much. But I've heard he made great contributions to this museum."

"I was twelve years old when he died, Miss Cooper. Killed by native poachers when he was leading an expedition. Greedy and ignorant men who took his life simply because he stood between them and some ivory animal horns. Killed because of the power of their superstition. My older brother, Kirk, remained on, in Kenya, doing my father's work. He'd be the one to ask about my father's contributions."

"You didn't stay in Africa?"

"I was sent off to boarding school in New England. My mother's health was quite fragile. She was hospitalized for long spells while I was growing up. I developed a preference for art, which was Mother's influence."

"Are any of your father's things here, in the Natural History museum?"

Poste extended his hand, palm upward, deferring to Mamdouba. "Oh, surely. Many, many of our finest African exhibits were brought back to us by Willem. I can arrange for you to see a catalog of the items, if you wish," Mamdouba said.

Mamdouba played to Chapman now, smiling a bit too broadly. "I imagine by the time you're through with this investigation, you'll be asking me to sign you up for one of our safaris, Detective."

"Don't count on it. I'm a Discovery channel guy. The only safari you'll get me on is in my Naugahyde chair in front of the television set. No mosquitoes, no wild boars, no hungry cannibals. Just tell me if you've got any vaults down here, okay, sir?"

I was ready to break up the group and take them down the hall, one at a time, to an empty lab that had been set aside for us. Mike wanted to ask each of them whether they had known Pablo Bermudez, the worker who fell off the Met roof, and I had scores of questions about their contact with Katrina.

"Any of you done any foreign travel this year?" Mike asked.

Each one of them nodded. He threw out a random sampling of foreign cities, then got to London. Both Bellinger and Poste responded that they had been there.

"When did you go, and with whom?"

"Can't be sure of the date," said Erik Poste. "Late March, if I'm not mistaken. Alone. I'd been to an auction of great Masters in Geneva and stopped there on the way back. Did a bit of museum business at some galleries. Twenty-four-hour layover."

"And you?"

"January," Bellinger answered. "Pierre Thibodaux took me along. The British Museum was thinking of deaccessioning some medieval objects. He wanted my opinion. Spent an afternoon there with him looking them over."

"Just the two of you on the trip?"

"And Eve. Eve Drexler. Just along for the ride, as far as I could tell. A perk for being a loyal soldier."

I put down my coffee and stared across the table at Bellinger. "Museum security's pretty tight these days. Do you recall signing in and showing any identification to be admitted?"

Bellinger took a deep breath and closed his eyes. "Probably so. Sure, sure."

"Do you remember how Eve Drexler signed in?"

He ran a finger around the rim of his mug. "I haven't the faintest idea. There was nothing particularly significant about—"

There was a knock on the door before Mark Zimmerly opened it and came in.

"Excuse me, Mr. Mamdouba, but I need to speak with you immediately."

Ever careful of his manners, the curator tried to calm the agitated young man. "In just a minute, Zimm. Step outside and I'll join you shortly."

Zimm hesitated before speaking, but looked to Chapman for help and decided not to wait. "You got a third-grade class from Scarsdale, sir. They're freaking out up there, the kids are screaming bloody murder."

Mamdouba stood up and moved briskly to the door, hoping to cut off the next sentence before any of the guests heard whatever the problem was.

"What is it, Zimm?" Mike asked. He beat the older man to the exit, ready to help.

"It's in a diorama, in one of the display cases on the main floor. It's—it's . . . an arm. A severed human arm."

26

The heavily tattooed upper arm of a large man was on the floor inside the glass case.

In the background, a halo of clouds floated over Box Canyon, above a purple haze that set the background for the jaguar diorama. The three carnivorous felines sat self-satisfied among the cacti and shrubs as they had for fifty years, but now they looked as though they had just enjoyed a fresh meal.

The slow-moving security guards had closed the gallery and ushered the frightened schoolchildren out of the building.

Mike and I stood in front of the glass, while Elijah Mamdouba and Richard Socarides had stepped back from the exhibit into the dimly lit corridor. Socarides was doing the curatorial version of "not my job."

"Elijah, African mammals is upstairs. I've not got a thing to do with the Americans. I couldn't begin to tell you what's gone on here."

"Looks like that's got some age on it," I said to Mike, bending over with my hands on my knees. "Like it had been tanned, almost, and preserved. Like an animal hide."

He had stepped away briefly to call his lieutenant and ask for the Crime Scene Unit to come over to do a run.

"Mr. Mamdouba, how do you get into these things, these dioramas?"

"Quite difficult, Mr. Chapman. Most of these are sealed. It's really a big production to get inside. When we do restoration, or when we touch up those wonderful background paintings, we have to remove the entire plate-glass window."

"I'm a bit more familiar with these, Detective. If Elijah doesn't mind. There's a door on the side of each diorama. Locked, of course. But above each one is a catwalk."

"A catwalk?"

"Technicians have to get inside every few months to change the lightbulbs. We've had terrible problems with lighting, you see. Fluorescent bulbs damaged many of the animals. Faded my poor zebra stripes terribly. It's narrow up on top, but that would be the way to drop something in with the animals."

"And the keys to those doors, who would have them?"

"Everyone who works in restoration, most of the tech guys, and there are probably a few masters floating around among curators and even custodians." Socarides reached into his pocket and came out with a chain, isolating a small key. He started to walk to the bronze door alongside the diorama.

"Whoa, buddy. We got a larceny here. Stolen limb, I suppose, and maybe a trespass. I got a couple of guys on the way over here to dust for prints and retrieve that arm from the case. Let's not be putting our paws on anything just yet."

It took almost an hour for the two detectives to arrive at the museum with their boxes of equipment. They set about meticulously examining the doorway before one of them climbed up to the catwalk. It was set fifteen feet above the diorama, so they ended up calling for a custodial crew and directed the removal of the window.

I waited for them to remove the arm with their gloved hands before trying to look it over.

"This guy's got some miles on him," Mike said. "Glad to know we didn't screw up the commissioner's body count overnight."

A small sticker was taped to the skin on its underside. Mike read from the tag: "68.3206."

He turned to Mamdouba. "Looks like a museum exhibit. Year and acquisition number."

The director of curatorial affairs seemed to be relieved. "That's a Metropolitan object. It's not our tracking system. What a cruel joke this is."

"They got human arms in an art museum?"

Mamdouba shrugged his shoulders.

I wrote the number on my legal pad. We would be seeing Thibodaux later today. I took Mike to the side while the detectives got the information they needed to complete their paperwork from Mamdouba.

"What's your guess?"

"Sometime between the close of business yesterday, and admission time this morning, some clown decided to feed the jaguars. Is it an unconnected bad joke? Or a message for the two of us? Maybe Katrina's killer is trying to throw us off guard. Depends on who has control of this grotesque piece of art. Must have been lifted out of some museum storage area."

"If her killer works here, maybe he's trying to get us to look harder at someone at the Met," I suggested. "Or vice versa. Shake us up a bit."

"He shook Mamdouba, all right. Human body parts, no matter how ancient and laminated, can't be good for the crowds."

We waited until the severed arm had been photographed and vouchered as evidence before making our way back down to the underground quarters of the exhibition. It was after two o'clock, and none of the members present for our morning meeting had remained to finish the interviews.

Zimm was around the corner in his office. "Sorry I sounded so freaked out when I interrupted your meeting this morning. You wouldn't have believed the commotion upstairs. There's a message for you to call your office, Ms. Cooper."

I looked at the slip of paper. "Laura called. Good news."

Zimm offered his desk phone and stepped out of the room with Mike, who was suggesting he keep his ears open to see what the scoop would be about the arm in the diorama.

I dialed Laura. "Just a minute, Alex. I'll patch you through to Ryan."

A moment of silence, then, "Alex? It went like clockwork. My Internet perv, Frederick Welch III, is now in custody."

"He went for the whole thing?"

"Showed up at the museum right on time. Met the undercover at the horse's ass, if you'll excuse me. Right behind the rear end of Teddy Roosevelt's steed, on the Central Park West steps. Opened up his overnight bag to show her that he had brought some weed and some pills with him—to relax her, for the first time—and walked right around to Seventy-seventh Street to register at the hotel."

"And you got it on tape? I mean, saying that she's thirteen?"

"She was perfect. While they're walking, she says to him, 'I lied to you. I'm really not thirteen. I won't have my birthday for another two weeks. I'm still only twelve.' He gave her a big squeeze and told her that was even better. He said he'd never made love to a twelve-year-old before."

"How'd he react when they slapped the cuffs on him?"

"Whimpered a bit. Didn't start to cry until Harry told him they had to do a lineup. Naked. They wanted to match his penis to the picture he sent on the e-mail. Bawled like a baby. Had to admit it really wasn't a self-portrait. Oh, Alex, I hope you don't mind. I asked public info to give the story to Mickey Diamond, for the *Post*. He says unless you solve your homicide case by midnight, I'm good for page one."

"Much as I'd like to, I won't be stealing your ink. What's he got?"

"A mug shot of Freddie, with a banner that mimics the AOL greeting when you log on to e-mail: YOU'VE GOT JAIL!"

"I like it. Good job, all of you. Oh, Ryan, would you tell Harry I may need to beep him later? We've got a witness coming into town who had an on-line relationship with our deceased. I may need a court order to search some of the museum employees' hard drives, and it could get more urgent by tonight or tomorrow."

"I'll tell him to expect you."

Mike and I trudged up the stairs, through the hallways, and out onto the brilliantly sunlit sidewalk south of the museum. "You could forget what time of day it is in there. No windows."

"Don't we need to fortify ourselves before Thibodaux? I'll buy you a burger."

We took the transverse across Central Park at Eighty-first Street and drove up Madison. At the corner of Ninety-second Street, we parked and went into "92" for a late lunch. I called Thibodaux to make sure that he was in. A woman answered, not Eve Drexler, and confirmed our appointment.

By three-thirty, we had been admitted to the director's office. "I'll have to get back to you about that later," he said to someone, hanging up the telephone. Then to us: "A bit humbling to be doing a job search after landing this position."

"We heard about your resignation last week, of course. We've got quite a way to go with our investigation and we're going to need—"

"My departure from the museum has nothing to do with your murder case, Miss Cooper. Despite what the newspapers say. And I have no plans to leave town."

"You already made yourself unavailable to us last Friday by going to Washington for the weekend. Perhaps we should begin by asking for a copy of your schedule."

"My trip to Washington was canceled, Miss Cooper. I never left the city."

"But—but Ms. Drexler told us—"

"Well, Miss Drexler was mistaken. I was supposed to deliver the keynote address at the annual meeting of the American Association of Museums. It was recommended to me the night before, as I was packing to leave, that because of the hint of *scandale*, as we say in France, it might be best if I developed a mild flu. The twenty-four-hour variety."

"So you didn't go to Washington on Friday?" I asked, thinking of Pablo Bermudez and his fall from the museum roof.

"I took the advice I was given and stayed at home."

"Did you come to the museum at all?"

"I slipped in early to pick up some correspondence that I could take care of from my apartment, but I really didn't want to deal with anyone here. This is all a bit embarrassing and uncomfortable for me. I wasn't anxious to be seen."

Neither did whoever pushed Bermudez to his death.

"I'm sorry Ms. Drexler felt it necessary to lie to us."

"I'm afraid she did that at my direction. I was not expecting a call from either of you. I just meant for her to hold to the original story. Not that the museum organization would get any press attention, but there would be less opportunity for the piranhas from the media to feed on, if they heard I had backed out of my speech."

"The man who died on Friday—"

"Another unforeseeable tragedy. Very bad timing for me."

"And for him," Mike said.

"Did you know Mr. Bermudez?" I asked.

"He was around these offices quite a bit," Thibodaux said, motioning in a sweep with his hand. "One of the most reliable workers here, so we used him a lot to help oversee the movement of fragile objects and paintings that had to go from place to place. Bright young man. I can't tell you I had any more personal relationship with him than that."

"Mr. Thibodaux, would you mind telling us the reason for your resignation?"

He stood at the window looking out over Fifth Avenue, his jaw clenched and his stance rigid. "It has to do with an inquiry, an antiquities dealer who's about to be indicted by your federal counterparts."

"What for?"

"There were a number of laws passed in the last twenty years, in countries all over the world, preventing the sale of ancient objects that would take them out of their respective countries. Our Egyptian man, Timothy Gaylord, for example. He can't acquire anything unless we know it was taken out of Egypt before 1983."

"What's the purpose?"

"Bleeding hearts argue that rich nations like ours are robbing the poorer ones, the ancient civilizations, of their cultural patrimony."

"Aren't you?"

"You think things are safer when they're left at home in some of these impoverished, politically unstable environments, rather than made available for the world to see and learn from, Detective? You think the Taliban's destruction of those magnificent Bamiyan Buddhas in 2001 was better than moving them out of Afghanistan? Imagine the risk some of these works of art are exposed to when left in their natural habitats."

"And the indictment?" I asked.

"This dealer had a habit of getting some unique treasures out of very undesirable locations."

"Smuggling?" I thought of Katrina's file that we had retrieved from Bellinger's office—the flea market fiasco—and how appalled she had been that Thibodaux had arranged to have the small ivory piece smuggled out of Geneva.

"Am I under oath, Miss Cooper?" He glared at me. "This dealer, they say, went so far as to create phony collections. Made up a fancy tale about an Edwardian collector in London who had owned the antiquities in question since the 1920s. Even baked the descriptive labels of the objects in an oven to give them some age."

"And you bought them."

"With a good number of other museums bidding on them. Yes, we actually bought some of them. I mean, think of it, Miss Cooper. Had this kind of legal reasoning taken hold a century ago, the museums of this country would be pitiful places. Wouldn't be a blessed thing in them."

"Is this about export policies or is it about theft, Mr. Thibodaux?"

"I'm stepping down, Miss Cooper. I'm hoping, quite frankly, that there will be a place for me back at the Louvre."

"Shit, what an advantage your paisanos had. They've been stealing for centuries. Napoléon wiped out the Egyptians in his 1789 campaign. Brought boatloads back to France." Mike removed a Polaroid photo of the severed arm that the crime scene guys had taken for us. "This appendage has one of your acquisition tags stuck on it. I'm sure it's mismarked but I'd like you to see it."

Thiboudaux looked at the mottled limb. "Some-one's having a bit of sport at your expense. President Raspen must be wild."

"Why?"

"Actually, it was my idea to send this over to be used in the bestiary exhibition. A most unusual treas-ure for a great art museum like the Metropolitan."

Who figured Thibodaux for a loony sense of humor? "A human arm? A real one?"

"I can't tell you how we fought to get this piece. It came from the Hermitage, which had a stunning col-lection of Scythian objects."

"Scythian? I'm not familiar—"

"It's a remote mountainous region in western Siberia. They left great treasures of solid gold. Much of it was appropriate for the joint show because they were known for their decoration of mythical beasts. The Russians wound up with all this art, which is lit-tle known by the rest of the world."

"And you brought it here?"

"My predecessors did, Montebello and Hoving. The Scythians were great fighters and kept herds of Mongolian ponies. So there were wonderfully worked leather saddles and gilded horse paraphernalia."

"The arm, sir, what the hell is that doing here?"

"These people lived in the Altai mountains, where the temperatures were quite frozen in the winters. Birds, animals, entire human bodies were preserved for centuries, more perfectly than in the dry deserts of Egypt."

Once again I was thoroughly confused. Would Katrina Grooten have been in such pristine condition because she had been in cold storage, or a warm, desicated crypt? And why was it that all these cultural mavens knew as much about safeguarding bodies as a forensic pathologist?

"This is the arm, Detective, of a Scythian warlord, probably third century A.D. Somehow, they preserved these human hides, just like animals." He put the photograph down on the windowsill and pointed at the serpentine tattoos that covered the deep brown skin. "See the combat motif, Mr. Chapman? Two stags facing off, muscles taut and legs poised to leap. And there, an eagle swooping down to grab its prey in its beak."

The mere mention of the word *warlord* had caught Mike's attention. "This guy's got something to teach all these tattoo-crazy broads today. If I see one more shamrock or rose or heart on the cheeks of somebody's ass or hiding in their cleavage—I mean, so pedestrian."

Thibodaux glanced up at Mike.

"I'm not talking romance or my personal life. I'm talking dead bodies I come across. This one's got style. So where was it?"

"It left the Met months ago. You ought to check with Mamdouba's people. Someone must have pinched it out of the exhibition stock to stir up trouble over at Natural History."

"Who knew it was there? Any of your people on the committee?"

"All of them, I would think. But all of Mamdouba's folks, too."

Thibodaux seemed to have charmed himself with his presentation of his knowledge of Scythian art and history. He was more at ease than when we had arrived.

Then Mike took another direction. "We found out an interesting little fact on Friday that we thought you could help us with."

The director tilted his head and nodded, confident he had gained Mike's respect.

"Katrina Grooten didn't exactly have a formal send-off. Nobody got to go to her apartment and pick out her favorite suit or little black dress to be laid out in. It was a kind of come-as-you-are deal, you know?"

Thibodaux tensed again.

"She had on some cheap woolen slacks and dingy old underwear. But the odd thing is—and Ms. Cooper here is my expert on retail—she had on a cashmere sweater. Hand-knit, high-end, ritzy Madison Avenue label. So we check it out. Is this just a coincidence or do you know somebody named Penelope Thibodaux?"

"My late wife, Chapman. I assume you were smart enough to make that connection yourself." He was angry now, almost spitting out words in Mike's direction.

"So you didn't know the Grooten girl, but your wife did?"

"My wife never met her. Look, I didn't recognize that photograph you showed me the first day. Surely you understand that. That—that—death pallor and, how do you say, that morgue shot, it didn't look anything at all like the young woman who worked here. I swear to you I wasn't trying to mislead you. And even then, I didn't remember her name. The last time I saw Ms. Grooten, she looked so full of life, so—"

"When was that?"

"Believe me, I've tried very hard to recall the circumstances."

"The sweater, you wanna tell us about that?"

"That would have been last summer. Late in August, perhaps. Eve can give you a date. It was at my apartment. Not what you're thinking, Detective. A cocktail party, a celebration for some of the trustees."

"And Katrina, why would she be at something like that?"

"We were courting donors for the Cloisters, trying to raise interest—and money—for some items coming on the market. Bellinger put the whole thing together. I'm sure it was his decision to include staff. And to decide which staff."

"Why at your place?"

He pointed out the window. "The apartment we live in—excuse me, I live in—is owned by the Met. It's

a penthouse on Fifth Avenue. We do a lot of the enter-
taining there. On this particular occasion it was a very
warm night. I had the caterer set the bar up out on my
terrace. The view is quite magnificent, looking over
the museum and the entire park. I remember that a
girl, an employee, that is, was cold. Actually shiver-
ing."

"But you said it was warm."

"That's what was so unusual. Everyone else was
enjoying the chance to be outside. I noticed how
uncomfortable she was."

I thought of the symptoms of post–traumatic stress.
This would only have been two months after Katrina's
brutal assault. I thought also of the signs of arsenic
poisoning that Dr. Kestenbaum had described. Chills
had been one of them.

"I offered her the opportunity to go inside, of course.
But she felt that Hiram Bellinger very much wanted her
to be part of the conversation with the trustees, since
she was so knowledgeable about the pieces." He fidgeted a bit. "I told her that I still had some of Penelope's
clothes in the apartment. I'm afraid I still hadn't
absorbed the finality of my wife's death."

"So you took her into the bedroom?"

"Sorry to disappoint you, Detective. No. I went in
and found this sweater in one of the drawers. Quite
frankly, I didn't know what it was made of, if it's the
value that concerns you. I brought it out to the young
woman and told her I'd be pleased if she kept it. It
would be a favor to *me*, since Penelope was—well—
gone."

He thought for a moment and then went on, "I

believe I inquired about whether she felt well enough to stay on, and if she had a way home. If I'm not mistaken, she lived near the Bellingers and told me that Hiram would see that she got home safely."

"You knew, of course, from Hiram that Katrina had been raped leaving the Cloisters one night last June?"

"That was the girl? But I never put that together." Thibodaux was agitated now. "I have a vague recollection that he told me about some incident in the park. That the employee in question didn't want the police involved, didn't want anyone to know what happened. What was I to do, Miss Cooper, violate her wishes? No, I had no idea that was Miss Grooten."

Mike was practically in the face of the director. "How about back at the Louvre? Want to tell us about your trysts with Katrina in Paris or Toulouse?"

"You've got a wonderful imagination, Chapman. But you're out of line. Dead wrong."

Mike opened his notepad and read the date, almost three years earlier, that Grooten had been hired at the Metropolitan. "That's exactly two months after you settled in here, isn't it?"

"There's always a turnover of staff with a new director. Check the numbers, you'll see that my predecessor took dozens of young scholars with him to his new posting. I'm sure there were many openings around the time of my arrival."

"And trustees who have told us they saw Katrina with you, at parties at the Louvre?"

"*Fou!* I would say to them in French. Completely mad."

"They would be wrong?"

"Look, Miss Cooper, can I tell you that Katrina Grooten was never at the Louvre, when you tell me she was working in France at the time? We had receptions there—two, sometimes three nights a week. Openings of exhibits, receptions for artists, historical celebrations. I had to be at every one of them. Was she ever there? I don't know. Was she with me? Certainly not. I would like to know who is telling you this rubbish. I've got enemies, for sure—"

"This information came from a supporter of yours, actually," I said. "That's one of the reasons I credited it."

Mike cut in, sensing Thibodaux was on the ropes. "Is that information more or less reliable than the fact that when you went to London in January, to the British Museum, you were seen there with Katrina Grooten?"

He reddened and shouted at Mike, "*Seen* there, Detective? I seriously doubt that."

"I'll make it crystal clear for you. I can prove that you signed in. And I can prove that Hiram Bellinger signed in with you. And even though I think my favorite medical examiner is gonna tell me Katrina was all boxed up in her sarcophagus, I can prove that you were cavorting around that museum with someone who was using her name. Dead girl walking?"

Thibodaux circled around Mike and sat in the chair behind his desk. "Hiram Bellinger's plan. Foolish and quite unnecessary."

"Which was?"

"The pieces we had gone to examine were French.

Medieval French. We had a similar problem with
their provenance, so it was going to be a little dicey
to bring them back. Bellinger figured that if we
decided to buy the collection, it would be wise not to
do so in either of our names. To protect our reputa-
tions, of course."

"The girl's reputation didn't matter, right?"

"Face it, Detective, she didn't have one. She was
just a beginner in this business. In her case, it could
have been the harmless mistake of a young graduate
student. Wouldn't ruin her career, as it could ours."

"So you're telling us that Bellinger did this, knowing Katrina was dead?"

"Absolutely not. He assured me it was safe to do
because she had just resigned from the Met and left
the country a few weeks before our trip, at Christmas.
She had mailed back her identification tag, as
required, which was all we needed."

"And Eve Drexler used it, to get into the British
Museum with you and Bellinger."

"Drexler's twice her age. Didn't anyone check the
photograph?"

Thibodaux's arrogance was unquenchable. "Now
who do you think would bother to look at her plastic
tag once they recognized me? There I am, director of
the Metropolitan Museum, bringing two members of
my staff to an executive meeting."

Chapman knew now that Thibodaux had been
lying the first time we met him, when he looked at the
photograph of Katrina but denied knowing who she
was. "That title, director of the Met—the title you
used to have—you think that cloaks you with the

power to do whatever you want, say whatever suits you?"

Thibodaux ignored him. But what did his lies conceal? Some knowledge of Katrina's fate, or just a strategy to keep himself out of a brewing scandal?

I thought of Katrina's letter of resignation that Bellinger had showed to us when we were first in his office. The single initial of the signature had appeared to be so easy to imitate.

"Did anyone else impersonate Ms. Grooten after her disappearance last winter?"

"Her resignation, Miss Cooper. We believed that she had left us voluntarily. She hadn't gone missing, so far as we knew. And no, I'm not aware of any other instances."

"Her employee identification, what became of that?"

"Miss Drexler would know. Or perhaps Bellinger. I never gave any more thought to Katrina after that day."

Few people had, it seemed to me.

"Before we go, Mr. Thidobaux, we'd like to make arrangements to see the museum's private vaults this week."

"Ah, now I know the culprit, Mr. Chapman. You've given up your source. Madam Gerst? A pity how a little jealousy can stir up such a pot of trouble. Arthur Paglin's vault."

"That one, and the others."

He looked Mike straight in the eye. "Which others, in particular?"

"I'm expecting you to tell us that."

"I'll have to check with our patrons, of course. It is not our privilege to enter them."

"It'll be my privilege with a search warrant."

I'd need a lot more specificity about their location to get any judge to sign off on a warrant, but I didn't blame Mike for trying.

"I'll get to work on that first thing in the morning. There are only two that I know of presently, besides the Paglin estate."

"It's an interesting concept, these vaults. Didn't anyone ever try the same gimmick over at Natural History?" I asked.

Thibodaux seemed delighted to point a finger across the park. "Every museum has its hiding places, Miss Cooper. Secret compartments, if you will. Elijah Mamdouba hasn't shown you the skeletons in his closet?"

27

Clem's flight had been delayed by thunderstorms west of London. When Mercer called to tell us that he had picked her up and was on his way to the hotel, Mike and I checked into her suite and directed security to bring them right up to the room.

Mike turned on the television in the living room and gnawed on an apple from an elegant arrangement of complimentary fruit and wine. He listened to a cycle of headline news then moved to *Jeopardy!* Before going to commercial break, Trebek announced that the final category was "Patriotic Poems."

I put my twenty on the mahogany side table and Mike did the same. "You may be Ms. Iambic Pentameter, but I get the prize for patriotic."

Trebek read the final answer, printed in the cobalt blue box that was enlarged on the screen. "'Author of poem, regarded as our national hymn, composed while standing on Pike's Peak.'"

"Suck it up, Chapman. It's mine."

"Wait, blondie. It's not Key, 'cause he didn't say national anthem. What the hell's the one that Kate

Smith used to sing?" I shook my head. "Hymn? Like 'Mine eyes have seen—'"

I swept the money off the table. "Who is Katharine Lee Bates?"

"You're right, Mrs. Falkowicz," Trebek told the only one of the three contestants, a librarian from Boone, North Carolina. "She wrote 'America the Beautiful' as a poem, and never even met the gentleman who set it to music, using a song found in a church hymnal."

"Wellesley College, class of 1880."

"So you had the alumni advantage this time. That's almost like cheating."

"And there's a street named after her in Falmouth, Massachusetts, which I drive by every time I take the ferry to the Vineyard. You've got to get around more, Mikey."

The door buzzer rang and I went to open it. Standing beside Mercer Wallace's six-foot-six frame was a woman barely five feet tall. Her dark brown skin and luminous green eyes were framed by a helmetlike shock of straight black hair. She stepped into the room and looked up at me as I introduced myself.

"I'm Clem. Clementine Qisukqut."

"Mike Chapman. I'm a homicide detective. I'm handling Katrina's case."

Mercer carried her small bag into the bedroom and placed it on the luggage rack.

"I'm sure you're exhausted. If at all possible, we'd really like to get started with some questions this evening."

"That's fine. All I did was sit the entire day. May I

just clean up a bit?" She excused herself and went inside, returning to the living area ten minutes later.

We all settled into comfortable sofas and armchairs and let Clem begin. She seemed anxious to tell us about Katrina Grooten.

"I met Katrina a couple of years ago, not long after she started working at the museum. It was a year before we began to spend time together on the joint museum show."

"But you were at Natural History, is that right?"

"Yes. I had a friend who was in the last year of a postdoc here in the States. He worked at the Cloisters before he went back to Europe. I met Katrina at a party at his apartment. It was a regular thing he did, to get some of the foreign students together. It gets quite lonely here, as you can imagine, since most of us arrive without family or a network of friends."

"Did you two become close?"

"Not right away. We didn't have that much in common. Our backgrounds were so entirely different, and our professional interests were, too. There's probably no small museum more beautiful than the Cloisters, but I don't quite see the relevance of Gothic art and architecture. I couldn't connect to whatever it was that fascinated Katrina."

"You're an anthropologist?"

"Yes. A cultural anthropologist." She smiled. "And it was quite the same for Katrina. She couldn't fathom my interest in primitive civilizations, even though the entire history of evolution was the underpinning of my work."

"How did that change?"

"Slowly. Mutual acquaintances kept bringing us together, unintentionally, of course. If there was an exhibit at the Met that one of the graduate students thought would interest others of us, someone would call or e-mail and we'd end up hanging out together. Sometimes go to dinner afterwards, usually in a small group.

"It was early last year, when the office for the bestiary show was set up at my museum, that she began to spend time at Natural History."

Clem had kicked off her shoes and had her feet curled up beneath her. "Would you mind very much if I had a drink?"

Mike walked to the cabinet under the television and unlocked the minibar. "Name it."

"Any Jack Daniel's there? I'll take it neat."

He poured two small bottles into a cut-crystal glass.

"I'm afraid I'm not your typical scholarly grad student. I'm a bit friskier than most, which is why I was booted out of here. I guess the first time I pushed Katrina's buttons was when I tried to do a little rabble-rousing about the meteorite."

Chapman was intrigued. He could sense that there was a more interesting undercurrent in the anthropologist's personality than he had expected. "No offense, Clem, but I can't see that's there much to get too worked up about in these great old museums. Space rocks?"

"Ah, but you're so white. Sorry, Mr. Wallace. You and Ms. Cooper, just like Katrina."

Mercer laughed.

"'The Mighty Quinn,'" Mike repeated. "Let's get right down to it, Clem. I was expecting a full-out Eskimo, and here you are with these piercing green eyes and no whale blubber."

"Danish mother, Mr. Chapman. Greenland's a dependency of Denmark. My mother went there to teach school when she was twenty-two. Married my father. Eskimos as long as the island's been inhabited." She lifted a clump of her shiny black hair and it fell back in place. "The hair and the skin, those genes were pretty dominant."

"What does that have to do with a meteorite?"

"The Willamette Meteorite, the centerpiece of the museum planetarium, you know it?"

"Yeah. Great hunk of rock. It's the largest one in the world, isn't it?"

"Fifteen and a half tons. And it was found in Oregon, on land that belonged to an Indian tribe. Clackamas Indians. The meteorite crashed to earth thousands of years ago. Museum explorers brought it back here and it's been on display since 1906, almost one hundred years."

"What's the beef?"

Clem was doing a good job on her bourbon. "To the Indians, the meteorite had great spiritual significance. It was something the tribe worshiped for centuries, representing a union between the earth, the sky, and the water."

"Didn't they sue to get it back?" I asked.

"Yes, and a few years ago there was a settlement. The tribe dropped its claims for repatriation in exchange for the museum's agreement to use the meteorite for education about its religious and cultural history. But there was a snag."

Mike was responding to Clem's enthusiasm. He listened attentively.

"Turns out before the deal was made, the museum had cut off a twenty-eight-pound chunk."

He laughed.

"You think I'm being silly? You know how much a collector will pay for a piece of a rare meteorite? Thousands of dollars an *ounce*. That twenty-eight-pound chunk is worth millions. Literally, millions."

"What became of it?"

"The museum traded the whole thing to a private collector, in exchange for a small piece of a meteorite from Mars. What does that guy do? He starts auctioning off tiny slices."

"Pissed off the Indians?"

"And me."

"So you rallied the troops?"

"You bet I did. Just a grassroots effort to help the Indians. We even got two of the buyers, including a chiropractor in Oregon—how's that for spiritual?—to donate smaller pieces of the Willamette slivers back to the tribe. I think it was Katrina's first attempt to understand the sacred nature of a primitive people."

"Wasn't any of her South African background—"

"Think about it, Mike. May I call you Mike? Katrina's parents lived their lives under the apartheid system. She was born into that society, educated in white schools. Goes off to study in England and France, and what becomes of her? Immerses herself in medieval studies, which transported her even farther away from the real world. She needed a soul, the girl did, and I tried to give it to her."

"This was before she was attacked?"

"Raped? In the park? Yeah. We began to make ourselves a bit unpopular with the administration here last spring. Didn't matter for her, because she worked for the Met. For me, it meant trouble. Had a sit-down with Mamdouba. Given a good talking-to. Stick to my specimens and stay out of museum affairs."

Mike sat forward on the edge of his chair. "I've heard a lot of motives for murder, Clem. I'm finding it hard to think a girl could die for slivers of rock."

"You're quite right about that, Mike. It's the bones. I do believe she died for the bones."

28

"What do you know about my country? Any of you?"

Mercer and I were silent. Mike spoke. "In 982, Erik the Red was banished from Iceland for manslaughter and shipped there. World's largest island. Pulled the wool over your ancestors' eyes. Went back and told everybody his new home was a 'green land' to make it more attractive, so he'd have some company there with him. That's about as much as I learned. Sorry."

"Not bad, as far as you went." She put down her glass and talked with her hands as she told her story. "My father's family comes from a very small village. It's called Qaanaag. Way up on the northwestern part of Greenland, in the Arctic region."

"No wonder you drink your bourbon without ice."

"You don't know what cold is. Polar Eskimos. A very small community of people, pretty well isolated from the rest of the world. And odd how my life is so wound up in this museum. Robert Peary had been searching for the North Pole since the 1880s."

"The admiral?" I asked.

"Only a lieutenant then," Mike said.

"The man who was president of the Natural History Museum at the time, Morris Jesup, struck a deal with Peary. Got him leave from the navy and financing for his expedition to find the pole, if Peary would agree to collect zoological specimens and geological information." Clem winked at Mike. "Guess what Peary set out to collect?"

"No clue."

"A meteorite. Something the Eskimos called the Iron Mountain."

"You're hung up on these rocks."

"At the time, it was the largest one that had been found. It took him three years of attempts before he was able to bring it back on his ship. Landed at the Brooklyn Navy Yard in 1897. It took fourteen teams of horses to cart this treasure to the museum.

"But Peary had much more valuable cargo on board."

"Like what?"

"Inuits. Six human beings, from this remote little tribe that had less than 250 members. They had helped Peary over the years with his travels, his hunting, and his collecting. They had come to trust him and work with him. He and his crew were the only white people they knew."

"But why did he bring them to New York?"

"He was considered a great man of science, Alex. That would be his reason, of course. But they were treated as spectacles and oddities, by the press and public."

"Was this the first time he'd brought people to New York?"

"Alive, yes."

"Surely he didn't bring dead ones?"

"The year before this trip he had exhumed a family of Eskimos from their native burial ground—favorites of his, whom he had befriended on his earlier voyages. There was a father, a mother, and their young daughter who had died in a recent epidemic, and had just been buried."

"Whatever for?"

"He sold them to the museum."

"But *why*?"

"Skeletons, skulls. For display. So rich white people could gawk at the aborigines. So scientists could study the Northern races."

"And on this trip?"

"Four adults. Two of them were widowers with young children. So there was a little girl, and a little boy who came, too. Along with five barrels filled with Eskimo remains from freshly dug graves." She closed her eyes and paused. "My great-grandmother was in one of those barrels."

The thought was unimaginable. No one spoke until Clem did. "She was better off than the ones who were breathing."

"Those who were alive, where did they live?"

"You've been to the great Natural History Museum? The six Eskimos were made to live in the basement of the museum."

"How could they possibly live in the basement?" The thought of the dank, dark place was forbidding in this day and age. How inhumane to have placed them there more than a century ago, before modern plumbing, temperature control, and electric lighting.

"Not well, is the obvious answer. People came to stare at the brown-skinned curiosities. Literally, journalists and curiosity-seekers crawled on the sidewalk to peek through the grating into the basement windows."

"Did they ever get out of the museum?"

"They had to, but not by choice. They became ill. The New York City heat was overwhelming to them. They caught colds, which developed into pneumonia for five of them. Tuberculosis for another. And all six of them wound up in Bellevue Hospital as patients. When their health improved, they were released back to the museum. Someone had the foresight to fix up more comfortable living quarters, on the sixth floor, where the caretaker was housed."

"Were they—?"

"Within six months of their arrival, two of the adults had died. Sadly, one of them was Qisuk, the leader, which left his little boy orphaned. Alone here in a strange world with no family or friends. The child didn't speak the language and only three other survivors spoke his."

"Didn't these officials think of taking the survivors, especially these children, back to their homes, to Greenland?" I asked.

"The ice and weather made it impossible to do in the middle of winter."

"Didn't anyone care about them?"

"Oh, yes, of course. One of the kindest was a museum employee named William Wallace. I think he was the superintendent of buildings at Natural History. He and his wife took little Mene into their home. He became part of their family. He was tutored in English, went to school with the Wallaces' son, became quite a good athlete and a relatively happy child. But within the year, each of the other five Eskimos who had arrived with him in New York had died."

"What did they tell the boy about his poor father?"

"Museum officials had learned a great deal about polar Eskimo funeral rites from Peary. They decided that the best thing to do, for Mene's sake, was to reproduce the traditional burial ceremony that his tribesmen performed at home. The boy had turned eight and was old enough to understand what was being done, and to remember the dignity with which his father was to be honored."

"So what'd they do?"

"Well, Mr. Wallace and some members of the scientific staff gathered on the museum grounds, in a lovely secluded courtyard behind one of the main buildings. The records show that the service was conducted at just about sunset."

"The boy was there?"

"Oh, yes. And just like the tradition in my father's village, he watched as the body was brought out from the museum, covered with animal skins and a carved mask that lay over Qisuk's head. It was placed on a base of stones, and then layers of more stones were stacked in a mound over the dead leader."

Clem's hands continued to illustrate the story she told. "Then his favorite kayak and tools were arranged beside him. A very impressive ceremony, meant to show young Mene the respect everyone had for his father. It ended when the child put his mark on the grave."

"What do you mean, his mark?"

"Another of our rituals. A loved one makes a symbol in front of the stones, between the grave site and the direction of the home in which his nearest kin lives. It stops the spirit of the dead from returning to haunt the living."

"And Mene did that?"

"It made quite an impression on the boy. Here in this strange country, he watched over his father's burial like the funerals of the great hunters he had seen in his homeland."

"Coop's a sucker for happy endings. Tell her things got better for the boy, okay?"

"They did. The Wallace family gave him a good life for a time. And because Mr. Wallace worked at the museum, Mene got to visit a lot. Upstairs, on the fifth floor, where the Eskimo artifacts were studied and cataloged."

"I'm surprised he'd want to be there."

"I'm sure he thought it was great fun. He had no idea he was being studied. Whenever Peary came back with specimens, over the years, whether it was an Arctic owl or native costumes and weapons, Mene could explain them to the staff. He was actually a favorite of many of the workers. Until the day he made a dreadful discovery."

"In the museum?"

"Yes. I guess he was almost eighteen at the time. By then, Mene was allowed to walk through the great halls of the museum, studying the exhibits he had never been permitted to see before."

Clem stood and put both hands up to her mouth, then spread them in front of her.

"He wandered around rooms filled with beasts and animals he had never imagined existed, seeing African habitats and South Seas tropical island lizards and fish, most of which weren't even pictured in his books at school in 1906."

I wanted to hear that the mark Mene had left at the head of his father's grave had worked to protect him, that he wasn't haunted by that restless spirit for the remainder of his life.

Clem had one hand out straight in front of her, the other folded over her heart. "And then he reached Room Three, which must have made him nostalgic for his home. There was an array of kayaks, sleds being led by their stuffed hunting dogs, primitive paraphernalia from Peary's voyages, and finally—a large cabinet that was labeled 'Exhibit Number Five. Polar Eskimo named Qisuk.' "

Imagine the impact of the betrayal, the trauma experienced by the boy who thought his father had been treated like the legendary warriors of his homeland.

"Mene was face-to-face with his father's skeleton, which had been mounted and hung in a glass display case in the museum."

29

"The young man fell to his knees and wept."

"How did something like that ever happen? How could they have deceived the child that way?"

Mike tried to break the tension. "He's lucky they didn't stuff his father."

Clem's glance was dead sober. "The way Mene told the story, he was never sure. Next to the hanging skeleton was a life cast of Qisuk."

"What's that?"

"The museum has an entire collection of them in the anthropology department. Workers would make molds, applying paraffin to the face of the dead person—sometimes to their entire bodies. Completely lifelike. Mene looked up and saw the melancholy face of his beloved father. He was sure they had skinned and preserved him, just like an animal."

"He wasn't right about that part, was he?" I asked.

"Try finding the records. See if *you* can get an honest accounting. Franz Boas, the great anthropologist, kept a diary—and mind you, he thought the whole charade was entirely appropriate. In his writings, he claims the museum officials staged the fake burial to placate the young child, so he wouldn't think his father's body had been picked apart by the scientists."

"What was actually under the animal skins the night they pretended to bury Qisuk?"

"A log. A piece of wood the size of a man."

"But surely—"

"If you think I'm making any of this up, Alex," Clem said, patting a notebook that she had brought with her and placed on the small desk next to her glass, "there are newspaper clips that tell the whole story. The fight for Qisuk's body—"

"Fight? Between whom?"

"He died at Bellevue Hospital. The doctors there wanted to autopsy him, but the museum wanted the same privilege."

"Was there a winner?"

"An agreement was reached between the two institutions. The poor fellow was to be dissected at Bellevue, and then the museum would be allowed to preserve the skeleton. Famous phrenologists inspected his brain and took measurements of his skull."

"Why the skull?"

"The idea was that the low cultural level of more primitive people was a factor in their receding foreheads. Not enough room for mental development. Just part of the racism intrinsic to the anthropological theories of the day."

"So what's to study?" Chapman asked.

"I hesitate to call the scientists bigots. After all, those were the Euro-American tenets of the nineteenth century. They were intrigued by the Eskimos, Mike. How did this nomadic, uneducated little tribe thrive in one of the earth's most inhospitable climates? It was worthy of scientific study, don't you think?"

Clem looked at Mercer, knowing he didn't need this lecture on the narrow-mindedness that had been pervasive not just in society, but within the well-educated scientific community. "The world's fair in St. Louis, 1904. Ever hear of it?"

"Judy Garland, Leon Ames, Mary Astor, Margaret O'Brien," Mike snapped back. "Meet me in St. Louis, Louis. Zing, zing, zing went my heartstrings."

"That's the charming side. While Judy was finding romance on the trolley, Qisuk's brain was one of the freakier exhibits. On loan from the museum."

"And all this went on while Mene was growing up, but he knew nothing about it? That his father's pickled brain was carted off to a world's fair? Is it possible that Wallace participated in this cruel charade while the boy was living in his home?"

"You'll never guess what Mene's adoptive father was doing as a side business, at his farm upstate."

"You're way ahead of us."

Clem sat on the arm of the sofa, flipping through yellowed clippings as she talked, showing me pictures of the young Mene with his adoptive family on the farm in Cold Spring.

"Have you ever heard of a macerating plant?"

None of us answered.

"It's a bone bleacher."

I shivered instinctively, thinking of what Zimm had described to us last week—one hundred years later—as the museum's new degreasing machine.

"Back of the house was a running stream, so Mr.

Wallace convinced the museum to let him set up his own operation there. A cheap way to clean the animal specimens. He just parked the dead carcasses in the running springwater until they were naturally washed and bleached."

"And Qisuk?"

"Mr. Wallace was personally responsible for bleaching the Eskimo's bones, so that the anthropologists could get on with mounting the skeleton. He did it in his own backyard, while Mene was living in the house and playing on the grounds of the old farm."

"It's unthinkable."

"On top of that, William Wallace lost his job at the museum—nothing having to do with Qisuk's phony funeral, which all the officials thought was fine—but because of financial irregularities. An early scam in which he was charging the museum for animal work he was doing for circuses and zoos. Billed the trustees for an elephant he had bleached for some circus troupe performing in the old Madison Square Garden."

"So who supported Mene? The museum president? Or Robert Peary?"

Clem laughed. "Peary had long before given up his interest in his Eskimo specimens."

"But the president of the museum, did he just abandon the child, too?"

"Pretty much so. Morris Jesup. He didn't put his money where his mouth was either. When Jesup died, in 1908, his estate was valued at thirteen million dollars. He didn't leave the child a nickel in his will."

"What did the kid do?"

"Mene? He was still just a teenager, but he began the battle that would last him a lifetime."

"Who did he fight?"

"The museum, its administration, its trustees." Clem licked her finger and scanned through the plastic-covered sleeves in her notebook. When she found the newspaper article she had been searching for, she turned the book around so that the headline was facing me.

I read aloud from the January 6, 1907, edition of *The World,* which pictured an imploring Mene on his knees, in front of a sketch of the massive museum facade. Above the entrance was the bold black print that shouted his plea: GIVE ME MY FATHER'S BODY!

"All the boy wanted," Clem said, "was to take his father's remains home to Greenland for a proper funeral. To be given his kayak and hunting weapons to bury with him there."

"What did the museum do?"

"Not what you might think. They gave him nothing. But it didn't take very much media heat, even in those days, to cause them to dismantle the display case."

"And do what with it?"

"Put it in a coffin, if you can call it that. A large wooden box with a piece of glass on top, so the skeleton was still visible within it. Moved it upstairs to the workroom where other skeletal models were assembled."

"But did they return it to Mene?"

"There was a new president by this time, a zoologist named Carey Bumpus. His view? We've got hundreds of skeletons here. How the hell do I know which of these bones is your father?"

"And Mene?"

"A very difficult life, never quite comfortable in America. When he was almost twenty, he finally got some of the Arctic explorers to take him back home."

"Did anyone know him there?"

Clem smiled at me. "A tiny place like that, a dozen years after the white men took six of the tribesmen away? Certainly. These people have no written language, only oral history. But the story of Qisuk and Mene had been told many times. And he still had aunts and cousins there. In a sense it got worse."

"But why?"

"Like a man without a country. Now he could no longer speak the Eskimo language."

"Did he stay?"

"Not for long. The loneliness there was as profound for him as it had been in New York City. He came back to America, wandering around New England until he finally settled in a town in New Hampshire, where he found a job in a lumber mill. But it was all short-lived. Mene died in the Spanish influenza epidemic that swept the country, before he was even thirty."

I turned the pages of Clem's book of documents, looking at photos of this young outsider throughout his life. There were images in which his velvety brown eyes seemed to express all the joyous promise of every childhood, but far many more in which the pain of his isolation dimmed the gaze as he grew into an adolescent and young adult.

"Before he died, though, was he able to arrange for his father's body to go home with him?"

"Never. It was one more broken promise."

I hesitated to ask. "To this day, has Qisuk's—?" I stopped, not knowing how to refer to the remains. It certainly wasn't an intact body.

"Natural History accession number 99/3610? That's all Qisuk was to the museum leaders."

The dead man bore the same kind of identification tag as a stuffed moose or prehistoric fish.

Clem went on. "Yes, in 1993, more than a century after the six Eskimos left their homes, their bones were returned to Greenland for burial. I told you, didn't I, that my father was born in the same village? It's called Qaanaaq."

"Yes, you did."

"My family was there at the time, in the beginning of August, when the funerals were held. I was at university in London, back for a visit, and we had gone north to see my grandfather. I'd been studying to be a librarian until then. It was learning the story of these ancestors, and the journey of Qisuk's bones, that changed my path. That's when I decided what I wanted to do was be an anthropologist."

"Did you go to the ceremony?"

"Oh, yes. A very traditional one. Quite moving, actually. They were buried on a hilltop near the water, with a pile of stones on top of the grave. And a marker with a simple inscription: THEY HAVE COME HOME."

She paused with her eyes closed, as if remembering the scene.

"And this story you've told us," Mike asked, "you

think this has something to do with the murder of Katrina Grooten?"

"Most definitely."

"Why?"

It all seemed so obvious to Clementine. "When Katrina started coming to the Natural History Museum to work on the joint show, she was amazed at all the skeletons that were there. She'd never given any thought to where they came from."

Neither had I. I had always assumed that they were thousands of years old, specimens found in remote desert areas, abandoned caves, archaeological digs.

"Guess she never saw *The Flintstones*," Mike said.

Clem was not put off by Mike's humor. She had a story to tell and was determined to do it. "It was Native Americans who really rattled the cages. While Robert Peary and his cohorts were studying my people, anthropologists were doing the very same thing with American Indians out West. Not just collecting their artifacts and tools, but digging up skulls from graves and hauling them back East to study, too."

"What became of them all?"

"Until a decade ago, the remains were in the collections of more than seven hundred museums, large and small, throughout your country. The bones of more than two hundred thousand American Indians are *still* sitting in wooden boxes and drawers at these institutions. But your native people had an advantage that mine didn't have, in terms of their numbers and their ability to organize."

"What'd they do?"

"Demonstrated, agitated, got new laws passed."

"Legislation?"

"Native American Graves Protection and Repatriation Act, 1990. Guess if your ancestors' brains had been diced up and studied, Mike, you'd have known about it, too."

"Slim pickings, ma'am. Well preserved in alcohol, but very dense matter inside thick skulls."

"You're not telling me every skeleton can be linked to a tribe?" Mercer asked.

"No, no. That's one of the biggest problems. Some of these museum collections are hundreds of years old. They're not matched to any tribe or cultural affiliation. Never will be."

Mike was still stuck on the Eskimos. "So if this law was passed here in 1990, how come your people—Qisuk and the others—still didn't get home for a few more years?"

"The legislation only applied to Native Americans. Museums were required to repatriate all the Indian bones that tribes asked for, but that didn't help my Eskimos a damn bit."

"Why did Katrina care?"

"Take this girl whose scholarship field was funerary art, Mike. For the first time in her life she came face-to-face with the reality experienced by most cultures of color, all over the world. No churchyards, no headstones, no marked graves. Our ancestors are sitting in cardboard boxes, collecting dust on museum shelves."

"In the name of science."

"I got under her skin at first. How could she have been so blind to this? Think of what the situation was in South Africa, where she grew up. I told her Mene's story, which mesmerized her. I told her about my own great-grandmother being shipped to the United States in a barrel. That got her riled up. Then she focused on the American Indians. I practically had to club her over the head before I could get her to understand her own country."

"The skeletons found there?"

"*Found* there? Hey, Mike, I'm not talking about *Pithecanthropus erectus* and the missing link. Those guys walked the earth thousands of years ago. Their remains were *found*. The ones I'm referring to, like my own relatives, were *stolen*."

Mercer was standing behind Mike, with his enormous hands wrapped around Mike's forehead. "His skull doesn't slope quite as obviously as you'd think, Clem. It's just impenetrable."

The detective in Mike was skeptical when he heard Clem refer to human remains as stolen. "Explain that. The story of your Eskimos is a very unusual one. That's not how all these bones got into collections."

"Maybe you don't want to hear me, but my colleagues and I have all the documentation to prove this." Clem didn't need a notebook to call up the facts she had mastered. "I told Katrina what had been happening all over Africa. In 1909, a black man named Kouw was dismembered and boiled just four months after he died. His widow and children watched and wailed, but the scientists won. Off to a museum with him. The diary of a famous anthropologist described how she kept vigil over a sickly woman till her death, in the 1940s, waited for her tribesmen to bury her, then dug her up and took her back to Cape Town."

"No government protection?"

"First half of the twentieth century in Africa? The natives didn't have a prayer. Only the missionaries tried to intercede for them. They kept some of the best records of plundered graves. These aren't the relics of cavemen. They're the remains of Khoisans—bushmen and Hottentots—many of whom have living descendants who have heard these stories all their lives."

"You think this had anything to do with Katrina's decision to go back to South Africa?"

"Everything. She had taken a job at the McGregor Museum."

I remembered that from our conversation with Hiram Bellinger. He thought it was a waste of her education. The McGregor specialized in natural history but had no European art department.

"So," Mike said slowly, "so you think you know why she wanted that job at the McGregor?"

"The bone vault, Detective. She wanted to get into their bone vault."

30

"What's a bone vault?"

"Nothing you're going to find in any museum directory, Mike. It's how Katrina and I referred to the stash of skeletons that every museum has in one hideaway or another. The South African Museum in Cape Town, they've got a locked storeroom with more than a thousand cartons full of somebody's grandmothers and grandfathers."

"And the McGregor?"

"Up in Kimberley. One hundred and fifty dusty boxes of bones, sitting under white fluorescent light."

"None on display?"

"No. The curators got wise to the controversy a few years later than the Americans. Took down the hanging skeletons in the late nineties."

"So, where's the McGregor vault?"

"That's the trick. She was going to try to find it and help to get the remains identified. To return them to the families that have been asking for them."

Mercer was fascinated. "Can they actually be identified at this point?"

"Some can. I think there's a new DNA process."

"Mitochondrial DNA," I told her. Tracing genetic material through the maternal line, through bone and hair.

"Katrina was to replace a woman who used to work at the McGregor, a friend of mine who had actually started to catalog the remains when they were taken off display three years ago. She had been doing this as a personal measure, hoping the day would come when the indigenous communities would be able to win their return."

"This friend of yours started to inventory them?"

"You didn't know how dangerous museum work could be, did you? Shortly after she undertook her project, she began to get death threats. First mailed to her office at the museum, then on her answering machine at home. Vague, of course, and anonymous, but good enough to scare her. She left South Africa and moved back to Kenya. It was after she left that the skeletons were all moved into storage and locked up."

"Why? What had she found?"

"Very specific information. Some of the entries had names of the bodies attached to the labels, even specifying the farms from which the corpses had been dug up. Bones that could be given to family members to help restore their dignity and validate their existence."

"And the others?"

"Simply an acquisition tag that says 'Bush-Hottentot' or whatever their local tribe was. They were considered subhuman, Mike. Their bones were displayed just as if they were animals. These people were denigrated in death as they had been in life."

"So you've got an organization to get into the locked rooms and retrieve the bones?"

"That's a very formal word for it, Mercer. Might be more accurate to call it a cabal. If we organized, there wouldn't be one of us to get inside the employment office of any museum."

"You enlisted Katrina?"

"I awakened her. I opened her eyes." Clem looked down at her notebook on the table in front of her. "These were atrocities committed in the name of science and education, and some of us feel we can do something to right them."

"Who else, besides Katrina, was involved with your work here in New York?"

She took a deep breath and shook her head. "You find out who killed her, and then I'll give you specific names. I can't put anyone else in harm's way until you do."

I placed my hand on top of her book. "It's not just their help we need. How can we know whether or not they're in danger if we don't know who they are?"

Clem stood firm. "Let me sleep on it. Let me hear what you know and with whom you've already talked." She raised her hand to cover her mouth, stifling a yawn, then stood and began to walk around the room, as if she were trying to shake off the jet lag. In London, it was well into the early hours of the next day.

"We should save some of this until the morning," I said, signaling Mike to cut off the questioning.

"These partners of yours, how do you communicate with each other?"

Clem yawned again and I tapped my watch face as I looked at Mike and Mercer.

"So if we let you get some sleep, you game to come down to Alex's office with us in the morning? Fill in the rest of these blanks?"

"That's why I'm here."

Clem walked us to the door of her suite, talking as she did.

"You must miss your job terribly," I said, remembering that Clem had told me she had given up the chance to work in her field, temporarily, for the less controversial role of working in the exquisite refurbished Round Reading Room of the British Museum.

"I had my reasons," she said, grinning. "It so happens that lovely library is directly above the African galleries. I'm not without my allies there. We're still stirring up trouble."

I arranged to pick her up at the Park Avenue entrance to the hotel in the morning, on my way down to the office, and we said good night.

"Ten-fifteen? I'm ready to eat the ferns in the lobby," Mike said. "Anybody for dinner at Lumi?"

We drove the short distance to the chic little restaurant on the corner of Seventieth Street and Lexington Avenue, and Mercer followed in his car. Lumi herself took us to the corner table, next to the maître d's stand, after I told her we needed a quiet place to talk about an investigation.

Over drinks we discussed Clem's information and came up with a plan for the following morning. I would draft an e-mail for her to send to a group of museum employees, to see whether anyone could be drawn out to talk to Clem about Katrina.

Mercer and I had our favorite pasta—cavatelli with peas and tiny bits of prosciutto—while Mike took forever to work on the osso buco he ordered whenever we ate there. While we were waiting for our espresso, Mercer's beeper went off. He excused himself and walked up the two steps from the restaurant door to the sidewalk.

He came back to the table to tell us he had to leave.

"It's your girl, Alex. Angel Alfieri, the fourteen-year-old."

The china cup clattered against the saucer as it dropped from my fingers. "They found her? Is she okay?"

"She's alive. It wasn't Felix—the cabdriver—that she went off with. Looks like she holed up with Ralphie, to make Felix *and* her girlfriend jealous."

"Thank—"

"Don't thank anybody yet. We got a hostage situation. She's in Ralphie's apartment, up on Paladino, and he's holding a loaded gun to her head."

31

I pushed away from the table and stood up to leave. Just as quickly, Mercer clamped a hand on my shoulder and I dropped back into my seat.

"I'll baby-sit. Do whatcha gotta do," Mike said.

Mercer was a member of the hostage squad, an elite group of detectives selected and trained to negotiate with some of the most unstable criminals in the most life-threatening situations. They responded to bank robbers with automatic weapons, holding dozens of citizens after a silent alarm trapped them at the crime scene; domestics in which a psychotic or intoxicated husband had a butcher knife to his wife's throat; and political disputes when dissidents invaded a consulate or residence. The cops chosen for the assignment came from every unit in the department. In addition to their regular squad duties, they were on call for these emergency situations whenever they arose.

Mercer had the intelligence, patience, and personal skills for the job. I had watched him coax deranged felons and jealous paramours out of their weapons several times in the years I had known him. Mike's temperament made him completely unsuitable for the job. He had no tolerance for a perp's threats or demands, and a shorter fuse than even I possessed.

We both watched as Mercer headed out the door to try to save the life of a kid who had jumped into water and was in way too deep over her head. I remembered that she had fabricated the forcible rape charge when Felix told her that he had had better sex with her girlfriend, who had Ralphie's name tattooed on her rear end. Undoubtedly, this was Angel's opportunity to get back at both of them by throwing herself at Ralphie.

"C'mon. Time to go home. We got a lot to do tomorrow."

I walked to Mike's car, unable to focus on the next day's work, completely distracted by the thought of the young girl looking into the barrel of a gun and wondering whether I had helped to drive her there.

"One favor?" I asked.

Mike pursed his lips and gave me a firm, "No."

"Ride up First Avenue, please? I swear I won't get out of the car. I just want to know whether her mother's out there. I'd like to see if she needs anything."

"What you really want to see is the kid, and you know you can't. Sticking you in her face would be like grinding sand in an open wound. I'll humor you, blondie, but only so I don't have to listen to you whine."

We reached the projects a few minutes before midnight. There was a police barricade at each end of the block. A lieutenant with a bullhorn was standing on the sidewalk, and Emergency Services had set up klieg lights that were directed at a window on the sixth floor. A small crowd had gathered on the pavement, behind the row of wooden horses guarded by uniformed cops, who were encouraging the onlookers to move along. An ambulance was double-parked at the curb in case the bargaining process was unsuccessful.

I searched for Mercer among the group closest to the lieutenant in charge, but I couldn't find his head. That was a good sign. He had probably been sent into the building to try to soothe the angry young man and convince him to open the apartment door and release his captive.

"There's nothing to see. It's a work in progress, Coop. Nobody hurt. They've got the right man for the job." Mike reached over and took my hand off the dashboard, squeezing it tightly as he did.

Three more officers came running from the opposite side of the street, passing in front of us to sprint to the building. They each wore the hostage squad uniform, a short black bomber jacket with a bright red logo emblazoned across the back: TALK TO ME. They were followed at a more leisurely pace by a uniformed boss, a beefy guy with a captain's shield pinned above a stack of ribbons and medals.

"Hey, Chapman, whaddaya think? You're at some goddamn drive-in movie with your date? Get your ass out of the car and make yourself useful. Send the bimbo for a cup of coffee."

The captain slammed his fist down on the hood of the car, yelling across the top of it to a lieutenant standing closer to the building. "Hey, Bannerman.

You know Chapman here? Homicide? Throw him in the mix."

Mike opened the car door to protest. "I've been rejected for hostage work more times than you've gotten laid. I'm no good—"

"Forget negotiating. The kid's got a gun in there. Who the hell knows which way this thing is gonna turn. Last month out in Queens the team wound up with a homicide/suicide. All the smooth talk in the world didn't help. Perp shot his captive in the head, then opened his mouth and plugged himself. We're taking every bit of backup we can get at this point. Act like a cop, not a prima donna. Yo, Bannerman, put this guy to work."

Then the captain leaned his elbow on the rim of the window. "You, sweetheart, why don't you grab a gypsy cab and go wait for Detective On-the-Job at home, snug under the covers?"

"Captain Ekersly, I'd like you to meet Alexandra Cooper. Assistant district attorney, New York County, in charge of—"

"Sex. Nice to meet you. Raymond Ekersly. You do good work, my guys tell me. I don't know what the hell you're thinking, up here holding hands with this cowboy when I got better things for him to do, but I suggest you get out of our way, okay? See you in court."

"I can just stay here while—"

"Vito. See that radio car with two auxiliaries sitting in it, up the block? Walk the DA up there and tell them to take her wherever she wants to go." Ekersly turned back to me. "Your place or his, sweetheart?"

"Coop's indicted people for less than that, Cap. She's not your sweetheart. She's nobody's sweetheart, okay?"

"I can't catch a break either way. Get to work, guys. I give up. East Side. Seventieth Street." I opened the door and stepped out of the car as the captain walked toward the projects.

"Your office at nine? You and Clem?" Mike asked.

"Sure. You know I won't be able to sleep." I hesitated before going on. "You want to come by when— when this is over, for a drink?"

"Always the optimist. Who knows when it'll be over? I'll really be ready to sack it in if this ends peacefully. Don't worry, I'll call you with the results. Have a nightcap on me."

I waved him off and followed Vito to the neighborhood auxiliary car, where two civilians who liked to dress up and play cop were keeping the street safe.

Six months ago, I thought as I settled myself into the backseat, Mike would have been on my doorstep the moment this crisis passed, to assuage my concern and distract me from my thoughts about the role I had played in igniting it. Now he had someone he wanted to be with at home. At moments like this I would have to learn to adjust emotionally to that new arrangement.

I barely spoke on the ride downtown to my apartment, wondering what Angel had said or done to cause Ralphie to flip out on her. Maybe she had taunted him with the fact that she was sleeping with him only to get back at Felix, or maybe he had become enraged when she disclosed that his girlfriend had been unfaithful. Mercer had to strike exactly the right chord to connect with the kid, or there was likely to be a homicide on my conscience.

When the driver reached the red light at the corner of Seventy-first Street and Second Avenue, he pulled over in front of an all-night deli. "You mind if we stop a minute and get some coffee, ma'am?"

"Tell you what. I need some, too. Could be a long night. I'll buy a dozen containers and some food to take back to the crew at the scene if you guys don't mind waiting ten minutes."

"Sounds like a good deal."

I filled the cardboard cups while the counterman sliced and wrapped an assortment of sandwiches, which I carried out to the car. "Help yourselves and spread the rest around. Thanks for the lift."

"You okay?"

I pointed to the driveway exit that led away from my building entrance, two-thirds of the way up the block. "That's home. I've been cooped up inside all day. The night air feels good for a change."

I went back in the deli to pour myself a cup of coffee and pay the tab. As I sipped on the hot brew, my friend Renee walked in to use the small ATM in the back of the store.

"What a nice surprise," she said, kissing me on the cheek. "I asked David if he'd seen you lately. He can tell by how early you take in your newspaper that you've been keeping terrible hours. I'm just getting some cash for the morning. Got a minute?"

Renee and her fiancé, David Mitchell, lived in an apartment on the same hallway as mine.

"Sure. Zac outside?"

"Yeah. Have any strength left for a short walk with me? I got stuck with the late shift."

David, a psychiatrist, and Renee, a therapist, had a handsome weimaraner named Prozac. I liked to think I was her surrogate mother. She had often comforted me when I needed some affection and a cold nose in the middle of a difficult night.

I went out to the sidewalk and knelt to greet the friendly dog, unlooping her leash from the top of the parking meter where Renee had tied her.

When Renee came out, I hooked my arm in hers and we set off to square the block, up to Seventy-second Street and around to Third Avenue.

"What are you doing with coffee at this hour of the night?"

"I'm so wired, I'll never sleep." I gave her an abbreviated version of the hostage situation, as she tried to offer reassurance and get my mind off the subject.

"How's Jake?"

I laughed. "I think it would be less stressful to talk about Felix and Angel at this point. Jake's traveling."

"Again? I was hoping to make a date for you to have dinner with us next week."

I shrugged my shoulders.

Zac stopped and sniffed at a wrought-iron gate in front of a brownstone. "You can have me, if that works. I'm not certain what day he's coming back."

I started forward but Zac stood her ground. "C'mon, baby. Time to go to sleep."

The smart, lean animal lowered her head and

growled softly. Renee and I turned to look behind us and saw nothing unusual.

"Let's go, Zac. Nobody there." I took two steps but the dog strained against her leash. Renee took control of the leather strap and we walked on to Third Avenue. After we turned the corner and got halfway down the block, I glanced back over my shoulder. No one was there, but I thought I saw the shadow of a figure tucked back in the opening of a storefront.

Zac found a fire hydrant to her liking and did what she was supposed to do. While she did, the light from the streetlamp found the shadow lurking behind us and stretched its length out into the asphalt street. It seemed to be ten feet tall.

"Okay, girl, home we go." I tried to speed up the process but the dog was stubborn.

"She's really unhappy about something," Renee said.

I broke into a jog and the hot coffee slurped over the side of the cup, stinging my hand as it dripped onto my skin. I threw the container to the ground as I saw the figure step out of the dark recess and onto the sidewalk behind us.

"Run, Renee. Just pull Zac and run, will you?"

The dog growled again and resisted Renee's urging. She must have seen the frightened look on my face and sternly commanded the animal to move. Despite Zac's vocalizing, I knew she was far too gentle a dog to attack, and Renee would have hurt herself before ever putting the sweet-natured weimaraner in harm's way. I blocked Renee's back with my body to give her a chance to get going, and tried to make out the face of the person on the sidewalk as I backed up.

Renee ran as the dog began to bark loudly, heading around the last corner to the short downhill slope of Seventy-first Street. "The garage. Go into the garage," I shouted at her. "Tell Jorge to call 911."

I moved sideways, like a crab racing across hot sand, looking back and forth between Renee and our pursuer.

Several cars streamed by on the avenue, oblivious to my fear. By the time I stopped to flag one down, the stalker would have gained on me.

Stalker. Stalker. Shirley Denzig? The dark night and fluorescent streetlights were playing their usual tricks with each other. Was the tall figure wearing a long-billed baseball cap a man, a stranger out for a late-night walk? Or was it the short, squat body of Denzig, elongated by an optical illusion in the dim glare of a city night?

Now he or she was running with us, slower than we were, but steadily in our direction. And now, as I stood at the mouth of the sloping ramp that led down to our building's garage entrance, I was shaded by the overhang, and the approaching figure came clearly into view under the bright streetlight.

Shirley Denzig. No question about it. The psychotic young woman had focused her attention on me again and waited for me outside my building tonight, just as the detectives were trying to close in on her after news of her latest scam at the Waldorf-Astoria.

Renee was inside the garage. She had disappeared from my range of vision, and Zac's barks echoed in the hollow space of the enormous underground parking facility beneath my apartment.

I speeded my pace. Denzig's short legs and extra weight kept her well behind me. I looked back again, anxious to know whether she was still carrying the gun she had stolen from her father's home.

When I ran down the garage ramp I could see the attendant standing to the side, his hand on the control button that would lower the heavy metal grating behind me once I was inside.

"Hit it now, Jorge," I yelled to him. "Close the door!"

I sprinted the last six yards and ducked beneath the electrically controlled jaws of the security device as it ground to a close, and rolled onto the oil-stained floor of the garage.

Shirley Denzig landed against the structure with all her weight. Dull thuds resounded on our side as she kicked against the metal.

Jorge helped me to my feet and I ran to his office, grabbing the phone from Renee's hand to explain to the 911 operator what to tell the cops.

Within minutes, we could hear the sound of the approaching sirens. Denzig's frenzied banging had stopped. She had disappeared into the night.

32

Jorge was adamant. And scared. He refused to open the garage door when the police started banging on it because he could not see who they were and had no idea who or what I had been running from. The cops finally gave up and came downstairs through the entrance that led from within the building's lobby.

"Would one of you guys mind taking my friend up to her apartment?"

"Are you kidding? You think we're leaving you now?" Renee said. "Besides, I'd like to know what all the excitement was about."

It took me ten minutes to explain the Shirley Denzig story to the police, who called in a description of her for transmission to other patrol cars in the area. They escorted us upstairs to our apartments, and arranged to meet me in the lobby at 7:45 in the morning, to make sure I got out of the garage without incident, so I could pick up Clem and get down to my office.

I ignored the blinking light on my answering machine and went in the den with Katrina Grooten's file, holding the portable phone on my lap while I tried to calm myself and concentrate on the investigation. If my adrenaline had not already been fueled by Angel's predicament, my episode with Shirley ensured that I would be unable to sleep.

I turned on the television to NY1, muting the sound, waiting to see whether they cut to live coverage of the unfolding drama in East Harlem.

Another hour passed, and then two. An out-of-control blaze in the Hunts Point section of the Bronx had spectacular flames that kept the local news crew engaged. My notes to myself were no longer making sense, the to-do lists I created for Mike were growing unreasonably long, and the relaxing weekend on the Vineyard seemed like it had ended a month ago.

At three-ten the phone rang.

"She's fine. Go to sleep now, girl." Mercer's deep voice allayed my worst fears.

I exhaled into the mouthpiece, too upset to speak.

"Hey, we got a pretty good track record for saves. I sure as hell wasn't gonna let that little punk break it for me. I'll be in late tomorrow. Catch up with you guys in the afternoon."

"Whatever you need. Thanks a million, personally, on this one. I've got to ask you, Mercer, did she go there because—?"

"She went there for exactly the reasons you think. And she liked it there fine, gettin' it on with Ralphie. Turns out he's dealing crack from the apartment. Kept her pretty well tuned up since she arrived. Angel decides to pocket some vials before she's ready to leave, to make a few bucks on the visit."

"I see it coming."

"He catches her, smacks her around. Now she wants to scoot, but she's got a black eye and he doesn't want to let her out. Angel threatens to snitch, and he's got a reason to go ballistic, 'cause he knows she's called the police before, to have Felix locked up. She picks up the gun and points it at Ralphie, but he grabs it back and can't think of any place to stick it except right up against that underutilized bundle of brains the child has. Neighbor hears screams, dials 911."

Maybe this is the wake-up call Angel needed. Why couldn't she come out of this like Dorothy in Oz and realize that at her age there's no place like home?

"Look, Alex, I'm whipped. I'll give you chapter and verse tomorrow. Angel's being treated at Mount Sinai, Ralphie's spending the night courtesy of my brothers in blue down at central booking. We recovered two guns, a load of ammo, and forty-two crack vials from his apartment. Everybody's safe and sound. Tell Mr. Chapman to let go of your hand and go home. See you tomorrow."

There was no point in telling Mercer that Mike hadn't waited out the siege with me. I turned off the tube, rolled over on the sofa, and fell asleep.

In the morning, I showered and dressed, met the cops in my lobby, who took me to the garage so that one of them could ride with me over to Park Avenue. No sign of my nocturnal stalker, so I let him out, continuing on to pick up Clem from the hotel at eight. We found a space on Mulberry Street and I tossed the laminated NYPD parking plate on the dashboard.

We walked through the small asphalt-paved park

that only twenty-five years ago had been the heart of
Little Italy but was now the center of a greatly
expanded Chinatown. Mike called it Tiananmen
Square. Men and women dressed in black mandarin-
style jackets bustled back and forth, carrying plastic
bags from the Canal Street fish markets and the Division Street vegetable trucks. Kids from the local ele-
mentary school played kickball. Nobody was speaking English.

As we emerged from the gates on the Baxter Street
side of the park, the sound of the screeching children
was replaced by the chants of about twenty adults
who were marching in two rows, up and down the
length of Hogan Place. Some of them were carrying
posters and placards, hand-lettered with an assortment of slogans. All of them were shouting in unison.

"It's safe and sane! End Battaglia's reign!"

I could read the signs now as we approached the
corner. It was a group from the American Alliance for
Sexual Freedom, protesting my arrest of their sadomasochistic spelling whiz, Peter Kalder. A few had
their organization logo labeled on large cardboard
signs while others had printed more original thoughts:
WHIP SOME SENSE INTO ALEX COOPER! and COOPER—
SHOW SOME RESTRAINT—STAY OUT OF OUR BED-
ROOMS! Stick drawings of me, cat-o'-nine-tails in one
hand and cuffs dangling from the other, would have
pleased Mike Chapman immensely.

Prosecutors and cops were weaving their way
among the demonstrators, visibly annoyed at having
to maneuver around the rowdy cluster to get to the
office entrance.

"Shit." I stopped in my tracks when I saw a *Post* cameraman waiting opposite the building. This was a good morning to avoid a photo opportunity, obviously arranged by the alliance. "Do you mind if we go in through the back door of the Tombs?"

"Whatever's easiest for you," Clem said, standing on tiptoe to try to read all the comments. "I never realized there was a unit like yours, just specializing in sexual assault cases. You must walk a tight line, trying to keep everybody happy."

"I gave that idea up a long time ago. Most people have no reason to know we exist until the unimaginable happens to them or a loved one."

"Doesn't this make the district attorney angry with you? He's elected, isn't he?"

"Battaglia's the best. He's got one rule, Clem, when we make decisions about prosecuting. 'Do the right thing.' Don't play politics with people's lives, don't try to think how something will spin in the next day's op-ed pieces, just try to do justice. He hates all the tabloid titillation with sex crimes, but he'll stand behind any decision his top people make."

"Lucky for you."

I pounded on the heavy door behind the building, where the grim green trucks of the Department of Correction were depositing the day's defendants who were being bused in from Rikers Island.

"Hey, Jumbo, can you let us in? There's a lynch mob at my front door."

The eight-to-four guard on the rear door of the Tombs was the size of a Mack truck. He pressed the button to open the wide mouth of the garage, and

Clem and I walked inside. The pens were still empty but the crew was getting ready to receive its allotment of felons-in-waiting.

"G'morning, Ms. Cooper. You need any help with that little commotion outside? I could round up some of my guys and show them what black and blue looks like, in living color."

"Save your strength, buddy. Nothing out there I can't handle with a tough hide and a decent sense of humor."

He took us through a lock-and-block system of corridors. The one behind us had to be secured before he could open the next door in front. There were five from the point at which he admitted us, until we emerged from the cells into the arraignment part, which would be called to order in less than fifteen minutes, at nine o'clock.

A rookie prosecutor I recognized, who was nearing the end of his first year in the office, was reviewing case files. He would be manning the court calendar for the rest of the day. He was puzzled to see me enter from the prisoners' doorway.

"Need anything here?"

"Just taking a visitor on tour. What's your name?" When he told me, I wrote it on a Post-it in my wallet, telling him I might be down with a search warrant later in the day, and asking him to tell the judge to expect me.

I stopped for coffee in the cafeteria in the courthouse lobby, which had long been known as the roach coach. We rode up on the elevators that carried convicted felons to the probation office. I tried to avoid eye contact with one of them—a taxi driver who two weeks ago had been found guilty of fondling an intoxicated passenger who had fallen asleep in the rear seat of his Yellow Cab.

The circuitous routing had added almost twenty minutes to the trip to my desk.

I unlocked the door and told Clem to settle in while I checked my voice mail and organized my desk after the long weekend.

"Here's what we'd like you to do." I set up my laptop on the table between a row of filing cabinets. "I want you to log on a guest account, so it will show your regular address. Last night at dinner, we drafted an e-mail that we'd like you to send."

"To?"

"You tell me. Our thought was that you would send it to the team that was working on the exhibition. Was there a user-group address?"

"Yeah. There was a special 'org' account set up for joint access by workers from both museums."

"Would it be logical that you could still get into it?"

"Sure. It's meant to be used by interested people in museums all over the world. A lot of them are former employees or student interns, and many are scholars who know the collections. We're all encouraged to send in suggestions for the exhibition. Things like that."

"Is everyone we talked about last night included in that grouping?"

Clem ticked off the names on her fingers and nodded her head in response.

"Did you bring your address book with you?"

"I followed all your instructions."

"Look through it and include anyone else you think had a connection to Katrina," I said. "Use your own greeting. I want people who know you to recognize your voice, if you will. Your language. And when they open the message, the header will show the hour you sent it as daylight saving time, which would make it pretty early back home."

"What will you do about that? Won't the e-mail display what time I sent it?"

"We've got a tech unit upstairs. I left a voice mail for one of the guys who works there, who was due in at eight. He'll come down to reset it for us, so it shows UK time."

"Good."

"Mention that you've been so worried since the police called you that you haven't been able to sleep." I handed her a slip of paper I had worked on last night. "Then tell them this."

I'm coming to New York later this week. I thought some of you who were also Katrina Grooten's friends might want to meet with me to plan a memorial service for her. She sent me a letter shortly before she died, as it turned out, and some of you may be interested in what she told me. Have the police been helpful? I'm wondering whether to give the information to them.

"It would be hard not to be curious about that, I guess. Most of the people we've talked about know

I'm not likely to want to cooperate with government authorities. They think I enjoy being a trouble-maker."

"That's the idea. Just the way people respond to you should be interesting. How did you set it up with your office in London?" I wanted to be sure that no one would answer Clem's phone there and give up the fact that she was already in Manhattan. She was safely under our collective wing at the moment, and it helped to know that while we tried to lure Katrina's killer into plain sight.

"Told my boss I had to make an emergency trip to Greenland, to see an ailing relative. Didn't leave them a phone number. Just said I'd stay in touch by e-mail."

"What will your secretary tell people?"

"No such luxury at my level. It's voice mail. I just changed the outgoing message to say the same thing."

"Anyone know where you're staying in New York?"

"How could they? I didn't have a clue myself until we got to the hotel lobby."

"Then why don't you get to work? I'm just going to stick my head into the district attorney's office to see how he wants me to deal with my sidewalk cheering section."

Rose Malone was untying her sneakers to change into the high heels that showed off her great legs. "I bet you needed those to dash through my swarm of admirers this morning. What time's the boss due in?"

"He gave the commencement speech at Stanford's graduation ceremony yesterday. He's flying back today, so he won't be here at all." She straightened up and whispered to me across her desk, "McKinney already came by to see him about it. I think he's going to have the Fifth Precinct squad commander cordon off the entrance and move the protestors around to the rear of the building. The police will call it a safety measure. At least it keeps them away from the judge's entrance and all the grand jurors."

"You think they have any openings in the appeals bureau, Rose? No witnesses, no lunatics, no controversies."

"Your life would be so dull you wouldn't be able to stand it. You thrive on this."

"I like challenges, I like creative investigations, I like the people I work with. *This?*" I pointed out her window to the sidewalk below. "There's no way to win. If the big guy calls in, tell him I'll do whatever he thinks is best. And that before the end of the week we should have some developments on the Grooten murder."

Mike was already in my office when I got back across the hallway. "That's some flogging you're getting downstairs. I came mighty close to firing off a few shots to disperse the crowd but I thought I might accidentally get lucky and hit one of 'em."

"I've got Clem working on her first e-mail—"

"Done and gone. Hank Brock was in here tinkering with the time function on the computer. Said to tell you he got it set to read like she's in London, okay?"

"Perfect. And I'm going upstairs as soon as there's a quorum in the grand jury." I'd be lucky if that happened by ten-fifteen. "I want to get some subpoenas ready for the Natural History Museum. We need a detailed floor plan and a list of anything that might be a private vault or closet."

"Got my first fish on the line," Clem said. I picked up my head and watched as she clicked on her new mail.

She read it aloud.

"When do you arrive and where will you be staying? Why don't we meet for coffee? Katrina was such a sweet girl. The police seem determined to bungle this entire thing. We should talk first."

"Who's it from?"

"That woman who works for Pierre Thibodaux. Eve Drexler."

33

"Keep her engaged," Mike said to Clem. "We know she had Katrina's identification tag when she signed into the British Museum meeting in January. It's at least worth talking to her about that when Coop and I meet with her again this week."

I thought of Ruth Gerst's nickname for Drexler: "Evil." "You think she'd be doing Thibodaux's bidding just because she was loyal to him, or did she figure she had a chance at consoling the widower and trying to replace Penelope in his affection?"

"Like she figured Katrina was getting too close? Let me tell you, if Eve could lift the lid onto that sarcophagus by herself, I'll eat my nightstick. It'd mean someone she trusted had—"

"The man who went off the roof?"

"Bermudez."

"She was the first one at the hospital, wasn't she?"

"Yeah, but that would have been her responsibility anyway."

"But Thibodaux admitted to us that he never actually left town Friday night. He could have gone himself. Maybe Eve had used him for muscle."

"What man off what roof?" Clem asked quietly.

I explained what had happened at the Met on Friday and asked if she had ever heard Bermudez's name. I walked to Laura's desk and picked up the package of news clips that the public information office copied and distributed to the executive staff every morning. It was particularly thick after a three-day weekend, and this one was stuffed with tabloid features about every stabbing, shooting, and sex crime that had occurred since Friday morning.

I flipped through the assorted stories that had been included in the handout because they related to the Grooten investigation. Sunday's *Daily News* had an obit of Pablo Bermudez, with a three-paragraph story that quoted Thibodaux, who expressed his sorrow at the tragic accident.

"Ever see him?" I asked Clem, showing her the photograph of the dead man, posed with his wife while on vacation in San Juan a few weeks before he fell to his death.

"He does look familiar." She took the paper from my hand and studied the picture. "I mean, workmen from the Met were in and out of our basement all the time. They delivered exhibits and picked them up. Some were friendlier than others, hung around and asked questions about the displays. A few guys asked to come back with their kids to show them the animals, the behind-the-scenes stuff."

"Do you think Katrina knew any of these guys?"

"I haven't a clue. If I had to guess, I'd say she wasn't one to chat up strangers. I mean, after the rape, she didn't like to be down in the basement alone. She was always looking for someone to cling to. It gets kind of creepy there when the place closes up at night."

I bet it does, I mused.

"How do you want me to reply to Eve?"

"Did you actually have any relationship with her when you worked at Natural History?"

"Not from her perspective. I mean, I saw her at a handful of meetings, I had to copy her on all my correspondence about the joint exhibition, but nothing personal at all."

"Why not thank her for writing. Tell her your plans are still up in the air. Maybe you should say you're already in Greenland, so she doesn't try to reach you in London." I smiled at Mike. "She seems anxious to talk about the Keystone Kops. Guess you should stop bungling and solve this damn case already."

Clem turned back to the computer and typed her response. "More mail. Whoops, it's from Zimm. He wants me to save an evening for him. Smart enough not to invite me to the museum. Not good for his reputation."

I thought that was odd. He was almost ready to leave for his new job in Chicago and hadn't seemed worried about harming his reputation at all.

She pressed the print function as she continued to read to us. "Police think Katrina was poisoned, he says. Mamdouba's put the lid on all of them. Doesn't want anyone talking to the cops out of his presence. They're tightening up the attic and basement. No more wandering in and out of labs and storerooms. He knows how close I was to Katrina. Like that."

E-mail was a strange phenomenon, as our Internet-related cases demonstrated. People who didn't know each other at all developed on-line relationships with the mere sending and receipt of several messages. They frequently revealed things in this impersonal medium that they would never have said to the same relative stranger on the telephone or face-to-face. They often talked without the filters they used in conversations, and I was counting on that fact today.

"Does it feel right to you?"

"What he says to me? That he answers so quickly? Yeah. I didn't know him well, but I'd guess his affection for Katrina is real. He'd want to know what she'd told me."

"Then chum up to him," Mike said. "Today is Tuesday, right? Tell him you're getting into town this Friday. You can see him over the weekend. Then ask him some more questions. Exactly what has Mamdouba told him? What areas that used to be open have been closed off?"

He turned to me. "I'm telling you, Coop. We need layouts of those floor plans today. Ready when we get up there."

"Laura can type the subpoenas as soon as she gets in. We can fax them up to the museum."

"You ready to pick up where we left off last night?"

Clem took her hands away from the keyboard and swiveled her chair to face us.

"When we knocked off, I was asking about the friends who were working with you on the return of the bones. Were all of them here in New York, at the two museums?"

"By no means. I guess five or six of us were local. We'd talk about it at dinner or when we got together." She smiled. "We're aware that it was nothing we were going to solve in a hurry."

"But the rest of them, how do you stay in touch?"

"E-mail, of course. The Internet."

That answer pleased me. Once she identified her cohorts to me, a search warrant or court order could help our computer jocks download their office hard drives and examine their Internet browsers for information about sites visited and people contacted.

"On an official level, have you had any support from museum administrators?"

"It's not a popular topic here. Try bringing up names like Qisuk and Mene. You'll get a passel of denials, and when you go to find the records, they've all been purged. With whom have you talked about Katrina's disappearance?" She caught herself. "Her murder?"

"At Natural History we've met with Elijah Mamdouba and the curator in charge of African mammals, Richard Socarides. Did you know either of them?"

"I've worked with both. Elijah's a mystery to me. He's a very kind man, but he's really between a rock and a hard place. I tried to engage him on this issue any number of times. As a black African, he would, one might think, have a keen interest in doing the right thing. But he's just a flunky for the trustees, and happy to be that."

"What's in it for the museums to fight this?"

"Think of the human time it takes to sort it all out. Then there's the money to help identify millions of skeletal pieces by DNA. Each and every scientific discipline has a reason to oppose the return. The paleontologists and anthropologists don't want to let these collections go. They think it's more important to know what my great-grandparents ate for lunch every day than to know they're resting peacefully. Every archaeologist alive thinks this concept of returning the remains disrupts their ability to do their work, both in the field—now and for the future—and in the museums."

Clem went on, "There's a gold mine in these vaults. Some of the collections are priceless. And nobody wants to upset that apple cart."

Mike laughed. "Not even the mammal man?"

"Socarides? Are you kidding? He sits on some of the most valuable bones in that museum. Have they let you see the elephant room?"

Mike and I both answered, "No."

"There's a maze of staircases that winds up to the attic. It's a fantastic sight. Tiers and tiers of huge elephant skulls. Below them, the actual bones from their bodies, all draped in plastic coverings. Then a wall full of their teeth, ten pounds each. You know what an elephant's skeleton weighs? Half a ton. And then you add to their value the fact that some were gifts of famous people. Those sad gray beasts shot by Teddy Roosevelt or donated by P. T. Barnum."

"I guess just the worth of their ivory would make them even more treasured."

"The tusk vault, that's what you'd want to see."

That word again. "Now this one's a specific place?"

"Oh, yes. But it's so well hidden within the museum that most of the people who work there don't even know it exists."

"Why does it?"

"It's supposed to be a secret, a very small room with a dark green steel door. I've never seen it. Built, of course, to prevent the theft of the tusks, which is why none of us were ever able to find out where it is. Millions of dollars' worth of ivory. Not only from the elephants, but, even more rare, from creatures like narwhals."

"These rooms, these special rooms, are there several of them, Clem?"

"Dozens. For a variety of different purposes."

It was clear that at our meeting the previous morning, Mamdouba hadn't been forthcoming when we asked about private vaults.

Mike looked over at me. "Suppose you could work up enough probable cause to get a warrant. You know, get us in the museum to look for something. Like—like arsenic. Like a boat ticket to Cairo. Could we take Clem in with us and get her to show us around?"

"I'm still stuck on the probable-cause piece. We can talk about it when we leave here. Maybe we can get Zimm to help us, without a warrant."

"There's probably nothing I can find for you inside that place that he doesn't already know about," Clem said. "You should push him to help. I think he had a thing for Katrina. He tagged along for a few of our dinners."

"As long as you bring that up, did you ever meet Pierre Thibodaux?"

"Several times, just at museum receptions and meetings. I wasn't part of his world, that's for sure."

"Did Katrina ever talk about him?"

Clem blushed. "I don't want to say anything that would make you think badly of her."

"She's dead. About six decades prematurely, if you ask me. I don't care whether she liked married men or monkeys, I just need to know the truth," Mike said.

"Katrina fancied Monsieur Thibodaux. I think she'd met him in France, actually, before she moved to the States."

"She talked about that?"

"Never. She denied it to me, in fact. But we were at a meeting once, in his office. Right at the beginning of the exhibition planning. Thibodaux noticed her immediately. Came right up and kissed her, both cheeks. Thought he had recognized her from somewhere. Maybe that little French museum she worked in before coming to the Cloisters. Talked to her for about five minutes."

"What did they say?"

"Sorry. English, Danish, Inuit. I don't know any French. I didn't stay around to listen."

"Did you get the sense that anything sexual had gone on?"

"Heavens, no. She may have wanted it to happen at one point, but after the—" Clem broke her sentence abruptly. "After last June—"

"After the rape?"

"Exactly. When that happened, she just lost her spark. Withdrew from all of us for a while. Then I got canned and moved away to London. I'll be devastated if Thibodaux had anything to do with—um—with hurting Katrina. I set her to work on him."

"How? What do you mean?"

"I saw the way he eyed her, and the way she responded to him. I didn't think there would be any harm in trying to use him as a sympathizer. Primitive artworks aren't exactly the centerpiece of the Met collection. Why would he care if we emptied out our closets?"

"I knew he lied to us about Katrina, from the first time we talked to him," Mike said to me before turning back to Clem. "Did he bite?"

"I think he nibbled at Katrina's skin a little." Clem laughed. "But he had no interest in our project to repatriate bones. She told me he gave her a tough lecture about the impossibility of returning artifacts to African communities. How the objects are displayed in our museums with a respect uncommon in their homelands. He told her they'd be in greater danger if they were sent back to some of the villages from which they came."

That sounded like the Thibodaux we had interviewed. I would try to get Clem alone later and see whether she knew any specifics that might contradict the director's description of his relationship with Katrina, things she would be reluctant to discuss in front of Mike.

"The others from the Met," Mike asked, "how well did you know any of them?"

Clem mentioned some names of her peers from the joint exhibition who worked at the other museum. I jotted down the ones who were not familiar to me.

"Any of the curators?"

"Well, Anna Friedrichs, of course, and Erik Poste.

They both were involved in the bestiary show, so we had regular meetings together. Timothy Gaylord, too."

Gaylord was due back in the city today. Perhaps he would be less of an enigma once we met him this afternoon.

"Do you know about their relationships with Katrina?"

"Superficial, I would think. Erik's family was South African, and his father had done a lot of work on the African continent. Exploring, hunting, collecting kind of things. And Anna, of course, had professional expertise in primitive art. We both thought they'd be good candidates to try to recruit, you know? Have some well-respected scholars to back us up."

"Did Katrina have any luck?"

"We failed on both fronts. The only one I asked her to approach alone was Thibodaux. He seemed so obviously taken by her. Erik Poste? We took him to dinner together one night. We knew he was coming over to Natural History late in the day—he did most of his work here in the evenings, when he finished at the Met. Must have spent our week's salary wining and dining him. He was shocked, that's all. So aggravated at Katrina."

"Why?"

"Erik didn't even listen to the stories we told him, about graves of real people that have been plundered. About the town in Namibia in which they were digging a new roadway. They found the graves of twenty-six white settlers from the 1930s, so they were moved and reburied with pomp and ceremony. In the same plot there was the grave of a black native woman and her baby. Those two remains were taken to the local museum for dissection and 'study.' Just a few years ago this happened. And Erik Poste? Oblivious to it."

"But what made him mad?"

"That Katrina had such a brilliant eye for medieval artwork. That he and Bellinger had agreed that she could begin to help with acquisitions for the Met and the Cloisters. Erik complimented her work, her memos, her opinions. It was quite a tirade. He berated her for throwing it all away because of some tribal voodoo. I don't think he heard a word I told him."

"And Ms. Friedrichs?"

"I don't know what's worse. Erik is completely absorbed in his work. It's all European and anything but primitive. Anna, well—this *is* her field. All her education and background have been in aboriginal cultures. She nodded her head and stroked us when we talked about what we wanted to do, but I don't think she cared a whit about helping us in reality. I think she's a phony. You know what Anna and I fought about on the committee for the joint show?"

"No idea."

"When Margaret Mead came back from the South Pacific, among the treasures she brought were shrunken heads. Maori tribesmen shrunken heads. They were on display for decades in the museum. It was only recently that they were withdrawn from exhibit. Anna wanted to bring them out of mothballs for the big exhibition. Taking on Margaret Mead is like taking on Mother Teresa. And trust me, Anna thinks she's the reincarnation of Mead, taken to a higher level and a haughtier locale."

"Why higher?"

"'Cause she's queen of all things primitive in a damn *art* museum, not surrounded by stuffed squirrels and T. rex fossils in Natural History."

I made some notes to ask Ms. Friedrichs about her feelings about the repatriation of human remains.

"You know this guy Timothy Gaylord?" Mike asked.

"Now there's a man with problems. Nobody knows quite what to do with mummies these days." Clem laughed. "The Met's got a fortune invested in Egyptian tomb relics. Used to be quite acceptable to dig up the dead. We put ours away."

"Your what?"

"Mummies. The anthropology department at Natural History also has a vast collection of mummies, even though nobody associates us with that kind of thing. They're mostly stored now, too. In big black metal boxes. Some of them were sent on loan from the Met half a century ago and never returned. Boy, did Gaylord want those back."

"Do you know where in the museum they store those mummies?" I was thinking that might be a likely place to secrete a sarcophagus without calling attention to it. Maybe even hide the remains of the princess that were removed to make room for Katrina.

"Used to be in the tower attic. But it got so cramped up there that I think they moved most of them to the basement." An even more logical place to keep the heavy limestone coffin, as we originally figured.

There was a knock on the door and Laura opened

it to say good morning and see if there were things she needed to do. I got her started on some assignments.

"I'll leave you and Clem to handle the mail," I told Mike. "I'm going to the grand jury, then to Sarah's office to see how she's managing the cases that came in over the weekend. And Timothy Gaylord. Would you give him a call to find out when we can meet with him later today?"

The meeting with Sarah and several of the assistants in our unit took almost two hours. An end-of-semester party at Columbia College had turned into a drunken orgy, and a Barnard freshman woke up naked in the bed of a guy she had never seen before and didn't remember meeting. A homeless woman had been raped while sleeping on the seat of a subway train, in the last car, shortly after it pulled out of the Times Square station. And a teacher at a local high school was arrested for exchanging top grades for oral sex with four of the sophomore girls in his biology class.

"Where's Mike?" I asked, after greeting Laura and coming back into my office.

"Two guys from the DA's squad came by looking for you. Told him something urgent was up and he flew out of here with them."

It was unlike him to leave without an explanation, but I assumed I would get one soon.

34

Clem handed me the printouts of her latest e-mail responses. "On the Natural History side, nothing from Mamdouba. That doesn't surprise me, though. Socarides is the guy in charge of African mammals. His is sort of intriguing."

It began with a courteous salutation and the appropriate expression of concern about Katrina's death. Then he launched into a defensive description of the uses of arsenic in taxidermy, asking for Clem's telephone number so he could learn as soon as possible what Katrina had said about her health in the weeks before she died.

"The others are from the Met staff. Bellinger and Friedrichs. I'd expect to hear from them. She worked so closely with Hiram, and I think she trusted him. And Anna—well, it would be strange if she didn't express her condolences. Nothing out of the ordinary. If I'd ever thought I'd have so many dinner invitations, though, I would have been back for a visit long before this. You've got everyone vying for my companionship."

"Keep tapping away at the keyboard, if you don't mind. Answer them all, okay? When you get some conversation going, why don't you mention that Katrina talked to you about the bones she was looking for. See if that gooses anybody."

I was on the phone with one of the guys in the Special Victims Unit when Mike reappeared in my doorway. "It's only a little bit past noon and I got my first collar. Piece of cake."

"A homicide I don't know about?"

"Nope. Part of your fan club." He made a ratcheting noise with the teeth of his handcuffs as he closed them and lifted the back flap of his blazer to loop them into the waist of his pants. "Your favorite stalker."

"Shirley Denzig? Picketing with the S and M group?"

"Yeah. Joe Roman and the guys from the squad came by to let you know they got a call she was downstairs, so I went along in case they needed me to ID her."

"But how did she know about the demonstration? Why'd she come?"

"The all-news radio station was running it. Courthouse brouhaha. Sex crimes prosecutor steps in shit at the DA's office. She couldn't wait to get here and add to your aggravation. They're fingerprinting upstairs as we speak. Grand larceny, three counts, from the cases at the Waldorf. Aggravated harassment for the calls to you. Oh, and we tossed in criminal possession of a weapon, third degree, for the loaded gun she's got in her backpack."

CPW third degree was probably the charge that would bring Denzig the most jail time.

"That should make you feel better. Remind me to tell you about last night," I said.

"You're joking, aren't you? Something happened after we split?"

"Save it for the right moment, okay?" I nodded in Clem's direction. No need to spook a witness with reminders of how crazily some of our defendants behave, how loosely tethered they are to reality.

I felt an enormous surge of relief at the news of Denzig's apprehension.

"You need to sign a corroborating affidavit for the complaint."

"A pleasure, Detective. Which of my esteemed colleagues is catching today?"

Mike lowered his voice. "McKinney's giving it to Ellen Gunsher."

"Not a prayer," I practically shouted the words at Mike, coming out from behind my desk to pass him to get to McKinney's office down at the end of the hallway.

He grabbed my elbow as I tried to brush by. "The gun. That's what she's supposed to handle. That's what her unit does. Let it go, Coop."

I pulled away and kept walking. "I'm not letting that case be assigned to a lawyer who's too cowardly to set foot in a courtroom, just because she's in bed with McKinney. What for? So she can plead it out to some cheap charge when I'm not looking?"

"He in?" I asked McKinney's secretary. The door to his office was closed.

"Can't be disturbed. There's a meeting—"

I knocked and turned the handle. "Hate to interrupt when you've got so much on your plate."

McKinney was stretched out on the worn leather sofa on the far side of his office, his shoes off and tucked beneath the small conference table in the middle of the room. Gunsher was standing by the hot plate under the window, brewing two cups of tea.

"Shirley Denzig. That's already been assigned. Sorry, there's been a phone dump and—"

"Yeah, Alex, but now there's a gun," he said, sitting upright and fishing for his loafers with his toes. "Who was working on it?"

"I made sure not to know. Chinese wall and all that. I'm just a witness. Sarah assigned someone to it ages ago."

"Well, Ellen can take it over and—"

"That's not happening, Pat. Someone with trial experience who can deal with three traveling salesmen who aren't going to want to come to town to testify—"

We kept cutting each other off, and Ellen took in the back-and-forth action like she was watching a Ping-Pong match.

"It'd be ugly, Pat, if you have to be a witness at the trial." He looked puzzled. "I understand you're the one who leaked the story about Grooten's body being found in Port Newark the night Mike and I were out there. The thing you tried to blame on Jake, remember? I'll bet when I check about who called the media in today for this little feeding frenzy about the S and M lunatic, some kindly source who owes me will tell me that there's no one in the universe who wanted to give my antagonists an airing more than you."

"Don't walk out of here until I'm finished, Alex. I'm not done."

"Sorry, Ellen. We don't need the gun traced. We already know she stole it from her father's garage. Hate to waste your time on something so trivial." I let the door swing shut behind me.

Back at my office, I reached over Laura and used her phone to dial Sarah's extension and let her know that Shirley Denzig had been arrested. "I don't care who you choose. Assign it to anyone who can pick a jury and lay a proper foundation to introduce a gun into evidence. Mike and I are going back up to Natural History this afternoon."

Mike was standing over Clem's shoulder, reading her mail. "Now we've got Erik Poste checking in. Very sorry about Katrina. Afraid he won't be in town this weekend when Clem gets here but he'd like to give her a call. Gives his number at the Met. Says he won't be there this afternoon 'cause he's going somewhere with Gaylord."

"Speaking of Gaylord—"

"Yeah, I got him. He'll be at Natural History all afternoon. We can talk to him there."

"What do we do with Clem?"

"Well, we sure don't want to out her at the museum. We want her on-line, don't we?"

"And secure, too. I got it." I called Ryan Blackmer's office to see whether Harry Hinton was assigned to testify today to the grand jury on the pedophile sting arrest he had made on Monday afternoon. He was, and Ryan expected him to be the first presentation at 2 P.M. Hinton would be available after that.

"We're going to leave you here in Coop's office with another detective while we go to the museum to do some more interviews and snoop around. Harry's a genius on the Internet. If something comes up that's important, he'll reach out to us. He'll take you back to the hotel any time you're ready to go. And we'll get together with you this evening to see where we all stand."

I ordered in sandwiches to feed Clem and kept her company until two-thirty when Harry Hinton appeared in my office, following his brief grand jury appearance.

I made the introductions and told Harry what we were trying to accomplish.

"Here's one more from Eve Drexler," Clem said as I was signing the subpoenas on Laura's desk. "I told her I heard she had been in London, at a meeting with Thibodaux and Bellinger at the British Museum. I said that someone from New York had recognized her, but when I tried to find them, to inquire about Katrina, I saw that it was Katrina herself who had been signed in at the meeting."

"Good thinking. What'd she say?"

"She's asking me not to mention it to the police until I meet with her first."

"That means Thibodaux hasn't had a chance to tell her yet that we know about it."

"She blames it on Bellinger."

"So did her boss, yesterday when we confronted him with it."

"You want to do this in real time?" Harry Hinton asked. "I can make this livelier for you."

"How?"

"CITU, over at headquarters." The Computer

Intelligence and Technology Unit was just a few blocks away at One Police Plaza. "They've got a new piece of equipment. Cost 'em sixty thousand dollars."

Mike was impressed. The department rarely spent that kind of money on anything.

"It works like a wiretap on a telephone. It can intercept on-line communications while they're in progress. This broad's writing to Clem. We can tap in and see who she goes on-line with next, if she's talking about your case. Maybe she forwards the info she's getting to someone, maybe she passes on what she knows. Maybe she knows stuff you two don't."

"You've used this before?"

"My boss is the one who applied for the money to buy the equipment. We can download the actual kiddie porn while it's being transmitted, even if it's encrypted."

"You've been holding out on me. What do you need to get started?"

"Court order."

The ability to find out what each of these witnesses was saying to the others, if they were communicating on-line, was a brilliant idea I had not thought possible.

"Keep an eye on Clem. Get Ryan up here and beg him to do the order for me. I can talk him through the facts he needs from my cell phone while we're driving uptown."

My hearty band of sadomacho fanatics must have wearied or made their point and disbanded after McKinney shifted them around to the rear of the courthouse and they'd had their fifteen minutes of fame on the midday news shows. We were able to get out the main door without incident. I left my car in Chinatown and rode up the West Side Highway with Mike, talking on the cell phone to Ryan and giving him what I hoped would be probable cause to get the interception going by this evening. There was at least the fact that one of the e-mail correspondents, who happened also to be a Met employee, had been using the dead girl's identification a month after her disappearance. I also told him the name of the young lawyer who might be able to expedite the request, since I had not yet been able to apply for the search warrants I had wanted without knowing the specific target sites at the museums.

Then I called Mamdouba to tell him we were going to meet with Timothy Gaylord, who was over from the Met, working on the joint exhibition in the museum basement. We wanted to come up to see Mamdouba when we were done.

"I'm afraid you've taken up all the time we have for this business, Miss Cooper. It's been very disruptive here, to the staff. Perhaps we can arrange that future meetings will be held in your offices?"

We had known this stonewalling would come at some point, but had not predicted the timing. "Certainly. But Mr. Gaylord is expecting us, and I believe Detective Wallace is already there." It was past the three o'clock hour that we had set earlier in the day.

Mike had stopped at the light at the bottom of the exit ramp. "Scare the shit out of him, blondie. Keep your toe in his door. Give him something to worry about."

I shrugged my shoulders and mouthed the three letters to Mike. He agreed.

"It's critical we see you today, just for a few minutes. It's about the DNA results on Katrina Grooten's clothing."

I imagined that great big unctuous smile of Mamdouba's wiping itself right off his face.

"But, Miss Cooper, I thought you assured us that Katrina wasn't sexually assaulted by her killer? You're confusing—"

"That's why we need to see you. We know that you have a DNA profile for every employee at the museum. We're going to need access to those—"

"Not before I have an explanation." His voice was sharp and angry now.

"Of course you will, as soon as we're done with Mr. Gaylord." I disconnected the phone before he could ask any more questions.

I dialed the medical examiner's office and hung on until Dr. Kestenbaum could pick up the call. "Got a minute to help me? I'm digging myself into a hole here with our witnesses. If I told you I had already-made genetic fingerprints of several of our suspects, and could probably get swabs from the rest of them, would it do you any good, given that there's no blood or seminal fluid?"

"I can let you know in a week," he said, ever cautious and professional.

"I'm about five minutes away from getting the investigative door slammed in my face. Why next week? What's that going to do for you?"

"I presented the case at our weekly meeting on Friday. The chief had a good idea. Whoever killed your victim had to do some heavy lifting. Getting the body from wherever death occurred to the place where he— or she—wrapped her in the old linen cloths. Then removed the lid of the limestone box, or at least had to slide it open and back into place."

"Help us, doc. What's your point?" We had parked on Columbus Avenue.

"Amylase. Possibly on the deceased's clothing. Or the linen. Maybe even on the exterior of the sarcophagus."

"Remind me. Amylase?"

"It's an enzyme found in body fluids. Saliva, tears—"

"We're not gaining any ground with this crew if I suggest the killer cried at the crime scene or kissed her good-bye." My impatience was palpable.

"And sweat," Kestenbaum said, finishing his sentence. "The person who did these things is very likely to have perspired, and we might well have a fair amount of DNA if his sweaty hands were on the clothing or coffin."

"You'll know—?"

"It's a very sophisticated test that we aren't equipped to do here. We're outsourcing the evidence to a private lab in Maryland."

"Best-case scenario?"

"We might be able to tell you who lifted Grooten's body into the box and closed the lid on her."

35

We entered the museum on West Seventy-seventh Street, heading directly for the basement offices of the joint bestiary exhibition. I called Laura as we walked, and she patched me through to Clem.

"All quiet."

"Give this one a try. Not a group mailing, but just to a few of them. The ones who've been answering personally. Tell them that the police want a sample of your DNA. Say that you've been told there was evidence that was found with Katrina's body, okay?"

"Was there really—?"

"I don't mean to be rude, Clem, but I can't answer your questions now. I can only ask for your help."

We sent her back to work and continued on our way. Security buzzed the group at work belowground, and minutes later, Zimm appeared to lead us downstairs. Mercer had arrived about a quarter of an hour earlier. The three of us left the graduate student in his office and made our way down the dark hallway to the conference room in which the Met curators were working. Erik Poste and Hiram Bellinger rose to greet us and Gaylord finished a telephone conversation before extending a hand.

"What's this about DNA?" he asked. "You've got no business—"

"Put the brakes on, pal," Mike said, motioning with his hand, suggesting that the three men resume their seats at the table. "Who was that you were talking to? Mamdouba?"

"No, that was Eve Drexler, actually. Something about taking evidence from us like we were suspects in this case."

The old axiom had proved itself once again, only now the technology had changed. Telegraph, telephone, tell a woman. Clem had spread the word about DNA to Eve, and she had alerted her team between the time we got out of the car and got down the stairs.

"Just a precaution, Mr. Gaylord. You see, every curator and worker at Natural History has to give a DNA sample."

"That's understandable, Detective. They're working with animal specimens, doing genetic analysis and tracking evolutionary patterns. They can't take the chance of confusing their own DNA with some relic or biological sample." He had declined Mike's suggestion to be seated and was pacing at the head of the table. "We work with art and ancient decorative objects," he said, incorporating Poste and Bellinger in his response. "If you're implying that I—I—we, had anything at all to do—"

Erik Poste tried to present a calmer face on behalf of the Metropolitan curators. "You make this sound like a game. Why don't you tell us what you know, Mr. Chapman? If there was some legitimate purpose to this scientific exercise, I think we'd find a way to work with you."

"Hey, I look like a man with time on his hands to play games? I got a girl who specializes in funeral exhibits and becomes one. I got an airborne man who goes off a flying buttress without wings or a safety net. I got a Scythian arm that fell into a jaguar den—you wanna talk exercise or you think maybe we got a job to do?"

"When we say we're interested in DNA evidence, gentlemen, we're not limited to blood and semen. Detective Wallace made an arrest last month in which the defendant was identified from saliva he left on the rim of a beer bottle at the crime scene," I told them.

"And I popped a guy in a homicide because we got his skin cells on the doorknob of the victim's bedroom."

"Skin cells?"

"Yeah, they slough off, just when we're holding on to something with ordinary contact. Windowsills, steering wheel of a car, the lid of a sarcophagus."

Maybe it was just the close atmosphere in the windowless cubicle, but the three men seemed to be squirming.

"It's painless, boys," Mike said. "I'll stop by the Met tomorrow with my Q-tips and plastic vials, and it will be over in a flash. Meanwhile, Mr. Gaylord, can we take you down the hall to ask you a few more questions?"

Gaylord sucked on the stem of his pipe as he followed me around to Zimm's office. There was no tobacco in its bowl, so I assumed this was a habit of his.

"D'you mind if we displace you for a bit?"

"Not at all," the young man answered. "By the way, Ms. Cooper, you know that girlfriend of Katrina's I told you about, the one who moved to London?"

"Yeah. The one whose name you couldn't remember."

"Clementine. I just heard from her today. I guess you guys have already been in touch with her." He looked from my face to Mike's to try to draw a response.

"We're trying to encourage her to come to Manhattan. We're hoping she has some information that will help us solve the murder. We'll talk about it later, Zimm, okay?"

Gaylord sat at the only desk in the room, his body perched sideways on the chair, one leg crossed over the other. The pipe seemed glued to his lower lip.

Mike was interested in basics. "Ms. Grooten was found in a coffin that was the responsibility of your department. You know more about the Egyptian collection than anyone in the museum. I expect there are things that you have control of that—"

"Look, Chapman, there were six or seven sarcophagi over here all the time. The shipments moved in and out regularly. Nothing anyone would take notice of. People here carted them around all the time."

"Yeah, but you must have had special knowledge

about how to do it. I mean, it took two of us to lift the lid on the piece the night we found it. How could anyone do that alone? Maybe I need you to tell us it would have taken more than one person to do that?"

"I assume you go to the movies, don't you? *The Ten Commandments? Cleopatra?* You've seen all those slaves building the pyramids and hoisting the sphinxes into place. Weights and pulleys, Chapman, just like the old Egyptians. Put a rope around the top and slide it off," he said, pounding on the desktop in front of him. "Drop your body inside, ease the lid back in place. A bit of privacy is all one needs."

"Over at your shop, too?"

"You've seen the maze in our basement. I can't say one would be any worse than the other. Let me ask you, has Mamdouba opened up his collection of mummies to you yet?"

"No, he hasn't. I had no idea there were any here until today. Can you show them to us?"

"If I knew where they were, I'd have spirited some of my own out of here long before now. The Met sent some on loan half a century ago and we've not seen them since. They've got one of the most famous mummies in the world here. Copper Man. The copper oxide gives him a rather unique green cast. Comes from the Atacama Desert in Chile, where my conference was held this past week. A several-thousand-year-old miner who was pinned in a shaft while hammering for copper. J. P. Morgan bought him for this museum in 1905. Clem can tell you more about him than I can."

That got Mike's attention. "Clem? What do you know about Clem?"

"I heard Mr. Zimmerly mention her to you just now. What do I know about her?" Gaylord removed the pipe from his mouth and swiveled on the chair to answer Mike. "A real pain in the ass, Detective. I know her name is Clem, and she was fascinated with this Natural History mummy because he'd come from the Restaradora Mine. I believe she told me her father was a miner."

Of course. Miner. Forty-niner. And his daughter, Clementine.

"Why did you find her so difficult?"

"Ms. Cooper, we run an art museum. The greatest in the world. It's not a haven for activists and bleeding hearts whose mission is restoring the karma of people who've been dead for hundreds of centuries. We're a shrine to the most superb paintings and sculpture ever created, masterpieces from every significant culture in the world."

Gaylord had both elbows on the desk, his pipe bobbing in my direction. "That young woman hounded my staff mercilessly. What did she think we were going to do—send fifty thousand objects back to Cairo just to satisfy her and undo the mummy's curse?"

"She wasn't really inter—"

"May I remind you? The Temple of Dendur—that magnificent structure, the crown jewel of the Met—that entire monument would have been submerged under water when the Aswan Dam was built. We saved that temple, dammit. We brought it here in boxes—six hundred eighty-two of them. One for each carved piece of rock. Most of the treasures we have would have been destroyed if left in their own war-torn and decaying civilizations."

"But the people themselves, Mr. Gaylord. I understood that Clem's concern was with the remains of people."

His free hand slammed on the desk. "Then what the hell does that have to do with me and my colleagues? We're as different from a natural history museum as night and day—in function, in purpose, in style. Clem and her Eskimos, Clem and her sacred Indian burial grounds—they're all Mamdouba's problems, not ours."

"These things don't trouble you?"

"Mr. Chapman, I can't change these facts, these histories. It's quite simple. European culture has always been venerated in art museums. The culture of aboriginal people was relegated, like curiosities of science, to natural history museums."

Gaylord stood up and replaced the pipe in his mouth. "There is a chasm between these two New York institutions that is far wider than the park that divides us geographically. In fact, the reason you find us all here today is because we're trying to reverse the disaster that Thibodaux started. We'd like to call off this joint exhibition."

"But there's so much invested in it already."

"Not nearly as much as Pierre had anticipated. UniQuest, the company that was giving us most of the commercial backing, is probably going to pull the plug. We got a call from Los Angeles today. Quentin Vallejo has put a moratorium on spending for the moment."

If Nina had been trying to reach me with that news,

I would have no way of knowing since my phone had been dead since the time we entered this basement area.

"A financial decision?"

"Basically, yes. I don't think any of us shared Pierre's enthusiasm for the plan. Besides, UniQuest is afraid of the bad publicity because of the Grooten murder. And apparently, while I was away last weekend, a man fell off the roof of the Met. They didn't like that much, either."

"Did you know him? Pablo Bermudez, I mean."

He bit on the pipe stem. "Hard worker. Always busy. Never had much to say."

Gaylord didn't seem to care deeply about the human factor. Lucky Pablo didn't splatter blood on any of the canvases when he hit the ground.

"So what will become of these offices and the objects that are here?"

"Anna Friedrichs is upstairs now, talking with Mamdouba. She's going to try to convince him to carry on with his own bestiary show. He doesn't need our input to pull this off. If we dissolve this union quickly and easily, we'll start to transfer the Metropolitan's objects back into our own quarters."

How do you secure a potential crime scene that is closeted away somewhere within hundreds of thousands of square feet, when you haven't yet identified the exact location? Better still, how do you do the same to two areas? I didn't want anything moved out until we had a chance to examine every possible hiding place under this vast roof.

"You know," Gaylord said, walking around us to

open the door, "that Bermudez fellow was first hired by Bellinger. I think he lived up near the Cloisters. If I remember correctly, he'd been the super in Hiram's building, which is how he was recommended to work with us. Maybe Hiram knows something about the man."

I remembered the obit said he had lived with his family in Washington Heights.

Gaylord walked, hands in pockets and head down, along the hallway to get back to the joint exhibition office. Peering after him, I could see that Bellinger and Poste were gone.

I called Zimm's name, and the bespectacled student emerged from a lab two doors away.

"Have you seen these guys?" I asked, thumbing my finger toward the empty room.

"They left a while ago. I told them I had another e-mail from Clem. She said she might be in town as early as tonight. She said Katrina must have found the vault she was looking for."

36

Mike, Mercer, and I were huddled in the corner outside Zimm's office.

"I've got the subpoena to hand to Mamdouba for the floor plan and list of rooms. The museum closes at five forty-five. That's half an hour. Clem's already telling people that she may get to town tonight. Why don't we have Hinton drive her up here and bring her into the place when there's no one around to see her. Then—"

"We'd still have to get her past a security guard."

"Like any one of them is going to have a clue?" Mike smirked. "The place will be emptying out for the night. Mercer, you can meet her outside the entrance. The guard'll be so busy dealing with Mercer and looking at his shiny gold badge that he won't even notice Clem. We need an insider to get us around here. Zimm's good, but he has no idea what we'd be looking for, necessarily. Clem would recognize the significance of anything she and Katrina discussed. She's snooped everywhere, I'm sure."

"You think Mamdouba will let us stay late, after closing hours?" Mercer asked.

"Other people are in here doing their work."

"You trust him? You ready to take him into our confidence about having Clem here?" Mike asked.

I responded by looking at each of them. "What do you guys think?"

Mike wasn't ready to trust anyone. "Let's get her here first. One of us will sniff around the attic with Coop, looking at bones. The other one will hold hands with an Eskimo in a quiet room till the coast is clear and she can show us what she knows."

I called Laura's number and asked her to put Clem on. "You just missed them. You can reach them on Detective Hinton's cell phone. He was on his way to the hotel with Clem. She was getting tired."

I wrote down the number she gave me. "Any messages?"

"Call Nina at home tonight. It's pretty important." That would be the UniQuest funding story. "Sarah wants to talk to you later if you've got some time. Eve Drexler called. I recognized her name from the case so I asked whether I could help."

"What'd she want?"

"To see whether I could give her a telephone number to reach Clem."

"What'd you tell her?"

"You taught me well. Told her I didn't know who that was and that I'd be happy to ask you. She told me not to bother you with it."

Eve was getting impatient with the e-mails. She wanted to talk to Clem. Or was she calling on Thibodaux's behalf? She was obviously spreading the news that Clem had planted with her about Katrina and the police investigation.

I dialed Harry Hinton's cell phone number. "Where are you?"

"Stuck behind a four-car pileup on the FDR Drive, just below Fourteenth Street."

"Think you can get Clem to the hotel, get her something to eat, let her put her feet up for half an hour, and get her to the Museum of Natural History by seven-thirty?"

I heard him ask if she was game and he got back on to assure me he could. "Well, we're down to only one guard to worry about," I told Mike and Mercer. "Traffic's bad and she wants a bit of a rest. No way they can make it before this place closes, so that will give us some time to get started. Let's find out which door they keep open so staff can come and go after hours. Harry'll call when they leave the hotel and one of you can walk Clem in."

Mamdouba was less than pleased to see us so near to closing time. His expression soured when I handed him the subpoena.

"Must I go to court?" he asked, reading the language on the small white document.

"No. You can see that the foreman of the grand jury modified the request. Instead of a personal appearance before them, you can satisfy your legal obligation by giving me everything we ask for. That's why my office called your assistant this morning, so you'd have the papers ready."

"Let me see what we've got for you." He left us in his colorfully decorated circular office and retreated to his assistant's desk. When he returned, he had an armload of papers.

The big grin returned to his face. "So, here you can begin." He unfolded a Xeroxed copy of a museum floor plan that stretched beyond the edges of his desk blotter. He ran his index finger from the Central Park West entrance door through the narrow lines that led into display rooms to the left of the Theodore Roosevelt Memorial Hall as he talked.

"Now, what you see here no longer exists like this. It's become the Hall of Biodiversity, as you know. But you can use this—"

"Wait a minute." Mike bent down and looked at the date below the name of the architectural firm that had done the plan. "This diagram was printed in 1963. You've torn up and rebuilt this place five times since then." He tapped the desk with his fist. "And we don't want the tourist version, Mr. Mamdouba. It's got to be current and it's got to be complete. I want details of everything that's below the ground floor and whatever is above the fourth floor."

"Mr. Chapman, there are seven hundred twenty-three rooms in this museum. You'll be here for a week."

"I gotta be somewhere for a week, and so far nobody's suggested Paris. Get me everything."

Mike pulled up a chair up to the side of Mamdouba's desk and began to fan out all the wrinkled maps that diagrammed the mishmash of corridors and stairwells in the museum's twenty-three interconnected buildings.

"But, but you can't do that here," the curator sputtered at him.

"Because?"

"We've got to have a meeting. A bit of an emergency."

"With people from the Met, about the exhibition breaking up?"

"Exactly."

"Is Mr. Thibodaux coming?"

"No, no. Not since he tendered his resignation. He's got nothing more to do with this. Some of the others from the Met are already here, and Miss Drexler is on her way with Pierre's files. I'll need this room, Mr. Chapman."

"Park us where you want us, Mr. Mamdouba. We're all yours."

"Tomorrow?"

"Right now. We got a lot of territory to cover and—"

"Yes, but I understand you're even bringing in help from overseas," he said quietly.

Mike met Mamdouba's supercilious smirk with one of his own. "I'm a patsy for reunions. Love it when the whole family gets together every now and then. We'll stay all night if we have to, sir. Is that a problem for you?"

"Of course it is. I have to keep the guards with you—"

"Like *we're* the security risk? Those guys have been sleeping on the job for aeons. There's more life in your dead T. rex than in the whole passel of mopes somebody stuffed and left guarding your treasures. Tell you what, you can check my pockets when I leave, if that's your concern. Mercer and I are not much on collecting crabs in formaldehyde, and Coop here has more jewels than she needs. What we could use is a quiet place to look over these lists."

Mike picked several sheaves of paper out of the large pile and handed them to Mercer and me while he continued to search for a more up-to-date floor plan. The directory I was holding appeared to be a comprehensive inventory of categories of collections. It was several hundred pages thick, bound together with a large metal clamp.

I peered over at Mercer's folder, which was equally weighty. It listed names of donors, going back almost a century, and the specimens they had contributed to the museum.

"Is there anything that itemizes your collections by name and refers to the storage areas or display cases they're in?"

"Everything that's now on exhibit is computerized. You'll find that printout here, too," Mamdouba said, thumbing through the stack he had given to Mike.

"Like that only leaves us looking for the other ninety percent?"

"Well, we're trying to get that all into the system, Miss Cooper. It's a dreadfully difficult process. Two million butterflies, five million gall wasps, fifty million bones. Is that the kind of thing you're interested in?"

"*Fifty* million? How many of them are human?"

"They're mostly mammals, Detective. The numbers are in these folders that my assistant organized for you."

"Settle us in somewhere. It's gonna be a long night. And one of those magnetized passes—we'll need to borrow one in case we go to the basement."

Mamdouba was quiet for a few moments, undoubtedly trying to decide whether to engage in a battle with us. With obvious reluctance, he went into his desk drawer and handed Mike a plastic pass with a VIP guest label on it. He was thinking, it seemed to me, about what space he could stick us in temporarily that would cause the least interference or notice. "Come down the hall after me, please."

He led us to an empty office about five doors away from his corner room. It was sparsely furnished, except for the shelves of mollusks that covered three walls from floor to ceiling. "If this is acceptable, I'll check on you later."

Limpets, snails, mussels, and oysters, all looking very gray in their pickled juice, watched over us as we set to work spreading out the floor plans on the empty desktop. "Start looking?" Mike asked.

Mercer sat on the window ledge, resting one of his long legs against an open desk drawer. "I'd concentrate on the level below the ground floor and the area up on five, above the offices," he said, handing Mike a red felt-tipped pen. "They've got to be the least populated spaces when the museum is shut down. Look for unmarked rooms or closets and circle 'em so we can take a peek."

"And compare the different generations of maps," I added. "See if something has been reconfigured and whether it's accessible now or not."

"Man, we're gonna have to come back with comfy shoes. We got miles to cover in here."

I made myself comfortable on the floor and looked

up at Mercer. "You and I need to cross-reference what we find. Why don't you start looking to see whether there are any familiar names from this case? Like is the Gerst collection mentioned, or anything about Erik Poste's father? Maybe there are references to items on loan from the Met, like the mummies Timothy Gaylord was talking about."

More than two hours went by and we were still drowning in paper. Mamdouba knocked on the door and pushed it ajar without saying a word.

"We keeping you?"

"On the contrary, Mr. Chapman. Just to let you know some of us will be here working late as well, in case that's helpful to you."

We had caught the attention of some of the staffers, and they were all probably too curious to leave when they stood the chance of seeing in which direction we might be moving.

He closed the door behind him and Mike spoke: "Damn. Looks like he'll try to outlast us. This could change the evening's plan."

"I've been through this twice," Mercer said. "Only name I recognize is Herbert Gerst."

"A private vault?"

"This doesn't show any such thing. Looks like he accounts for two of the elephants, a load of mammals—okapi, elands, and every other endangered species you can think of—and a whole bunch of crawling things that should be in little glass jars. But they're spread out all over the museum."

"And I've circled places where I think you could find arsenic," I said, "starting with the taxidermy department. I suppose I should let Dr. Kestenbaum go through these lists, too. I have no idea where else to search for it."

"Hey, it never occurred to any of us that the damn stuff was being used for so many different purposes in either museum. Somebody's gonna have to account for all of it."

My beeper went off and it was Harry Hinton's number. I called him from the phone on the desk. "We're on the way," he said, "and Ryan's still working on a court order for the computer interception. Maybe we'll have it up and running for you by morning."

"No luck for tonight?"

"Nah. Jumped on it too late."

"Mercer will meet you at the corner of Columbus Avenue and Seventy-seventh Street in fifteen minutes. Tell Clem I'll run interference inside."

Mike kept poring over the interior layouts and contrasting the areas that we had accounted for as either open display space or rooms we had seen when Zimm had taken us through the place last week. Mercer and I took the elevator down to the ground floor. We showed our identification to the guard and told him Mercer was going out to meet another detective, but would return right away.

The man was slumped back in his chair, the brim of his cap pulled down on his forehead with his eyes glued to a science fiction magazine. The small black-and-white monitors on the stand beside him showed the entrances and exits within the network of courtyards behind us; twilight was descending, making it even more difficult to distinguish between the various gray walls of the abutting structures.

I thought of making small talk to distract him, in case he might recognize Clem from her days of employment here, but he was as oblivious to me as he was to the television screens he was supposed to be viewing. I turned my back to him to be certain the long, high-ceilinged corridor was still empty. The poor lighting forced me to squint to see beyond midway, but the cavernous space would clearly make footsteps audible if anyone approached.

Minutes later, Mercer and Clem jogged toward the doorway. My square-badged companion, nose-deep in aliens and space pods, was grateful when I told him I'd swing open the door for my partners without needing his help. He waved me toward it and kept reading. Walking briskly on either side of our petite charge, Mercer and I led her around to the first elevator bank we came to and disappeared from view of the guard's watch station.

When we reached the last leg of the walk back to our small room, I left Mercer and Clem at the entrance to the hallway. Passing the open door where Mike was at work, I continued on to Mamdouba's corner turret. The door was closed, but I could hear voices inside. I gave the two of them a signal to come ahead to the mollusk room, then followed them in, locking the door behind me. The three of us rearranged ourselves in the cramped space to make room for Clem to sit. She had been glad for the short break, having showered and eaten a light dinner from the room service menu.

"Will this hold you guys?" She dumped out the

contents of a small shopping bag. "Hope the city can afford the bill. It was all in the room, and I figured you might get hungry."

I laughed as Mike grabbed the glass jar of pistachios and Mercer reached for a couple of candy bars. I opened the bag of M&M's and washed them down with a few gulps from a can of soda that the three of us shared. We left the minibar bottles of scotch and vodka for the end of our night's routine.

"That's using your brain. I thought I'd have to eat bugs. C'mon," Mike said, flattening the creased floor plans with which he'd been familiarizing himself, pointing to the basement areas surrounding the joint exhibition offices. "Make yourself useful. Can you give us any more specifics about what's kept in these rooms?"

She talked us through some of the places where she had worked, guiding us with the capped tip of a pen. "It's deceptive. See this? It's a wall that separates two buildings. From the main floor it flows through like it's connected, but from where you're looking? You can't get there from here."

"Maybe we ought to go see these places," I said. "It'll give us a better sense of how we'll have to maneuver and what to specify when I draft a warrant."

"Let Mercer stay here with Clem, going over the rooms. Start figuring out where the bones are for us. You and I'll check out this part of the basement. See if anyone's still around."

I heard the click of the lock as Mercer closed the door behind us. We paused for a minute, and listened to the shrill voice of a woman, coming from Mamdouba's anteroom. I couldn't recognize from its pitch whether it was Eve Drexler, Anna Friedrichs, or the curator's assistant, who had stayed after hours.

Mike and I took the elevator to the lobby. The glass eyes of dozens of wild beasts, frozen in the safe confines of their dioramas, seemed to follow us down the vast corridor that led away from the museum's southwest corner toward the basement entrance Zimm had used to lead us downstairs on earlier visits.

Clem was right. The place was eerie at night. Vast spaces followed after one another with every turn and change in direction, each one dimly lit at best. Elegantly detailed Art Deco light globes suspended from ceilings on brass chains had the look and effectiveness of another era.

Every thirty feet or so, a modern fluorescent fixture had been stuck in place, looking like something you'd see in a bus station rest room.

We descended down the dismal staircase to the section of the basement we had seen before. Zimm was still at his desk, working on the computer, three jars of repulsive arachnids at his side.

"Mamdouba said you might be down. Anything I can help with?"

I had my legal pad and pen ready to take notes. "Just back for some detail we missed. You alone down here?"

"Nope. Lights are still on. I think we've got a full house tonight." He smiled at Mike and me. "You're sure stirring up some excitement."

We avoided the exhibition offices and headed to the far end of the hallway. Doorway after doorway, I sketched a record of whether the rooms were open or locked, what form of animal specimen seemed to be floating in the jars on the shelves, and what the climate conditions were.

Where had poor Katrina Grooten's body been stored all these months? The possible options were overwhelming. I made a note to pin down Dr. Kestenbaum for a date to come back to take temperature controls to help determine the most likely surroundings for the creation of an "Incorruptible."

For more than an hour we worked our way in and out of small storage rooms and smaller laboratories. Each time we reached a fork in the road, I'd take one side and Mike the other, agreeing to meet back at the intersection in fifteen minutes. We worked our way through three separate basement areas without any findings of significance.

By the time we got to the fourth subbasement, I was beginning to feel at home with the chemical odors, artificial lights, and countless numbers of dead things that filled every shelf, drawer, and closet.

"Your call, Coop," Mike said, reading from a small sign on the wall in front of us after he pulled a hanging string to turn on an overhead bulb. "Wasps and winged things to the left. Dinosaur fossils to the right."

"No bugs for me."

"They're not alive."

"No bugs, period. I owe you, okay? There's no choice here."

I started down the narrow corridor to my right, trying the doors and finding several of them locked. The fifth knob gave easily, and I groped along the wall till I found the light switch.

This hallway had possibilities. Here was a room labeled *Barosaurus Femurs*, with leg bones larger than tree stumps. A quick scan suggested nothing small enough to be human, but I could not reach the higher shelves or see their contents. I marked it on my pad for a return visit.

Door after door yielded similar fossilized parts. Some rooms were all dinosaur heads, with hollow eye sockets four feet in diameter and horned nostrils that stood taller than my waist. Others had nothing but vertebrae lined up end to end. It would be hard to discern, without an expert guide, whether any other species remains had been mixed in with these antiquities.

I reached the end of the gray hallway and pushed against the last door, meeting with resistance as I did. It opened slowly, operating on a rusty old air pump hinged on the wall behind it. I leaned against the door to secure it in place while I studied the contents of the room. This one stored even smaller bones, and I walked to a rack against the far wall to study a tag that appeared to have some written description on it.

As I bent over to read it, hoping the bare bulb from the far end of the hallway would provide enough light for me, the door came loose from its anchored position. I heard a loud whooshing sound as it sprung away from the wall and slammed shut, leaving me alone in the confined space with a century's accumulation of dust-covered animal skeletons.

I tried to tell myself that I was too tired to be upset. I talked to myself like a mother calming a six-year-old child. They're just bones, I kept repeating, as I tried to get my bearings and make my way back to the door in the dark. There's nothing in here to hurt me. I'm in a museum, the most child-friendly museum in the world, and my favorite policeman is fifty yards away.

I reached out to hold on to a shelf to help me feel my way back to the exit. I brushed against the rough surface of a ragged piece of cartilage and moved my hand upward to grasp the cool steel of the rack instead. Inching along step by step, I startled myself when I struck a glass object, banging it against something else.

It was a large glass jar.

Shit. I stopped in my tracks. Like dominoes, the jar I hit had knocked against its neighbor, rattling the one behind it until another in the next row toppled on its side and broke. The noxious fluid inside splashed to the floor, releasing both a foul smell and whatever pickled creatures had been sleeping inside.

Now panic set in. I looked up at the shelves over my head. Dozens and dozens of mason jars lined the walls above me. The only light in the room was the iridescence emitted by the bright pink dye that illuminated all of the bottled skeletal remains. Some kind of prehistoric crawlers were in those bottles, unidentifiable wet specimens that glowed against the darkness of the room.

I took another step forward, sliding on the slippery substance from the broken jars that coated the floor. Two more steps and I heard a crunching noise below my heel, as though I was walking on some kind of hard-shelled insect. My foot slipped on the wet slime, and again I grabbed for the shelf. The entire rack was on wheels and it rattled wildly as my bug phobia took firm hold.

I reached out my left hand to feel for the door, still clutching the end of the metal shelves. I gripped the knob when I found it and pulled hard with both hands. It wouldn't give. Stay calm, I told myself. It was hard to open from the other side, so now it's just stuck again. I yanked with all my strength, my hands greasy from the sweat I was working up. I couldn't budge the knob in either direction.

I felt along the side of the door for a light switch. Nothing. There was no fresh air in the room, and some sightless fossil with a prickly snout and a snake-like body was eye level with me, daring me to rescue both of us from this claustrophobic cell.

Patting the pockets of my jacket and pants was another useless gesture. I opened the lid on my cell phone and powered it up, but was unable to dial any number from this black hole in the museum basement. I used the point of my pen to try to jimmy the catch on the lock, but it was way too old and sticky to respond.

Feeling behind me, I stepped back and began to scream for Mike. I yelled as loud as I could, kicking against the door like Shirley Denzig had done at my garage the night before. I stopped yelling and listened for the sound of footsteps, but the walls were so thick that I doubted he could hear me any better than I could hear him.

Now the fumes from the liquid I'd released were filling the room. I mustn't get dizzy, I told myself. I did not want to be down on this floor with whatever had dripped out of the large jar, that much I knew.

Turning in place, I looked again to the far end of the space. In the ghoulish pink glow I could make out the square design of a small window high on the wall that might give out onto the courtyard. It was covered with a shade, and too tiny to get through, but if I could break it open it would give me some air and maybe someone would hear my shouts.

Behind me, I thought I heard the doorknob rattle. I spun around, stepped toward it and yelled Mike's name again as loud as I could. Nothing. Had I imagined the noise?

I wiped the sweat from my forehead but the thought was already planted in my brain: What if this was no accident? What if we had surprised the killer by coming down to the basement tonight? What if he—or she—had trapped me in this room after I walked in alone, and then gone back to do something even worse to Mike? What if Mike never got here to open this door?

I moved to rest my back on the rack but I landed against it harder than I had intended. It rocked and swayed, and the small set of wheels on the end closest to me spun off and whirled across the room. The shelves slanted downward, and everything hurtled to the floor.

Glass jars crashed and split into pieces, spraying their contents all over the floor. The odor was unbearable, and I coughed and choked on the fumes as they rose from beneath me and invaded my mouth and nose. I was almost panting because of my fear, and the faster the breaths came, the more the odor was drawn into my nostrils and throat.

Animal bones slid off the shelves and over my head and shoulders. I took three steps toward the window and reached up to brush something out of my hair.

Beetles. Thousands of beetles had been stored in the jars and now littered the room, some of them landing on my body as they fell. I choked again, this time fighting back the urge to be sick.

What had Zimm told us? Beetles were used all over the museum to eat the flesh off dead specimens. These must have been sealed into jars with their last meals, then left to rot on dusty trays in the deserted room.

The rational spirit within me kept saying that someone would surely find me before daylight. My other internal voice reminded me that whoever had slammed the door shut would be back to finish me off, if these awful creatures didn't do it first.

I walked as carefully as I could toward the wall with the window. Beneath it was a metal tank, the same kind of enormous vat that Zimm had shown us—the kind in which the prehistoric fish had been stored in its alcohol bath. Would the lid of that tank support me so that I could climb up onto it and try to break open a pane of the small glass opening behind the window shade?

Again the jiggling sound of the doorknob, and this time, with renewed urgency, I froze in place and screamed, "Michael! Mike Chapman. Get me out of here. I can't breathe."

Exquisite silence. I coughed and gagged on the dreadful smell that permeated my clothing and everything else in the room.

I pressed on the lid of the six-foot-long tank. It felt

like a thin layer of stainless steel, and I was concerned about putting my weight on top of it. I could make out the label affixed to it because of the oversize lettering in bright red ink. There was a skull and crossbones with the words FIRE HAZARD.

Of course it was a fire hazard. A tank that big full of alcohol to serve as a preservative would be enough to light up the west side of town. Add that to my list of ways to kill someone in this museum.

I looked back up at the window. These were double-glazed, we had been told, as another climate control. I had nothing except the wooden heel of my shoe with which to try to break one of the panes. So far, I had managed to destroy everything else made of glass. I might as well take a shot at this.

Before removing a shoe and exposing my foot to whatever was slopping around on the floor, I lifted the lid of the container to see how sturdy its support would be. I didn't need to drown myself in ethyl alcohol.

I removed a tissue from my jacket pocket, as a precaution, and covered my mouth as I opened the vat. But there was no strong smell of alcohol at all, so I used both hands to rest the top against the wall.

The pink iridescence above my head highlighted something gray inside the box. I bent over to see what was there. I gazed at the face of a small mummified head.

37

I let the lid drop back into place and decided to take my chances that it would hold me. I didn't believe in the mummy's curse but there were way too many dead things in this room to keep me from losing control before too long. Hoisting myself onto the end of the vat's closed surface, I pulled off my shoes and stood atop it in my bare feet.

Pushing the faded shade to the side, I raised my hand and began to bang away at the window pane. It seemed like nothing short of a sledgehammer would have any effect.

Again there was a noise at the door. I poised myself, arm in the air with my weapon aimed at it. The door opened and the light in the hallway reflected off the top of Mike Chapman's black hair.

"You getting high from these fumes, blondie? I got a box of Krazy Glue I can give you to take home. What the—"

"Somebody locked me in here!"

"Will you get down from there? What are you doing by that window? You can't kill yourself by jumping *up* from the basement to the courtyard. Save your strength."

"The missing princess—the mummy from the sarcophagus that Katrina was in? She's in this vat."

"You afraid she's gonna walk? That why you're standing up there, looking like something scared the crap out of you? C'mon, let's get going. Get off that thing."

"I can't."

"What do you mean you can't? Let's go."

"Look at the floor, Mike."

"This room's a mess. Must be some kind of lab. How can you stand it in here with that smell?"

"I broke those jars. It's not a lab. It wasn't like that when I got in here."

"Why'd you do that?"

"I didn't do it. I didn't mean to do it. Someone locked me in here."

"What are you talking about? The door wasn't locked. It was just tight. I had to lean all my weight against it, but I don't have a key."

"Didn't you hear me screaming the first two times you tried the door? You should have let me know you were there."

"What first two times? I just came down here looking for you now, 'cause you weren't back at the staircase where we said we'd meet. I gave you an extra ten minutes, then just started trying all the doors. This was the last one."

"I'm telling you that someone closed me in here, then came back and locked the door. I heard them jiggling the handle, I swear to you. I'm not crazy."

He walked toward me, crunching broken glass and beetle shells on his way. "These creepy crawlies got to you, Coop. It was just your imagination. Zimm and I were the only ones over here."

"Zimm? We left him in the other building."

"Yeah, but he decided to catch up with us. See if he could be useful. I sent him back."

Somebody had been playing with the door when I was locked inside. Why had Zimm followed us here? "It's not my imagination. I'm not moving till you tell me you believe me."

Mike stood in front of me, reaching up to grab my legs behind my knees. "I forgot my cape. We'll do it fireman's carry and not Sir Walter Raleigh style. Forgive me."

He lifted me over his shoulder and across the littered floor, my shoes in hand, to the hallway. Then he went back inside and looked into the steel container.

"Egyptian princess. Twelfth Dynasty. That girl just can't find a quiet place to sleep. C'mon, I need to clean you up before we go upstairs."

I took Mike's hand and let him lead me down the corridor. There was a men's room next to the stairwell and he took me inside.

He ran cold water, soaked a paper towel in it, and began to wipe my face and hands. "It's a bad night when a broad a couple of thousand years older than you looks better than you do."

I bent my head toward him and shook it at him. "I'm getting used to that fact. Anything stuck there? Any b—"

"Clean as a whistle." He handed me his comb and I ran it through my hair.

"I know you think I'm exaggerating, but I'm telling you the truth."

"Later, kid. We got people waiting for us upstairs. And now I gotta call crime scene and get them working on the mummy. And you," he said, tugging on a strand of my hair, "you're not out of my sight for a nanosecond, got it?"

I nodded and walked up the dingy staircase in front of him.

Retracing our path to the fourth floor, I knocked on the door and identified myself to Mercer. He opened it and told me that Mamdouba wanted to talk to me. He had come to ask me a question and expressed his annoyance that I was down in the basement with Mike.

Mike walked to the turret with me and held the door for me to go into Mamdouba's office. The curatorial director was standing at the window, having pulled himself up to full height and assumed the most clipped, formal version of his manner.

"Inasmuch as I have been gracious enough to be your host, in President Raspen's absence, and inasmuch as I have cooperated with you in every way possible, I think it is extremely rude—to say the very least—that you have brought Miss Clementine Qisukqut into this museum tonight."

Mamdouba raised his finger to shake at me. He was furious. "Police business, that I have great respect for. Trusting you and your detectives is one thing. But sneaking in here with a former employee who was discharged from this institution—discharged because of her untrustworthiness, her calumny—well, *this*, I tell you, Miss Cooper, with *this* you have broken every rule. Your little trick on me is over. You'll have to go. At once."

My apologies were lame and unsuccessful. I tried to interrupt to tell him that we had just found the mummy from the sarcophagus, but Mamdouba wouldn't be distracted from his tirade. The more I tried to excuse our ruse, the angrier he became.

"But you even joked about the fact that she was coming to town."

"To town, perhaps. To my museum, without my permission—no."

I wanted to know who had blown Clem's cover. I didn't think the leak was all that serious, since Clem's e-mails to some in the museum group had suggested that she might arrive in Manhattan that very night, but Mamdouba's discovery certainly foiled our plans for the rest of the night. He wouldn't tell me anything.

"Bring your Trojan horses in here, madam. Now that you've made a fool of me, let me tell them what to expect from this point forward."

I wasn't sure whether to move.

"Get your friends," he barked. "It's almost ten o'clock. I'd like to go home. *Get* them!"

He stood in the doorway of his anteroom and watched Mike and me walk back the short distance as though it were a gangplank. I opened the door and gave Mercer and Clem the word that someone had spotted her, and that Mamdouba was waiting to rap our knuckles and kick us out into the night.

Clem caught up with me as we walked toward the corner office. "Don't blame yourself. I'm sure it's my fault. I was getting a little frisky with those last e-mails. I'll let you read them. I think I was too excited to exercise much caution. Zimm probably figured out I was already here. He may have thought he had to blow the whistle on me, for his own sake."

The four of us took our places in the curator's circular turret. Clem spoke first. "This is not the way I hoped to come back, Mr. Mamdouba. I think you know how much respect I have for this great museum, for the work of my colleagues, for—"

The bantam administrator wanted no explanations. He gave Clem a tongue-lashing for her unauthorized entry into the facility from which she had been banned months ago. I broke in to try to convince him that she had only come at my urging, at my direction. Mike jumped in to defend me, and only Mercer stood with calm reserve, behind Clem's chair, his powerful hands on her tiny shoulders.

"This will mark the end of your comings and goings, Miss Cooper." Mamdouba crushed the subpoena and threw it in the wastebasket.

"May I have a moment with you?" I motioned to the anteroom. I did not want to be discussing witnesses and evidence in front of Clem, but I wanted to impress upon the director of curatorial affairs the kind of access we needed from him and why we had taken the chance that we did. Traipsing through his displays in the daytime, with dozens of police officers in the midst of hundreds of schoolchildren, would be far less appealing than our clumsy efforts to operate more discreetly after dark. He also needed to know about our discovery in the basement, which we hadn't disclosed to Clem.

I followed him out to the anteroom and closed the door behind us, for privacy. I made my pitch and explained how the search warrants would have to be executed, and what other requests I would make to the grand jury to compel his cooperation, but he had reached the end of his very short rope. The subpoena was only a piece of paper. He could rip it up and throw it away, but we still had the power to hold him in contempt.

"This is an institution of science, Miss Cooper. Make your case somewhere else. Go back to the Metropolitan. That's where the dead girl worked, no? You have abused the privilege of being inside our walls, madam." The little man was screaming now.

The door opened behind me and both Mike and Mercer joined us in the anteroom. Mike was ready for an argument while Mercer, as usual, took the diplomatic approach. He backed me away with a motion of his arm, and I took a seat on a nearby sofa to let him cool Mamdouba down.

"Ms. Cooper's been known to step in shit from time to time. Maybe this wasn't her brightest idea," Mike said, "but we're trying to solve a murder without shutting your doors to the public."

"You'd have absolutely no reason to do that. No right. We won't stand for it. You don't even know where this girl died. All you have is a body somewhere in New Jersey." He lowered himself into the chair at his assistant's desk and wiped the sweat from the back of his neck.

"And a coat check from a cold day last December, right here in your lobby. And maybe enough arsenic to finish off every one of us. Let's all be sensible," Mercer said. "Why don't we work out a schedule that meets with your approval. We'd like to keep you on our side, sir, okay?"

The two detectives outlined the way they wanted to proceed. Mamdouba was too agitated to listen closely. There would be no way to work out an agreement tonight.

"I'm sorry, Mr. Wallace. It's very late, I'm quite tired, and I need to speak to the president herself before I can give you an answer." He got up and walked to the door of his office, standing back as he pulled it open so we could go in and claim our trespassing Inuit.

I stood at the entrance and looked inside the perfectly round room. No one was there. Clementine Qisukqut had vanished.

38

Elijah Mamdouba brushed past me and strode to the center of his suite. He swept around and shook his fist at me. "Your fault, Miss Cooper. Enough games."

I was dumbfounded. My heart was pounding and my head ached as if it were caught in a vise. It was as if two people were staring at a picture and seeing entirely different things: I knew something terrible had happened to Clem, while the director assumed she was the cause of the trouble.

Mercer raced in and started for the first of four doors that were set back into the walls of the room.

"Don't touch that, Detective." Again, Mamdouba was shouting at us. "She's playing with all of us. You step into the tiger's lair and you are surprised when the tiger bites you? We had no reason to trust Miss Clementine, and neither did you."

It was as though her disappearance had relieved him of all the tension the evening's events had created. He leaned forward, hands on his thighs, and broke into the heartiest of belly laughs.

Mercer opened the first door only to find an empty coat closet, wire hangers on hiatus until the chill of fall returned. He pulled at the next knob to reveal a small bathroom, toilet and sink.

Mike was livid. "What the hell are you laughing about? Where's the girl?" He crossed the room and turned another handle. Pitch black. He stepped forward into the darkness and reemerged immediately. "Where are the lights?"

"She's run away on you, Mr. Chapman. There's the devil in that—"

Mike poked his head into the opening and yelled Clem's name. "It's a goddamn stairwell, Mercer. I can't see a friggin' thing in there."

He backed up around the large desk and bumped into Mamdouba, sticking him in the chest with his forefinger. "I don't give a fat rat's ass if Teddy Roosevelt falls off his horse and the animals come alive in their cages. Get every guard in this place on his feet, sound whatever kind of alarm you've got, get me a handful of flashlights, and tell me where the hell these stairs go. Coop, go back and get the floor plans. Hoof it."

Mercer was on Mamdouba's phone with the chief of detectives' office. "Get Emergency Services here. Send me some patrol cars. Close off the streets around the museum. . . . They *what*? Don't tell me they can't. They do it to blow up Snoopy and those rubber cartoon characters for the Thanksgiving Day parade. Shut it down tighter than a crab's ass. You got subway entrances north and south of the place. Block 'em off."

I ran back to our workroom and grabbed the maps off the top of the desk.

"What's wrong with you, man? Why the hell didn't you tell us there's a secret staircase in there? You think Clem came over here from London to play games? Someone grabbed her right from under our noses. Use your brain." Mike stormed back to the staircase. "What does this lead to and who had access to it?"

Mamdouba was in his fourth mood swing of the night. The displeasure that had turned to defiance and then briefly become hysteria had now sobered to misery. "It's not a secret. There's no reason for anyone to know about it. It's, uh, it's vestigial."

"I left my thesaurus at the station house. Help me."

Mamdouba had called the security command center and alarms were screeching overhead and echoing in the vast hallways beyond.

"*Vestigial.* Useless, like your appendix. Built a century ago, when these corner towers were constructed. They've been out of use ever since elevators were put in. The steps are narrow and dark and dangerous. Nobody uses them."

Now Mercer was talking to the head of the hostage negotiation squad: "That's the point. We don't know who's got her or where she is. It's not premature. You damn well better have a team up here because if we find the girl and she's alive, I'm gonna need all the help I can get. Pronto."

Three guards rushed into the room, the leader looking to Mamdouba for information and direction.

"That flashlight. Toss it," Mike said.

"Do it." Mamdouba nodded his head.

Mercer took another flashlight out of the second

guard's hand and threw it to me, grabbing a third for himself.

"I'm going up. You go down," Mike said to Mercer. I started to follow them into the darkened stairwell but Mike shouted at me to go back. "You're only trouble, blondie. Stay here with the guards and man the phone. Chief of D's on the way."

Mamdouba was playing with a panel of light switches on the landing. I could hear the click as he flipped them but no lights came on.

His office had erupted into total chaos as guards responded from stations all around the museum. The one who seemed to be their leader was giving them orders to fan out and start scouring every crevice of the building, looking for a short, dark-skinned woman with black hair. They were not licensed to carry weapons, so most of them had only their flashlights in hand.

Within minutes, three patrol cars had arrived at the museum. A uniformed sergeant and three cops were the first to get to Mamdouba's office. "Hey, Al, what gives?"

"You know anything about the murder investigation, the girl who was found—?"

"Chapman's case? Seen it in the papers. Body in the back of the truck somewhere in Jersey. You caught the guy tonight? Who's missing?"

I gave them the briefest version of the events to get them going. The sergeant sent two guys to follow Mercer and Mike, while he and his driver remained with me.

"What's her 'scrip?"

I tried to be patient as I told them what Clem looked like, so they could send out a radio broadcast to the other officers arriving at the museum, as well as to those patrolling the neighborhood.

"Name?"

I spelled it for him while the driver took notes.

"Odd one."

"Inuit."

"What?"

"Eskimo."

"APB the North Pole, Al." The sergeant laughed, as concerned about the situation as Mamdouba had been at first.

Mike and a young cop came back into the room. "You want to get reamed at Compstat next month, Paddy? Stand here making stupid friggin' jokes while you're about to notch up one more murder count in your precinct. Get me every man available in Manhattan North."

"Now you're joking. It's just a museum."

"You ever been up on five, Coop? Or beyond it, to the attic?"

I shook my head in the negative as Mike went on. "We're gonna tear it apart upstairs. You won't believe what it looks like. You could rent out rooms to a dozen people and no one would know they're living up there. Or dead. There's a zillion cubbyholes and lockers and cases. Where's Mercer? Anyone with Mercer? Call him, Coop."

I dialed his phone from Mamdouba's desk and was sent into his voice mail. He must have reached the basement already, where his cell phone wouldn't work. I tried Zimm's extension and got no answer.

"Do you know who else is working in the basement?" I asked Mamdouba.

"Several of the team were here until an hour ago. Gaylord, Poste, Bellinger, Friedrichs. They were all up here. But it's late, they may be gone. Zimm, I told him not to leave until he heard from me, in case I needed any last-minute errands completed tonight."

Mike was giving orders to NYPD cops, who were arriving in pairs every five minutes or so, and to the bewildered security guards. "You see anything alive and moving under this roof, corral him or her and bring 'em . . ."

He looked at me, not knowing what to say.

"IMAX theater. Off the main lobby."

"Paddy." He turned his attention to the sergeant. "Interns, grad students, science dorks, janitors. Nobody leaves. What did they see, what did they hear? Bones. I want anyone who knows where the bones are."

Mamdouba muttered softly, "They are everywhere, Mr. Chapman. Upstairs and down."

The sergeant had a police walkie-talkie and was communicating with his men on the street. "Somebody at every entrance, every doorway. Dumpsters in the courtyard, check 'em. Flood the place with whoever shows up."

"Can you turn off that damn system already?" Mike was on the phone with headquarters again. The internal alarms had been clanging for twenty minutes. If there was anyone who had not realized there was an emergency, he had already met the taxidermists.

Mercer was practically panting when he came back

into the office. "Door from the staircase doesn't open on three. On two is an office like this one. Lock must be a hundred years old. Shouldered into it and it gave way. Dusty, empty, nothing in the closets except bottles full of lizards. First floor's a bookshop. Took it all the way down to the basement."

"Where the exhibition offices are? See any of the—"

"No, you heard Clem. Can't get there from here. It's spookier than shit."

"Herps." Mamdouba again.

"What?"

"Snakes. Herpetology. They're all dead, Mr. Wallace."

"You still do not want to be in there. Tank after tank—pythons, constrictors, anacondas—all in some kind of alcohol solution."

"You see anyone?"

"Nope. This one's a labyrinth of storerooms and closets. Racks of metal shelves on wheels with specimens. I left the cop who followed on that side. Call him some backup, will you? Still as a tomb. He's checking out every inch of it."

"Did you get over to—?"

"The exhibition area? Yeah. Had to climb back up to the lobby and over to where we've been in before. Got the kid to go—"

"Zimm?"

"Yeah. Told him what happened and sent him—"

"How'd he react to the news about Clem?"

"Seemed appropriately freaked out. I have him doing a sweep to see who's still here, round them up.

I'll go back to meet him and let him take us through every back alley he knows down there. Sarge, I need guys to open every door."

"Did Zimm say he knew Clem would be here tonight?"

"Mike, I didn't stop to do an interview. I'm trying to find her alive, okay?"

"Anyone else there?"

"That sour broad. Anna Friedrichs. She's dragging up here after me, taking her sweet time." Mike handed Mercer the basement floor plans that Clem had helped him to decipher. "Take this with you when you go back down. Sarge, your walkie-talkies. Give 'em up."

Mamdouba, who had been speaking on the phone, now turned to us. "Mr. Socarides is still in his office. Mammals. He'll go with you to the fifth floor, Mr. Chapman. He's responsible for—well, for many of the bones."

"Humans?"

"Animals. But he knows the storage area."

I thumbed through the pages detailing collections and donations. "Can he help with these names?"

"Certainly."

"We'll bring this list with us, then."

"You're not coming, kid. Go with Mercer. Help him."

"Stay put, Alex."

Mercer didn't want me in his way either. I wasn't exactly a good-luck charm.

Each of them took a few of the men and women in blue and set out on their paths to the nether reaches of the gigantic museum. Twenty-three buildings. Seven hundred and twenty-three rooms. We didn't need a precinct to search it, we needed an army.

Now the noise was coming from the street outside. I walked to the window and looked down at the intersection of Columbus Avenue and West Seventy-seventh Street. Dozens of RMP's were blocking the intersection, and several big trucks of the Emergency Services Unit were positioned beneath the old granite facade. Sirens wailed the arrival of more and more officers, and flashing red bubbles atop black unmarked cars signaled the presence of detectives and police brass.

Anna Friedrichs looked terrified when she entered the room. "Is Clem all right? Have you found her?"

I told her how Clem had disappeared. "Did you read her e-mails today? Did you know she was coming to New York?"

"By the end of the day we all knew she was coming to town to talk with the police. But later in the week, I thought. It was Zimm who just told me she hinted about coming tonight."

"He told you that? When?"

"Now. Just now. She trusted him, I guess. Said she'd look to see if his light was on when she got to the museum. He took that to mean at night. Tonight."

"Get him up here." I flapped my hand in Mamdouba's direction. "If you can't reach him by phone, send two of your men to bring him up here immediately. D'you know who else he told?" I asked, turning back to Friedrichs.

"He's so upset with himself it's hard to be sure. He

knows he told Erik Poste and Hiram Bellinger. He's not sure who else was around."

I handed her the list of collections and donor names. "How familiar are you with this museum—I mean, the physical layout?"

"I, uh—I only know about some of the companion works to mine."

As curator of Africa, Oceania, and the Americas in the Met, she covered the most primitive societies, the ones to which Clem had introduced Katrina. "Human bones, skeletons, things like that. Can you show us where they're kept?"

She looked at Mamdouba for help. "Upstairs? Have you seen the closets on five?"

"Sarge, give me two men. I want to go up the main staircase and catch up with Chapman. Would you keep looking, Ms. Friedrichs? Any names, anything you see on those lists that might connect us to something—a particular storeroom, a special place, a priceless exhibit—that someone didn't want Katrina Grooten to find. As soon as Socarides gets here—"

"I'm ready, Ms. Cooper." He was standing in the doorway and had his own flashlight in hand. "Anna, let me take a look at those lists."

I followed the two police officers into the hallway, anxious to make myself useful in the pursuit. "I think it's more important that you come with me. She can study the papers. I've tracked them against each of your names—all three of you, plus Bellinger, Poste, Thibodaux, Drexler. I don't know what else I should be looking for."

Socarides scanned the papers, as though trying to

match names with the faces of people present. The
obvious collections that referenced aboriginal artifacts
had been circled, as had many of the African and
Pacific Islands groupings.

"You missed one," he said, slapping the papers
with his flashlight. "Goddamn it. You missed Willem.
Let's go there first."

Socarides passed us and started jogging toward the
huge staircase and up to the fifth floor. I stood frozen
in place for a few seconds, certain I had cross-checked
every name in my case folder.

I ran after him, taking the flat marble steps two at a
time, pulling myself upward by the brass banister that
gleamed against the murky gray walls and plastered
ceiling.

He stopped at the top of the landing to get his bearings, and I reached his side. I remembered what Ruth
Gerst had told us. Poste's father, Willem, had been a
great African explorer and adventurer. Erik was on
expert on museum history, someone had said. He had
grown up in museums. After his father's death, he
came to the States to live, with his mother.

"Where do we go? I'm sick that I didn't make the
right connection."

He was stalking down the hallway as he talked.
"Nobody thought to tell you his name and you obviously never thought to ask. A prosecutor should know
better than that."

"Poste? It's Willem Poste," I repeated, trying to
keep up with his long strides.

"Willem Van der Poste, Ms. Cooper," he said, passing the lists back to me. "Look under the *V*'s. Like

many Boers who moved to America after the Second World War, Willem's widow dropped that formal, aristocratic part of the surname. Too Teutonic. Too Germanic. Look at your papers again and you'll see all the properties donated to the museum by Willem Van der Poste."

Fifty million bones hidden beneath these rooftops and thousands of them had been collected by Erik Poste's father. Dinosaur fossils, mammalian teeth, human skeletons.

Socarides was taking me down the endless corridor to find Van der Poste's bone vault.

39

Cops were swarming in and around the fifth-floor offices and storage cabinets. Even with the overhead lights switched on, the hallway was all dark corners and angles, old wooden cabinets with broken drawer pulls filling the wide spaces between doors, and exhibits shrouded in plastic drop cloths covering every flat surface.

I could hear Mike's voice a football field or two farther down the way, yelling orders to try to organize the crew that was racing about, testing and yanking doorknobs while waiting for security guards with passkeys to let them into every locked entryway.

Socarides turned a corner and charged off in a perpendicular direction. I shouted to Mike to follow us and kept running after my determined guide.

The passageway led deep into the museum's interior. Our footsteps echoed in the immense space of our surroundings, while Mike trotted behind us, calling Clem's name every few seconds. None of this area was accessible to the public. Cool, dark, and dry, it seemed as remote from the popular displays of the forty exhibition halls that enchanted busloads of schoolchildren as the tip of the Empire State Building appeared looking up at it from the sidewalk.

We stopped behind Socarides at the old-fashioned door of a small room. It was a solid panel of oak with a foot-wide glass window at eye level. Black lettering that once announced the occupant's name had long ago been scraped off the pane. The handle wouldn't give. I stepped back and Socarides smashed against the glass with his flashlight, reaching in to open the door.

Inside the dreary room, I found the switch and turned on the lights. Fish skeletons. Thousands of them. Stained with a pinkish dye now familiar to me, they emitted a supernatural glow as they rested upright in bottles filled with ethyl alcohol, from the floor of the room to the fourteen-foot ceiling.

Chapman and Socarides were ahead of me, moving farther along the seemingly abandoned hallway, shattering window after window to get inside cubicles and cabinets, eyeballing their contents, as they worked their way toward a dead end.

"Next one over. This stuff used to be up here, I know," Socarides called to us. We ran back to the main hallway and down another lifeless wing of storage space.

Four more tries at small, dreary rooms yielded an incalculable number of drawers filled with the still bodies of birds. Feathers, beaks, bills, and tiny little vertebrae everywhere.

Mike slammed the last one behind him and stopped to take a deep breath.

"Here, Detective. Over here."

I followed Mike a few yards farther down the corridor to the twelve-by-twelve-foot storeroom into which Socarides had hacked his way. Both of us stepped inside.

Human skeletons, six of them suspended full length, hung in a row facing the entrance door. Each of the macabre sextet was hooked at the base of his cracked skull by a shiny brass hinge that attached to the top shelf, several feet above our heads.

Long, bony fingers met me at eye level, dangling from the chalky remains of these forgotten souls. I half expected them to lift in unison and reach out to grasp some part of my neck or throat.

Behind them and on each of the walls of this secluded den were stacks and stacks of bones. I swiveled to my left to get out of Mike's way as he ran his flashlight up and down the space beside the door, looking for light switches. Now I was facing three rows of skulls, human heads with protruding teeth, hollow cheeks, and black sockets that once held eyes which would have returned my stunned gaze dead-on.

"What's here? What do you know about this?" Mike asked.

"It is Willem Van der Poste, Erik Poste's father," I said.

The beams of our three flashlights probing up and down the shelves made it even creepier. I directed the light to the far side of the room to find more skulls, these with hair still clinging to the decaying scalps.

"Some of these were his. The man amassed a huge collection of African artifacts. But he did it in the employ of dozens of different patrons. Great white hunter kind of thing."

"This his private vault?"

"No, no. He never had the money for that."

Leaving that door open, Socarides led us to the adjacent space, letting Mike break into it and scan for better light while he talked. "Rich trustees and museum aficionados back in the twenties and thirties made pilgrimages to the Dark Continent. Some for big game, some for the sheer excitement, some to plunder the ivory and gold and rubber."

More bones. The rest of the bodies that must have connected, at one distant time, to the forlorn heads in the room we had just left. Bones in boxes, neatly labeled with a first name or a tribe designation or a simple question mark.

"Willem's father was a Boer. Went to South Africa at the turn of the last century. Developed a reputation as the most spectacular shooter of the lot. Bagged half the beasts that made up the basis of the original museum collection here. The man to see, in Africa."

Into a third room, stacked again with human remains. Mike stepped back into the hallway and cupped his hands, yelling for reinforcements, then asked, "Whose rooms are these?"

"They're not designated as anyone's. These—these *things* are just waiting here for someone to decide what becomes of them in this age of political correctness. There—up there, Detective."

Socarides's flashlight stopped on something that glinted in the dark. Mike grabbed a bookcase wedged into the space behind the door and slammed it to its side, skulls scattering across the floor. He climbed onto its edge, two feet off the ground, to reach the top few tiers of shelves.

Guns. A rack of hunting rifles spread out across the uppermost space. "Eight of 'em up here. Looks like there were a couple more here once, if this was ever full."

He wiped his hand to see what amount of dust had accumulated in the several inches that separated the long guns from each other. One level below were pistols and handguns. No way of really knowing how many had been on the shelf earlier than today and whether any had been taken recently.

Mike stood on his toes and reached behind the row of pistols now clearly visible to me as I tried to give him more light.

"This one of yours?" He balanced against the sturdy wooden shelf with one hand, handing me a couple of the guns while pulling into Socarides's view the tip of an elephant tusk that must have been four feet long.

"Ivory, Detective. Willem Van der Poste's private insurance policy, if I had to guess. Every hunter had a stash of some sort or other, and his tusks were probably hidden here against the day he'd get back to the States and need to convert them into cash. Sell them on the black market."

Mike backed down off the shelf. "Got a few of 'em up there. Worth what?"

"Fifteen, maybe twenty thousand apiece. Maybe more."

"Nobody back there, Chapman," a cop called in after checking the rooms beyond us.

"Open every room. Check every inch of this place." The uniformed cops hustled as Mike gave out orders. "Where to?"

Socarides was running out of ideas. "Maybe he got her out of the museum. Maybe they're not—"

"That's great. I'll let you know when the chief gives me that news. I'm a worst-case scenario kind of guy. I don't feature 'em on the Jitney, on their way out to the Hamptons. Where else could you hide inside here? Where else would—?"

"The basement. I mean, there are several basement areas, each separate and—"

"I know. We got people down there."

"There's the attic, above us. Vast spaces, locked storerooms. No reason for anyone to be up there, no one to disturb them once they got there."

"Can you get to it from the staircase in Mamdouba's office?"

"Frankly, I didn't know there was a staircase in his office. No idea where that leads."

Back to the main hallway, Mike was running ahead of Socarides and me, screaming to security guards to point him to the access to the attic. The older man nearest that end of the building was clearly so intimidated that the keys jangled in his grip as he tried to work them in the lock of the massive door. I laid a hand on his forearm and asked him to give them to me, which he seemed eager to do. When I found the right one, Mike leaned against the panel and headed up the stairs.

Again we followed. Still enveloped in the semidarkness, I tried to orient myself to our location, after having altered our route so many times downstairs. Uniformed cops were coursing through the immense space. If anything could rattle the bones and wake the dead, it would be this stampede of cops who were entirely at home on urban streets, in subway stations, housing projects, and city parks, but thoroughly perplexed by this labyrinth of hidden rooms and concealed closets.

Chapman had gotten his bearings before I did. "That's southwest," he said, pointing. "Mamdouba's office. That would be the corner the staircase would lead up from."

He took off in that direction and I loped behind him. "Coop, give it a whistle."

I put two fingers in the corners of my mouth and blew as hard as I could, the cab-stopping kind of signal that could be heard blocks away, that Mike had never mastered. He called out after I got the attention of half of the troops. "Over here. Move all this shit, all these cabinets that are blocking doorways. Anything obstructing any entryway or exit. We're looking for a woman's body. Breathing or not. Find her. The guy may be packing."

There must have been eight or ten attic areas like this over the entire complex of buildings that made up the museum. This was only one of them. Although it led out of Mamdouba's corner turret, there was no way to tell whether it connected to the rambling set of contiguous halls.

"Soc, what's up there?"

Under the eaves, still high above our heads, was a steel catwalk. It was not much wider than a balance beam, with chain guylines that bordered it as it crossed the width of the immense room.

"Never been there, never noticed it. Must be for maintenance, for structural repairs."

"Hey, Pavlova, you wanna be useful? Make all those ballet lessons your old man paid for worthwhile? I don't think my feet'll fit on the damn thing."

I loathed heights as much as I hated vermin, snakes, and spiders.

"Bird's-eye view, Coop. Different perspective. Give it a shot."

I stepped out of my shoes, handed my flashlight to Mike, and started to climb the rusty rungs of the ladder that was welded in place against the south wall of the room. The metal dug into the middle of my soles as I climbed higher, trying to focus my eyes on a water-stained spot on the wall above my head. Anything not to look back down.

The solid plank felt good beneath my feet. I glided out onto it, clutching the side rails with all the strength in my hands, and moved forward by planting heel in front of toe in a regular cadence.

The first stretch was the most unsettling, from the wall more than twenty feet across to the first block of storerooms. The open space below me was more than twice that height.

I paused to look down at the tops of the structures below. Some appeared to be permanent fixtures, sizable rooms that must have been built into the original architectural plans for the storage of items and artifacts not on display. They were topped by strips of wooden board, and although it was impossible to see whole objects in between the slats from this distance above them, I could make out the shapes of large, dark masses as well as the occasional glimpse of something that contrasted with that, something light. The whiteness of bones was what it looked like to me.

I propelled myself ahead, stopped, and noted that there were other, more modern cabinets—gray metal lockers that looked like they had been added as the collections outgrew the original design space.

Then I was out over open hallway again, clinging to my side railings and measuring my steps. Storerooms and cabinets. More open corridor. Storerooms and—

I froze over the third cluster of storage rooms. I looked down. Shadows and opaque radiance coming through the skylights that dotted the eaves above me danced atop all the surfaces I saw below. I steadied myself with both hands and crouched lower.

I was sure of it now. It wasn't the flutter of white clouds or the brilliance of the moon from the skylights. It wasn't the confusion of dozens of flashlight beams intersecting one another from the floor far beneath me.

Something had moved in the darkness. Something in one of the vaults.

40

"Stop panting and tell me how certain you are."

I had managed to turn around and wriggle my way back to the ladder and down to Mike. "No question."

"Could be rats you saw from up there."

I thought of the last time I had spent a lonely night hunting down a killer. "Trust me, Mike. I know rats. That was no rat. It was definitely a big human."

"One? Only one?"

"All I could see was one dark figure moving from one side of an enclosed space to another."

Mike turned to a bright-eyed young cop who was standing behind him. "Want a gold shield? Go downstairs. First find Mercer Wallace. Detective, SVU. Big guy, blackest man you ever saw. Think Shaft. Tell him we got the perp up here. Then look for the highest-ranking boss you can lay your hands on. I want Emergency Services, hostage squad, medics. Everybody else stays downstairs. And one boss. Only one. Tell 'em I said that. Come back. You're gonna be my lackey for the rest of the night."

He told Socarides to get down to Mamdouba's office and remain there.

Taking me by the hand, a finger held up over his mouth telling me to keep quiet, Mike moved in the direction I had suggested, the third tier of storage rooms. He waved the men closest to that area away and settled us back into an alcove between cabinets to wait for Mercer.

We were face-to-face, inches apart, in the narrow space that separated two glass-fronted cabinets that were filled with shrunken heads, pulled from display decades ago. I put my hands on Mike's chest, reaching up to whisper to him.

"What do you think you're going to do?"

"You got any bright ideas? I don't think. I'm saving my brain to donate to the museum. Thinking's what they pay the bosses to do. That's why I need Mercer here. Me? I'd just shoot the guy's friggin' balls off, Clem or no Clem."

"But if she's alive—"

"That's why I'm being so well-behaved. Let it quiet down until the hostage guys get here. Let him think I called off the dogs and he's safe for the night."

"Safe? Safe to do what?"

"Maybe he'll try to use Clem as leverage to get out of there. Face it, Coop. The flip side is that maybe he's already killed her. If he thinks we're all in the dark and we're figuring Clem was already sprung from the museum, or that just like Mamdouba thought, she was playing a game with us and disappeared on her own, he could walk out of here—leaving her body—and just stroll across the park to his office. Depends how delusional he is, what he thinks he pulled off."

I bowed my head and pressed it against Mike's shoulder.

"Cheer up, blondie. If she's in there, we'll get her out." He sniffed a couple of times and I looked up. "It's midnight and you still smell good. How come?" We were squeezed into tight quarters and he was trying to lighten me up.

"Eau de formaldehyde. Stuffed moose musk. Cartilage number five. Beetle juice. You've got a good nose." I looked up at Mike. "Erik Poste?"

"That's my best guess, too. Knows the museum inside out. Has his old man's stash of bones here. Access to guns. Works with arsenic. Knew what Katrina and Clem were up to. Now all we have to figure out is why."

The cops had stopped turning everything upside down and inside out. A calm was settling over the great, grim hall.

"You know what the *Jeopardy!* question was tonight?"

We had missed it this evening, and Mike was offering me a distraction until Mercer got here.

"Category: 'World-Class Thieves.' I would have bet a thousand. You?"

"Double or nothing." I gave him a wan smile. The storeroom was still now. Maybe I had been mistaken once again tonight.

"The answer is: 'Jack Roland Murphy.'"

I shook my head.

Mike's mouth was against my ear. "You gonna pay up? Look at that skylight, Coop. See it?"

He tilted my chin up toward the eaves. "Nineteen

sixty-four. Miami Beach boy Murph the Surf climbed up the ledge of this old granite building and lowered himself right through that very hole in the roof to steal the Star of India—J. P. Morgan's sapphire. It was the size of a golf ball, kid. Warm night, the alarm system was disarmed and the window was wide open. Just whacked the glass case with a claw hammer and the guards never even knew he was there. Probably the same guys who are working tonight. My pop worked the caper. You owe me two grand—"

I heard footsteps pounding far down the hallway. Mike stepped out of our alcove and held out his arm, commanding Mercer and the woman with him to stop. I recognized Kerry Schrager, from the DA's squad, who had been trained recently for the hostage team.

"Don't move a hair. I'll explain."

As soon as Mike walked away, I was convinced I heard scuffling in the small room. I listened for voices but heard none.

Within minutes, Mike, Mercer, and Kerry walked back to our staging area.

"Here's how we work it, okay?" Mercer said. "Nice and easy. Kerry and I—"

Mike was itching to get started. "Tina Turner. 'Proud Mary.' I don't do nothing nice and easy. I vote for rough. Where are the snipers?"

"On the roof."

"Snipers?" I looked up again. "But we don't know where Clem—"

"Exactly. They're just sitting tight. We don't know

what kind of guns your man has in there. Case he gets crazy, we got firepower. We got Emergency Services at the top of the staircases on every side of the room, a medic with 'em, and a boss in each corner. Kerry and I do the drill. We're in charge. You two know more of the facts, so you stand by in case I need info."

The first rule in hostage negotiation was establishing a perimeter. Sending one man or team in to work with the hostage taker, but having everyone else backed up at the ready.

"We think our pal in there is Erik Poste. D'you find anything in the basement to help connect this to him?" Mike asked Mercer.

"Arsenic?" I asked, fearing he may have used it again on Clem.

"Eve Drexler thinks she found the answer to that. Thibodaux did, actually," Mercer said. "Looks like every time Bellinger submitted an order for arsenic for his work at the Cloisters, Erik Poste requisitioned a bit more of it for the restorations in his department at the Met."

"He probably never even touched the stuff they've got in taxidermy over here, but he wanted it to look like someone from *this* museum could have been responsible for the poisoning," Mike said. "So if he wasn't expecting to see Clem tonight when he headed over here, he probably didn't bring any of his private supply along with him."

"We're gonna give it a shot. Our method," Mercer said, talking to Mike. "You gotta be patient and stay out of my way. We've never lost a life, and I'm not planning to start tonight."

Mike kneeled on the floor and sketched out the exact location of the storeroom in which we thought Erik Poste was holed up. Mercer stood and turned away from us, and Kerry followed him down the narrow alleyway between compartments. The outlines of their bodies were swallowed up in the murky darkness, and all that stood out was the sharp scarlet lettering on the back of Kerry's jacket: TALK TO ME.

The pair positioned themselves adjacent to the enclosed space, but not in front of it. "Mr. Poste," I heard next, Mercer's deep bass voice speaking softly and gently. "Erik? This is Mercer Wallace."

No reply, no sound at all. The negotiator never refers to himself as a cop, never mentions rank. Never reveals the fact that there's an arsenal backing him up.

But now there was movement behind us. I turned to look, and two men dressed in jet-black jumpsuits were climbing onto the catwalk. High-powered rifles were slung over their shoulders, and they kept walking—with far more confidence than I had evidenced—out over the spaces on either side of Mercer's position. Snipers were inside the museum as well as above it.

Mercer squatted a bit closer to the storage area. "Erik. I want you to listen to me." He needed to find a way to engage his target in a dialogue without striking the wrong nerve. It was a delicate task at best, and this one, with so many unknowns, was like sitting on a powder keg.

Mercer's goal was to find out what had become of Clem. It would be one thing to force an end to Poste's standoff if he was alone, but if he had Clem, and she was still alive, it would be an entirely different operation. He didn't want to start his conversation with the subject of the body in the sarcophagus. There would be little way to fool Poste out of the knowledge that he was facing a life sentence for the murder of Katrina Grooten.

Develop an intimacy, Mercer had told me when I had asked him about how men and women were trained to do this work. Start by grounding the subject and connecting him to people and things he cared about, wanted to see again.

Mercer kept talking, even though there was no response from within the storeroom. "I've got a patrol officer bringing your wife over here, Erik. She wants to see you. She wants you to come out of there safe and sound. Nobody gets hurt, that's the plan."

Mike put his mouth to my ear. "What if hates his wife, huh? That'd be the last straw for some guys I know. They'd just as soon blow their brains out than have to face the little woman after a night like this."

Mercer went on speaking for more than ten minutes without any kind of response. He had been given enough of a briefing before he came upstairs to know what in this world meant something to Poste. "The kids, Erik. Think about your children."

Still no sign of life.

"I've been talking to Mamdouba and he was telling me about your father, about the work he did in Africa, how brave he was. What a great character he was."

Kerry backed up to where we were standing, toying

with the small receiving device wrapped around her ear. Someone was transmitting information to her. She looked up and my eyes followed her glance.

One of the men on the catwalk was making motions with both of his hands. He looked like a mime, pretending to be lowering a rope to the ground. I couldn't see anything dropping.

I held my hands out, palms upward, and mouthed to Kerry, "What's going on?"

Mike put his mouth against my ear again and whispered. "Fiber-optic camera. It's no thicker than a sewing needle. They can slip it between the slats on top of the storage room and we'll be able to see what's inside. Who's with him, whether she's—you know."

Three minutes later, Kerry nodded her head and gave us a thumbs-up. "Clem's there. Looks like she's alive." Information kept coming in from whoever was viewing the monitor at the command center within the museum. "She's bound and gagged. Looks like gauze. No movement except her eyes." She paused to receive more word. "Yeah, her eyes are open. She's okay."

No doubt the gauze was the same kind of old linen rag that had been wrapped, mummy fashion, around the body of Katrina Grooten.

"He's got a pistol in his hand," Kerry said, "and a rifle across his lap. He's sitting next to the girl. He's got her lying on the floor, hog-tied from behind."

"Can Mercer hear the commentary, too?"

"Exactly what I'm getting. It's being relayed to both of us."

The negotiators were not permitted to decide whether or when to take the door. These new high-tech devices took much of the guesswork out of the job. If the perp wasn't cooperating, the chief of detectives would eventually make the call about whether to storm the storeroom or wait until fear, hunger, or exhaustion caused the bad guy to give in.

"Talk to me," Mercer said again, calmly and evenly. "Talk to me, Erik. We've got to resolve this situation."

Those three words were the squad's motto for a good reason. They had to get the subject to open up. Find out what it is that would draw him out of the situation. If they could absorb him in conversation—sports, weather, stamp collecting, European paintings—they could keep him preoccupied, away from his captive, and they could eventually wear him down.

It had worked dozens of times, I knew. When it failed, the results were deadly.

Mercer focused on the work of Willem Van der Poste. Someone, maybe in a phone call to the wife, had suggested that Erik had idolized his late father. "Mamdouba's got photographs in his office, Erik. Fascinating pictures of your father. Pictures of you as a young boy with him."

It seemed to me that Mercer had talked for more than half an hour before he got a reaction of any kind. Poste didn't speak a word until Mercer asked him to put down his guns.

"I know you've got them in there, Erik. You're not going to shoot anyone. You want to tell me what we can do to bring you out of there?"

"You all figure I won't use the guns, do you?"

The sound of his voice echoed in the corridor. It was Poste, all right. It sounded eerily calm, but greatly magnified. I didn't think that was his intention, but rather a product of the acoustics in the vast hall.

"How about you let the girl out, Erik? Then we can—"

"What's in it for me, Mr. Wallace? You're going to allow me to go home?" Poste laughed.

"I'm going to find out what has you so upset, and see if we can fix it. Mamdouba says—"

"Don't give me any crap about Elijah Mamdouba. Nobody can fix it, Wallace. It's a different world now. My father was their hero. The men who were putting this place together thought he was the best thing that ever happened to them. Today, he's a pariah here. I'd come with him as a child, when we sailed back from Africa. Everyone who worked in the museum worshiped the ground he walked on."

"That's still true."

"They're all about saving the planet and preserving the species now. You think it was scientists who brought back all those creatures downstairs? They were hunters, for Chrissakes. They did it for sport. At least my father was honest about it. Rich Brits and Americans. Piles of money to throw away on trips to the heart of darkness. If these people didn't like to kill the beasts, Wallace, how the hell do you think they filled the dioramas downstairs?"

Mercer didn't have an answer. "Did you go with him on safari when you were a kid?"

"It had all changed by then. When my father was

young, before 'civilization' reached Africa," Poste said mockingly, "the supply of wildlife seemed inexhaustible. He learned to shoot to defend his home and family, to put food on the table."

I could hear scuffling now, as though he was changing position.

"Those fools who came over on expedition would shoot whatever they could find. 'You've got your elephant,' my father would say. 'You've got what you came here for.' 'We'll have another one then. One for the museum, two for me. And after that, Willem, we'll take some gorillas. Maybe shoot a cannibal or two.' *You* might have been in danger, Wallace. The old T.R. spirit. Bully. Everything was bully."

Mercer had him going. The way I understood it, this was a good thing, for Clem's sake.

"And your father?"

"He warned the sportsmen, the museum trustees, all about the situation. Told them there weren't enough animals to satisfy them. Nobody listened to him."

"But his things, his collections are all—"

"They're all forgotten is what they are. I used to hold on to his great hands, all callused and hard, and walk through the halls with him. His name was everywhere, on all the display labels. He was a giant to these people—the board, the administrators. 'That one's mine, Erik,' he used to tell me. And then the story to go with it. 'That crowned eagle, see it? It had picked up a monkey—a full grown one—to carry off for a feast. Got it with one shot, right in its own nest.' Now Willem Van der Poste is taboo. Everything that once was his is stuck in a box or a closet. Mamdouba? He couldn't find an elephant tusk if his life depended on it."

"Is that what you want, Erik? You want to—"

"I have what I want, Detective. I found exactly what I want."

He was walking now, in the confined space. We could all hear the steps.

"The girl," Mercer said, his voice louder and more firm. "Don't touch the girl."

41

Everyone moved at once.

Mercer stood up and stepped closer to Poste's enclosure. Kerry left us and eased herself in behind his position. Above us, the two snipers lifted their guns to their shoulders.

"Take it slow, Erik. Step back from the girl. Leave Clem alone. I want to hear what you have to say."

Within seconds, Poste must have complied with the order to get away from Clem. Mercer held his arm up in the air, circling his forefinger and thumb to signal things were okay for the moment.

Kerry walked back to us. "He's got something in his hand. Like a small arrow, best they can tell. He's been rubbing it up and down his forearm, sort of scratching himself, while he was speaking to Mercer. That last time? He leaned over behind Clem and began to dig the point of it into the back of her hand."

"The guns?"

"He put them down when he started to talk."

"Which is worse?" I said aloud to no one in particular.

"There's a whole shelf full of sharp objects that the camera's picking up. It's scanning around now, while he's pacing. Arrows of all sizes. A lot of primitive weapons," Kerry said, listening to the transmission that was going to her and to Mercer.

"Poison-tipped hunting darts," Mike said. "Probably part of Papa's stash."

"Your friend wanted bones?" Kerry asked. "All around her. Human skulls, shelf on top of shelf. A couple of skeletons hanging right over her head."

"Be careful what you wish for," Mike muttered.

"He's spooked now," Kerry said. "He's trying to figure out how Mercer knew he was so close to your witness."

"Can't he see the camera?"

"It's lens is smaller than a pea, Coop. It's just above him, flush against the wooden boards. With good light he'd have trouble spotting it, and he's got no light at all."

Mercer tried to connect to him again. "You gotta let Clem out of there. Then you and I can strike a deal, okay?"

"It's too late for a deal. I know that."

"Why? You haven't hurt her, have you? She'll be okay."

"And you'll just forget about her timid little friend? Katrina? Will you do that for me?" He was teasing Mercer now, knowing we were as stymied as he was.

Mercer put his hands on his waist and stretched his neck back. He had tried for an hour to keep Poste from mentioning the dead girl. Once Katrina got in the mix, Poste knew he was looking at a long haul in state prison. No one-way ticket home.

"He's picked up a head from the shelf. Nope, put it down. Back to the weapons. Some kind of ax or hatchet." Kerry's commentary was chilling. With all the sophisticated weaponry in the hands of the cops who ringed the museum attic, Poste had Clem locked inside with a stockpile of primitive death tools.

"Katrina figured it out. Well, that's not really true. It was Clementine here who planted the seed. D'you know what happened to the big-game hunters when the animals died out? When the men who were glorified by this museum—Akeley and Lang and Chapin—were finished killing them off, quite unnecessarily?"

"Why don't you tell me, Erik."

"They became grave diggers. That's what she calls them, don't you?"

"He's back at her side," Kerry whispered. "He's prodding her in the spine with an arrow. A different one this time." She slipped from our alcove and walked into place a foot or two away from Mercer, ready to assist him.

"You're dead meat if you move from here, Coop. My orders," Mike said, following behind Kerry.

From each corner of the room, teams started to move closer to where we were centered. No one was going to let Poste do any damage to Clem. Some boss was struggling to decide how and when to break in on him. At some point, when the talking stalled and the hostage was at risk of serious physical harm, the team would resort to brute force.

"I don't understand what you mean, Erik. Tell me what you're talking about."

"Came a time when there were no longer animals to sell to the great museums of America and Europe. The greedy bastards had wiped out some of the most extraordinary creatures on the face of the earth. White rhinos, okapi, forest gorillas. You can count them on your fingers today."

"That's not your father's fault. That didn't—"

"We've got company, haven't we, Wallace? A lot of company listening in on our chat? The acoustics up here don't favor you, Detective. Sounds like you've got all your cops back in place."

"What's your beef against Clem? Just open the door and we'll get Mamdouba up here to talk to you. He'll give you anything of your father's that you want."

"Imagine what the man was reduced to, Wallace. All his skill, all his passion. You do something unique, do it for a lifetime, better than anybody in the entire world. All of a sudden your universe implodes, your heart's torn out of you, you become an anachronism, and you can't even support your family. The animals may have become scarce, Mercer, but there was no shortage of human remains."

Now I had no one to repeat to me the transmissions of the visual scene of Erik Poste and Clem inside the enclosure as I stood alone in my slim alcove. I could only judge danger by the reflex reactions of the men above me on the catwalk. Erik must have been right on top of Clem.

"Everybody wanted them, every museum in the

world. Not just here. Even in Africa. Paid the hunters—paid anyone who'd do it, actually—to dig up the graves. Old ones, new ones. Made no difference. Clem knows it, don't you? These proud institutions competed against each other for human remains."

"Clem knew about your father?"

"No, no, she never made that connection until today. How could she? They'd taken his name off everything in this place long ago. She was close, though. Awfully close."

"Katrina, did she realize it?"

"That last night in December. Fell into her lap, really."

More noise now, coming from the stairwell. Four men, like a quartet of weight lifters, were carrying a battering ram down the long corridor. They were moving into position to break down the door to Poste's hideout. Clearly they felt Clem was at greater risk inside, with the guns, the axes, and the killer.

Mercer, Mike, and Kerry stepped farther back and made way for the Emergency Services team. I froze as I saw them each draw their guns, Kerry and Mercer gesturing as they received directions through their ear-pieces about how to take the room behind the battering ram.

"Want to tell me how that happened, Erik?"

"Not really, Wallace. Then what else will we have to talk about? That might end our conversation—"

The ram crashed through the door. I clenched my teeth, waiting for the sound of gunshots.

42

"C'mon, Alex. Clem's okay. She's going to be fine."
Kerry waved me over to the room. No shots had been
fired as Mercer and the others had charged into the
small space.

One of the ESU men had cuffed Poste and removed
him so that Clem did not have to be near him. Mike
and Mercer were untying her bonds as two medics
rushed in behind me to check her vital signs and ask
about injuries.

I stopped long enough to tell Poste that I'd like the
chance to talk to him when we went downstairs in a few
minutes. No need to read him his Miranda rights now
and give him time to think about lawyering up.

"Don't waste your time, Miss Cooper. I've got
nothing to say to you. If you'd stayed locked in the
basement all night, none of this need have happened."

I didn't have to tell Mike that I had been right. He
glanced at me and I knew he understood.

Clem was crying now. She was upright with her
back against a rack full of human skulls, a blood pressure cuff around her arm, Mercer massaging her
wrists.

Mike got out of the way and made room for me. "I'm great with stiffs. Tears, tea, and sympathy is your turf."

I kneeled down beside her and she reached her free arm around my neck. "Take it easy, Clem. It's all over."

I could feel the scratches on her forearm as I embraced her. I showed them to the medic.

Clem managed a laugh. "You know how many times I've dropped one of those arrows on my foot? Margaret Mead would be appalled at how often the interns did that. That poison has a shorter shelf life than a carton of milk. They've probably been in this room for thirty or forty years. It's the guns that terrified me."

Mike had stepped out into the hallway to examine the firearms. "Not loaded. None of 'em. I'm not even sure they would work at this point."

"I feel so stupid," Clem said, looking up at him. "I would never have done what he told me if I'd known."

"Hey, you're alive. Whatever you did was right. We thought the same thing you did," Mike said.

"We're gonna take her over to Roosevelt," one of the medics said, referring to the nearest hospital. "You can talk to her there. We gotta have her checked out."

"I'll go with you in a few minutes. I need to talk to the detectives first. Please?"

The medics weren't happy but they picked up their equipment and stepped out into the hallway.

Clem was sitting on the floor, cross-legged, rubbing her ankles while she talked. "He told me some things about Katrina. About why—"

She looked up at me, biting her lower lip hard with her teeth, as though that would shut off the flow of tears. "That's why I thought he was really going to kill me. And kill himself. He had the guns. Then the arrows, which he knew had poison tips. Then he picked up one of the hatchets."

That hatchet had probably caused the chief of detectives to give ESU the order to break in.

"Did you know about the staircase in Mamdouba's office?"

"No. Never heard about it. Those turrets are coveted space. Honchos only. Never spent much time up there."

"Did he have the gun when he surprised you?"

"I didn't see him coming. Of course"—she smiled—"when Mamdouba took you out of the office, to the anteroom, I couldn't resist the chance to get up and go behind his desk. Look over the papers he had there while you guys were arguing with him. That's the bit of me that will never change, I suppose."

"And Poste?"

"The door opened. I turned my head and he was pointing the gun right at me. Grabbed my hand and told me if I made a sound I was dead."

"He knew you were there?"

"No, I'd guess he knew *you* were there. He's probably the only person who would have known about the staircases. He played in them when he was a boy, visiting the museum with his father. That's what he told me when we got up here. Even knew whose office it used to be."

"But why was he there?"

"Listening to your conversation with Mamdouba, trying to overhear what you had figured out about the murder so far. Especially once Zimm told him I might be coming tonight. Just listening. He didn't expect to find me there alone. That's why he had no escape route planned. No idea how to get rid of me. Just a place to hide me until he thought it out. Just this, this—" Clem struggled to put a name on this gruesome assemblage of human remains.

"This bone vault," Mike said.

"Did Erik know about what his father had done?" I asked.

"About desecrating the graves, you mean? Not when he was a kid. Not until about a year ago, when he started to work on the joint exhibit. It was his brother who told him."

"Brother?" Mike asked.

"In one of our interviews, he told us his older brother had stayed on in Kenya, remember? To do his father's work." At the time, I assumed that meant guiding safaris, going on museum explorations.

"Kirk Van der Poste. He's the half brother. Eight years older than Erik. His mother passed away of malaria. The father married a second time, then died when Erik was twelve. When he wrote to Kirk that he was coming to the Natural History Museum to work on an exhibition, that's when Kirk told him that all the collections their father had brought here were being dismantled and stored away. Even worse, being given back to native tribes."

"How did Kirk know that?"

"From his contacts at the McGregor, in South Africa."

"Hadn't either of them been here since they were kids?"

"How could they get up here into these store-rooms? They had no more access than total strangers. Last year was the first time Erik set foot in this museum since his father was killed. Just think what an opportunity the exhibition work gave him. A free pass to wander around up here, looking for anything he wanted."

"And Kirk, he wanted the bones?"

"Everything else that went with them. When those graves were plundered, along came all the looted pieces that no one else valued at the time. Bronze cast-ings, Swahili wooden grave markers, terra-cotta pot-teries. They must all be stashed away in here, with rhino horns and elephant tusks. Hundreds of thou-sands of dollars' worth, collected by Willem Van der Poste. Bounty to sell to museums, and for even higher prices on the thriving black market."

We were standing in the middle of a small fortune in bones.

"How did Kirk know?"

"He had heard enough back in Africa to understand what his father was doing. Plus, he'd inherited some of his father's early field journals."

"The what?"

"Field journals. The records of all the expeditions, the ledger entries that documented the museums where things were sold or stored. Erik Poste was indif-ferent to our mission to return the bones. He just thought it was foolish political correctness. All museums had baggage. Things were different fifty, a hundred years ago. But he knew that Katrina would stumble—had stumbled upon something much more valuable the last week of her life."

"The arsenic, did he talk about that?"

She nodded. "He started out defending himself to me. Telling me that he had only tried to make her sick. Sick enough to want to go home to South Africa. That the small amounts of it he put in her drinks, when they were together at the museum working late into the evenings, would never have killed her."

Dr. Kestenbaum had told me the same thing. If the occasional poisoning had stopped, Katrina would have recovered when she reached South Africa. When the ME got back the toxicology results on Katrina's hair samples, they would reveal precisely when the poisoning had started and what the doses had been.

"The rape, he knew about that?"

"Anna Friedrichs told him." She insisted to us that she had, although Poste had played dumb during our interviews. "He took advantage of that. And of September eleventh, too. Everyone thought, even Katrina herself, that her physical symptoms were the result of the stress of the sexual assault and the terrorist attacks. Like everyone else she was anxious about more bombings and the anthrax scares that made us all so nervous."

Each of us remembered the torment of those painful fall days.

"Yet she didn't want to leave New York until she could find the aboriginal bones that she hoped to get back to Africa. Poste just wanted to speed up her exit, weaken her resolve."

"Something must have changed his mind."

"Right before Christmas," she said. "He thought this was what I was referring to in that e-mail you had me send, Alex. That's why he was so driven to ask me about it. When Katrina was offered the job at the McGregor Museum in Kimberley, she knew they had already begun the process of trying to identify the stacks of skeletons they have, to return them to the native peoples, to their tribes, for burial.

"One of the curators phoned her. Asked her what she knew about Willem Van der Poste's specimens, whether she could get a look at them and ask Mamdouba's help in arranging the return of the bones. The man who called her had dealings in Africa with Kirk. Knew that Erik Poste worked at the Met. He suggested she approach him for help making a pitch to the museum administrators. Thought Erik would want to polish up his father's reputation."

"Again, he turned her down, right?"

"Yes. But she came up with another idea. To enlist the help of Van der Poste's widow, and get her support for doing the right thing."

"Erik's mother?" He had mentioned his mother to me, when he told us about moving to this country as a child. That she was ill. That because she was hospitalized he was sent away to boarding school. "She's still alive? How did Katrina find her?"

"Museum records. Correspondence they had with her after Willem's death."

"But she must have been very sickly to have been

hospitalized for so long so many years ago," I said.

"She was sick, all right. Mental illness. Profound depression, which she's suffered from all her life. And Erik had severed his relationship with her when he was still an adolescent."

"You knew about this?"

"No, no. But Erik assumed Katrina had told me. He kept talking about his mother when he was tying me up. I'm putting it together from the pieces he was rambling about."

"Did his mother meet with Katrina?"

"Not only spoke to her. Mrs. Poste gave Katrina the field journals, the ones from Willem's later years. The ones that Kirk didn't inherit. He had a lot more to hide than smuggled ivory."

"What—?"

Clem inhaled and looked at me. "He didn't die the way Erik told you he did. Not as some noble hunter protecting the animals from poachers."

"What happened?"

"Willem Van der Poste was leading a safari. All amateurs. He was trampled by a bull elephant, nearly crushed to death. He made the tourists go on with several of the guides, expecting them to send back more help to carry him out of the jungle. He couldn't hunt, couldn't move his legs at all."

We stared at Clem silently, waiting for her to speak again.

"Days passed. He ran out of food, out of supplies." She glanced around at the bones on the shelves surrounding us. "It's unthinkable, really. He shot his servant, his bearer. The native who had introduced him to Africa and protected him over the decades. Cannibalized him—"

"You don't need to go on. We get the picture," Mike said. "No wonder his wife wanted to change her name."

And no wonder she never emerged from the depression that engulfed her after learning the truth.

"So one night last December, when Katrina had come back from the sanitarium with the field journals that would completely shatter Van der Poste's reputation, she made the mistake of showing them to Erik. Naively, she thought they would make him see our side of the issue. Make him want to help the aborigines who had been so mistreated for so very long."

"He must have decided to kill her that very night," I said.

"With a massive dose of arsenic," Mike added. "Somewhere in this mausoleum."

I looked around the room at the sinister collection of skulls and skeletons. "Up here?"

Mercer didn't think so. "She may have found this room. Lots of others like it. He probably killed her in the basement, though. Zimm took me to some places you couldn't find without sonar. Remote, cool, dry. Big empty bins that would hold a dead animal twice the size of Katrina. You wouldn't see it, you wouldn't smell it. Once he gets his sarcophagus in place, just lifts her in and slides the lid shut."

"You think Bermudez was an accomplice?"

"Unwittingly." Clem tried to get on her feet and I helped her stand. She flexed her feet to make sure the circulation had been restored. "I asked him if the guy who fell off the Met last week had helped him—you know—hurt Katrina. I thought maybe he killed himself, out of remorse for what he had done."

"What did he tell you?"

"How stupid I was. Stupid, I guess, to think he'd let some janitor help him. Bermudez was in charge of the crew who loaded the sarcophagus onto the truck for shipment. He must have seen the story in the newspaper about Katrina. That's when he showed up in Poste's office. Poste says the guy guessed that he knew something about Katrina's death and demanded money. Blackmail. Poste gave him a down payment. Said he'd meet him with more money later in the week. Everybody knew about the poor man's Friday morning check of the water treatment center, apparently."

"He admitted pushing Bermudez?"

"He just laughed at me and told me they parted ways on the rooftop last Friday."

43

The entire spring sky was spread out overhead. The hindquarters of Ursa Major, the Great Bear, were clearly defined in the familiar shape of the Big Dipper. The North Star pointed to Leo, arcing eastward to the constellation of Virgo. And just rising in the northeast for the first time was the sparkling white summer star, Vega.

I leaned my head against the back of the seat, in the rear row of the Hayden Planetarium Space Theater, and listened to the chief of detectives brief the press corps on the arrest of Erik Poste, who had just been taken out of the museum in handcuffs. It was four-thirty in the morning and I was sitting by myself as the reporters fired questions at the police brass and the exhausted detectives.

"You're telling us he acted alone?"

"That's right. Detective Chapman will explain a bit of the background about Mr. Poste and his father," the chief said, stepping back from the podium and giving Mike some play.

"That accident at the Met last Friday? Related to the Grooten death?"

The chief stepped in front of Mike and took control of the microphone again. "We're not going to go into the evidence we've got at this point, but it's safe to say that we're no longer treating that as an accident."

"How about that arm in the diorama? The one that freaked out the schoolkids?"

"My latent print unit tells me that there are fingerprints of value on that. We'll be doing comparisons with our suspect, of course. Mr. Poste did have access to the master keys that open the diorama cabinets."

"You think he did that just to cast suspicion on the custodial workers over here?"

"You're just speculating now, Mr. Diamond. I know you can build an entire story around that arm, so I'll just leave it to your editors' judgment. If that's what they call it at the *Post*."

The other reporters laughed. They had most of their information and were ready to leave.

Mr. Mamdouba tapped the chief on the shoulder and said something to him.

"Before you guys go, Elijah Mamdouba—the director of curatorial affairs here—would like to say a few words."

Some of the reporters took their seats. Others ignored the diminutive figure and filed out to call in their stories.

"This is a very strange circumstance for us, ladies and gentlemen. Very awkward indeed." He was speaking to a small audience, maybe twelve or thirteen reporters were left in the room, but he was clearly hoping his words would be printed for millions to read.

"It was in one of the two most magnificent rooms

in the city of New York, at the Temple of Dendur in our sister museum across the park—a mere week ago—that my colleague Pierre Thibodaux first learned of the discovery of Miss Grooten's body.

"We inform you about the conclusion of this tragedy today in this other stunning arena here at the planetarium, part of our spectacular Museum of Natural History." He gestured around him at the superb new facility at the Rose Center, the most powerful virtual-reality simulator in the world.

Mamdouba was not wrong. Both of these brilliant institutions were the city's finest showcases. Acres and acres of exhibits, millions and millions of paintings, objects, specimens, and artifacts. Thousands of dedicated scholars and scientists who devoted their lives to assembling these unrivaled collections of art, in one case, and scientific wonders in the other.

"Over time," Mamdouba went on, "we have reflected within our walls and our laboratories the society in which we live, in which we study and are educated. Overcoming the ignorance of those who went before us has become an inevitable part of our process of growth, whether it was about evolution or the environment, about racial stereotypes, animal extinction, or space exploration."

I couldn't think of any places in the entire country that were responsible for the education and enlightenment of more people than the Metropolitan and the Natural History Museum. How ironic, then, and how bizarre, that a quiet young scholar had met her death because of her work beneath these roofs.

Mamdouba was finishing his remarks. "That the

scientific community once used human beings from primitive cultures for their research in such profoundly disturbing ways has caused every museum in the world to do some soul-searching. That animal specimens were so necessary for examination and studies that affected their own viability on our earth created a paradox in terms of conserving those very creatures that have become endangered."

He went on about scientists and visionaries, explorers and anthropologists and paleontologists, the mission and the paradox, the vision and the tragedy. The reporters stayed until he spoke his piece, riveted again by the marvels that had been brought together under this splendid tangle of rooftops.

When he finished speaking and the reporters departed, I sat in my plush seat and waited for the chief to dismiss the detectives. I closed my eyes.

When I opened them five minutes later, having dozed off, some motion in the seat bottom of my chair jolted me awake. The room was empty, except for Mike, Mercer, and me.

"Liftoff," Mike said. "Time to wake up. Zimm's got us tickets for the five A.M. early bird special. He's in the control room with the janitor. Thinks you deserve a private display."

Speakers and woofers that vibrated to give the audience the sense of a real space launch at the start of the show were wired into each seat. Mercer was holding a bag of microwaved popcorn that he must have found in some lab worker's office, and Mike was pouring Clem's minibar bottles of scotch and vodka into three plastic cups.

Tom Hanks's voice-over began a narration about our search for other forms of life in the universe.

"There's Orion," Mike said, pointing over Mercer's head to a formation of bright stars.

"Last thing I want to see this morning is a hunter."

"How about Andromeda, the princess?"

I sipped at my drink and smiled at him. "Don't go there."

"She was chained to a rock, left to be devoured by a sea monster, to appease the gods. Saved by—well, by one of those winged horses whose names I never remember. Let's just say saved by Mercer and me. We'd never let it happen to you, kid."

We clicked our plastic cups and the glorious night sky above us began to move.

Acknowledgments

The two institutions that form the backdrop for Alexandra Cooper's investigation are among the most extraordinary museums in the world. They have contributed immeasurably to the culture of our country for more than a century.

In addition to the many pleasure-filled hours I have spent inside their walls, there are wonderful books that reveal their histories and the range of their treasures. Among those I found most helpful were: *Stuffed Animals and Pickled Heads* by Stephen Asma; *Give Me My Father's Body* by Kenn Harper; *Making the Mummies Dance* by Thomas Hoving; *Dinosaurs in the Attic* by Douglas Preston; *The Mummy Congress* by Heather Pringle; *Merchants and Masterpieces* by Calvin Tompkins; and *A Gathering of Wonders* by Joseph Wallace. As always, the archives of *The New York Times* had a splendid assortment of facts and features.

The usual suspects sustained me throughout the long process of writing the story. My devoted colleagues in the Sex Crimes Prosecution Unit of the Manhattan D.A.'s office, and in the Special Victims Unit of the NYPD, will always be the best in the business. Nothing makes me prouder than the thirty years

I spent working shoulder to shoulder with each of them. The men and women of the Office of the Chief Medical Examiner of New York, pathologists and serologists, were my heroes before September 11, 2001, and will be forever.

I am grateful to everyone at Scribner and Pocket Books, and to Esther Newberg at ICM, for standing beside me patiently every step of the way and supporting me so enthusiastically.

The booksellers, librarians, and loyal readers who hold me in their hands have all my thanks.

Friends and family make everything possible, over and over again. And my adored husband, Justin Feldman, who is cheerleader and critic, believed in me from the beginning, which is the greatest gift.

ABOUT THE AUTHOR

Linda Fairstein, America's foremost expert on crimes of sexual assault and domestic violence, led the Sex Crimes Unit of the District Attorney's Office in Manhattan for twenty-five years prior to her retirement in 2002. A fellow of the American College of Trial Lawyers, she is a graduate of Vassar College and the University of Virginia School of Law. Her first novel, *Final Jeopardy,* which introduced the character Alexandra Cooper, was published in 1996 to critical and commercial acclaim and was made into an ABC Movie of the Week starring Dana Delaney. *Likely to Die* in 1997, *Cold Hit* in 1999, and *The Deadhouse* in 2001 also achieved international-bestseller status. Her nonfiction book, *Sexual Violence,* was a *New York Times* Notable Book in 1994. She lives with her husband in Manhattan and on Martha's Vineyard.

POCKET STAR BOOKS
PROUDLY PRESENTS

THE DEADHOUSE

Linda Fairstein

Available in Paperback
from
Pocket Star Books

Turn the page for a preview of
The Deadhouse

It was hard not to smile as I watched Lola Dakota die.

I clicked the remote control button and listened to the commentary again on another network.

"New Jersey police officers have released a portion of these dramatic videotapes to the media this evening. We're going to play for you the actual recordings the three hit men hired by her husband to kill Ms. Dakota made to prove to him that they had accomplished their mission."

The local reporter was posed in front of a large mansion in the town of Summit, less than an hour's drive from where I was sitting, in the video technicians' office of the New York County District Attorney. Snowflakes drifted and swirled around her head as she pointed a gloved hand at the darkened facade of a house, ringed with strands of the tiny white lights of Christmas decorations that outlined the roof, the windows, and the enormous wreath on the front door.

"Earlier this afternoon, before the sun went down, Hugh," the woman addressed the news channel's anchorman, "those of us who gathered here for word of Ms. Dakota's condition could see the pools of blood left in the snow during the early morning shooting. It will be a grim holiday season for this forty-two-year-old university professor's family. Let's take you back over the story that led to this morning's tragic events."

Mike Chapman grabbed the clicker from my hand and pressed the mute button, then jabbed at my back with it. "How come the Jersey prosecutors got to do this caper? Too big for you to handle, blondie?"

As the bureau chief in charge of sex crimes for the New York County District Attorney's Office for more than a decade, sexual assault cases—as well as domestic violence and stalking crimes—fell under my jurisdiction. The District Attorney, Paul Battaglia, ran an office with a legal staff of more than six hundred lawyers, but he had taken a particular interest in the investigation of the professor's perilous marital entanglement.

"Battaglia didn't like the whole idea—the risk, the melodrama, and, well, the emotional instability of Lola Dakota. He probably didn't know the story would look this good on the late news broadcast or he might have reconsidered."

Chapman lifted his foot to the edge of my chair and swivelled it around so that I faced him. "Had you worked with Lola for a long time?"

"I guess it's been almost two years since the first day I met her. Someone called Battaglia from the President's office at Columbia University. Said there was a matter that needed to be handled discreetly." I reached for a cup of coffee. "One of their professors had split from her husband, and he was stalking her. The usual domestic. She didn't want to have him arrested, didn't want any publicity that would embarrass the administration—just wanted him to leave her alone. The D.A. kicked it over to me to try to make it happen. That's how I met Lola Dakota. And became aware of her miserable husband."

"What'd you do for her?"

Chapman worked homicides, most of the time relying on sophisticated forensic technology and reliable medical evidence to resolve his cases. He rarely dealt with breathing witnesses, and although he was the best detective in the Manhattan North Squad when he came face-to-face with a corpse, Chapman was always intrigued by how the rest of us in law enforcement managed to untangle and resolve the delicate problems of the living.

"Met with her several times, trying to convince her that we could make a prosecution stick and gain her trust to let me bring charges. I explained that filing a criminal complaint was the only way I could get a judge to put some muscle behind our actions." Lola was like most of our victims. She wanted the violence to stop, but she did not want to face her spouse in a court of law.

"It worked?"

"No better than usual. When reasoning with her failed, we relocated her to a temporary apartment, arranged for counseling, and sent a couple of our detectives to talk to her husband informally and explain that Lola was giving him a break."

"Happy to see the local constables, was he?"

"Elated. They told him that she didn't want us to lock him up, but if he kept harassing her, that wasn't a choice I would allow her to make the next time he darkened her doorway. So he behaved . . . for a while."

"Until she moved back in with him?"

"Right. Just in time for Valentine's Day."

"Hearts and flowers, happily ever after?"

"Eight months." I turned back to glance at the screen. Flakes were caking up on the reporter's eyelids as she continued to tell her story, reminding me that undoubtedly snow was piling up on my Jeep as well, which was parked in front of the building. A picture of Ivan Kralovic, Lola's husband, appeared as an insert on the bottom right corner of the screen.

"We've got to take a short break," the reporter said, repeating the euphemistic phrase that signaled a commercial interruption, "then we'll show you the dramatic footage that led to Mr. Kralovic's arrest today."

"And at the end of those eight months, what happened? Did you lock him up the second time?"

"No. She wouldn't even give me a clue about what he had done. Called me that October to ask how to get an order of protection. After I greased the wheels to expedite it for her in Family Court, she told me she had rented an apartment on Riverside Drive, moved to a new office away from the campus, and settled her problems with Ivan the Terrible."

"Don't disappoint me, Coop. Tell me he lived up to his name."

"Predictably. It was in January of this year that he cut her with a corkscrew while they were enjoying a quiet dinner for two. Must have mistaken her for a good Burgundy. Sliced open her forearm. He raced her to St. Luke's and it took twenty-seven stitches to close her up."

"They were together for just that one evening?"

"No, he had coaxed her back for the holidays a month earlier. A seasonal reconciliation."

Chapman shook his head. "Yeah, I guess most accidents happen close to home. You nail his ass for that one?"

"Once again, Lola refused to prosecute. Told the doctors in the ER—while Ivan was standing at her bedside—that she'd done it herself. By the time I heard about it through the university and got her down to my office, she was completely uncooperative. Said that if I had Ivan locked up, she would never tell the true story in a courtroom. She had learned her lesson by trying to reunite with him, she assured me, and wasn't going to have anything further to do with him."

"Guess he didn't get the picture."

"He stalked Lola on and off. That's what led her to hide out in New Jersey, at her sister's house, some time in the spring. She called me every now and then, after Ivan threatened her or when she thought she was being followed. But her sister got spooked—worried about her own safety—and brought Lola to the local prosecutors over there."

"Let's go to the videotape," Mike said, spinning my

chair back to the television screen and hitting the sound button on the clicker. The film was rolling and the reporter's voice-over was providing the narrative. The scene appeared to be the same large suburban house, earlier in the day.

". . . and you can see the white delivery van parked at the side of the road. The two men walked up the steps in front of the home, which is owned by Ms. Dakota's sister, carrying the cases of wine. When the professor opened the door and came outside to accept the gift bottles, both men put their packages on the ground. The one on the left presented a receipt that Dakota leaned over to sign, while the man on the right—there he goes now—pulled a revolver from beneath his jacket and fired five times, at point blank range."

I leaned forward and watched again as Lola clutched at her chest, her body pushed backward by the force of the impact. Her eyes opened wide for an instant, seeming to stare directly at the lens of the camera, before they closed, as she fell to the ground, blood oozing from her clothing onto the clean white cover provided by the preceding day's dusting of snow.

Now the camera, held by a third accomplice in the van, zoomed in for a close-up and then the man seemed to lose control of the video equipment as it apparently dropped from his fingers.

"When the killers played their tape for Ivan Kralovic in his office at noon today, after the Summit Police Department released the news of Ms. Dakota's death to the wire services, they were rewarded with a payment of one hundred thousand dollars in cash."

Back to a live shot of the chilled reporter wrapping up her story for the night. "Unfortunately for Kralovic, the gunmen he had hired to kill his estranged wife were actually undercover detectives from the county sheriff's office here in New Jersey, who staged the shooting with the enthusiastic participation of the intended victim."

The tape rolled again and showed the supposedly deceased Dakota now sitting upright against the front door of the house and smiling for the camera as she removed the outer jacket that had concealed the packets of "blood" that had spurted and flowed so convincingly moments ago.

"We've been waiting here, Hugh, hoping this brave woman would tell us how she feels now that she has taken such dramatic steps to end years of spousal abuse and bring to justice the man who wanted to kill her. But sources now tell us that she left the house here this afternoon, after Kralovic's arrest, and has not yet returned." The reporter glanced down at her notes to read a comment from the local prosecutor. "The District Attorney, however, wants us to express his gratitude to the county sheriff for this 'innovative plan that put an end to Ivan's reign of terror, something that prosecutors from Paul Battaglia's office and the New York Police Department across the Hudson River have been unable to do for two years.' Back to the studio—"

I pulled the remote away from Chapman and slammed it onto the desktop after shutting off the set. "Let's go back to my office and close up for the night."

"Temper, temper, Ms. Cooper. Dakota's not likely to win the Oscar for her performance. You peeved 'cause you didn't get a chance to do the film direction?"

I turned off the light and closed the door behind us. "I don't begrudge her anything. But why did the Jersey D.A. have to take a shot at us? He knows it hasn't been our choice to let this thing drag on as long as it did." There wasn't a seasoned prosecutor anywhere who didn't know that the most frustrating dynamic in an abusive marriage was the love-hate relationship that persisted between victim and offender, even after the violence escalated.

My heels clicked on the tiles of the quiet corridor as we snaked our way down the long, dark hallway from video to my eighth-floor office. It was almost eleven-thirty at night, and the tapping of an occasional computer keyboard was the only noise I heard to suggest that any of my colleagues were still at their desks.

Only a handful of cases went to trial this time of year, in the middle of December, with lawyers, judges, and jurors all anticipating the two-week court hiatus for the holiday season. I had been working late—reviewing indictments for the end of the term filing deadline, and preparing to conduct a sex offender registration hearing after the weekend—when Detective Michael Chapman came over to tell me the eleven o'clock news was leading with the Dakota story. He had been down the street at Headquarters to drop off some evidence at the Property Clerk's Office and called to see if I wanted a drink before knocking off for the night.

"C'mon, I'll buy you dinner," he now said. "Can't expect me to last the midnight shift on an empty stomach. Not with all the dead bodies I'm likely to encounter."

"It's too late to eat."

"That means you got a better offer. Jake must be home, cooking up some exotic—"

"Wrong. He's in Washington. Got the assignment on that story of the Ambassador who was assassinated in Uganda, at the economic conference." I'd been dating an NBC news correspondent since early summer, and the rare nights he was free in time for dinner took me away from my usual haunts and habits.

"How come they keep giving him all that third-world stuff to cover when he seems like such a first-world guy?"

The phone was ringing as I opened the door to my office.

"Alex?" Jake's voice sounded brusque and businesslike. "I'm at the NBC studio in D.C."

"How's your story coming—?"

"Lola Dakota is dead."

"I know," I said, sitting down in my chair and turning away from Chapman for some privacy. "Mike and I just watched the whole bit on the local news. I think she's got a real future on the stage. Hard to believe she went for all that phony ketchup and—"

"Listen to me, Alex. She was killed tonight."

I turned back to look at Mike, rolling my eyes to suggest that Jake clearly had not seen the entire story yet and didn't understand that the shooting was a setup. "We know all that, and we also know that Paul Battaglia is not going to be thrilled when the tabloids point the finger at me, for not putting this mess to bed a couple of—"

"This isn't about *you*, Alex. I've heard the whole story with the Jersey prosecutors and their sting operation. But there's a later headline that just came over the newsroom wires a few minutes ago, probably while you and Mike were watching the story run on the air. Some kids found Lola Dakota's body tonight—her dead body—in the basement of an apartment building in Manhattan, crushed to death at the bottom of an elevator shaft."

My eyes shut tight and I rested my head on the back of my chair, as Jake lowered his voice to make his point. "Trust me, darling. Lola Dakota is dead."